"Tell me the worst thing you've ever done," she said suddenly. "It doesn't matter what you say. You can't top me."

"Somehow, I really doubt that."

She stared at him, and for just a second her face was illuminated by the overhead flares set off by the local soldiers—a cry for help. From anyone. She looked beautiful, despite the cuts and bruises. Beautiful and strong, and he wondered why the hell he would notice that now.

"I slept with the man who held me hostage. Willingly. I seduced him, because I wasn't about to be a victim. I stayed in control. I made my own choices," she said, her teeth gritted at the memory of what she'd done. "I wasn't forced. They're going to say that I was and I'm going to have to agree. But that's a lie."

What she'd just told him was something she'd never reveal to anyone else. And now she needed the same thing from him. She was daring him really, and he'd never been one to back down from a dare in his life.

She's not going to remember any of this, so just tell her.

"I killed my stepfather," he told her.

HARD TO HOLD

STEPHANIE TYLER

A DELL BOOK
NEW YORK

A Dell Mass Market Original

Copyright © 2009 by Stephanie Tyler

Published in the United States by Dell, an imprint of The Random House
Publishing Group, a division of Random House, Inc., New York.

DELL is a registered trademark of Random House, Inc., and the colophon
is a trademark of Random House, Inc.

ISBN 978-0-440-24434-9

Cover design: Lynn Andreozzi
Cover illustration: © Alan Ayers

Printed in the United States of America

www.bantamdell.com

2 4 6 8 9 7 5 3 1

For Zoo and Lily—

I couldn't do this without either of you. And for

my grandfather, who served in the United States Navy,

and whose influence I felt during every step

of writing this book.

ACKNOWLEDGMENTS

Writing a book is never a solitary process, and I have many people to thank for their enthusiasm and unyielding faith in me.

First and foremost, a special thanks to my editor, Shauna Summers, for her wonderful insights and guidance through this entire process.

Thanks to everyone at Bantam Dell who helped make this the best book possible, cover to cover—from Jessica Sebor, who always goes above and beyond to help; to the art department, who rock my world with their awesome covers; and to Pam Feinstein, for being such an amazing copy editor.

Special thanks to Boone Medlock and Bryan Estell, whose military insights and personal stories were invaluable.

Thanks to authors Lynn Viehl, aka PBW, and Holly Lisle, for giving so much of their time to mentor and share their own experiences with so many writers via their blogs. I can't tell you how much this helped me.

Finally, last but never least, thanks to my fellow authors whom I'm proud to call friends: Lara Adrian, Maya Banks, Jaci Burton, Alison Kent, Amy Knupp, and especially Larissa Ione, for all their support in ways too numerous to list.

PROLOGUE

"We want to be in a situation under maximum pressure, maximum intensity, and maximum danger. When it's shared with others, it provides a bond which is stronger than any tie that can exist."
—**SEAL Team Six Officer**

Lieutenant Junior Grade Jake Hansen had already muttered the word *motherfucker* as many times as he possibly could in under a minute's time. He'd used it as noun and then a verb, planned on continuing to think of new and inventive ways to utilize it in his vocabulary until his Navy SEAL teammate and best friend finally told him to shut up so he could *motherfucking* bandage Jake's bleeding biceps.

It was a flesh wound, but it still hurt—and bled—like hell. Not that he'd ever admit that first part. And there was no way he was stopping, although Nick hadn't bothered to suggest that. Probably because Nick had been running with a stress fracture along his shin for the better part of the afternoon, at the tail end of a mission that had gone totally to shit after the first five minutes.

Those first five minutes happened three days ago. Now they were intent on getting the hell out of Djibouti, Africa. The water—and the point of convergence with their team sharpshooter, senior chief and CO—was only five miles away.

"Just rebel fire—not aimed at us," Nick spoke quietly into the mic attached to his headset as the gunfire continued to pop, lighting the backdrop of the night sky to their west.

"Could've fooled me," Jake muttered, his anger directed more at himself for letting the bullet catch him than at the random firefight. This country was full of small skirmishes and all-out wars, but none of that had been SEAL Team Twelve's concern this trip. They'd been forced to scatter to complete their mission to secure the missing equipment and the intel it contained. Now they were headed home.

Nick was still listening to the voice on the other end of his headset, intently enough to make Jake switch on his own earpiece.

"Hostage reported . . . one klick north . . . seen and left for dead by the rebels," the team's senior chief was saying, although the line was breaking up fast.

"Who reported the hostage?" Jake asked.

"Source was verified reliable. Red Cross relief workers got a call about the incident, and also heard it from the refugees moving north. They were scared to stop and take her—didn't want to draw attention to the fact that she'd survived. She's American. Can you get there?"

"Confirmed. We can get there," Nick said.

Jake mentally traced the route—one mile back the way they came. Toward the line of fire. He and Nick began to hump it, weapons drawn, and still listening to the report.

"...Senator Cresswell's daughter...a doctor...first name, Isabelle, last name, Markham...thirty-one...missing and believed kidnapped for seventy-two hours..."

This way, Jake motioned as they cut through some thick underbrush and headed up a path off the main road. It was easy to see how they'd missed the small hut in the first place—it was completely camouflaged by brush and entirely invisible in the dark.

Trap? Nick motioned.

Jake walked the perimeter slowly while Nick followed, weapon drawn. No wires were apparent and when they walked around the front, he saw the structure had no door.

Seen and left for dead. Jake's stomach had turned on hearing that atrocity, but the reality hit him like a punch to the gut when they actually found Dr. Isabelle Markham. All his doubts about the veracity of the report fell away as he and Nick moved forward into the darkened room. Nick took the sweep, speaking quietly into the mic and Jake turned his off and dropped to his knees beside the prone body.

"Jesus," he whispered.

She lay on her stomach, hands tied behind her back, cheek to the dusty floor, her mouth gagged so she couldn't yell. Eyes closed. Pale. Naked. Gingerly, he brushed a hand down the back of her neck. She didn't stir, and he was frozen.

Nick knelt opposite him, his fingers on Isabelle's wrist.

"There's a strong pulse," he said, before he turned to work on freeing her hands.

Jake untied the filthy gag and pulled it out of her mouth. She made a quick gasping sound but didn't wake up.

"Doesn't look like there's head trauma. We need to turn her, make sure she's not bleeding anywhere," Nick said. He threw the filthy ropes that had once bound her behind him as Jake unbuttoned his jacket, trying to ignore the fact that his fingers felt like lead, and placed it over her where she lay. There was no way to put it on her fully without actually turning her and exposing her more.

He'd been in the military for eleven years—since he was fifteen, had seen shit both before and after his enlistment that could turn a man ugly or crazy or cold.

He'd gone none of those ways, no matter how hard others might argue, but nothing he'd ever seen or done had prepared him for this. Because, even though she was down, Isabelle Markham was not out. He could tell by the set of her shoulders, defiant, even in sleep, could tell by the way her hands were bruised and her nails broken, because she'd fought back. She was still fighting and he wasn't sure why that affected him so deeply, but it did.

"Can she make the trip?" he asked Nick, who was assessing her facial area with a penlight, and at the sound of his voice, Isabelle stirred and finally opened her eyes. They were a dark hazel, her pupils dilated from fear and pain, and they locked onto his with a force he felt physically.

"Dr. Markham, you're safe. We're with the U.S. Navy, and we're going to get you out of here," he said, placed his hand lightly on her shoulder.

"Can't move me," she whispered, her voice breathless, as if it hurt to speak. "Not far."

"What's wrong?"

"Ribs...broken. Too close...to my lung," she managed. "Not safe."

"We need a vehicle to take her out of here."

Nick nodded his assent, then asked, "Ma'am, can we turn you?" even though she was staring up at Jake.

"Yes. Onto...right side," she whispered after a long moment, as though she realized they'd see her completely exposed.

She'd been through so much already, neither man could stand that she'd have to bear more humiliation. But the firefight was drawing closer, and Jake forced his emotions to lose to logic.

"Let's do it, then. On my count," he said. "One, two, three."

He rolled Isabelle to her back as one unit by pushing simultaneously on her hip and shoulder, avoiding her side completely. Nick had already laid the jacket out underneath her and Jake noted a dark bruise by her temple from a blow hard enough to knock her out. Tears streaked her face, fresh ones, and her breathing was labored, and still she held it together.

But when she grabbed at the jacket sleeves, she let out a cry at the pain that small movement gave her.

"I've got it," Jake told her. He eased one of her arms gently into the jacket, and while Nick did the same to the other, Jake made a quick assessment of the injuries he saw on her body.

She was filthy, her body smeared with dirt and blood.

He immediately focused on the worst of it, a large mass of bruises on her left side, where she'd indicated the broken ribs. It looked like she'd been kicked and he sucked in air between his gritted teeth and wished he could find the men who did this to her. All of them.

She stared up at him as though she could read his mind and he reached out and buttoned the jacket, covering her body.

The jacket only reached mid-thigh, but she'd already relaxed. Then Jake pulled a clean T-shirt from his bag. One of the only things he had left since they'd been forced to drop nearly everything but their first-line gear to hop and pop their way to the border.

"Dr. Markham, I'd like to put this on you," he said. She looked at him, slightly confused. "I don't have any pants for you, but I can put this on so you're covered."

"Name?" she asked.

"I'm Lieutenant Junior Grade Jake Hansen," he said. "And this is Ensign Nick Devane."

She nodded and Jake wound the shirt between her legs, tying it firmly around her hips. She didn't take her eyes off him for second, and he maintained as much eye contact as he could.

"You need to try to drink something," he told her, once he'd pulled the jacket down again.

"Yes," she said.

He eased her onto her right side and she braced herself with her right arm under her head. Then he offered her water from his canteen, which she took down in small sips, her breath coming faster as she attempted to hydrate.

He was going to have to run an IV. He could give her a

light dose of morphine too, for the pain, if she'd help him rule out abdominal injuries. She'd need something if they were going to move her even the shortest distance, because there was no way she was walking out of here on her own two feet.

"Dr. Markham, we've got to get you out of this place, at least," he said.

She shook her head no. *Dammit.*

Nick had walked toward the door to try to make contact with the team and to assess just how much time, if any, they had to get out of range of the next skirmish headed their way. For right now, it was suddenly all quiet, which worried Jake more than if there had been major fire. Too quiet always equaled trouble.

Nick motioned for Jake to come to him.

"I'll be right back," Jake told her. She grabbed his wrist. "I'm not leaving—just moving to that corner. You can watch me the whole time," he assured her, and she did just that.

"What's up?"

"No comms," Nick said. "One of us is going to have to go on ahead and bring back help, unless you want to build a board."

It was an option—the easier one, probably, but not the best solution for Isabelle. They'd end up jostling her too much and if they got caught along the way, covering her would prove difficult.

"I'll stay," Jake said, and Nick, his best friend and brother, looked at him. "Come on, man, this is no time to play big brother on me. Besides, I outrank you."

"Asshole," Nick muttered, but he didn't argue. They

were on limited time. Rendezvous with the helo was at 0500. Three short hours away. Keeping Isabelle here was the path of least resistance—it was the safest place, since the rebels thought she was dead already.

"At least move her to the side, out of view of the doorway," Nick said.

"I'll do that myself. Go now, before you lose the dark," Jake said. For a second, the men clasped hands, fist over fist in the familiar ritual they'd been performing since they were eight years old. Nick edged out the doorway, and within seconds Jake lost sight of him.

He immediately turned his attention back to Isabelle.

"I'm going to run some fluids and then give you a small dose of morphine. Then I'm going to lift you—carry you over to the corner," he told her when he crouched down beside her again.

She nodded, continued watching him prepare the IV and find a strong vein in her forearm. Once he got the bag running, he pinned it to his own shoulder to keep it the correct height and flowing, and then he injected the morphine.

"That should work quickly," he said. She nodded, and within five minutes she was telling him that he could attempt the short move. He picked her up carefully, ignoring the burning pain in his own arm, watched her face carefully for signs of major discomfort as he transported her five feet to the corner on the right side of the door. The corner where he'd have the best element of surprise if someone came knocking.

When he laid her back down on her right side, he checked her color, her breathing. Labored, but no worse.

"I'm okay," she said.

"Do you know how long you've been here?" he asked as he attached the IV bag to the thatched wall behind her.

"What day is it?"

"Tuesday. It's 0200 hours—close to two in the morning civilian time."

"Not long. Maybe since this morning."

Good. That was good. Nick and the others would hump it back within an hour at most, and if Isabelle had made it this long, she could make it just that little bit longer.

He cradled the M4 in his right arm and sat next to her on the floor.

"Why did the other man leave?" she asked.

"He's going to get help."

"I thought you were help."

"Dr. Markham, everything's going to be fine. You just rest," he said. But the morphine, mixed with her nervousness, made her more talkative.

"I think we're on a first name basis," she said. "You said you were Navy?"

"Yes."

"I didn't think they sent sailors out to rescue hostages."

"I'm with the SEALs, Isabelle. This is the kind of mission we're built for. You're going to be fine."

She nodded slowly. "When will my mother know I'm all right? That I'm alive?"

"She'll be notified as soon as we can get you out of here. You're our first priority—not your mother," he said.

"She wouldn't be happy to hear you say that."

"Then it's a good thing she's not here."

"A very good thing...don't need to hear *I told you so, Izzy*..."

Sometime during her last sentence, she'd fallen asleep. He waited until her breaths grew even before spending the better part of half an hour getting familiar with her legs, putting antiseptic on the larger lacerations and getting angrier with every bruise he encountered.

His reaction was visceral, on a level so deep he couldn't explain it or shake it and he had to force himself to cover her legs when he was done. The jacket's sleeves reached mid-palm on her, but despite the heat, her skin still felt cool to his touch. Shock, probably.

Her dark hair had fallen loose, and as he brushed some of it off her cheeks, his fists tightened on seeing the fingerprint-sized bruises along her neck.

She's going to be fine.

He forced himself to leave her for a few minutes. Staying low to the ground, he checked the door, spent a few minutes assessing the new pattern of gunfire that started up suddenly. The sound came from the opposite direction Nick had run to, and Jake calculated that his teammate should be at the convergence point by now. The problem they'd run into was getting a vehicle, but his teammates were nothing if not resourceful.

When he returned to Isabelle's side, he found that she'd opened her eyes at the staccato of the now steady machine-gun fire. It was definitely drawing closer. She automatically reached a hand out for his free one, and he let her take it, twine her fingers through his.

"We're all right," he said.

"Have you killed a lot of people?" she asked.

"Enough."

"And you have enough ammo to kill more?"

She thinks we're going to die. And hell, she might be right, but it wasn't a possibility he allowed himself to dwell on once he'd written his letter and got on the helo. Death was always a stark and sobering reality and he'd be a fool—and dead long before this—if he didn't acknowledge that reality every single time he took a trip.

"The gunfire sounds a lot closer than it really is," he said.

"Liar."

"Normally, a good one." That got a small smile out of her, but it faded quickly. "The rebels are more interested in one another than us."

"I'm not worried about the rebels. I'm just not sure . . . he said he was coming back to get me."

He'd assumed that the rebel soldiers did this to her, took her from the village she'd been working in and dragged her to this remote hut. But something in her voice told him that wasn't true, and coupled with his earlier suspicion of just where the intel of her location originated from, the warning bells in his head rang louder than ever.

"Who did this to you, Isabelle?" he asked. She shook her head and he wondered if he should press further. She'd be questioned by the FBI and CIA and various other agencies because of who her mother was anyway, and she didn't owe him any kind of true confession. It would be enough for him if he could get her out of here safely.

"He wouldn't be stupid enough to come back here," she whispered. "If he does, you won't let him near me, right?"

"He won't even get close. Tell me who did this to you."

"I can't."

"Sometimes admitting it the first time's the hardest," he said.

"And sometimes it's the worst thing you can ever do," she shot back.

He didn't argue, because he couldn't. Admissions had never been high on his list of priorities and he'd always been more of an *It's easier to ask for forgiveness than permission but I'm not planning on asking for either* kind of guy.

A small sob caught in her throat. Her face contorted in pain and she held her side and winced.

"It's okay. Just try to relax. You don't have to tell me anything," he said, stroked her cheek with his thumb. "I'll give you some more morphine."

She didn't argue as he sent another dose through the IV line. In a few minutes, her eyes got that hazy look again and her breathing was better, but she still wasn't content.

He realized why almost immediately, as smoke and dust rose in his nostrils. The rebels were burning down this part of the jungle, cutting a swath so refugees and the opposing army couldn't hide from them.

He and Isabelle were directly in that path.

"Rebels are smoking out the survivors," she whispered, and damn, he wished she didn't know that. "We've got to get out of here."

He was backed into an impossible situation—moving Isabelle now, at the rate he'd have to evac her . . .

"I know the risks," she said, and he didn't have time to second-guess either of their decisions. Instead, he cut a piece of the blanket away and tied it over her mouth and nose, stopped the IV for the time being and tucked it against her. Then he marked the floor so Nick would know his next position, if his team was able to make it close to the hut at all.

Bag slung over his chest, he picked Isabelle up and he ran, a different route than the one he and Nick had taken an hour earlier. The foliage was thick, and he tried to stay on the main path as much as he could, prayed that no one would come running from the opposite direction.

He ran until the smoke wasn't heavy, until the shots sounded more distant, until he knew he couldn't risk jostling her any longer than he already had.

"How...far?" she asked when he laid her down between some overgrown brush that held just enough coverage from both the road and the field to camouflage them.

"Two miles," he said.

She opened her eyes and stared at him steadily. "I thought you'd be faster."

He fought a smile. "Stop talking. Just breathe."

They were out of the way for now, maybe a mile west of what was being burned. If no one came for them in the next half hour, he'd move them again.

He got down low, lay on his side parallel to her body and put his face close to hers. "Just try to relax. My team will find us soon. They've never let me down. And I'm not going to let you down."

She nodded, like she wanted to believe him.

"Are you going to keep fighting, Isabelle? Or am I in this alone?" he asked, and the way she answered caught him off guard.

"Tell me the worst thing you've ever done," she said

suddenly. "It doesn't matter what you say. You can't top me."

"Somehow, I really doubt that."

She stared at him, and for just a second her face was illuminated by the overhead flares set off by the local soldiers—a cry for help. From anyone. She looked beautiful, despite the cuts and bruises. Beautiful and strong, and he wondered why the hell he would notice that now.

"I slept with the man who held me hostage. Willingly. I seduced him, because I wasn't about to be a victim. I stayed in control. I made my own choices," she said, her teeth gritted at the memory of what she'd done. "I wasn't forced. They're going to say that I was and I'm going to have to agree. But that's a lie."

What she'd just told him was something she'd never reveal to anyone else. And now she needed the same thing from him. She was daring him really, and he'd never been one to back down from a dare in his life.

She's not going to remember any of this, so just tell her.

"I killed my stepfather," he told her. "Self-defense. He tried to kill me first." *Nothing more than the rules of engagement.*

"How old?"

He paused. "I was fourteen," he said, was about to tell her he didn't want to talk about this anymore—couldn't, really. She was asking so much of him, things he'd never willingly give away. He didn't do submission well, and she was nearly tearing his heart right out of his chest with every question.

And when she took his hand in hers, he wondered what

the hell to do next. "Tell me what else I can do for you," he said.

"Kiss me," she whispered, and he figured she must be zoned out on the morphine and the pain and there was no way she realized what she asked him.

But his own eyes had finally adjusted to the dark, and one look in her eyes, clearer now than they'd been minutes earlier, told him that she was in full control of her senses.

"Isabelle, I—"

"I don't want to die knowing that the last man who touched me hurt me."

"We're not going to die."

"Can you promise me that?"

"I don't make promises. But I know what my gut tells me."

"Please, Jake. Don't make me beg for this," she whispered and, *ah shit,* he'd already leaned down toward her involuntarily.

He put his mouth on hers, the taste a welcome relief from the dust and stifling heat. How she could taste so sweet in the middle of all this hell was a mystery.

Her arm curled around his neck, holding him there in a sudden burst of fierce protectiveness and passion that bonded them more strongly than he would've thought possible.

When he pulled back, her breathing was faster. He couldn't tell if it was her injury or the kiss or both, but she murmured, "Put your hands on me," in his ear. And he did, lightly through the jacket, the way a man would touch a woman he wanted—caressed her arm, her breast, her belly, let his hand linger on her hip and thigh as if his touch could heal everything.

He watched her face carefully while he caressed her, in case it was too much, but she didn't stop him. And when he finished, he brought a hand to her cheek and rubbed a thumb over the bruise on her forehead.

"Thank you," she whispered, her voice tight. "I know, after what I told you—I know that couldn't have been easy."

"I don't do things out of pity. Never did," he said, pressed his lower body against hers carefully, so she'd know the effect she'd had on him. Because the most important thing right now was to make her smile.

And when she did smile, he forgot about her injuries and the fire and the gunshots. He was going to have to run with her again, and soon, because he refused to let this be the end of the line. And he couldn't help but kiss her again, a long deep kiss that wasn't ever going to be enough. His hand rested on her hip and her hand closed around his for the second time that night.

He pulled back when he heard the low hum of a motor over the riot of gunshots.

Saved. Fucking finally.

"Is that for us?" she asked. He turned to her to tell her yes, but she'd already drifted off to sleep. Actually looked peaceful, her fingers still twined through his.

He knew it would be a long while until he found peace again.

CHAPTER

1

two months later

Isabelle Markham knocked lightly on the heavy metal door, heard the sharp *What?* come from the other side and thought briefly about turning away.

"The SEALs who rescued you are stationed here. I'm sure you'll run into them at some point. Will that be a problem for you?" The admiral—and the man she knew simply as Uncle Cal—eyed her sharply across the desk, his words a final test.

"That's not a problem," she said, right before she signed the final papers that declared her commitment to the U.S. Navy as a civilian consultant for the next three months.

She'd meant it. It was *not* a problem. She needed closure

on this situation. She'd start working on base tomorrow and didn't want any surprises to throw her off the finely honed balance she'd fought for over the past two months.

She pushed her way inside the office and found herself face-to-face with the man who'd saved her life.

Jake Hansen stood well over six feet tall, dressed in full jungle camouflage BDUs. In Africa, his hair had been completely covered by a dark green bandanna. His whole face, except for his eyes, which were somewhere between the color of steel and smoke, had been camouflaged with paint—most of which had begun to fade. As the hours had worn on, she'd been able to get glimpses of what lay behind the SEAL's mask.

She remembered the medic wiping the greasepaint off her own face during the transport to the hospital.

His hair was longer, blonder than she'd have guessed, but the rest of her instinct had served correct. He was one of the most handsome men she'd ever seen—rugged good looks really, made even better by the way he didn't seem to notice it.

He just stared at her, like if he looked at her hard enough, she might disappear.

"Lieutenant...Jake...I'm Isabelle Markham." Her voice seemed to echo in the small room and she forced herself to breathe.

"I know who you are," he said, and she tried to hold back a smile at hearing his voice again. The tone was low, rough, just like she'd remembered, a voice that had forced its way into her dreams.

When she'd been stuck in the hospital, right after the

rescue, she'd wake up in the middle of the night reaching for his hand, sure he was right there next to her.

She still found herself seeking out his touch, but now it was from the comfort of her own bed.

"I really wanted to see you—to thank you. For saving my life," she said. She wondered how such an important sentiment could sound so completely lame, but it was nothing less than the truth.

He walked toward her and for a second she wondered if he was going to . . . hug her or something. But he only shut the door behind her.

"How did you find me?" he asked, and no, it wasn't exactly the type of reunion she'd been hoping for.

"I . . . Admiral Callahan told me where you might be. He knows my mother," she said, and maybe she could sound more like she was in high school. Jake didn't make her feel any better, because he just sighed, shook his head and mumbled stuff under his breath.

He'd done that a lot in Africa. She'd found it comforting then. Now, not so much.

"I don't remember much about the rescue," she said quickly, because she saw the partial horror in his eyes. Obviously sharing secrets in the dark when their lives were in danger was one thing, but the cold stark reality of daylight was a different story entirely. "I mean, they told me what had happened to me—what you did for me, but I was really out of it. It's all one big blur."

He relaxed slightly, but his guard was still up.

When the FBI and CIA questioned her, she'd just kept thinking about Jake, focusing on his gray eyes, pretended she was telling him the story. Because he was the only one who knew the truth—her truth—the only person besides her who ever would.

And he'd understood. If he hadn't, he never would've bared his soul to her. She hadn't been sure if he'd topped her story, but she had to admit they were neck and neck.

"You shouldn't have come here," he said finally.

"*You're welcome* would've sufficed and been a much nicer response."

"If you're looking for nice, you really did come to the wrong place. I don't need thanks for doing my job. And besides, it wasn't a one-man mission," he said.

"But you stayed with me. Stayed behind when you didn't have to."

"That's my job," he said tightly and she wondered if he was going to ask her to leave his office.

"I know. But it still meant a lot to me," she said quietly. He stuck his hands in his pockets and looked up at the ceiling for a second, as though the sentiment caught him off guard. She knew that didn't happen often.

"Do you want some coffee or something?" he asked finally.

"Coffee would be great."

"I'll be right back." He motioned for her to sit in one of the chairs that flanked his desk, which was piled impossibly high with files.

She heard the door close behind her and she sat in the hard wooden chair and tried to take in as much as she could of his office, as though this room could give her more of a glimpse into the soul and psyche of a man who routinely risked his own life to save people he didn't even know, and most likely would never see again.

He really seemed to prefer that last part.

A recruiting poster for the Navy hung to the left of the desk and, she discovered on further inspection, covered a large hole in the wall. A broken chair, the likely culprit for the hole, lay in pieces underneath the poster.

On his desk, on top of the piles was a book on policy and procedure, an iPod and an empty box of donuts. A uniform hung from a dart in the wall behind the desk—dress whites with an impossible array of medals across the chest.

It was the space of a man who wasn't around much to care about what his office looked like.

The door opened behind her sooner than she'd expected, and Jake handed her a Styrofoam cup of steaming liquid. He hadn't asked how she liked her coffee and she took a tentative sip. It was light and sweet, just the way she liked.

"How did you know how I take my coffee?" she asked.

He sat across from her and gave a small shrug. "Because that's how I take mine."

"So everyone who drinks coffee with you has to take it the way you do?"

"Yes," he said simply. He sat behind his desk, stretched his legs out so his feet rested near hers.

"Are you all right?" he asked finally.

"Yes. I'm fine," she said firmly, and for a second she swore she saw the hint of a smile on his mouth. "What?"

"You've answered that question a lot. Too much, probably."

"You're right but—"

"You're fine, right?"

"I am."

"I'm not arguing."

"I want to go back there. To Africa," she said.

"I'm sure I'll be back there too," he said. "And don't take this the wrong way, but I really hope I don't see you there again."

"You think I'd be putting myself at risk unnecessarily."

"What I think at this point doesn't matter. Shouldn't."

"Why can't you have an opinion on my life? Everyone else does," she muttered.

"That's exactly why I don't."

He was just the way she'd remembered—the way she'd figured he'd be in an everyday, normal situation. He was not handling her with kid gloves, didn't look at her like she was a victim, and she knew she wanted to do more than just thank him.

"I'd like to see you again," she said before she could stop herself. These days, more so than before, it was all about taking chances, about really living and not letting fear win. She'd come out of this stronger. She was just having a problem finding someone who could deal with her strength, who could see through to her softer side.

"Are you asking me out? Because I'm more than capable of asking you out if I wanted to."

Yeah, she hadn't wanted to be treated with kid gloves. "So you're saying you don't want to?"

"I didn't say that, Isabelle." He leaned forward on his elbows, his strong hands flexing on the desk between them. "It's just that I don't like doctors. I mean, as a general rule."

God, those eyes . . . they could be a weapon all on their

own, and she was sure she wasn't the first woman to fall for him.

And he wanted nothing to do with her.

Dr. Isabelle Markham was thirty-one years old, had been to Brown undergrad and Harvard Medical. Top of her class. Area of specialty—reconstructive plastic surgery.

She could've gone anywhere.

She'd chosen to volunteer with Doctors Without Borders, aka Médecins Sans Frontières, and she'd been doing stints four months at a time for three years. Working in local clinics on her off time. There had never been any trouble until her mother ran for the Senate last year—and won. The threats started soon after.

In Africa, she'd been betrayed by her own bodyguard, an ex–Special Forces soldier who'd been kicked out of the Army years earlier, turned merc and, finally, turned on his own country. Jake just couldn't figure out why and the FBI agents who'd debriefed him hadn't been interested in sharing.

And Jake had visited her every chance he'd gotten those first two weeks she'd been in the hospital. It was three hours away from base and he'd arrive at three in the morning or later, watch her for a bit while she slept and slip out before anyone noticed him. He watched her bruises fade and the machinery and tubes removed, saw all the signs of progress, including her deep, easy sleep.

He saw the way she sometimes reached out for something with her hand, tighten a fist around empty air, and he'd tighten his own fist at his side and tell himself that this was all so fucking ridiculous. And then he'd been called away and spent the last month in the mountains of Afghanistan, gathering intel and getting shot on his way out of the country, which seemed to be his MO these days.

He'd come in late last night, gotten stitched, thought about calling around and gathering some intel of his own about Isabelle and figured that she had to be back into the normal routine of her life.

Before he'd left the States, he'd discovered that she was engaged.

But she sat across from him now, her dark hair long and loose down her back. She looked beautiful and carefree, like she'd recently made the best decision of her life. And her left hand was bare.

He'd never really been scared of anyone or anything in his life, but this woman, the possibilities she held out to him, shook him in a way he'd never been prepared for.

"What do you have against doctors?" she asked.

"They ask a lot of questions."

She stood up, dropped her empty coffee cup in the garbage can. "Why don't you think about it."

He willed his beeper to go off, the phone to ring, a small war to break out—anything—and wondered why he suddenly needed saving from a woman.

He couldn't do this—not with her.

She says she doesn't remember anything.

An odd sense of disappointment settled over him, even though there was no way to deny the palpable connection between them. If she didn't know *what* had happened, she knew *something* had.

Kissing her like that—touching her—had not been professional. He'd let his guard down completely. Like he hadn't already learned how bad the consequences of doing something like that could be.

"Are you used to getting what you want?" he asked.

"Aren't you?" She smiled before she walked out of his office, shutting the door quietly behind her.

He didn't even have time to wonder what the hell he was going to do now before his cell phone rang. He glanced at the number, flipped it open and said, "I'm fine."

"*Shot* is not *fine*," Kenneth Waldron, the only man Jake ever thought of as Dad, shouted across the line.

"Is that what your tarot cards told you?"

"I don't need any cards. I told you last month, something big is barreling down on you."

"Yeah, well, it missed me. Mostly."

"Jake..."

"I'm fine," Jake repeated, his hand automatically passing over his right side, still heavily bandaged. "Flesh wound. I'm just getting ready to run some drills."

"I wasn't necessarily talking about gunfire, by the way. And put your brother on the phone."

He didn't even bother to say, *They're not here.* Instead, he waited a beat, and Nick and Chris burst through the door of his office, arguing as usual.

Sometimes having a father who was psychic was a real drag. "Which one?"

"Whichever one won't lie to me!" his father roared.

Jake looked between Chris and Nick and figured it was a draw. He tossed the phone to Chris while Nick took the rest of his coffee and drank it in one gulp.

"He's fine, Dad," Chris said. "Why would I lie?" He paused to listen. "Well, yeah, you've got a point there."

Kenneth Waldron was known as Twist to his earliest friends, *cher* to his wife, who'd died twelve years earlier, and Dad to his three grown boys. At work, they called him Kenny to his face and Crazy behind his back, and tonight, during a meeting with his newest group of wannabe rock stars who spent more time pissing out the windows of moving cars and smashing bottles onstage than actually singing, the boys in the band began to call him Boss.

"Your pitch is off. Stop holding back and open up your voice. And I want to hear you play the shit out of that bass!" he yelled over the din.

He'd become some sort of legend in the music business, managing the most unmanageable of rock bands, taking them on when every other manager in town with a lick of sense dumped them on their asses and left them crying in the street. And he made them. Kept track of them. Fathered them and brought them to the top of their game.

Everyone always wondered how he did it. Why he did it. Hell, it was the easiest thing going compared to what he'd reared. Was still rearing, as his three sons continued to raise hell and heaven and everything in between.

He was young for the business, just turned forty-three, with a biological son who was twenty-six, and two adopted sons about the same age. He'd married Maggie when they were both just seventeen to escape his family, moved in with hers along the swamps of the Bayou, St. Charles Parish, and got her pregnant within the month. By then, he'd already been managing some local bands, and by nineteen, he and Maggie started their own company and signed with a city label to recruit the new talent.

They'd moved to New York to be near the city when Christopher had been thirteen. Already six feet, six inches tall, he would put on another three quarters of an inch before he finally stopped growing. He'd been used to being homeschooled back in Louisiana, but in actuality, he'd been used to running wild and doing pretty much whatever he'd wanted. He'd grown up rock and roll, had the talent and the voice to forge his own career in music but had never seemed all that interested in that kind of life. Which was why he'd gotten suspended on his very first day of private school in New York for lighting up a cigarette in the middle of the cafeteria.

When he'd been dragged to the principal's office, cursing anyone within earshot in Cajun French, Nick and Jake were already there. For what, Kenny couldn't remember clearly, although it was most probably for skipping school, which the two of them had had a tendency to do on a regular basis. They'd both been on the verge of expulsion.

Maggie had gone in to collect Chris and came home with the two other boys as well. They'd each gotten suspended for two weeks, because they'd all started fighting—with one another—right outside the principal's office, for no other reason than there was nothing better to do. Or at least that was the explanation Jake gave to him later on that same afternoon, when Kenny had bandaged a cut on his neck and discovered an even bigger problem.

To this day, Kenny couldn't remember when the boys

officially moved in, but it seemed as though after that first day they'd never left.

It had seemed right, he mused as he lit another cigarette and waited for the band to get their shit together onstage. He'd corralled them in a strip joint earlier that afternoon, attempting to get drunk and stupid, and he'd dragged them out and babysat them until they were ready to go on.

The band members thought they'd been caught because someone turned them in, but in reality, it was because Kenny had what the Cajuns called *the sight*. Chris had it too, something Maggie's mother had pronounced immediately upon seeing Chris seconds after he was born with one blue eye and one green.

What they dubbed the *psychic Cajun bullshit* drove Nick and Jake crazy, although Chris had pretty much refused to use his after Maggie died. And if anyone could fight a mental force of nature, it would be Chris.

Kenny disappeared, both mentally and physically, from the boys for a year after Maggie's death—there on the surface, with phone calls and brief visits in between his band's tours, but grief had taken its toll on him. In that year, his already fragile and wild sons had gone out of control, and he hadn't been sure if he could bring them back.

Some days, he wasn't sure if he ever had. And recently he'd been up half the night, pacing holes in the floor and worrying about all three of them. Because something just wasn't right.

"I think you need to stop worrying about us now," Chris had announced not that long ago over dinner, as Kenny fought not to ask about the cast on Nick's leg, or the two on Jake's forearms or the heavy bandage on the side of Chris's neck.

"I think you need to get a hobby," Nick said, and Kenny had wisely not brought up the fact that Nick had spent the better part of an hour turning the answering machine into some kind of detonating time bomb because he'd been bored.

"I think you need to get laid," Jake told him, his gray eyes steady and serious. Kenny had laughed and silently agreed that Jake was probably right.

But still, he worried. Worried when Nick caught a cold or his voice rasped more than usual, worried when he noticed that Jake wasn't sleeping well or that Chris needed to eat more and smoke less.

He wondered if they'd ever settle down, but as each year passed and they climbed to new heights of crazy rather than calming down with age, he'd begun to think that there weren't women born yet who could handle his boys for longer than a night. If that.

He'd talk to them more tomorrow night. For now, he lit another cigarette and prepared to storm the damned stage to get the current group of boys who stood in front of him under control.

CHAPTER
2

When Isabelle had announced her intentions to go back with Médecins Sans Frontières after the first of the year, her mother, in conjunction with Uncle Cal, had come up with a different plan for her.

For the last month, she'd tried the normalcy her mother had so desperately wanted, tried to reconnect with the man she was supposed to marry that following year and went to work in a big city hospital practicing her specialty. But more often than not, she was called down to stitch up people with small cuts who didn't want scars to mar their outward appearance. And she'd discovered that she and Daniel were practically strangers—and probably always had been.

She was being smothered. There was too much comfort,

too much sympathy, too much of everything she never wanted, and she'd known she couldn't spend the rest of her life like this.

Uncle Cal brought an opportunity to her attention, a way to do the work she wanted and be in a protected environment, and so here she was, doing consultant work for the Department of Defense and actually working in the Naval Hospital. Uncle Cal had pulled more than a few strings to allow her to actually practice on base, and she was grateful for the change.

She touched the side that still twinged when it rained or when she twisted wrong or worked too long without rest. The orthopedist she saw assured her that would fade, and until then she thought of the pain as more of a badge of honor. A mark of survival.

They'd caught Rafe, her bodyguard and protector for months while she'd worked in the Congo and its outlying regions. He'd kept her safe, and then, without warning, he'd betrayed her. For money.

Even so, Uncle Cal had managed to convince her mother that the Navy would provide Isabelle with the best kind of protection from further incidents. Even the FBI had told her she would be better off working for an organization that didn't put her in the middle of such dangerous places.

In the meantime, she was ringing in the first week of the New Year with a never-ending parade of Marines on a training mission. Except they seemed to be doing less training and more hurting themselves than anything. She was on call nearly twenty-four seven, reminding her of her residency—without the support staff.

"Think I'll be all right for BUD/S training next month, Doc?" A Marine named Al, who seemed much too young to see any kind of combat, looked up at her expectantly. Shrapnel had caught him across the forehead, and the gash had bled like crazy.

"You've got to tell me what BUD/S is first," she said.

"BUD/S is the first part of training for SEALs," Al explained. "It's supposed to be the hardest thing a man can do."

She doubted Jake would say that it was the hardest—not by a long shot—but she just nodded. "It sounds intense."

"Yeah—the first weeks are the worst, especially the part they call Hell Week. Once you pass that, you're secure, but there's still a lot more that goes into being a SEAL."

"And that's what you want to do?" she asked.

"Yes, ma'am," Al said, so earnestly she stifled a laugh.

"You should be ready," she said. "And I can make sure this doesn't scar."

"S'okay if you can't. Scars are fierce."

"Scars aren't going to get you through BUD/S. You met any SEALs yet, Doc?" a Marine named Luke asked her. He'd already been in twice today. "There's a group of them around this month. Just got back from a trip—they're always good for morale."

"I've met a few," she said. It had been twenty-four hours since she'd walked out of Jake's office, and she'd been too busy to think much about their interaction.

Today, she'd worn blue scrubs, her ID badge tied to a black string that hung around her neck and kept getting in the way. She'd pulled her hair back in a loose knot and she'd forgone makeup, but that didn't seem to matter because she'd been asked out about fifteen times. Obviously, none of the Marines had a problem dating doctors.

"You know they learn how to kill eighteen different ways with just their bare hands? Imagine what they can do with a weapon." Luke was talking to Al now, revving the young man up with what Isabelle believed to be a cross between bullshit and fact, with the truth lying someplace in between. "Man, some of those guys are just legendary."

"You know anything about that guy Jake Hansen I keep hearing about?" Al asked.

"Jake? He's crazy. You'll probably never meet him, Doc," Luke told her. "He hates doctors. Usually gets one of the other guys to stitch him up or does it himself."

"Interesting," she murmured.

"See that file box? They say that entire thing is his." Luke pointed to a scarred, khaki-colored, four drawer cabinet wedged into the corner of the infirmary.

Isabelle had tried to open it earlier, but none of the keys the old doc had left behind fit the lock. "It sounds like you might need to fill me in, then—you know, in case he ever shows."

That was all she needed to say before the fish stories began, each man trying to outdo the other with what they knew about Jake.

"They say that Jake went straight to BUD/S from boot camp. That never happens. I hear he joined the Navy when he was fifteen—best fake ID they'd ever seen, so they let him stay," Al piped up.

"He's got to be the youngest guy to ever make the SEALs," Luke said. "His BUD/S instructor was thrown out of the Navy for excessive torture during a SERE training session. Supposedly, he almost beat Jake to death, but he survived. Top in his class."

"SEALs are overrated. I could take him," a Marine named Zeke on the periphery of the conversation, with a bandage around his head, called out, and that made Isabelle laugh out loud.

"Supposedly, he's got this really sick tat of an eagle on the back of his skull. Had to go all the way to Belize to get it."

"Sweet," Al said, rubbed the back of his own head.

"Hands down and stay still," she said and he complied immediately. It felt good to have that command back in her tone.

"He never sleeps. Ever. And, after one trip, he lost over half the blood in his body. He comes back to base and he's on his feet after a few transfusions. For the rest of the week, he dragged around an IV pole and kept a Hep-Lock in his arm but he finished all his drills and made quals. The old doc didn't appreciate that much," Luke said.

Isabelle had to fight to keep from rolling her eyes.

"He sounds like a friggin' machine. The man of steel," Al said.

"I hear he's got to have it like three, four times a day. Sleeps with three women at once just to satisfy him," Luke said, and that was information she could've gone without knowing. She shot him a look but he just shrugged.

"He's definitely not the type to settle down and be domesticated," one of the nurses, who'd come in to grab some antiseptic, agreed with an edge to her voice that made

Isabelle bristle inwardly and wonder if that nurse had tried and failed herself.

Isabelle didn't have any desire to tame Jake Hansen. No, she wanted him wild as anything. She was sure that she was the woman who could handle him. She just wondered if he'd be able to reciprocate, and figured that now was as good a time as any to find out if he was strong enough for her.

And then Zeke addressed his next comment right to her. "I've come to realize that most men who need this much hype never live up to it."

She had a strong feeling that didn't apply to Jake, but she didn't tell Zeke that. Instead, she eyed the old file cabinet and made a mental note to requisition a blowtorch and a pickax ASAP.

"New doc's been putting her hands in your drawers."

How Max, a captain with Naval Intelligence, managed to say shit like that with a straight face was beyond him, but Jake was still happy for the heads-up. It was one of the many reasons he'd planted the silent alarm inside the old filing cabinet in the first place.

The old doc never looked in there, knowing that if a SEAL bothered to darken his doorstep it was because there was a bone sticking out somewhere and there wouldn't be time to look through any file. The files in that cabinet were bogus, placed there years ago to satisfy the mass of curiosity seekers looking for the legend of Jake and his SEAL teammates or whatever shit they were feeding the young recruits this week.

He hadn't counted on them feeding it to young doctors too, but he guessed no one was immune to vast quantities of bullshit these days.

The real SEAL medical files remained somewhere under lock and key, taken out only when a severe enough injury warranted them. Until then, team members committed to memory one anothers' medical history, medication allergies and the like, to make for light travel and easy ground medic.

"What's the guy want with my stuff?" Jake asked.

"Not a guy. Woman. Civilian—friend of the admiral's. Tall. Long dark hair. Hot as—"

Jake clenched a fist around the pencil he'd been using and snapped it in half. Because there was no way in hell Isabelle was working on this base. She would've mentioned that yesterday.

"Are you all right?" Max asked. Max was the go-to guy, handled all the comms for the team when they were in the field. He was their lifeline, and always seemed to have all the right information at just the right time.

"Yeah, fine," he said. Max shrugged and turned back to his computer. Jake threw the pencil in the garbage and pushed out into the cold January air, wishing he was healed enough to go for a run or a swim or something that could get rid of this extra tension before he went to see Isabelle.

Because he was not fine at all. He'd been having the nightmares again. Although they'd eased considerably over the past years, they were now a nightly ritual. That hadn't happened since he was fifteen and went through boot camp.

Fuck.

He'd come into the Navy half-shattered, half-wild and not expecting the process to do much for him except keep him out of jail.

He'd been wrong. The military had saved him, nurtured him. Understood him, maybe more than he ever expected a woman to.

He'd been placed in BUD/S from boot camp on a dare—they'd been trying to break him. They never succeeded. There was nothing they could do to him that he hadn't already endured in some way, shape or form, but in this case, enduring was just a step on the road that led to what he wanted to do.

He didn't need his past leaking out for the rest of the free world to see.

He slipped into the infirmary through the back door that led to the small hallway in between the treatment rooms and the doctors' offices.

Isabelle was sitting behind a desk filling out paperwork. Her hair was pulled back from her face and she bit her bottom lip as she concentrated. Her foot tapped against the desk to some beat only she could hear, and for a second, he almost walked away.

Instead of knocking, he leaned against the doorjamb until she noticed him, which took a few minutes. He was used to that, had mastered the fine art of seeming to appear out of nowhere. It was useful in both his job and in real life, although it tended to scare people.

Isabelle shifted, looked up and gasped. Her pen screeched across what she was writing, ripping the paper, and she threw the pen down. "How long have you been there? Why didn't you just knock?"

"Why are you looking through my stuff?" he demanded.

"I'm not . . . I wasn't." She paused and got herself together, and he realized that the woman in front of him was a terrible liar when she was caught off guard. Bad for her, good for him.

There's nothing about Isabelle Markham that's good for you.

"You couldn't be bothered to tell me that you'd be working here—on base?"

"I wasn't sure how you'd react," she said.

"I react a whole lot better to honesty," he said. "Jesus Christ."

"I was planning on telling you yesterday—I just got distracted," she said, and then her cheeks flushed.

He willed himself to ignore that. "I don't get it—you're not Reserves and I know you didn't go through OCS. Why are you here?"

She crossed her arms in front of her like a shield. "Now who's looking through someone else's files?"

He ignored her. "I don't see a huge need for plastic surgeons on this base."

"The DoD feels differently. I've been hired as a civilian, with the option to enlist."

"You've been doing more than consulting."

"I don't have to explain this to you, but the admiral pulled a few strings for me. If I decide I want to enlist, I'll complete Officer Candidate School when I'm fully healed and then I'll be reassigned to a base that deals primarily with reconstruction."

That made *him* pull back for a second. She was still in

danger. The admiral might be letting her think she wanted to be here, but Jake had no doubt that she was here for her own protection.

"If it makes you feel any better, I didn't look through your file," she said.

"It doesn't. Besides, I know you didn't look through it, because it's not kept with the other files. It's somewhere buried deep, or else it's been burned or shredded to the point where I exist only to a very select group of people."

"It's not like I'm going to tell people about you."

"You can't tell anyone about me. Can't mention me, can't mention what I look like. Nothing. And you especially can't mention that goddamned rescue story."

He'd pushed it a little too far that time, which was something he tended to do. All the time. But he didn't usually get choked-back tears from the people he'd pushed. Clenched fists, yes, and she had those too.

"That *goddamned rescue story* is important to me. You asshole. You complete and utter asshole," she said. "It must be great to be the man of steel, to let nothing bother you."

"I never said that," he said quietly, but it was too late.

"I promise, my *goddamned rescue story* and I will never bother you again," she said, and then she turned and walked out past him, that same determined set to her shoulders he'd seen the day before.

Admiral James Callahan knew how old Jake Hansen was when he'd enlisted, even though he'd pretended to buy the fake birth certificate, doctored to trick the admiral into thinking Jake was seventeen going on eighteen. Jake had forged that part of the document poorly to draw attention away from the fact that he was really fifteen going on sixteen. He'd had no way of knowing Cal had done the same thing himself some twenty years earlier.

Cal figured the boy would never make it through the first day, never mind the first week, and then there'd be no harm, no foul.

Jake turned out to be one of the best men the Navy had ever seen. Or so the drill sergeant told the admiral after the first week of boot camp. Wanted Jake to go through BUD/S.

"He's fifteen," Cal had said.

"Almost sixteen. If he passes the training, he'll be seventeen by the time he sees combat. We can keep him back if he needs to be older." Captain Harry Lopez had sat across from Cal in his barracks, over whiskey and cigars. It had been close to midnight, and the base was quiet.

"He's fifteen."

"He handles himself like he's older. He was born for this," Harry had argued.

Cal remembered holding Hansen's file, complete with the police report and the psychologicals obtained from the kid's supposed adoptive father, figured that by the time Jake entered his office, he'd have the intel read and be able to put any hint of softheartedness aside.

He'd been wrong. Since that day, Jake's file had been stored in a very special place, out of public consumption, and Jake remained one of the best he'd ever come across.

Jake would help Cal protect the daughter of one of his best friends. He was the perfect, and most obvious, choice.

"You asked to see me?"

Cal looked up to find Jake standing by the door, having completely bypassed his gunny and a locked door. "In," he said.

Jake moved across the expansive office silently and sat in front of Cal's desk. He actually looked patient, but Cal knew better. "I've got a job for you."

"I've already got a job."

"It's a favor."

"I'm listening."

"There's a family friend I'm worried about. She's working on base now, and I need some extra protection for her," Cal said. Jake nodded, like he knew, and Cal wondered if Jake had bugged his office. Because he never put anything past Jake. "It's the doctor your team rescued."

"That might not work out so well," Jake muttered.

"Jesus, Jake. What did you do? She's only been on base for two goddamned days!"

"*I* didn't do anything," Jake said, and sighed, as if Cal was bothering him.

The boy never did have any fear or what counted as common sense. He got away with more than most, and should've ended up under someone's boot long ago.

"You never said you knew Dr. Markham," Jake said finally.

"There wasn't a need for you to know. You saved her life—that was the important part," Cal said. "I had to tell her you and your team were stationed here. She'd come across you eventually. She was asking for you. About you."

If Jake was surprised at that, he didn't let on.

"You're the best one for this job. The only one I feel comfortable asking."

"How much protection are you talking about?"

"As much as you can give her over the next few weeks. Until we finish collecting the intel we need. But it's all on the QT, which is why I need you." Speaking of hides, Cal thought about Isabelle's mother and how she'd have his if something happened to her daughter again. Isabelle had been lucky so far. But Cal knew that the man who'd taken her would make good on his threats—Rafe had refused Cal's last payment, sent back a message that simply said, *Time's up.*

Cal had two former CIA men on the case and a constant feeling of a noose tightening around his neck.

"Wait a minute. She's not going to know anything about this?" Jake asked, his voice tinged with concern—and anger.

"It's in her best interest that she doesn't."

"She deserves to know," Jake said.

"That's not your call."

"What am I supposed to do? Get myself shot so I can be under her constant care?"

"You were already shot—maybe it's infected. Hell, I don't know; figure something out, dammit. She's as stubborn as you are and it took all I had to get her off a plane headed back to some damned shithole and onto this base. What does that tell you?" Cal slammed his fists on the desk and paused to collect himself. "I'm not asking you to marry her, Jake. Just don't let her get hurt again."

"I need more information."

Cal glanced at the picture on his desk—him with

Isabelle's father, Sergeant James Markham. Nicknamed Ox and as stubborn as one. The man who'd died saving Cal's life.

Cal stared Jake down, but the younger man didn't flinch. Cal hadn't expected him to. "I can't give you anything now. You've jumped into the fire with much less than this before."

"I want a name," Jake said. "You can't send me into war if I don't know the enemy."

Cal's nostrils flared even as he saw Jake's own private war flash in his eyes. "He was a private contractor Isabelle's mother hired. Rafe McAllistar."

"He was never caught," Jake spoke more to himself than to Cal, let out a low whistle and shook his head.

"We told Isabelle that he was. That's why she can't know about this protection."

"You think he'll come after her again?"

"I have reason to believe so, yes. And you are not to investigate this further. I have people on it."

"You sure he works alone?"

"Yes, I'm sure. But he's former Delta. Formidable."

"She's vulnerable as hell," Jake muttered.

"Which is why I chose you."

"She needs more secure protection than I can give."

"If the threat were imminent, she'd have it. This is a precaution. Like I said, you've trusted me before on much less than this."

"Guess I have." Jake stood, reached across the desk with his right hand out. Mission accepted.

Cal shook it and Jake turned to leave the room.

"One thing, Admiral," he called casually over his shoulder. "She's going to have to stay with me."

Cal curled his hands into fists and stood. He should've known Jake would try to back him into a wall. "With you and two other SEALs?"

"Can you think of a safer place?" Jake asked.

"Yes. Many safer places, and none of them include living with three single men," Cal said. "She'll stay with me."

Jake sighed and shook his head. "Then I'll move back in with you," he said, and Cal had instant flashbacks to that brief period of time, ten years earlier, when that had been tried and abandoned within a forty-eight-hour period.

"That won't work."

"I didn't think so," Jake said.

"Boy, you are really pushing it with me."

"There's a connection between you and the senator. Isabelle doesn't belong with you."

Cal stared at him before answering. "This isn't a joke."

"Do you think I want to move her into my house, my space—my life?" Jake asked, ran a hand through his hair, and Cal knew he was tugging the man past the point of frustration. Which was never a good idea.

"I know how much you value your privacy," Cal said quietly.

"I can't do limited protection for her, Admiral. You and I both know that kind of thing never works. If you want me to do this, you're going to have to let *me* do this."

Cal sat back down. "You'll start tomorrow. She's to know nothing about the situation. Just keep her safe, Jake. Keep her safe any way you have to."

Jake nodded and left the office without another word.

CHAPTER
3

Nick hadn't been with a woman since he'd gotten back on U.S. soil from Afghanistan, which was some kind of record he never wanted to have to beat. It had been nearly forty-eight hours, thanks to Jake's gunshot wound and the subsequent paperwork that needed to be handed in immediately, plus the debriefings and the physicals, and right now Nick craved the kind of release only hot sex—or a good demolition—could bring.

Of course, being out with the man you called *Dad* could put a severe cramp in both those options.

"I didn't want to come here to watch the battle of the fucking bands in the first place," Jake was complaining to Chris.

"I need to get laid," Nick told his brothers.

"Go for it," Chris said, then downed another shot.

"It's not like I can leave with someone—not with Dad here," Nick said.

"Like he didn't know about all the other times, starting with freshman year in high school," Chris said and Jake and Nick groaned in unison at that image.

"Freshman year wasn't my first," Nick said at the same time Jake asked, "Are you trying to make sure I can never have sex again?"

"Dad probably gets more ass than any of us combined," Chris said, and Nick and Jake groaned again. Chris just laughed. Tonight, he wore a white T-shirt, which made the fact that his eyes were two different colors stand out even more. One was bright blue, the other an intense green, and they gave him an unbalanced, slightly crazed look. Once people got to know him, they realized that it wasn't just a look.

"He's got to stop with the mind-reading bullshit," Nick muttered.

"Just don't start a fight tonight," Jake warned and Nick immediately figured that a good, old-fashioned fight could work to distract him for a while, since the band about to take the stage looked like Mötley Crüe gone wrong. Until he felt the tap on his shoulder and turned to see Kenny Waldron, the man he'd called *Dad* since he'd been fourteen, staring all of them down.

"I'm here to show off the new band, not my sons' excellence at bar fights," he said.

All three men held up their hands in silent surrender. Like they were being put under house arrest.

"Hey, we don't start them," Chris protested, and that much at least was true. There were guys who knew they were SEALs, wanted to pick fights with them just because of that. Sometimes it was because other men's girlfriends looked at them a little too long, but hey, they couldn't help that either.

Kenny rolled his eyes at them, and then his stare stayed on Jake for a few minutes too long. He opened his mouth like he was going to say something, but the band started in and he got distracted.

Score one for Jake. And speaking of score, Jake should be chomping at the bit worse than Nick was. Jake was definitely tense, but he appeared off the market tonight—not looking around for any kind of action, the way he normally would. Which could only mean that Jake was already in some kind of major trouble.

Nick looked around and his eye caught on one woman who looked familiar. It took him a minute, but he was finally able to place her. "Hey, Dr. Markham's here."

"Who's that?" Kenny asked.

"The woman Jake pissed off today," Chris said and Jake shot him a look, which he ignored.

"You saw her today?" Nick asked.

"It's a long story," Jake mumbled and Nick knew there was more to it than that. A lot more. But he was content to let Jake shrug it off if he wanted. He'd get the full story from Chris later on.

"Were you rude?" Kenny asked.

"I was the way I always am," Jake said. Chris choked on his beer, Kenny started lecturing Jake in Cajun French and Nick figured that this was a perfect time to slip away.

When Zeke had offered to show her around town, Isabelle had agreed only after he'd understood that this was in no way, shape or form a date. She wasn't going to accept at all, but she still had the ball of anger welling in her chest every time she thought about what Jake said in her office.

It was, of course, partially her fault, but he didn't have to be so arrogant. Or dismissive.

The more she thought about it, the more she realized that the whole idea that she and Jake had some kind of connection was something she must've made up in order to get through her recovery.

She'd done the therapy, dealt with the *It's not your fault* thing. That part was easy. She knew that. She knew she'd be able to handle another man's touch—one man's specifically—because on a small level she already had.

Were you just going to announce to him that you were waiting for him to be your first?

"You look really serious right now. Too serious for my first night of leave," Zeke said.

She had to actually think for a second to focus on what day of the week it was. *Thursday.* She was pretty sure of that. "Sorry. I guess I'm just tired," she said. "Too many of you guys to patch up."

He touched the butterfly bandage on his forehead. "I promise to try to be more careful."

"I don't think that's possible."

Zeke smiled. He was trying so hard, and he was handsome and nice, but her heart wasn't in this at all. "This is a new band—it's supposed to be great," he said.

She nodded and took a small sip of her beer. She didn't feel much like drinking, really had wanted to stay home and pull the covers up over her head. But that's what Uncle Cal and her mother wanted. Uncle Cal had even tried to give her some kind of curfew.

She'd waited until he'd gone to bed and then she'd snuck down the back stairs and met Zeke at the end of the block. She was more than prepared to run away from all of this. She'd never felt so lost in her life.

No, she wasn't holding it together as well as she'd thought. And she'd forgotten her wallet back at the house, so if she was really going to run away, she'd have to borrow money to do it.

Zeke was saying something to her, but she'd stopped paying attention, because Jake was walking toward her. Looking right at her.

She swallowed hard, steeled herself for what might well be another argument, although she didn't think so.

He was nearly to her when some guy—a bodybuilder type—grabbed Jake's shoulder from behind, for absolutely no reason at all that she could see, and yanked him back toward the middle of the room.

She watched as Jake turned, attempted to shrug it off and walk away, but the man had other ideas, this time grabbing the front of Jake's shirt.

Jake looked calm enough. He even smiled. And, within seconds, he held the guy by the throat.

"Oh, man, this is going to be good," Zeke was saying. "Just check this out."

She watched as a tall man with different-colored eyes stepped in between the burly man and Jake—recognized him as one of the SEALs in Africa who'd taken care of her on what seemed like the longest ten-mile ride ever, to reach the helicopter.

She recognized a third SEAL, the one who'd been with Jake when she'd been found. He seemed more interested in keeping the fight brewing than stopping it. And sure enough, within minutes a melee broke out, moving closer to the raised stage as more and more men got involved.

"Get back, Isabelle," Zeke told her, and she moved to a corner of the bar. The bartender motioned for her to come stand near him, behind the bar area, and she didn't argue.

Zeke flung himself into the crowd and for a few minutes she lost sight of both him and Jake—chairs and fists flew, bottles smashed and it seemed the entire bar, save for the women, were involved.

Except for the band, who never stopped playing. Even when people were actually rolling on the stage around them.

And then Jake managed to materialize right by her side, his shirt ripped at the collar, his hair messed and falling across his forehead.

"I was out of line," he said as soon as she made eye contact. "I didn't mean to belittle your rescue. But it's the way I deal with things, the way I have to handle things if I want to do my job well. And I do my job well."

He was standing so close, mainly, she figured, so he could be heard over the raucous music and the fight that continued behind him. "Can you understand that? I've never had this happen before."

Am I in this alone, Isabelle?

"Yeah, well, me neither," she said, and the corner of his mouth pulled slightly up.

"You still think I'm an asshole."

She shrugged. "What do you care what I think?" she asked, right before the mirror behind the bar shattered. Jake grabbed her, shielded her body with his and pulled her toward the door of the bar.

"I'm taking you home now," he said, after he'd given her a once-over to make sure she was okay.

"But I'm here with someone..." she protested, although she didn't fight being in Jake's arms.

"I don't care who you came here with, you're going home with me," he growled.

He took her by the arm and walked her past the crowd, past Zeke, who didn't even protest, and into the cool night air. He'd marked her as surely as if he'd tattooed his name across her forehead. "Let's get out of here before the police come."

"Do a lot of people try to pick fights with you?"

"Only the stupid ones," he said. "I'm not supposed to fight back. I'm just allowed to use minimal force to defend myself."

She nodded, because she got it. Jake's hands were officially deadly weapons. And then she noticed the dark stain spreading on his T-shirt. "You're bleeding."

"Shit. My stitches must've ripped." He yanked up his T-shirt and she saw the bloodstained gauze bandage.

"When did this happen?"

"Recently."

"Was it a gunshot?" she asked, but got no answer.

"Okay, I get it—all that information is classified. I'll just take you to the nearest emergency room."

"I'm not going to the hospital." He looked at her as if she'd suggested they go to the ballet.

"That's what people do when they're bleeding, Jake."

"Not me. Especially not when I have an expert right here."

"You expect me to do this?"

"What? You haven't forgiven me yet?"

"It has nothing to do with that."

"Then you're going to let me bleed to death for no good reason?" he asked.

"You're not bleeding to death," she muttered. He cocked his head and looked at her, and her insides got all quivery. The way the girls she used to make fun of in college said theirs did when a cute guy talked to them at a party. "Okay, fine. Where am I supposed to do this? I can't take you back to Uncle Cal's house."

"You're staying with your uncle?" Jake said, trying unsuccessfully to hold back a grin.

"Yes. For now. Until I find a place of my own," she said defensively. "He and my mother are slightly overprotective, in case you haven't noticed. Of course, it backfired a bit."

"Hey," he said, touched her shoulder. "Protection isn't always a bad thing."

"So I've noticed," she said. He still had a hand on her arm and she liked it. "Where are we going?"

"My place. You'd better drive," he said, handed her the keys and helped her into an ancient Chevy Blazer that looked as if it had recently been dragged through a swamp. "Storm's rolling in fast, but we'll beat it home."

The familiar burning smell that she always associated with snow was heavy on the air. "Just for the record, I haven't completely forgiven you," she said, when he got into the passenger side. The inside of the car was much cleaner than the outside, and the engine started up immediately with a purr she hadn't expected.

"Yeah, I know," he said. "But I hope you're not expecting me to apologize again, because what you got was pretty much it. And be careful, because she's fast." He patted the dashboard.

"I'm stitching you without any pain meds," she told him.

"I wouldn't have it any other way, Doc." He settled back against the seat as she pulled out of the lot seconds before she caught sight of the flashing lights of the police in the rearview mirror.

The house Jake directed her to was huge—a big white clapboard with at least four floors and set back from the other houses by a large acreage of land.

"This place is great," she said, after she parked and she and Jake headed up the main walk. The door was unlocked, and when he pushed it open she found herself in a spacious entranceway that was the size of a nice studio apartment. "Better than great."

"This is actually my father's house," he said.

"You live with your father?" Now it was her turn to smirk. "How old are you?"

"He doesn't live here anymore. His main residence is in L.A. This was a summer house and my brothers and I took over. And I'm old enough," he said. "Let's do this in my room—I don't need everyone coming home and fussing over me."

He started up the stairs, grabbing the medic kit he told her belonged to Chris, and she followed him.

His set of rooms took up nearly the entire second floor of the sprawling house.

The staircase opened up onto the main room, which had two couches—one leather and one cloth—surrounding a large entertainment center, magazines and books scattered all around. Jeans on the floor. And a pair of handcuffs.

"Is it easier if I lay on the couch or the bed?" he asked.

She tore her eyes away from the cuffs and glanced through the opened door of the bedroom to the rumpled king-sized bed. "The bed's higher."

"Come on." He walked into the bedroom and she followed. He pulled a chair up to the bed for her. "Will this work?" he asked.

"You're bleeding here too," she said, reached up to check a cut above his eyebrow. "I didn't notice that before. Must've happened when the mirror shattered. Are you cut anywhere else?"

"I'm fine. Don't worry about it. I'll just put a Band-Aid on it."

"Now you're going to tell me how to do my job?" she asked, and he sighed and mumbled under his breath as she started going through Chris's bag for supplies. It was impressively stocked, and she realized that Chris was probably responsible for most of Jake's medical care. "Get on the bed."

He sat on the edge and pulled his T-shirt off, and

through the bandage she got a glimpse of corrugated abs and a chest so hard she had a tough time tearing her eyes away.

He smiled, put his phone and beeper on the nightstand and lay on his back on the gray comforter.

"I'll do the small one first," she said as she sat in the chair next to the bed and pushed some hair off his forehead. It was an automatic gesture, one she did all the time with patients, but her hand lingered a bit too long on his hair.

They'd shared an intimacy most people never did with anyone—a life or death situation that brought them so close to the edge, and yet there was so very little she actually knew about him.

Her stomach started up with those stupid butterflies, especially because he was watching her carefully.

He doesn't like doctors. Or questions.

"How long have you been in the Navy?" she asked as she swiped the cut with Betadine.

"Are you going to ask me everything you would've found in my file?" he asked.

"Are you really going to go there again, especially now?" she asked as she held up the needle filled with local anesthetic, because even though he deserved it, she wasn't about to cause him any more pain. Well, physical pain. She was sure the questions pained him a great deal, but he wasn't getting out of that.

"I've been in long enough."

"That's the same thing Uncle Cal says when anyone asks him."

"Yeah, well, the admiral's been in a lot longer than I plan to be," he said.

"You're not career military?" She'd leaned over him now, began to work on the gash just above the dark blond of his eyebrow. He'd closed his eyes, but she didn't kid herself for a moment that he'd relaxed.

"I can't see myself staying on if I can't be in the middle of things."

"No interest in training?"

"And listen to guys whine about how tough it is to pass muster?"

"You never complained?"

"Not to anyone who mattered," he said.

Her fingers moved fast; she was in the zone, that place she knew well where she could help and heal. "From what I hear, you never complained at all."

"You've heard the rumors," he said. "That legend bull-shit."

"There's usually some truth to rumor." She pulled the thread tight and snipped the end. "This one's done."

He opened his eyes. "You're going to spoil me, Doc. I'm not used to getting stitched by a plastic surgeon."

"From what I hear, you're not used to getting stitched by doctors at all. And this one shouldn't leave a scar."

"They all leave scars," he said, and when she looked at him, he was staring up at the ceiling.

She began to peel off the layers of bandages on his side. Once she got to the actual wound, she was pleased to see most of the old stitches had stayed in place.

His cell phone rang and he grabbed it and spoke while she got to work.

"Yeah? No, that's not a problem. I received that package already," he said. "I won't be sending it back."

He listened intently for a few more seconds before he hung up. "You're going to keep asking me questions, aren't you?"

"Yes."

He groaned and she ignored him.

"Were you ever married?" she asked, because the thought of sharing Jake with anyone, even in the past tense, did not sit well with her. She took his snort as a resounding *no*.

"What about you?" he asked.

"I was engaged. But it wasn't going to work out. We'd drifted apart before my last tour with Doctors Without Borders. We were never really all that together, I guess. Good on paper, though."

"Another doctor?"

"Yes. Nice guy, but he never did understand what I was doing in Africa. He never would've understood me working for the Navy." She finished her work, rubbed some wet gauze over the wound, to clean up some of the blood and Betadine, and sat back in her chair.

"I'm sure a lot of people won't get the appeal. I mean, you're sure not going to make the money you'd make on the outside," he said.

"It's not about that. Even though Uncle Cal had to spend a little time talking me into it, in the end, the decision was easy. I feel like it's in my blood. My father was career Navy. KIA. I mean, I was little when it happened, but I still remember." She stopped for a breath. "That probably sounds really stupid and idealistic."

He paused for a second, then he ran his own fingers through his hair. He was still staring at the ceiling. "My stepfather was a Marine for a while. Tried out for the frogmen twice but never made it, so when it was my turn, I made sure that I did."

She opened her mouth to say, *He must be proud of you,* but nothing came out. Because she knew it wouldn't be true.

The pause on her end went on a little too long. Jake turned to look at her, his eyes the color of a dark storm cloud and she had a strong feeling he'd gone down this road on purpose.

His lips pressed into a thin, grim line, his eyes locked on hers, but he didn't make a move to get up off the bed. "You remember *everything* about the night of the rescue, don't you?"

"Jake, if I could just—"

"Answer me." The inherent command in his tone couldn't be ignored.

"Yes," she said. "Just let me explain."

"I don't want explanations. And I don't want to have to explain anything to anyone."

"I didn't realize that I was just anyone," she said angrily, moved forward to finish bandaging up his side so she could get out of this room and this house.

But Jake had other plans. He leaned up on one elbow, put his other hand on the back of her neck and pulled her mouth to his. He kissed her—hard—and she let him, because he was kissing her as if both their lives depended on it, like he wasn't mad at her anymore. Like somehow there was another apology in this kiss, and so much more.

He tasted like chocolate and mint and whiskey, and she put her hands on the mattress, next to him, because she was nearly off her chair and within a minute would be on top of him. Her body pulsed, her nipples puckered tightly until they were nearly painful against the lace fabric of her bra and longing for his touch.

As much as she wanted that, dreamed of that, as much as her body seemed to suddenly demand it, she still pulled away from his mouth.

"Jake," she whispered against his cheek, even as his hands stroked her lower back. "I'm not..."

"Ready for this. I know," he said. His voice was ragged, and he continued to hold her for a few seconds before pulling it together and taking his hands completely off of her.

Her own hands shook slightly as she sat back down and finished fixing the bandage. "You need to stay on the antibiotics," she said, as though her body wasn't aching for his.

"I will." He sat up facing her and pulled his T-shirt on quickly. "You'll stay here tonight. I'll have you back before the admiral realizes you snuck out."

"I never said I snuck out."

"You didn't have to. T-shirts and shorts are in the dresser. Help yourself. I'll just be out here on the couch if you need anything." He started out the door.

Her heart beat impossibly fast and she rubbed her mouth with her fingers. Her lips felt full, tingling. The way he'd kissed her, like he wasn't afraid she'd break if he'd really touched her, had nearly broken her.

But she hadn't. There *was* something between them—

she hadn't imagined it. And in his room, she was more at home than she'd been in a long time.

"Isabelle?"

She turned to see him standing in the doorway. "Yes?"

"Lock the door," he said, before closing it.

She hesitated for only a moment before doing what he told her, although she realized that it was merely a formality. A lock wasn't going to keep Jake Hansen out of her bed or out of her life.

At least not for long.

CHAPTER
4

The lock wouldn't keep Jake out at all, mainly because it hadn't worked for years. But Isabelle didn't know that, and he knew it would make her feel safe—and keep him honest.

The bar fight had gotten his blood going, but that kiss ramped it up to a nearly unbearable level.

And you pride yourself on control.

She'd saved him a trip to the hospital and stitched him up. He'd thanked her by getting angry and then kissing her, all within the space of two minutes.

Smooth. The perfect bodyguard.

At least he'd held it together for the stitches. Marginally.

He hadn't lied to her about not liking doctors as a rule.

Sitting still while Isabelle worked on him had not been easy. Closing his eyes had helped, but opening them had been an even better distraction, because she looked beautiful. Beyond beautiful. She was down-and-dirty hot in jeans and a skimpy shirt that showed off her curves.

Thinking about that wasn't helping anything.

She'd been on a date. With a Marine.

You're the dumb-ass who turned her down.

Her boots were next to the couch, her black leather jacket on the coffee table, and it took everything he had not to rifle through the pockets. Force of habit and she had nothing to hide, but still, his nerves were taut, on edge. Ready for action. Action he wasn't going to be getting from the teams for quite a while and longer from Isabelle, judging by her reaction.

She was pretending to be all right—she wasn't even close. He got stupid around her, and anything that made him stupid couldn't be good for him.

He wanted her with a fierceness he couldn't begin to understand, wanted to protect her, comfort her—make love to her until neither one of them could see straight.

He turned onto his good side on the couch and threw down the book he'd been attempting to read. The way the lights flickered, he expected power to go out at any minute.

Sleeping wasn't an option. He couldn't afford to have a nightmare with her right there. Besides, he was officially on duty now, and even though the town and its surrounding cities were locked down by the storm, and the house alarms—and his personal ones—were all set, he'd be power sleeping only. Focusing on endurance techniques.

He shifted in another attempt to find comfort, but his

body was too long for the small space, and pulling out the couch was something he always avoided.

Pullout couches reminded him of too many days long ago, when he was eight years old with a dead mother and a mean drunk for a stepfather in a shitty, one-room apartment in Brownsville. Dirty linoleum, dingy Formica countertops with the metal edging coming loose, sharp enough to slice you if you were unlucky enough to be thrown against it. He'd been unlucky a lot, had slept on a pullout couch from the time he was old enough to remember. Neighbors gave him food and sympathy, when all he ever wanted was the food. Sympathy would make him soft. Sympathy always got him more pain and almost got him killed.

Steve—his stepfather—was a former heavyweight boxer who got his start in the Marines and liked practicing his moves on his stepson. Every once in a while, when the whiskey hadn't completely taken hold and turned him, Steve would actually show Jake some of the moves.

In that twilight zone, suspended between the light and dark, Steve would bellow, *You're gonna have the moves just like your old man, right son?*

Son. Jesus Christ.

Yeah, just like you, Dad, he'd agree, because he'd never been stupid and a night of peace with no beating was something he'd learned to cherish.

Two stiff jabs, right cross.

Steve's footfalls, heavier than they should've been, slammed without finesse on the old floor, even though in his mind Jake was pretty sure the old man thought he was Muhammad Ali.

If that doesn't take 'em down, go for the body shots . . . go for the ribs. Knock the wind out of them, then finish with an up-percut to the chin...

Long after Steve passed out, Jake would practice those moves and the hand-to-hand combat Steve had shown him from his days in the Corps—*Spring-stance, power-point position, knife your hands, son*—because someday Jake would be big enough to really use them.

Someday, Jake had. The buildup of anger and frustration had pushed him past his capacity, had created a far too potent mix for a young boy to handle on his own.

Here, you will learn endurance and survival techniques. Captain Harry Lopez's voice echoed in his mind from that long-ago day during the SEAL Qualification Training when Jake had just turned sixteen not long after making it successfully through Hell Week. *If and when you are unlucky enough to be taken prisoner, you will need this course. Here, you will learn to control what can be controlled, to stay fit, both mentally and physically. You will learn to not encourage beatings, to develop support networks and to create your plan to escape. Most of all, you will begin to understand how much the desire to live affects all of your decisions.*

Jake had proven that desire more than once. But here, on the couch, if he slept now, he'd just be eight years old again and waiting for something to happen.

Jake met Nick that same year, when Steve had taken a job as a janitor at some fancy prep school in Manhattan; Jake's acceptance and tuition there had been a part of the bargain. Steve worked the afternoon shift—it meant he could sleep in and sleep off the drink from the night before and still leave his evenings free.

Nick was still trached at that time, refused to talk even

though he was more than capable of it. He'd been labeled slow and stuck in a Special Ed class. Alone. Privileges of the rich, turned into cages for their children who weren't considered perfect.

Nick and Isabelle had a lot more in common than they knew. Jake knew too that being rich didn't protect you from anything at all.

His sons were just lucky that Kenny had a bigger emergency to deal with, or else he surely would've tracked down at least one of them. Which would have in turn roped in the other two, because their philosophy of *leave no man behind* extended well past their military missions. Always had.

Kenny's private jet had been the last aircraft allowed to take off from Virginia—he'd managed to outrun one storm but he knew he'd end up catching it in New York.

Le bon Dieu mait la main.

"What's that, sir?"

He looked up at the young nurse behind the main Emergency Room desk and realized he'd been speaking aloud. "Sorry. I was just...it means *God help.*"

"Yes, well, we could always use some of that around here." She gave him a brief smile—the smile of someone who saw too much pain and suffering on a daily basis, and he wanted to grab her and tell her this was all taking too big a toll on her. But he didn't. She most likely thought him crazy already.

He'd arrived at the hospital in time for the ER resident to declare the bass player of one of his more famous bands dead as of 2:03 A.M.; in time to pay the insurance bill for the lead singer, who was having his stomach pumped as Kenny signed the forms. The only upside to the weather was that the paparazzi hadn't gotten wind of this yet.

"Are you done with those forms, sir?" the nurse asked, for the third time, and no, he wasn't. He'd had to put down the pen she'd given him to fill out the forms several times already; the vibes of every single person who'd touched it that night—their fear, their pain—bursting through and getting under his skin.

Repeating the short Cajun prayer helped moderately.

Hospitals were not great places for him to be. Too many people in distress, too chaotic. He couldn't see the dead, but places like this put his psychic nerve endings on edge.

"I'm done," he said finally, threw the pen down on the counter and shoved the clipboard toward the nurse whose name tag read Penny. His mind clouded and an image began to form . . .

Non. Sa c'est de trop.

"That's too much," he muttered, rubbed his arms and refused to let images in by walking away from her.

If he kept moving, things were better, the feelings less intense. Unfortunately, the waiting room at this big city hospital was packed to the gills and the roar in his brain wouldn't subside until he let something through.

He settled in by a free windowsill, closed his eyes and pressed his forehead to the cold glass. The anniversary of Jake's stepfather's death was this week, which always made Jake's aura more sensitive. But something bigger was going on with Jake, and Kenny still couldn't put his finger on it. The panic here wasn't helping.

When he opened his eyes, he saw that the snow had already begun to fall.

Nick found the company he'd been seeking after the fight ended and right before the police were called into the bar. He'd slid out the back door, more in an attempt to avoid his father's wrath than the law, and he'd run into a pretty woman whose name began with an *R*. Rachel, maybe. Or Rochelle. She'd been eyeing him all night, gave excellent head and had scratched the shit out of his back when she came.

He'd been on his way home when his cell rang. It was Chris, who was in a situation at the convenience store a few blocks from their house.

And yes, the situation was *exactly* what Nick thought it would be.

When he stormed inside the small store, he saw the clerk—a new guy, probably not even out of high school, huddled in the corner by the register, looking confused.

"Where are they?" Nick asked him.

"Middle aisle. That guy said it's the warmest place in the store. And then he told me to get the hell out of his way."

"Sounds about right," Nick muttered as the sound of a woman's screams rang across the store.

In the middle aisle he found the screaming woman lying on an inflatable raft, her head facing him, Chris sitting in between her legs, and this was not the way Nick planned on ending his night.

"Do you have some kind of magnetic force inside your

body that pulls them toward you?" Nick asked over the sound of another bloodcurdling scream.

"Honey, you're doing great," Chris told the woman, and then addressed himself to Nick. "I was just buying some stuff for breakfast." Chris adjusted the beach towel over the woman's midsection. "This is Kristin."

Kristin craned her neck to try to see behind her. "He says he's done this before."

"He has."

"He said his mother's whole family were midwives."

"Yeah, they were." Nick couldn't help but smile at the mention of Maggie. Midwifery was something she'd given up once she and Kenny left Louisiana, but, like Chris, she'd always seemed to find herself helping someone give birth in the most unlikely of places.

"You have no idea how much this hurts," Kristin half yelled.

"She should've been in BUD/S," Nick muttered.

Chris stared at him. "Breathe, Kristin. Just breathe, like I told you. But don't push yet."

"I need to."

"Not yet," Chris said.

"Why don't we get her to the hospital? The road's not closed yet." Nick knelt down by Kristin's head.

Chris peeked under the towel and shook his head. "No time."

"I can't have my baby here," she implored Nick, as if he were the only reasonable one in the room. "I had a birth plan. My husband is supposed to be with me. I had a craving for mint chocolate chip ice cream and now I'm having a baby on the floor. This isn't in the plan!"

"Have you tried calling your husband?" Nick asked, used a towel from the pile to wipe some sweat off of her brow. Chris had already prepared an area for the baby, had the usual supplies from his ever-present medical kit close at hand.

"Gary's in the Pacific until next week. I'm not due for another two weeks," Kristin explained.

"He's a Marine?"

"No, a pilot. He's training to fly F-14s."

"You must be proud of him," Nick said and her face crunched into a grimace as she nodded. A long, low moan followed and Nick took the opportunity to ask, "You're going to keep her out here?" as he snapped on the sterile gloves and checked the bulb syringe, the sterile chuck and the O_2 tank, just in case.

After doing this for so many years, Chris was nothing if not prepared. His car was like a walking triage center.

"If you saw the back room, you'd understand," Chris said, and yeah, it looked like Kristin was going to give birth right beside the tampons, which was kind of ironic.

"Did you see Jake leave?" Chris asked him, then turned to Kristin. "Don't push yet."

"He left with the doctor," Nick said.

"Who'd you leave with?"

Nick opened his mouth to answer but noticed Kristin looking up at him. "Don't you have a contraction to have or something?"

"Is he always this much of an asshole?" Kristin asked Chris.

"He's usually much worse. Women seem to love it," Chris drawled.

Nick didn't bother protesting.

"She can't have the baby here—my boss will kill me." The clerk tugged at Nick's sleeve as Kristin clamped down with a death grip on Nick's hand.

"No choice, my man. Deal with it," Chris told the guy, then smiled, his widest *It's all gonna be fine* smile, and said, "It's time to push," with his eyes looking even more different-colored and crazy. Kristin turned to Nick for reassurance.

"He's done this before. You're in good hands. Really." Nick always wondered what the hell these women must be thinking at a time like this, when a crazy man who wasn't a doctor was telling them to push.

Kristin screamed again and clamped down harder, twisting Nick's fingers, and he also wondered if she'd break any of the bones in his hand by the time she was done, because she was not letting go.

He always got this end of the job, but at this point there really wasn't any end of the woman he wanted to be near. He got the whole joy-of-life thing, but this part was messy and complicated and he'd try to imagine what went wrong during his own delivery.

Chris always tried to tell him that watching a woman give birth should be cathartic for him. It never was.

"Head's out," Chris said. "Mouth clear. Okay, let's get the shoulders free, Kristin."

"Breathe and push," Nick said. "Grab your knees, look at me—focus on me." She nodded frantically and pushed until Chris nodded.

"One more time should do it," he said, and Nick repeated

his focus speech. Kristin pushed and then burst into tears of relief when Chris said, "Stop. He's out!"

"He? It's a boy?" she asked through her sobs. Nick moved away from her, draped a clean towel across the floor and took the baby from Chris. His back to Kristin, he performed a quick APGAR—score of nine—before he cleaned off the kid with the warm water he'd asked the clerk to provide. Chris reassured Kristin as he delivered the placenta, while Nick wrapped the baby in a fresh towel and handed Kristin her son.

"Oh, my God . . . I can't believe this." Kristin looked between the two of them. "He's all right?"

"He's fine, you're fine. Everything's fine," Chris said, just as the power sputtered out.

An hour later, parked outside the ER, Chris lit a cigarette and took a deep drag. "Dad said tonight was going to be nuts."

"I figured he said that because we were all together," Nick grumbled. "He's really got to start specifying this shit."

"How specific do you want him to get about your life?"

Nick stretched. "Not very. Besides, he seems most involved in Jake's now. Which is fine with me."

Chris rubbed his chin. "Something's going on with that doctor."

"Yeah, and by *something* you mean that she wants him, right?"

"That's the vibe I caught. From both of them," Chris

said, peered out the front window. "Getting shittier out here."

"We're not supposed to get involved like that. Not with someone we rescued."

"Yep. I know." Chris flicked his cigarette out the window and lit another.

"He's having the nightmares again."

"Yeah, I know that too."

Nick put his head back and sighed. "Let's get home before the weather gets worse. It's going to be slow moving and I don't feel like sleeping in the car tonight."

"She's naming the baby after me, you know." Chris maneuvered the old Jeep out of the parking lot and skidded out onto the main road, catching the wheel expertly just before they went into a tailspin.

Nick shook his head and laughed. "They all name the baby after you," he said, as his and Chris's beepers began to ring in tandem.

"It's a fine night for training," Chris said as he pointed the car toward the base.

CHAPTER
5

There was no way she was going to be able to sleep tonight, alone, in Jake's bed. Sleep had never come easily, but here, surrounded by the pure, masculine scent of the man she'd been longing for, Isabelle's senses were on overdrive.

Lights off, she stared at the ceiling as two hours ticked away. The blinds were open and the glow from the street lamps came through the windows. The tink of hail against the glass was an unsteady beat. Even though the house was well made, the wind still found places to force itself inside with a low, desperate howl.

When the streetlights went out, the room was suddenly too dark. She pushed the comforter off and felt the chill, and then she tripped over the night table while heading for the door.

"Isabelle? You all right?" Jake's voice came, low and reassuring through the door. She paused with her hand on the latch before she unlocked and opened it.

He was holding a flashlight, pointed down toward her feet so he didn't blind her.

"Did I wake you?" she asked.

"No." He walked over toward her and handed her the flashlight. "I'll grab a few lanterns. This happens all the time around here. We keep talking about putting in a generator, but we're never here long enough to make it happen."

"Don't you need this to find them?" she asked as she followed him with the flashlight into the hall.

"I work well in the dark," he called back.

"I'll bet you do," she murmured to herself.

"Did you say something?"

"I'm just a little thirsty—can I have this water?" she asked, pointing the light at the coffee table.

"Go for it."

She sat on the couch and took a long sip of water. Then she grabbed the blanket Jake must've been using and wrapped herself up in it.

Within minutes, Jake set two lanterns on the table in front of her. They provided enough light, though the room was still dim, basked in a hushed glow.

He didn't sit next to her, but rather stayed standing as if he were on some kind of emergency alert because of the power situation.

"Does your side hurt?" she asked.

"No."

"Would you tell me if it did?"

"No," he said with a small shake of his head. "So was that a date?"

"What are you—oh, you mean at the bar?"

"Yes, at the bar. With that Marine."

"By *that Marine,* do you mean Zeke?" Maybe she'd been right earlier to think Jake was just the tiniest bit jealous.

"Zeke, Deke, whatever. You can't date a Marine."

"Well, that's good to know. I didn't realize there were rules about these things."

He gazed at her, half a frown on his face. God, he was handsome, even frowning. He moved toward the doorway between the bedroom and the living space and put his hands up overhead, holding on to the door frame. She was about to tell him that that was a good way to pull out his stitches but found his curiosity more interesting.

"It wasn't a date, exactly. But I don't see why it matters to you—you didn't seem to want me around."

"I didn't expect you. There's a difference. I don't like surprises."

She pulled the blanket around her a little tighter. "Yeah, me neither." There was silence for a few minutes but it wasn't uncomfortable. The storm's intensity seemed to pick up slightly, and she wondered if she should just let what happened earlier drop. But she couldn't. "I'm sorry—about lying to you about what I remembered."

"Forget it. It's all right that you know. Only fair." He paused. "You really want to go back there, don't you?"

"Yes," she said quietly, waited for some kind of response, something that told her she was crazy for even considering it—but again, like the last time she'd mentioned it to him, none came.

"I thought you told your uncle that you were going to give OCS a try," he said instead.

"I'm planning on it. That's why I'm working in the clinic on base rather than a naval hospital. My uncle thought this would give me a better idea of what military life would be like. I don't want to be stationed at Portsmouth. I want to be where the action is. I know I can be useful in the field." She paused. "But I want to go back to Africa one more time before I go into OCS."

Jake didn't say anything, just watched her carefully. No judgment, but she'd love to know what he was thinking—something he hid very well.

"You probably think I'm being stubborn and ridiculous and getting into things I shouldn't. That I need to think before I act instead of just going by my instincts," she offered.

"Why would I think you should give up traits like that?"

He was completely, utterly serious. And in that moment, she knew for sure that she could love him. "So you wouldn't have me change a thing?"

"No."

She blinked back tears, because no one had ever told her that. Everyone always wanted her to change in some way— her mother, her ex-fiancé, even Uncle Cal. "If I went back to Africa, you wouldn't try to stop me?"

"I think it's a dangerous place."

"And?"

"And what? There's no secret meaning behind what I'm saying. It's dangerous."

At least he wasn't mincing words with her. "It was beautiful there despite everything. I could finally think. Breathe."

If she closed her eyes and really concentrated, got past the fear of her final days there, she could see the familiar faces of the staff, the families she'd helped. The brightly colored kangas she'd wrapped the newborns in. The nights she'd drink warm orange Fanta from recycled bottles and watch the sun go down.

"I met a good friend there," she said. "A photographer named Sarah. She was born in Zimbabwe—white—her family was split up when they had to give back their land," she said quietly. "She was wild, fun. But so...alone. She was gone by the time I was taken. I was supposed to keep in touch but I feel like I'd have to tell her what happened. And I can't—I'm not supposed to talk about it. I wasn't even supposed to tell her who my mother was."

"But you did," he said.

"I could trust her. She'd been through so much herself."

"Maybe you'll cross paths with her again one day," Jake said.

"Maybe. But once I'm commissioned, I won't be able to go back with Doctors Without Borders either. They frown on military personnel," she said.

"Why's that?"

"They sometimes try to sneak in weapons. Handle things more aggressively. They tend to have a certain... bearing," she said wryly. "So if I can't go back to Africa with Doctors Without Borders, I'll go back with the military. Uncle Cal said that the DoD wants to put some plastic surgeons overseas. In the field. Where they're most needed."

"They usually don't put women in front-line roles," he said.

"From what I hear about the DoD, doctors are needed so badly, they're making those decisions on a case-by-case basis," she said.

Jake nodded slowly, and she couldn't tell if he approved of the DoD's decision or not. "Was Doctors Without Borders good to you about what happened?" he asked instead of commenting.

"Yes, they were. But they don't know all the details," she said quietly. "You don't really either, I guess."

"I know that you fought like hell. You don't owe me any more of an explanation."

"I know," she said, her voice softer than she'd intended. "His name was Rafe. My mother hired him to watch out for me. Doctors Without Borders thought he was working for them and now they think Rafe kidnapped me for money because he found out who I was. They don't know he was supposed to watch me. And they didn't want any of this leaking out to the press." Her heart beat faster as the sentences tumbled out faster—terser—than she'd wanted them to.

"And they'll take you back?"

"If I go before OCS. Besides, Doctors Without Borders says that if you haven't experienced some kind of violence working with them, you haven't been doing it long enough."

Jake was silent for a long minute. "You signed a contract with the DoD," he reminded her.

"For three months," she said. "The opportunity I have is for a short stay in April. Six weeks, replacing a doctor who needs to go home for a family issue. That's long enough for me to accomplish what I need to do. Then I'll come back and wait until I'm cleared for OCS."

"You've got a plan," he said.

"I guess I do." That thought made her feel a little lighter. "But the plan's the easy part. Breaking it to my mother tomorrow night at dinner's another story."

"Sounds like it'll be a rough night."

"I really want to see her. We get along well. Lately though, everything turns into a *how is Isabelle handling everything* fest."

"She's worried."

"Yes. She also feels guilty." She sighed and pushed her hair behind her ears. "But I don't blame her for what happened. She was only trying to protect me."

"You'd been to Africa without bodyguards before. What changed?"

"The two times I'd gone alone were before she'd gotten elected. Once she took office, everything got riskier. Her political views are pretty radical—she pissed a lot of people off with her pro-war stance and she'd started to receive some threats. Then there was a direct threat."

"About you?"

"Yes—about a kidnapping. Right after that, she made a few calls about bodyguards and came up with Rafe's name as the most capable. Another senator had used him for protection when traveling through some of the African nations during a goodwill tour of the embassies. He said the guy was the best. Even so, she begged me not to go back, but she had her life to lead and I had mine. I wouldn't back down. Still I know she totally blames herself for hiring Rafe."

She wondered why all of this was so easy to talk about with Jake—conversations she'd previously had only with herself, going over each and every argument in her mind as if preparing for battle.

"Are you worried?"

"I'd be lying if I said no. But I can't let the fear get to me. I won't," she said fiercely, and she wasn't sure which one of them she was trying to convince more.

"Recognizing your fear's never a bad thing," he said.

"You know, you're the first person who hasn't asked me why I'd want to go back."

"You're the first woman who hasn't asked me why I do what I do. How I can."

"Because you want to be in control—it's important to you," she said. Because she recognized those traits in him as easily as she recognized them in herself.

"No one's ever really in control, Isabelle." His gray eyes flickered over her coolly. She didn't believe him, not fully, and she had a strong feeling he didn't really want to believe it himself.

"We're a lot more alike than you think."

"You'd better get some sleep," he said gruffly, as if he knew she wasn't buying his answer.

"I won't be able to." She couldn't go back into that bed, toss and turn among his sheets and pillows again. Not without him, and *with him* wasn't an option. *Yet.*

"Are you hungry?"

"Maybe a little."

"You could make us food, then," he said. And he was completely serious. "Stove's gas—it'll light, no problem."

"This is your house, what about *you* making us breakfast?"

He shook his head impatiently. "I don't cook. And I want pancakes. Can you make pancakes?"

She wanted to refuse but was struck with the sneaking suspicion that she was well on her way to being unable to refuse him anything at all.

That thought sent a small shiver through her as her gaze settled on his muscled forearms, tanned despite the frigid temperatures outside and finely dusted with blond hairs, his biceps flexing as he continued to support himself by holding on to the door frame over him.

"Come with me," he said suddenly, as if he'd made some kind of internal decision. He moved forward and grabbed one of the lanterns, then handed her the other. She'd assumed he'd be leading her down to the kitchen, but instead she found herself following behind him up a flight of stairs to another block of rooms set up just like Jake's. These were beautifully furnished, clean, but it was obvious no one used them on a regular basis.

"What's this?" she asked, held up the lantern so she could see the rooms better.

"Room for rent," he said, and she whipped around to stare at him.

"You're serious."

"I don't joke all that much, Isabelle."

"Why would you think I'd want to move in here with you and your brothers?"

He shrugged. "I guess you like staying with the admiral. Being smothered."

"You know I don't."

"I know you're halfway between wanting to be alone and being too scared to actually do it."

"How do you know that?"

He stared past her toward the window, his jaw clenched. "I've been there." Then he fixed his gaze on her. "Take it or leave it. No strings."

She walked through the rooms—there was a definite feminine touch to the furnishings. Classic, not frilly. But still, a woman had lived here once.

She turned to him. "It's perfect. I'll take it. And I'll pay rent."

"What about the cooking?" he asked, and she sighed. "I mean, I know you'll be busy when you go through OCS, but until then, you should be pretty free with just being the base doc."

"You're really impossible."

"That shouldn't surprise you. Besides, you don't want easy."

She didn't bother to tell him that he was right, because he'd probably heard it all too often. "Speaking of *not easy,* do you think I'll have a tough time in OCS?"

He shrugged. "Everybody does."

"Even you?"

He gave her a sidelong glance. "I thought you were going to make me breakfast."

"Something the man of steel found hard," she mused, and he ignored her.

"You're going to have a tough time if you decide to go

through with it. Why not just keep doing what you're do-ing?"

"Because I want to go back to doing what I was doing—go back to helping out where I can make a difference."

"And you think you'll be under the protection of some kind of magic bubble if you're with the military? Because you won't be."

"I know that. God, I know that. I'm not an idiot," she said, at the same time realizing that she was indeed a little bit of one, since that had been her exact thought process. Which made her next words come out more fiercely than she'd intended. "I'll know how to protect *myself* better."

"Hey." He moved closer to her, touched her arm. "If you want to learn how to protect yourself, I can help you."

But the anger and frustration had built up quickly in-side, the way it always did lately, without warning. "Why does everyone suddenly want to help me? It's like I've lost the ability to do anything by myself. Even you think I can't do anything myself."

"I didn't say that—"

"No, that's right, Jake. I get it. Path of least resistance. Don't admit to anything."

He backed away from her, one hand held up in a show of surrender. "What do you want from me, Isabelle?"

So much. She wanted so much—too much, probably. More than he might be willing or able to give.

Not that she'd asked him.

She walked toward him and he straightened up and squared his shoulders even more, as if he was putting up some kind of physical shield.

"What do *you* want from *me*, Jake?" she asked. "You

must want something. I don't think you ask every woman you meet to move into your house with you and your brothers."

"How do you know?"

"You don't seem like the type."

"And I know you're the type who doesn't like to ask for help. You know, it's all right to need it."

"Not where I come from," she muttered. "Surgeons are trained to be solitary. Competitive."

"Were you competitive in Africa?"

"I was solitary."

"Sounds like you still want to be." His hand fisted by his side, without hers in it, and no, that's not what she wanted at all.

She grabbed his hand, forced his fingers open—he didn't resist much—and put her palm to his. Fingers twined together, she stared into those amazing gray eyes that looked at her as if she were the only woman for him. "Do you think there's something more between us than the rescue?" she asked.

"I don't know," he admitted.

"Are you willing to find out?"

He didn't answer, stared at her until a steady beep from downstairs caught both of their attention.

Cal heard the wind slamming the house from his bedroom. He lay in the center of the king-sized bed, surrounded by books and papers, just the way he'd left them when he'd fallen asleep after his phone beeped to remind him to take his blood pressure medication. Which must've been when Isabelle left the house.

Dammit. Old man, losing your touch. Cal had been right to put her with Jake.

Jake had her now. She'd be safe with him. Well, as safe as you could be with a single, red-blooded American male who was as highly trained as a man could possibly be.

Cal certainly wasn't too old to remember what it was like to want it twenty-four seven.

Instinctively, his hand went to the phone and he dialed the familiar phone number. It was 0400. The time didn't matter—she'd be awake, and the shroud of darkness always helped ease any of the lingering guilt. By dawn he could pretend it didn't happen, even though there was no reason to pretend anymore.

"Jeannie." His voice sounded tired to his own ears, although he'd risen at this exact time every morning since he'd been seventeen.

Jeannie Cresswell's voice caught as she answered him. "Cal, is she—"

"No, she's fine. Everything's fine." Dammit, he should've thought before he called like that. Annoyed with himself, he pushed the covers away, let everything else tumble to the floor in all directions, and again, he thought about getting a dog for company rather than waking up with only paperwork.

He was too solitary a man for even that small luxury.

"Okay, good. That's good." Still there was worry in her voice that was never going to leave. "You paid him again, right? He said if you didn't continue to pay him..."

"I'm taking care of Rafe," he lied, the way he'd been lying to her for the past two weeks, since the money was due. The third payment in a string of never-ending payments, and one Rafe had refused.

Kowtowing to the mercenary's wishes hadn't been doing either Cal or Jeannie any good anyway. No, it was time to smoke the man out, then take care of the situation for good. Cal's past had haunted him for too long, and he was sure this was the right way to deal with this.

The only thing Cal wasn't sure of was how precarious the situation was going to be for Isabelle, or for how long. When Isabelle was first kidnapped, he'd assumed, along with everyone else, that the motive was solely money.

When the second demand came in, he knew better. That's when he'd called in his own favors to some feds who'd gone the military route first, men who were as loyal to Cal as he was to them. Together, they'd convinced Jeannie that slamming the lid on the FBI investigation was for Isabelle's own good. There was too much at stake—and neither Isabelle nor Jeannie deserved to get caught up in any of it.

"You're sure this is the right thing for Izzy?" Jeannie was asking. "Are you sure not telling the FBI about Rafe's demands is in her best interest?"

"Isabelle's going to be safe here. I wouldn't have arranged all of this if I didn't know it would work," he said, more to himself than to her, as if he could make it true by repeating it enough.

He yanked opened the window curtain and put his forehead against the cold pane of glass, closed his eyes and let Jeannie's voice ease his heart.

"I know that, Cal. You'd never let anything happen to her. Not like I did."

His words nearly caught in his throat. "She's a grown woman. You can't stop her from doing a job she wants to do."

"You did."

"I had to." God, he'd pulled strings, yanked them so hard, walked over people's heads and threw fits until he'd gotten exactly what he'd wanted through special permissions from higher-ups.

He knew that wasn't going to be enough, but it was a start. The clinic wouldn't hold Isabelle's interest for long. She'd heal fast, get clearance and she was determined to go back out into the field, one way or another. Stubborn, just like James. His best friend. The one he'd betrayed in a way a friend never should.

"Is he . . ." Jeannie couldn't even finish her sentence, stood at the door wearing sweatpants and a tank top. She'd been studying—had a year of college left and then planned on law school.

Cal stared at the wife of his best friend for a minute and realized what she was asking. "No. God, no, Jeannie . . . I'm sorry. I shouldn't have startled you. Shouldn't have come here like this." Still, he didn't make any move to leave and she didn't make any move to let him inside.

"Then why did you? Come here, I mean."

"I wanted to see you."

"I'm married, Cal. To your best friend."

"I know that, Jeannie. Don't you think I don't know that? That I think about how stupid I am every time I see his ring?"

"You're not the marrying kind. You've told me that before

and as much as I didn't want to believe it, I know it's the truth. You couldn't give me what I need."

But that wasn't the truth, because he could give her what she needed in a way that James was never able to touch. Jeannie always told Cal that it was hard to feel heat for a man when her heart was somewhere else.

Somehow, James knew that too, understood, accepted when she'd wished he wouldn't have, wished he'd let his anger and frustration mount and yell and scream. Show any kind of emotion at all.

But no, James would never do that. He was too good of a soldier, too buttoned up. Always in control.

And Cal, wearing a pair of old blue jeans and a black T-shirt, a cigarette tucked behind one ear, was anything but buttoned up. He knew he'd be stripping off her top and rubbing her bare chest by the end of the afternoon.

He'd pushed her right into James's arms. On purpose. Knew they'd be the perfect couple. As much as Jeannie had protested that she could never love James the way she loved Cal, she'd been better off.

Cal knew that love wasn't the most important thing— never would be. No, he'd never let it be.

CHAPTER
6

When Isabelle checked her beeper, she found a page with a call for any and all emergency and medical personnel in the general vicinity of the base and insisted that she and Jake head to the scene.

Jake had insisted on carrying her to the car so she wouldn't fall—after he called her stubborn—and buckling her in when she couldn't pull the seatbelt far enough to extend over the huge parka he'd dressed her in.

"Ready?" he asked, even as he gunned the car down the long driveway—without his own seatbelt on. He wore a gray skullcap and a black fleece pullover and gloves with the fingers cut off.

She gripped the dash, the door handle, anything to

steady herself and wondered just how crazy he really was. She made a mental note to check him for tattoos on his scalp, as per the rumors. As soon as he stopped the car from skidding all over the road.

"Jake..." She pushed her legs out straight as if there were an invisible set of brakes on her side of the car.

"Relax. I was number one in my class for combat driving." He did seem perfectly calm, even as the car took another sickening turn and plowed through a huge pile of snow.

"Were you the only one in that class?"

"You're funny without sleep. But you wanted to get to the scene fast, remember?" he added, as if it were all her fault that he was driving like a complete maniac.

"I'd like to get there in one piece."

"You will. You think that Marine can do better?" he asked with a smirk.

No, not better. Not even close. She'd gotten dressed in warm, borrowed clothes in the space of ten minutes, had tried not to mull over the fact that he had several new toothbrushes under his sink and just what that meant about his supply of overnight guests. He'd laced her into a pair of his boots that were ten sizes too big for her and somehow managed to do it without making her feel like she was ten and helpless.

"How bad is it?" she asked as she clomped down the stairs. One glance at the blanket of unplowed snow told the story.

"Pretty bad," he said.

"Are you going to be able to get through this?"

"Are you doubting my abilities?" He stood close enough to

make heat surge through her body. Again. "Because you really shouldn't."

"No. I'm not," she said, and he smiled. *God, she liked it when she could make him smile.*

"Okay, seriously, do you always drive like this?" She clutched the dashboard now, since the seatbelt was no match for Jake's *number one in combat driving* driving.

"Yes."

"How do you still have a license?"

"I need a license?" he asked innocently.

"I think I'm going to be sick," she said as he muttered something about *women loving to exaggerate,* a sharp *dammit* on the heels of that as he rounded the corner and found the road blocked.

He didn't say anything, took a wide turn to get on the highway that made the contents of the car shift hard, including her.

She had to brace herself with her arm against the dashboard when he pulled sharply to the side, blatantly ignoring the police cars straddling the middle of the road and going around them.

She saw the bus in the distance—on its side and tilted toward a slight embankment leading down from the road along the back side of the base.

"Stay here until I check on the scene," Jake said, but she was already letting herself out of the car, Chris's triage bag in hand. She nearly slipped before getting her footing and heading closer.

Of course, Jake managed to get there first.

"Ma'am, you can't be here." One of the officers attempted to stop her.

"I'm a doctor. I can help," she called as she moved toward Jake.

"You've got to clear this bus out," Jake was telling the officers, and even though he didn't strain to be heard, the inherent command in his tone cut through the chaos immediately.

She stood next to him as he started barking orders, taking over a situation that he wasn't officially in charge of, even though her heart was pounding and the urge to jump in was great. Jake held her arm as if holding her back—and she got it. Safety first.

She heard the word *Marines,* and figured out that it was a busload of soldiers headed back to base after a training exercise.

Things started moving as he directed the soldiers to help the men who could actually walk themselves off the bus.

It had skidded on a patch of black ice and turned onto its side, had continued a slow slide off the road and into the woods. The engine appeared to be smoking, but she couldn't tell if that was just because of the frigid cold.

There were several people who'd been thrown—she'd need to get to them immediately, while Jake continued his evacuation. It wasn't as bad as it could've been, but without the right equipment, and given the weather, things were going to get worse fast.

An ambulance skidded to a stop near Jake's car and she said a mental prayer of thanks and took off toward it.

"I need METTAGS," she said to the EMTs. Between the three of them, and Jake and the troopers, they could cover this scene for a little while. "Please tell me you've got more people coming."

"They're on the way," one of the EMTs said, and handed her some tags for triage.

She turned to seek out Jake, waved to him, as if asking, *Now?* He nodded and motioned her onto the scene. "Let's get moving."

She worked her way, along with the EMTs, through the crowds to the people who lay closest to the bus. After the first five minutes, she threw off her coat in favor of moving faster. The sweatshirt would have to be enough for now.

The tension, the fear, all of it fell away as the adrenaline surge kicked in. The gloves Jake had lent her were big, even with the fingers cut away, but without them, her hands would be frozen and useless. The rest of her body had stopped feeling the cold, anything except the unerring need to help as many of these men as she could. Moving forward—that's what it was all about.

Now she knelt in the snow, going back over those victims she'd first assessed an hour ago and labeled with black tags.

The bus driver couldn't be saved. Isabelle had labeled her with a black tag and instructed the EMTs to give her a dose of morphine, even though the woman was unconscious and barely breathing—Isabelle hated the thought that she'd be in any more pain than she had to be when she passed.

It was obvious on just a quick assessment that the driver hadn't been wearing any kind of seatbelt. Earlier, Isabelle had watched as the Marines who'd gotten off the bus first had had to drag her away from the stepwell. The woman's head had struck the windshield even as her body made impact with the dashboard. She'd most likely had massive cranial hemorrhage before she'd even been thrown from her seat.

Finger on the woman's fading pulse, Isabelle heard a soft moan, swiveled to find a young man who sat with his back against a tree. He was half hidden by the foliage, looking dazed.

"Can you walk?" she called out.

"Me?"

"Yes, you. Can you walk? Can you try?"

"I think so. Yes." The man nodded, pushed himself up.

"Good. Come here to me," Isabelle urged. The bus driver's pulse was slowing rapidly. Within seconds, there was nothing more for Isabelle to do but help the young man move toward the ambulance. He probably had a mild concussion. One of the lucky ones.

Luckier than the young man who was still reported to be on the bus.

Isabelle was yelling orders, her voice firm. Commanding, even, as if she'd been born into situations like this. The weather conditions were night and day from what she'd dealt with in Africa, but she'd definitely handled crises. And handled them well.

She was bossy. Demanding.

She was perfect.

She'd even asked if he knew initial triage protocol, asked him to repeat it back to her and then told him to follow it.

Like a page from his own book.

Care under fire—ambulate, ventilation, cap refill and follow simple commands. With that in mind, he focused his efforts on directing two men, who appeared to be unharmed except for some bruises, to get everyone who was already on their feet and walking away from the bus.

He'd collared one of the EMTs earlier, told him to stick to Isabelle's side like glue. Jake had managed to keep her in his sight most of the time, but scenes like this were hard, and he was being pulled in five thousand directions. Sticking by her side when he was needed other places, desperately, wasn't going to work.

"Is everyone off?" he asked the last men moving slowly away from the main scene.

"There's one guy left—he's trapped," one of the Marines said. "The cops said to leave him—the fire department's on their way with tools."

"Entering's too dangerous right now. A fire crew is on the way that's equipped to handle this," a trooper confirmed. Yes, the trooper was right about the first part, but there were no crews getting through in time to help. Jake had been on scene for over an hour and there was still no sign of the fire department

The bus was going to take a long, slow slide sooner rather than later. If he mentioned that to anyone, panic would ensue. Instead, he did what he did best—disappeared behind the triaged groupings and the trooper's yellow tape and made his way onto the bus.

According to reports, the remaining man was all the way at the back of the bus, his shoulder wedged beneath a seat. Dangerous to move him, deadly to leave him.

Great choice.

"I'm coming for you," Jake called back into the semi-darkness. The only light was alternating flashes from the ambulance and police car lights, and they weren't enough.

Until the beam from a flashlight hit him square in the face, blinding him.

"We're back here," a familiar voice said. A way too familiar voice. He stopped dead in his tracks. His stomach dropped as he inwardly cursed himself, and the EMT.

"Put the light down," he said. The beam moved and he saw that it was indeed Isabelle kneeling down near the patient.

"He's stable. A lot of pain. I can't get him out from under the seat," she said calmly, right before she bit the plastic cap off a syringe and spit it to the side.

I can't get him out from under the seat. As if she'd tried. Which she probably had. "Are you fucking crazy?" he asked.

"Are you?" Her voice was quiet, and yeah, *he* was. Everyone knew that. But she wasn't supposed to be. She was supposed to be rational and logical. Doctor-ish.

Jesus Christ, this was not good.

She'd already turned her attention back to the patient.

"What the hell are you doing in here?" he demanded, stayed where he was to calibrate the vehicle, which meant fighting every urge to grab her and carry her off the bus.

"Are you going to yell at me or help me?"

"Lady, you're in so much trouble here."

She glanced down at the boy she was helping. "He thinks he's all tough because he's a SEAL," she said as she continued to thread the IV calmly. The bus shifted slightly and she caught herself with one hand as she held the bag above the boy's head with the other. "You're going to be fine."

"Isabelle, you need to get out of here."

"I'm not leaving my patient."

"I'll bring him out to you. You need to stand up and walk past me. Right now. No arguments."

He didn't want to risk scaring either her or the Marine, but too much movement was not what this bus needed.

She heard him, loud and clear, looked like she'd just figured it out for herself. It was the look of someone who'd done something without thinking and now thinking was *all* she could do.

The wind, which had picked up to a steady howl through the broken windows of the bus, wasn't helping.

"You'll be fine," he reassured her. "Just walk toward me. Steadily. We're going to meet in the middle and change places."

She grabbed her bag and pulled the straps over her head and one shoulder before she stood. Carefully. She stepped over the trapped man and started walking toward Jake.

The bus shifted slightly and she stopped, stared at him.

"You're fine. Breathe. And keep walking," he told her. Her eyes were wide, and she exhaled the breath she'd been holding and kept moving.

As she passed him, they were chest to chest for a few seconds, her face inches from his, and he fought the urge to pick her up and carry her to safety.

"He's really wedged in there," she said quietly. "I've given him something for the pain, but I didn't want to knock him out completely. He's got feeling in both legs, and I figured I'd need him to cooperate."

"Cooperation is exactly what I need," he said tightly.

"I didn't see any other way. I'm sorry," she said.

When she'd gotten completely past him, he started to move toward the back. "Keep going. Get off the bus. Wait for me outside."

"Be careful," she called over her shoulder, and her words gave him pause, made him actually freakin' laugh in the middle of this non-laughable situation.

A second later, he knelt down by the guy's head and used his penlight to make his own quick assessment.

The kid, because *shit,* that's all he was, was scared. Partially in shock. His entire shoulder and arm were trapped beneath a dislodged double seat and his breathing was coming in short, quick gasps. Jake wondered what he'd been like before Isabelle had given him pain meds.

"What's your name?"

"It's Shane King, sir. I told the doc she shouldn't have come on here by herself."

"She's not the best listener." Jake reached out and grabbed Shane's foot. "Feel that?"

"Yes, sir."

"It's Jake. Please just call me Jake."

Whatever damage Jake might do by freeing the kid was better than death, so he barked his words out to the young soldier—a command, not a question—because in his experience, fear was always a stronger motivator than sympathy. "When I lift this, you're going to pull yourself out."

"Yes. Okay."

The lift was pure adrenaline, the way it always was when there was danger in the mix and especially as he felt the bus shift slightly under his feet. The kid felt it too, slowly but surely squirmed his way out from under the seat, his shoulder and arm hanging uselessly by his side.

He was even attempting to lift himself to his feet—half fear and half bravado, but he was *moving*—as Jake lowered the seat back down as gingerly as possible. Even so, the bus shifted again, a sickening lurch that left him and the kid staring at each other.

"Let's go." Jake moved as cautiously as time would allow, put himself on the kid's good side. "I'm going to lift you. It's going to hurt like hell."

"I want to walk off."

The bus shifted backward, hard.

"I'm assuming you want to live more," Jake said, grabbed the kid and hustled off the bus. He'd barely set foot off the hunk of twisted metal, the kid's whimpered cries in his ears—and *shit*, the kid would be lucky if they could save the arm at all, never mind the scars he'd incurred all along the side of his face and neck—when he felt the backdraft of the bus's whoosh down the hill, toward the ravine.

It wasn't a huge drop, but where the kid had been positioned, he would've surely been crushed.

A few people close enough to see what had happened began to yell and point toward the bus. Jake walked calmly past them and placed Shane on the ground.

"We need a stretcher over here," Isabelle yelled from where she was helping someone up off the ground, and two EMTs with a stretcher raced toward him. At least four had arrived on the scene, which was good.

He helped lift Shane gently onto the stretcher.

Shane grabbed Jake with his good arm. "You saved my life. You and the doc."

"You'll owe me one in the field," Jake said, shook Shane's hand before they loaded him into the ambulance and was immediately accosted by the trooper who'd told him to stay off the bus earlier.

"You don't listen well, do you, boy?" The guy got right in his face, put a hand on his shoulder—and no, Jake didn't much like either of those approaches. Especially the *boy* part.

"Get your fucking hand off me," he said, low and calm enough to make the guy follow his directive almost immediately.

"Cut the crap—I need all the hands I can get," Isabelle called out. She'd moved from a few feet away, assessing another patient, and as much as he wanted to be pissed at her, he couldn't be. Mainly because she was still yelling at him, and saving her life and Shane's didn't garner him any special favors in her book.

He liked that last part. A lot.

The trooper backed off and Isabelle pointed to a man sitting in the snow near him. "Jake, get him up. Run an IV. Now."

Who knew that getting a command from a woman would be such a turn-on? And he'd much rather throw her back into the car and pull off her clothes and take her, the primal urge invading every single muscle in his body.

She knew it too. He saw it in her eyes, the way she held his stare as she put on fresh gloves. The way she licked her bottom lip before she mouthed *Now* again and he got to work.

Jake had been about to grab that policeman by the throat—Isabelle was pretty certain of that. He probably wanted to throttle her too, but they'd gotten Shane off the bus. That was what mattered.

She'd deal with the consequences later. The mantra of her life lately, because getting on the bus had been more instinct than actual thought.

On her very first trip to Africa—God, she'd been so green—she'd stepped out of the Range Rover after driving for fourteen dusty hours, only to be yanked at with no greeting by a young African woman. Isabelle had run with her twenty feet farther up the road to where a man lay gasping for air, and she'd performed an emergency tracheotomy. Trial by fire. No time for thinking, just action.

The problem was, she needed to learn to balance those two things again.

As the light snow turned to rain, she got the young man to an EMT, pointed out the bus driver and turned to find Jake.

He was helping to change a tire on one of the ambulances along the far side of the road.

Even though her body was still humming from the urgency of the situation, every single hormone pointed her solidly in Jake's direction. Watching his forearms flex and his hands maneuver the tire onto the jeep, his body slicked from the rain and the ice, seemingly impervious to any and all weather, made her want him, right here in the middle of nowhere.

Maybe she had a fever—that would explain the sudden,

pulsating heat that flushed her from face to thighs and between her breasts, and fueled all the fantasies she'd had about Jake over the past months.

"Isabelle, get into the car!" he called over his shoulder, and yes, he knew she'd been watching him. But he was right—the snow had turned into a light icy-rain mix and her teeth were chattering and so she went to the Blazer and turned the keys in the ignition and pulled the jacket Jake had lent her—the one he'd thrown back in here at some point to keep it from getting soaked—over her.

The heat came on surprisingly quickly, although based on the way the car felt under her when she'd driven it last night—never mind the way combat man drove it this morning—she should've known that there was nothing ordinary about this car.

Warmer now, she stretched to try to keep her lower back from stiffening up. Between the cold and the heavy lifting she'd done, she was going to be really sore by tomorrow morning. Although one glance at the sky reminded her that it was already morning. Dawn had started its arrival when she wasn't looking.

Jake was outside the passenger-side window, right next to her, but his attention to the barely noticeable lightening sky was rapt.

As the day broke without much fanfare to wash minimal light over the snow, she hesitantly put her hand flat against the window. Although he still hadn't turned to face her—still kept his face turned toward the rising sun—he flattened his hand on his side of the window directly over hers through the glass.

Still, she knew getting close to Jake was not going to go down easy for him. She wouldn't have it any other way.

There was no other way for Sarah Cameron to get the shots she needed than to be in the middle of the action. She maneuvered through the brush as quietly as possible, heart pounding.

This was a checkpoint search gone terribly wrong. She'd been put on the scent by a mercenary named Al who knew Sarah was in need of money—she always needed money, now that her family's farm had been taken. She'd become a provider from age sixteen, unable to go to university, where she would have studied journalism and photography. Instead, she remained in her homeland to photograph her country's ills for profit.

Most of the time, it turned her stomach.

So did child soldiers, bought and sold like chattel, kept in line with promises of riches and a steady diet of drugs and threats.

She'd given up trying to understand it—now she spent all her time simply trying to capture the moment. And live in it too.

She didn't expect to live very long, and realized that over the past few years, she'd gotten to the point where she didn't care very much about that. It should've concerned her—would've concerned the old Sarah. But that was years earlier, and that woman no longer existed.

Sell your soul and your country for money. Yes, she had, wasn't proud of it, but her family needed her help. This was the best she could give them.

When Mugabe had taken power in Zimbabwe, the coalition government, along with ZANU, decided that it was time for the Africans to take back the land from the whites. It didn't matter that seven generations of Sarah's family were born and raised in Africa, that her father had worked hard to buy that land.

The worst part was that Sarah understood on an intellectual level what the new government was trying to accomplish. Why it had to happen. But she hated seeing everything her family had worked so hard to build destroyed in a single afternoon of violence and despair, hated suddenly being looked upon as an enemy and a traitor in the country that had nurtured her for sixteen years.

A country she loved.

Over the past years, the violence in Zimbabwe had escalated furiously. It was almost not safe for Sarah to go back without an escort. Not safe for her family to be there.

As if in response to that, Sarah herself stayed in some of the most dangerous places her country had to offer.

She'd been living at this clinic in Burundi for the past three months—it was one of the larger ones and she was pulling double duty, taking pictures for the book on Médicins Sans Frontières, or as the Americans called it, Doctors Without Borders, as well as documenting the ever growing political violence in the area.

The people at the MSF clinics were good to her—she was often a help translating, could teach the logistician a thing or two about fixing the ancient Land Rovers that took doctors and patients back and forth to airports and bigger hospitals when necessary.

That was over as of next week—these shots should pay

rent for her parents for the next few months. For her, maybe another week in a hotel in Kagera Region before looking for more work.

This wasn't the worst thing she'd ever done—her stomach still twisted in knots over what she'd helped Rafe do two months earlier—for the promise of money and training.

"The rumors aren't true, Sarah," he'd reassured her again last week. "Isabelle was fine when I left her. Safe. The American soldiers took her and we got our money."

"She was a friend."

"People like us don't have any friends," he'd said, and yes, that part was the truth.

She'd done her part, had thrown the clinic in Djibouti off the track for the first forty-eight hours Rafe had taken Isabelle and made sure no one had reported her missing. She'd also been the one to phone the Red Cross a day later to let them know Isabelle's location—and Rafe had been sending Sarah money ever since in small increments. Too small, but it was something. Until last week, when he hadn't shown up with cash and she'd been forced to take on this job.

He had promised to be at the clinic tomorrow in the same breath he'd promised he'd start to train her. Even though she carried her own weapon—a 9mm Glock—and could handle an M16 as well. As necessary, she had learned a variety of self-defense moves all guaranteed to help her take down opponents much larger than herself. Still, all the male mercenaries she'd known before Rafe had refused to train her. Including Clutch.

Clutch was the one she couldn't seem to get out of her

mind. She'd been attempting to snap a picture of the elusive merc when he'd caught her. And then she'd spent what seemed like forever in his bed, in his arms, until she hadn't wanted to leave. And she hadn't left for anything other than photography work in the vein of what she was doing right now. Dangerous work.

She'd come back to his house shaken one night after a near capture and asked him to train her. Clutch had offered her an office job instead, one she'd promptly turned down.

She couldn't help but think if she'd taken that job, where she'd be today.

She couldn't worry about that now. Not when the situation she was supposed to capture was unfolding before her camera's lens. The African driver had been unsuccessful in trying to deal with the soldiers by himself, and his passengers were being ordered out of the car.

You could save them . . . should save them. But she didn't. She'd had to learn to steel herself, even more than she'd done before. Get rid of sentimentality.

She didn't want to have to depend on Rafe and his money. She didn't want to have to depend on anyone. She'd come too close to that with Clutch, felt herself getting comfortable. Soft.

She almost laughed out loud at that, as if she could ever be soft. No, she was all hard edges and angles. Clutch had been the one to surprise her with his sentimentality.

This checkpoint was two miles away from the clinic—she'd fired up the ancient Land Rover and come here because the American newspapers paid well for pictures like this, pictures they were too afraid to come in and get themselves, and for good reason. She spoke the language, had the connections, and even so, her sense of survival often overrode her need for money.

This time, the man she'd been hired by was an adventure seeker—a man who traveled the world in search of dangerous places but who didn't have African citizenship, which would allow him to pass through the continent the way Sarah herself was able to do. She'd done work for him before—he paid on time and liked her pictures.

Camera balanced on one knee, she lit a cigarette with her free hand, let it dangle from her mouth as she refocused the lens. Things were going to get uglier at any moment— the soldiers were bearing arms and yelling, and the three men and one woman, all of whom appeared to be missionary types, were frantically digging in their pockets for anything that would allow them to cross the line.

When the soldiers began to force one of the men onto his knees, Sarah snapped pictures and crossed the line herself.

CHAPTER
7

Jake might've been sweet—well, *sweet* was probably the wrong word—when he was outside the car, but once inside with her, he let her have it. With both barrels.

"What the hell were you thinking?" He slammed the car into reverse and took to the road with a vengeance. "You know what, don't bother to answer that. I know the answer—you weren't thinking."

"I was working. Doing my job. And I'm tired of people telling me what I can't do," Isabelle muttered, well aware of how defensive she sounded.

"I never said *can't,* Isabelle. Obviously, you're more than capable of getting yourself into trouble."

"I want to do exactly what I feel like doing—I want to do everything. The way I used to."

"Your uncle would kill you if he knew what you did."

"When did you become my keeper?"

He didn't answer, just muttered and shifted in his seat. "You're stubborn."

"Yes. I'm not an easy person. I never have been."

"You're not back to the way you were," he muttered.

"How do you know?"

"You're taking stupid chances. That's how I know."

"You took the same chance I did."

"I'm trained to take chances like that, Isabelle. Last time I looked, surgeons don't get that kind of training."

"So it's all right for you to do something dangerous—"

"You should've let someone—anyone—know what you were going to do."

"Did you?" she asked.

"It's different for me." He curled his hands around the wheel and took a hard turn. "Look, I get it, all right? Probably more than anyone. But you've got to give yourself some time."

"I don't have the patience for this kind of healing," she admitted. "Surgery's simple. There's a start and a finish. It's not something that can go on indefinitely. I'm not used to open-ended things."

"You shouldn't have done something like that when you're having trouble in small spaces," he said, and she jerked her head toward him in surprise. "If you'd had a panic attack, collapsed, I might not have been able to get to both of you without the bus pitching backward."

"Are you done with the lecture?" she asked as he swerved

into a parking space outside the clinic, not wanting to think about how easily he'd assessed her vulnerabilities.

He slammed the gears into place, stared out the windshield for a second before he spoke. "I scared you last night—when I kissed you."

That certainly hadn't been what she'd been expecting. Did he scare her? He'd turned her on, gave her back the sexual feelings she'd been pushing down anytime they surfaced. The thing was, she'd known that would happen once she got around Jake, had hoped for that.

"It wasn't the kiss," she said, hated the way her face flushed.

"It was because I held you, pulled you down." He held the steering wheel with both hands, hard enough to whiten his knuckles.

She wanted to reach out, caress his hands and loosen them from the wheel, but kept her hands in her lap instead, balled into fists so tight her short nails bit into her palms. "You didn't do anything wrong. It's not that I don't want you to hold me. I just didn't expect it."

"I should've known better." He said it much more to himself than to her. "Pushing you like that didn't help anything—it's making you do things you shouldn't."

She stared at his profile for a few seconds before slamming her door open and climbing out. "I didn't go onto the bus because you kissed me, so fuck you, Jake. Just fuck you," she told him before she slammed the door closed.

She turned away before his eyes could catch hers—that made it easier to walk away from him, because really, she didn't know for sure if she was telling the truth. She'd wanted Jake's arms around her, tugging her down, his touch making her hot and satisfied.

She didn't want to think about why she couldn't let that happen yet. Didn't want to think about why she went off so quickly, like a lit firecracker with a busted fuse, anytime Jake tried to help her—because that would mean revisiting those awful days.

Anyone holding her, touching her, beyond Jake that first night was too much. She got panicky when people hugged her or stood too close. At work, those two weeks she was back, she'd forgone the elevator in favor of the stairs whenever she could.

She'd gotten so claustrophobic there that there were two separate times she swore she actually saw Rafe at the hospital—once in the cafeteria where she'd met Daniel for lunch and the other in the empty corridor leading to the blood labs.

For an hour afterward, her hands had trembled—never a good thing for a surgeon's patients to see. She'd had to tell herself over and over, *It wasn't him. He's in prison. He can't hurt you again.*

At least he'd never followed her into her dreams. That was one place she eluded him. During the day, the minefields were too numerous for her to avoid.

Even at the clinic, she sometimes felt the walls closing in. She'd stand outside, taking deep gulps of air until she felt better, the way she found herself doing now at the entranceway; she'd do that and tell herself she was healing.

She wondered how many times she'd have to tell herself that before it became true, before her body stopped reacting with fear when she thought about what happened.

No, going back to Africa was the right thing to do, the only way to allay those fears—until she did that, she was sure she wouldn't feel complete. Going back to Africa wasn't anything like her rushing onto that bus this morning—and she'd keep telling herself that until she believed it fully.

Fuck you, Jake was certainly nothing he hadn't heard before and many times over. He'd expected to hear it from Isabelle sooner than later, but if he couldn't be honest with her about everything, at least he wasn't going to hold back when he thought he could help her.

She was pushing her limits, a reaction to the fear.

He'd been pushed beyond any limits he thought he had, especially in the military, sometimes so far he wasn't sure he'd come out of it. But he always did, whether of his own accord or because of the skill of his instructors. He had people watching his six.

Who did Isabelle have, really? Beyond him, there was Cal, who was lying to her, and her mother. He hadn't heard her speak of friends, anyone, really, beyond a brief mention of her ex-fiancé and some photographer.

She hadn't been lying when she said she was solitary. He wondered if she'd ever be able to let him in.

She was killing him. This assignment was killing him. And to top it all off, now his side was killing him. He didn't think he'd pulled his stitches. Much. But he sure as hell wasn't going to tell Isabelle that. She would've laid him out on his back in the snow to fix him up.

And yeah, he'd had enough dreams about her on top of

him already not to deal with that well in a public place. So he brought himself over to Doc Welles, who'd thankfully gotten iced in overnight on the base and saw Jake right away.

The man was the admiral's personal doctor. The only one Jake would allow to touch him, unless Jake was unconscious, and then, who gave a fuck anyway.

The only doctor you'd willingly let touch you, save for Isabelle. Which had been a mistake.

Now, stripped down to just his boxer-briefs, that odd, vulnerable feeling had already started. Jake shifted on the paper-covered table as the urge to get up and get out got stronger by the second.

"Just relax and take deep breaths," Doc Welles told him, reached out and put a firm hand on his shoulder for a few seconds. "Your pulse is fast—are you in that much pain?"

"No. Not much pain."

"Try to relax. It's just me," Doc Welles said.

Jake nodded, managed to do all right while the doctor had the stethoscope against his chest. As the doc moved around toward his back, the familiar burst of panic tightened his throat.

"Relax. You're doing fine," Doc Welles repeated. For the ninetieth time.

Jake nodded, closed his eyes and tried to think about anything else. Didn't matter—he was automatically transported to that terrible place, and the only comfort he could give himself was that he'd come out stronger in the end. Stronger than he was at fourteen, when his grades sucked and he partied too much because he hadn't given a shit.

He'd been wise beyond his years, wild as anything, and

he'd never let on to anyone that his home life was a living hell, even to Nick, who'd known about the abuse from the time they'd become friends. Chris had discovered it as well, that first day they'd met—and fought—in the principal's office.

Neither of his brothers told. No, that had happened in a much different way.

That particular day, when Principal Reilly cornered him on the back stairs of the school, Jake felt a small tug of fear. That in itself was strange, because he had no fear of authority. No one could ever hurt him as badly as he'd already been hurt.

Still, Jake thought briefly about running, the way he had yesterday when he'd been called down for the school physical. The school brought in the district's doctor for those students who hadn't had their annual physicals done when September rolled around.

Normally, Jake didn't have to deal with that. But this year, a particularly brutal beating had left him unable to go to the doctor his stepfather usually brought him to, one who ignored the abuse.

The truant officer knew Jake and his hangouts too well for Jake to think about skipping any days during the first two weeks of school, and Jake knew better than to ask his stepfather for any kind of absence note.

"Don't you dare fuck things up for me at that school," Steve had warned him countless times. He was still the custodian at the K–8 school, while Jake had moved on to the high school building.

And now here he was, behind the curtain, with the principal and vice principal on the other side in case he tried to bolt.

There was no place to hide, so he'd taken off his shirt and waited while the doctor checked his ears and listened to his heart and maybe, just maybe, he wasn't going to have to turn around.

The doctor reached over Jake's shoulder to put the stethoscope on his back and froze.

"Turn around," the doctor said, his voice oddly gentle and completely different in tone than it had been minutes before. When Jake hesitated, he became impatient and physically turned Jake himself, twisting his body on the table.

There was a gasp—and Jake knew that hearing it from a grown man couldn't be good. It had been a long time since he'd looked in a mirror himself.

But the noise brought the principal through the curtain. "Holy shit. Holy mother of God."

Jake stood there stock-still, eyes shut, and just fucking prayed it would be over soon.

"Jake, look at me." Principal Reilly was in front of him, his eyes kind. Too kind. Christ, he hated that more than anything. "Who did this to you?"

And Jake, who'd already perfected the art of lying, told him calmly, "I fell off my bike," even though he knew it wasn't going to work this time.

"I have to report this," the doctor said.

"Let me call his father in first," Mr. Reilly said. In his effort to save Jake, the principal severely miscalculated.

Jake remembered fighting the urge to retch as Reilly said things like *A man-to-man talk in front of a social worker could stop the abuse.* He'd spoken of anger management classes and family therapy and, finally, of foster care.

Steve's not my fucking family, he'd wanted to say, wanted

to tell Reilly to call in Chris's mother and father instead, because they got it. Kenny especially, because as much as he'd wanted to confront Steve when he'd discovered the abuse two weeks earlier, he'd understood how much worse things could get for Jake if he did so. The bond between Jake and Chris's family that had cropped up within hours of meeting them had surprised the shit out of Jake, who'd long since grown to hate surprises of any kind.

In retrospect, Jake understood what Reilly had attempted to do. In fact, years after Jake had left school he had gone back to thank him for trying. He could tell Reilly still harbored deep guilt about what happened, hadn't realized he was fighting years of conditioning. Jake had a perfect opportunity that day and he did nothing. A big part of that had to do with a fierce pride and an equally fierce guilt of his own.

He hadn't thought about all of this in years. Hadn't had those damned nightmares in years, until . . .

He shut his eyes tight and pictured Isabelle standing in front of him, strong and happy, color in her cheeks, and his anger dissipated into a strange sense of peace.

"Your stitches didn't rip. Actually, they look great. And new," Doc Welles said and Jake opened his eyes and checked out his own side. It was bruised and swollen, but he'd had worse.

"Yeah, well, they pulled last night. Dr. Markham did these."

"Who?"

"She's new on base, working at the clinic."

"Ah, the plastic surgeon. Yes, she's good." Doc Welles wrote something on the chart. "Still on the antibiotics?"

"Yes."

"I'll put in my report to your CO. I'll clear you for light duty in two weeks if everything stays the way it's going. Which means don't overdo it," Doc Welles said sternly.

"I hope he didn't rip his stitches." The low, controlled drawl of Jake's CO, John "Saint" St. James floated over him.

Jake looked at Doc Welles, who didn't even glance up as he wrote on Jake's chart. "He didn't."

Saint sent a pointed look in Jake's direction. "With me."

Jake put on his shirt, thanked the doc and walked out of the office with Saint.

"You're supposed to be home. Resting." Saint frowned at him as they walked along toward the meeting room where Team Twelve worked, fought and planned together.

It was a look Jake was more than used to, since he'd pushed Saint well beyond his normal boiling point more times than either man could count and knew that this time Saint was nowhere close to reaching that threshold

"I'm resting. Trust me," Jake muttered. "I don't want anything to hold me up from getting back to active duty."

"You're behind on your paperwork," Saint said.

"That has nothing to do with active duty, Saint. But it'll get done," Jake assured him, thought about the pile of file folders he'd dumped somewhere on his desk that were most decidedly nowhere near getting done. But hell, Saint didn't have to know everything.

"It'd better," Saint said, gave him a firm pat on the shoulder even though his eyes were elsewhere.

Jake followed his gaze, looking across the lot in time to see the team, including Nick, readying to hump it down the beach for an extended morning PT session. Ten miles in full gear. The air's chill would help, but by the end of the first mile they'd be pulling for breath in the icy air, their senior chief yelling about their times, calling them *lazy-assed bastards* and threatening to take away everything from leave to their balls, and yeah, things were normal around here.

"I know you want to get back. But don't push it," Saint said. Jake glanced at his CO, the man rumored to have wrestled alligators for money in his younger days, the same guy who'd had his appendix and gallbladder removed and walked out of the hospital before his anesthesia had completely worn off because he refused to be catered to.

Saint had taken on Team Twelve when it was in its formative years—when it seemed like it was going to become the place for those SEALs who were just slightly too far over the edge to deal well with much authority. Saint gave the right kind of authority, understood the men's wild streaks, knew when to rein them in and when to let them run with it.

There aren't a lot of options for military men unless they're smart when they get in. The smart ones get an education so they can do something beyond backwater security, Saint drilled into his men's heads, over and over, encouraged them to take more classes, to better themselves, not to fall into the lure of private contracting.

Saint might have to do some more talking to Nick. Not that Jake planned on bringing up Nick's activities to Saint. Right now he was more than grateful for Nick's contact into that world—if Jake couldn't get the intel he needed on his own, he'd have to turn to other avenues.

When she'd first gotten word about the kidnapping of her daughter, Jeannie Cresswell had refused to leave her office. She'd stayed right next to the phone on her desk until it rang with good news, had refused food, drink, and well-meaning idiots who told her everything would be all right.

She'd only trusted Cal to tell her so, because she didn't put stock in fools.

Two long months had passed since her daughter came home and still things weren't returning to normal.

She'd kicked off her shoes right after she'd climbed into the limousine that would take her to see Isabelle and Cal. Now she rubbed her feet against the soft carpeting in a restless pattern as she stared out the window at the busy Friday evening traffic, heart heavy with the knowledge that the man she'd hired to protect her daughter was at large.

Jeannie had envisioned having to meet Rafe at three in the morning under the cover of darkness in some seedy part of town, sans bodyguards. Instead, he'd made an appointment and come to her office.

He'd come to her and she'd handed him everything he'd needed to hurt her only child. Unknowingly, but that didn't matter—the guilt would haunt her forever.

"*I know she's been to more dangerous places,*" she said. "*However, now that I've taken office—*"

"*You've received threats.*"

"*Yes. How did you know?*"

"*I've been doing this long enough, Senator Cresswell. You know my credentials.*"

"*From what I know about Doctors Without Borders, they*

won't allow bodyguards of any kind. They won't even allow weapons, which to me is utter foolishness, bringing young, impressionable people into the organization and giving them no way to protect themselves."

"We all know where you stand on gun control, Senator."

"Yes, I suppose you do."

"Don't worry about me getting into the program under a different cover. That's my job. I'll take care of that and the entire situation. Leave it all to me."

Those words, a blanket of comfort at the time, now tortured her every waking moment.

"Leave it all to me," Cal told her.

"But if we tell her that Rafe's been captured and she finds out otherwise, she'll never forgive us," she said.

"If we tell her he's still at large, she'll never be able to get on with her life," Cal countered as they stood in the sterile hallway outside Isabelle's room in step-down care, where her daughter lay healing. "This isn't a high priority case for them. You have the authority to call them off. In the meantime, I'll put my own people on the case. They'll be able to accomplish more without the red tape, and without risking the press getting involved."

The FBI and CIA had completed their questioning and for the past week Isabelle asked daily, sometimes twice a day, if there was any word on Rafe.

The only time Isabelle looked content was when she slept, clutching an invisible hand in her own.

Jeannie had let Cal tell the lie, had watched the relief settle in as Isabelle believed what she needed to believe.

You owed her that much.

She touched the locked charm she wore around her

neck, a picture of Isabelle on one side and James on the other. James never would have let her lie to Isabelle.

Five years together, twenty-three years gone and the memories were still so fresh.

She'd been so young when she'd met James, but she'd never been innocent. Growing up a military brat had taken care of that quickly, especially having an Army captain for a father and a two-star general for an uncle. Jeannie's own first words were a jumbled combination of curses and direct orders, or at least that's the way her mother always told the story.

And even though she'd grown up with and dated military men almost exclusively, in her mind it was all just about passing the time. Besides, she'd always been drawn to men she couldn't fully have, the type who refused to buckle under to her charm. And the way she'd looked in her teens and twenties, men like that were few and far between, and by the time she was seventeen, she'd never been swept off her feet with any of them. James had been no exception.

For one thing, he was Navy, not Army, and beyond that fact alone, she'd firmly set it in her mind that she wasn't going the military route. She was going to college, higher education, shaking off the family service record.

Her father had wanted a boy, but was resigned to her path, as if he knew she'd have different plans.

"Women always have their own minds," he used to say, and she could never tell if he thought that was good or bad. Knowing him, it was neither—it just was.

But James had been relentless in his pursuit. It was flattering, heady. And it had torn her interest away from her own pursuit of another man who had never wanted to be tied down.

Yes, she'd made the right choice at the time. The proper choice. James had been there to pick up the pieces when she was eighteen, and now, at forty-six, she was still waiting for Cal to come and put all the pieces back together. Because he owed her in so many different ways, and she intended to see he made full payment on his promises this time.

CHAPTER

8

After clearing a few would-be Marines for boot camp, the clinic was unusually quiet, so much so that the ringing of her office phone made Isabelle start. She'd been concentrating on the forms in front of her, health forms—the ones she needed to complete for her MSF tour, and for some reason, pen was not hitting paper as easily as she thought it should.

She picked up the receiver.

"Dr. Markham," she said, was greeted with silence on the other end. "Hello—is anyone there?"

Someone was there . . . She wondered for a second if it was Jake but realized that he'd call her cell, not the office phone—he'd programmed his number into her phone last night before they'd left for the accident scene. If he was ever going to call her at all.

She wasn't going to apologize to him—and memory served that he also sucked at apologies.

"Hello? Is anyone there?" Still no answer and she hung on the line for a few more seconds, an uncomfortable feeling growing in her gut before she put the receiver back in its cradle.

It was at times like this that her instincts crawled, thoughts of what-if crept into her mind and the four walls began to shift and move in toward her.

Stop it. You're safe. Rafe is locked up tight.

In the deepest, darkest recesses of her mind, she often wondered how long a man with such specialized training could be kept under lock and key.

"Clara, I'm going to lunch," she called out as the older nurse passed her doorway.

"Physicals start up again in an hour."

"I'll be back before then." She closed the door and changed quickly into her running clothes, bundling up more than she'd like to combat the chill her body would need to fight through before she got moving.

The phone rang again—she stared at it for a second and then ignored it, pushing through the back door of the clinic to the outside.

It was not the best weather to exert herself, especially the way her side ached, but the thought of running on the treadmill in the gym was too confining. She wanted to be—needed to be—outside, with no limits to the wide-open space around her.

Her sneakers hit the hard sand right along the surf line,

her breath coming in icy puffs in front of her, and *dammit*, she was going to go farther than two miles this time, even if it killed her. And judging by the sad way she was breathing and the stitch in her side, it might do just that.

Every step took her farther away from the clinic, farther away from a job she wasn't comfortable in . . . farther away from her memories of Africa and the papers sitting on her desk.

Too far from Jake.

She turned about-face and headed back in the direction she'd come.

Jake had enlisted Max—owed that man more favors than he cared to think about—to help him access files he shouldn't be allowed to touch.

When Max decided to collect, it was going to be a bitch.

Even so, Jake wasn't getting very far—files for Delta operators were locked down tighter than his own and there were still places he couldn't let his fingers travel for fear of backlash. He slammed the lid of the laptop down hard and stared at the map of Africa he'd printed, until his eyes crossed.

It was past 1800 when Cal called his cell.

"I'm taking Isabelle home tonight." The admiral dispensed with hello. "Her mother's having dinner at my house. She'll have her own security team with her."

"I'm not invited?" Jake asked, pictured the frown on the admiral's face as he crumpled the map and pitched it in the trash.

He'd been checking on Isabelle throughout the day—

without her seeing him. He'd spent the better portion of the morning skulking around the clinic, and an hour watching her run down the beach. Her form was good, but she'd been hurting.

Since she'd be taken care of for a few hours, he was on his feet, headed to his car and on to plan B.

"I'm still not happy about her moving in with you. The senator's going to be even less happy."

"I'm not in this to make anyone happy, Admiral."

"I might not tell the senator."

"Isabelle will. She won't go for lying."

"Now you know her better than I do?" Cal asked. "Don't answer that."

Jake hadn't planned on it, mainly because he didn't understand how he knew the kind of things he already did about Isabelle. "I need to tell Nick and Chris about all of this."

"No," Cal spoke sharply. "There's no need for that. You can do this job alone. I told you, the threat's not imminent. If and when it becomes so, I'll take matters *back* into my *own* hands."

"Every threat is imminent, Admiral. That's what makes it a threat." Jake kept his voice quiet and calm even as his heart rate increased. He clicked the phone shut, knowing the admiral had been the one to hang up first.

With a sharp squeal of tires he was off the main road and onto a back dirt trail that would get him off base and toward the edge of town fast.

Yeah, he'd tell himself that this was all in Isabelle's best interest. Right now, it was the only thing he had.

And still, he tried to get rid of the sickening feeling that

Cal was jerking his chain, but he couldn't shake it. And Jake had always lived by his instincts.

The one day he hadn't listened to his gut, he'd nearly died. No, that wasn't true exactly—he had listened to his instincts but he'd followed Steve back to their apartment anyway, to let what was supposed to happen play out.

In the end, his will to live happened to be stronger.

His phone rang again as he pulled into the bar's parking lot, all the way on the opposite end of town. *Dad.* "Did you make it home all right the other night?" Jake asked, hoping to ward off any questions. "We left messages for you, but we never heard back. We were worried."

"Don't try that reverse psych bullshit with me, young man. Do you want to tell me what's going on with you?"

"Nothing."

"Jake—"

"I can't talk about this."

"Can't or won't?"

"Normally it's a fifty-fifty split, but this is *can't.*"

"All right. I just know how you don't like surprises."

"What surprises are you talking about?" Jake asked, keeping his voice low as he entered the unusually quiet bar.

"I thought you didn't want to talk about it."

"I can't talk. But I can listen."

"It doesn't work that way," his father told him. "Just don't ignore your instincts."

Jake sighed as he hung up the phone, shook his head at his father's perceptiveness and wondered if Chris was also going to be able to see right through to what he was doing. Luckily, his brothers were on base through the night for training.

And this time, Jake wasn't about to ignore his instincts. He could lie to himself and pretend that his interest in the merc named Rafe was purely professional, but he didn't. Isabelle was far more than just a job to him, and he'd spent many a night forcing himself not to think about what he'd do to the guy if he even got close to him, because that would screw with his own control.

The closer Jake got to her, the more he hated lying to her. Lying didn't sit well with him—never had.

He'd exhausted all the typical routes, which he'd assumed would happen. Rafe's records were highly classified, so much so that it was as if the man didn't exist. Part security, part deniability, all necessity for Special Forces.

He'd have to turn to other avenues. And so he planned on seeing if Nick's contact, the man named Clutch, could help.

Clutch was a former Delta sniper who'd turned private contractor once he'd discovered how much cash his skills could net him on the open market. If anyone had a shot at knowing Rafe's movements, it would be Clutch.

A merc who wanted to disappear in Africa could easily do so—the skill set of a former Special Forces soldier was wildly appreciated. Rafe would find himself a ton of work.

Nick had met Clutch years earlier when his old team and Clutch's Delta group worked a mission together. Nick had also done some private work for Clutch last year— nothing since, not since Kenny got ahold of him—of all of them—and demanded they stop putting themselves in unnecessary danger.

As far as Jake knew, Nick hadn't gone back, even though his brother still talked about joining Clutch once his time with the SEALs was over. Chris tried to talk Nick out of it, especially out of private contracting work while he was still employed by the U.S. military, although he knew it wouldn't do any good. Nick had a need for speed and danger that always had—and would—outweigh both his brothers'.

Jake made it through BUD/S because there was no torture they'd put him through that he hadn't already survived. Nick made it through because he was completely desensitized to pain and he was constantly searching, craving, for ways to feel.

Chris made it through because he had that little edge of crazy that made it necessary for men like him to succeed.

After hearing about some of Nick's work, Jake had thought about joining Clutch more than once, but knew his nightmares would follow him to Africa. Trying to outrun them would be stupid. So would trying to outrun his feelings for Isabelle.

Before last night, he'd tried to sort his feelings logically and finally figured that what Isabelle felt for him had everything to do with the rescue and nothing to do with love. Okay, there was an attraction there too—he'd be an idiot not to see or admit that.

But there was something more, something he'd all but admitted to Isabelle herself—the same things that made him bypass some very willing women as he walked through the bar, in favor of finding out more about the guy who'd hurt Isabelle. A part of this job Cal had not put him in charge of.

When Isabelle found out about all of this—and he had no doubt that would happen sooner or later—she would freak. There was no getting around how badly all of this was going to blow up in Cal's face. In Jake's too.

He had to decide how badly he cared.

"What can I get you?" The bartender—a guy Jake had never seen before—put a napkin down in front of him.

Jake folded it in fours and put it back down on the bar. "Just water."

The bartender nodded, as if the request was nothing out of the ordinary. He poured Jake his water and slid it across the bar to him.

"Go ahead toward the back room. Vic is waiting," the bartender told him.

Jake had never had to call in this particular favor before, but he'd heard enough about Vic and the way he helped like-minded people in the military community—and beyond—connect. A brief knock on the heavy gray metal door and Jake found himself looking up at Vic. The guy had to be as tall as Chris, around six-five, but bodybuilder big. For a second, Jake thought it might be the same guy who picked the fight with him the other night at Craig's, but he wasn't.

"What do you need?" Vic asked after Jake walked into the back room and closed the door with a thud.

"I'm looking for Clutch. Tell him it's Nick's friend Jake. He'll know."

Vic frowned. "That's what they all say. I'll dial in. You've got to talk to him here."

"I'll need privacy."

"Yeah, you all do." Vic dialed, a cigarette dangling from his mouth. He waited, rolled his eyes toward the ceiling. "Freakin' Africa. They keep changing the area code without telling anyone. Hey—Clutch? Yeah, someone named Jake looking for you. Friend of Nick. What? Hang on." Vic leaned forward and stared into Jake's eyes. "Gray. Weird color."

Jake snorted.

"Here." Vic handed him the phone and ambled from the room, shutting the heavy door behind him.

Clutch had been tired of waiting for the phone call, the one that had come night before last, just like he'd known it would. The voice on the other end of the phone had triggered relief rather than the fear he'd experienced three years earlier, when he'd been taken out of Delta Force, shipped off to Africa to work for GOST—Government Operatives Specialty Team—a secret group of mercenaries funded by the government.

If GOST hadn't called then, it would've been tonight or tomorrow or next year, but they were always going to call, had promised him that he'd never truly be free.

Up until now, he'd been lucky, and he nearly laughed out loud for using that word in conjunction with himself. Laughing was easier last night with half a bottle of whiskey inside his belly, burning through his veins, nearly making him forget his own name. Tonight, his head pounding, he remembered it all too clearly.

Bobby Juniper, we need you back.

He'd played the message on his answering machine over and over, until he broke the tape. And then he'd smashed the machine and the office phone into little pieces and threw it in the driveway and ignored Juma and Moody's calls asking if he was all right.

It hadn't mattered—they'd continued to call his cell phone.

If he didn't come back and do the job GOST needed him to do, they'd kill him or expose his true identity to the people who'd been looking for him for the past eighteen years.

Clutch didn't know which would be worse. And so 1300 saw him sitting at his desk in his house in Ujiji, staring blankly out into the night with his bags already packed. Until Vic called through with a guy named Jake, a friend of a SEAL named Nick who'd done some work with him in the past. Crazy motherfucker, that one.

"Don't you know Army boys and squids aren't supposed to get along?" Clutch asked.

Jake's voice came clearly across the crackling line, a man determined. "What's that—the *once in, never out* bullshit they teach you?"

Bobby Juniper, we need you back . . .

"Look, I'm trying to track a merc who worked as a bodyguard in Djibouti a few months ago. At the Doctors Without Borders clinic. His name's Rafe McAllistar."

Clutch held the neck of the beer bottle so tightly his arm began to shake. Slowly he released his grip and set the bottle down heavily on the desk in front of him. "I know him."

Or at least he *had* known Rafe once—today he didn't recognize the man who'd blown his shot at becoming a Delta Force operator, two months away from completing his training, by defying a direct order. These days, Rafe was a man who would do anything and everything for money. Obviously, turning on his own clients wasn't something Rafe stopped at.

"Do you know where Rafe is now?" Jake persisted.

"After the senator's daughter was kidnapped, he took off. I assume he's hiding."

"How did you know about the doctor? It didn't make the papers."

"It doesn't need to make the papers for our community to know about it. We had plenty of guys approaching the senator after it happened, offering real protection from the guy. She refused. Said she had a friend who was taking care of things."

"Tell me what this guy's all about."

"I've got nothing to say that you'll want to hear."

"I don't have a choice."

Where had he heard those words before? "Rafe's gotten into places over the past couple of years that I wouldn't be able to touch, and I've had more training than him." Clutch didn't know if it was the fact that Rafe just didn't care that made him so good . . . and so dangerous. "He's as deadly as they come."

"He's never done anything like this before, like what he did to Isabelle?"

"Not to my knowledge. Mainly, he's hired to do the impossible—to break in where no one else can; he's also responsible for the assassinations of some important people over the past years. He's damned good at what he does, Jake. I know you and Nick are trained, but this guy's a master of disguises. He's above and beyond, and he's a loner."

A man with a death wish.

"Can you catch him?" Jake asked after a moment of silence.

"I can't make you any promises."

"The senator's daughter also mentioned a photographer who'd been hanging around the clinic."

"What's the name?"

Clutch could hang up now, leave the way he'd planned, and not to do the job he was supposed to do—no, this time he was disappearing for good. If GOST found him, he'd take the consequences. If they turned him in to the men who'd been looking for him for eighteen years, he'd be dead.

But even before Jake spoke again, Clutch knew what the man was going to say, knew that leaving wasn't an option.

"I've only got a first name—Sarah."

Sarah. Soft and warm, curled up next to him, tangled in the sheets . . . tangled around him in mornings that seemed to last forever.

But it hadn't been forever. It had been a year. She'd stayed with him on and off, refusing anything more than some food and his bed and his body.

She'd gotten some crazy idea that he could train her, she'd wanted to become what he was, when all he wanted to do was to shed his skin and walk out of this lifestyle, would do it in a second if there was another way for him to survive in this country. And there she was, so willing to step into what he would willingly cast off.

She was innocent to him, even with the tats and the guns and the wide eyes that had seen too much and never, ever pleaded with him for help with anything. And then the one time she did, he'd turned her down.

"*We can work together.*"

"*Sarah, the things I do, things I've done . . . you have no idea.*"

"*I've grown up here, among men like you. I'm not innocent.*"

"*I won't let you do this.*"

"*You have no way to stop me.*"

He hadn't—but pushing her into Rafe's arms hadn't been part of the plan.

Live or die, Sarah. Figure that out first and the rest will be easy, he'd told her as she'd walked off his porch.

Clutch hadn't seen her in six months, had heard the rumors that she'd started working with Rafe and hadn't wanted to believe them.

"I'll try to find her and dig up any intel on Rafe. Leave your number with Vic—I'll get back to you." Clutch severed the connection but continued to grip the big black phone, feeling it all come down on his shoulders.

How could he have been so wrong about Sarah?

You've been wrong like that before, he taunted himself.

Now he'd have to hunt one of his own. What Rafe had done hit Clutch too close to home for comfort, a story confirmed as fact by some rebel soldiers who Rafe had paid to leave the woman alone for the American soldiers to discover.

He had no idea why Rafe had done what he'd done, but Clutch had no doubt as to why he'd left the senator's daughter alive after he'd collected his money.

She was a message to someone. And messages like that weren't something to be ignored.

CHAPTER
9

When Isabelle's day at the clinic ended, Uncle Cal was waiting for her outside her office in his khaki uniform, shoulders back with the stiff military bearing she'd grown familiar with.

She'd never called him last night, or at any point today; she bristled inwardly at the thought of having to check in with anyone at her age. Her mood wasn't helped by the fact that she was still pissed at Jake.

She readied to meet her uncle's comments head-on, but none came.

"We've got dinner with your mom tonight. I figured you'd need a ride home," was all he said, nodded curtly to a few passing Marines who saluted him.

She'd forgotten completely about dinner after clearing one after another of the never-ending stream of patients, staying too busy to think about the way she and Jake had left things earlier. The fact that he was, no doubt, still pissed at her. "Thanks."

He nodded and she followed him out to his car. For the first few minutes, she slumped in the seat nearly boneless, the hard day coming off her in waves. Uncle Cal was wrapped in his own thoughts as well, and normally this shared solitude cemented the easy bond between them. Tonight, the silence just made her feel guilty.

Finally, she spoke. "I'm sorry, Uncle Cal—about last night. It's just that—"

He held up a hand. "Please, Izzy, it's all right. You don't need an old bulldog like me policing your every move. The fact that you had to sneak out was embarrassing, to say the least."

Yes, for both of them. What had she been thinking? "I shouldn't have worried you."

"Lieutenant J. G. Hansen called me this morning."

She couldn't hide her surprise. Still, it made sense—her uncle and Jake were close. There was probably some kind of *look after her* directive going on, although she doubted Uncle Cal would be pleased that she was actually moving into a house with Jake. Unless . . . "Did he mention that he's got rooms for rent at his house?"

"He did." As always, the tone of his voice was unreadable as to whether or not her moving in with Jake was an issue. Without elaborating further on that thought, he put his car in park in the driveway, next to the long, black Town Car her mother always traveled in, and turned to her.

"Some paperwork from Doctors Without Borders came to your mother's house yesterday."

Shit. *Shit.* Her mind worked quickly, but her uncle was already getting out of the car after giving her the heads-up. She caught up to him before he got halfway up the walk.

"Uncle Cal, I'm not going to be happy at the clinic—not for the long term."

"Things will get better. You're paying your dues."

Uncle Cal, of course, knew the truth as well as she did. Most of the military staff was still suspicious of Isabelle, and didn't have a problem showing it. The younger nurses were slightly nicer. But being shunned in itself didn't bother her too much; her female friends—any friends, really—had always been few and far between and she'd never minded.

The girls she'd met in college were long gone—medical school had kept her too busy to keep up with those friendships. Medical school had been too competitive, especially among female surgeons, and she'd preferred to keep mostly to herself.

She automatically touched her side as she thought about Sarah next and wondered where the photographer was.

Evening number three in Djibouti. Isabelle had been exhausted, attempting to plow through the constant paperwork, the forms required by MSF in order to keep track of medications and money spent.

A quick flash of light made her look up, startled. Instinctively, she hid her face behind her hand. "Oh, I don't really like . . . I'm not really used to . . ."

She'd spent a lot of time avoiding photographers and the

press in general, had become so good at it that most reporters forgot that Senator Cresswell had a daughter.

"Hey, it's all right. I get it." Sarah put the camera down on the table. "Cameras can freak people. Some cultures think that cameras can steal your soul."

"You don't agree?"

"I think that a lot of people's souls were never there to begin with." Sarah took the top off a Fanta and handed the drink to her. "You're doing well. Even Rafe was impressed and it takes a lot to impress him."

"You've known him before this?"

"We've been at a few of the same camps together. I know what he is."

"A logistician."

"Sure, we can go with that." Sarah lit a cigarette. "It's okay. I'm not going to tell anyone. But most doctors don't come here with their own bodyguards."

"I'm not most doctors."

Sarah smiled. "I know that too."

Sarah got her in a way that few women did, mainly because she was as complicated as Isabelle herself was. Their friendship had been one that not many people would understand and yet it was the most comfortable one Isabelle could ever remember having.

She refused to believe that Sarah had any involvement in what happened. She'd had too much taken away already.

"Izzy," Uncle Cal called to her—he was already at the front door and she followed him quickly into the house.

Her mother was waiting in the living room.

"Izzy!" Her mom threw her arms around her. The affection was always surprising to Isabelle. In her political world, Jeannie Cresswell was stoic, her bearing regal. In private, she was warm and funny and Isabelle always wondered if living that kind of a double life was wearing or just necessary.

"Hey, Mom." Isabelle returned the hug, the familiar scent of her mom's ever-present Chanel No. 5 immediately bringing Isabelle a sense of comfort. Although she and her mom weren't always physically close, they had a pretty tight bond that Isabelle was grateful for, despite her mom's overprotective nature, which had started with her family's military background and had gotten worse with the political lifestyle. Isabelle could never get a firm footing as to what exactly her mother wanted from her and she'd given up early, had focused on doing what she herself wanted to do, and after a long while, there was an easy, if uneven, peace between the two women.

The last trip to Africa had nearly broken that peace completely.

"You look good, honey." Jeannie held her at arm's length. "Still too thin, though. Are you eating?"

"I am, Mom. It's good to see you." And, really, it was.

Her mother had been there every day, nearly nonstop, for the first week Isabelle had been in the hospital. They'd been watching Isabelle closely for pneumothorax; it had been something of a small miracle that her lung hadn't collapsed or been punctured on the carry Jake had to perform. He'd run over some rough territory and in order to gain the speed necessary, he hadn't been all that gentle. The extra morphine he'd slipped her might have helped, and so had the hold he'd shifted to after he'd run a short distance with her in his arms.

She'd refused a lot of the pain meds they'd wanted to give her once she'd arrived at the hospital, hadn't wanted to be groggy. Her entire body remained on full alert, even while she slept. And she'd been forced to speak to the FBI and the CIA and the military and a steady stream of people who kept asking her the same questions.

She'd given them all the same answers, different than what she'd told Jake. Identified Rafe by picture over and over, knowing her life was never going to be the same.

She forced her thoughts away from that, caught sight of the envelope near her mother's bag as her mom and Cal shared a brief hug.

Jeannie motioned for her to sit next to her on the couch. "I had lunch with Daniel today," she said.

Isabelle bit back saying anything, held her mother's gaze for a few seconds in a big game of chicken. Jeannie gave in first. "He misses you, Izzy."

"You came to try to talk me into going back to Washington once my three months here are up." She wondered if her mom had that idea before or after the MSF paperwork arrived at her doorstep. Typical, the political approach—start soft and friendly, reel them in and then strike hard.

"Can I have the envelope from Doctors Without Borders, Mom?" she asked quietly. For a long moment, her words just hung there like a heavy weight pulling at all of them, until Jeannie leaned over to reach into her bag and then handed the now all-too-familiar packet to her. Isabelle flipped it over, saw her mom hadn't opened it, but that didn't matter—the return address clearly marked it as Médicins Sans Frontières.

She tore the envelope open and saw the completed paperwork—they were letting it go through. She'd worried, at first, that MSF would stop her from going because of what happened.

When she looked up from the papers, she found her mother staring at her and when she glanced toward Cal she found him staring out the front window, hands clasped behind his back. "It's only for eight weeks this time."

"You are not going back there. She is *not* going back there." Uncle Cal turned at the sound of her mother's voice and her mom looked between the two of them.

Isabelle turned to Cal. "You stopped me once. But I'm not going to comply with everyone else's wishes this time. I've got to make myself happy."

"How can going back there make you happy?" Jeannie held a hand to her throat, and Isabelle knew she couldn't explain it to her. Her mother would never understand ... and that was all right.

"Izzy, you signed a commitment to the Navy," Uncle Cal started.

"I'll honor that. And then, when I'm done with this Doctors Without Borders assignment, I'll decide. I'm not going to be able to go through Officer Candidate School yet. I can't even run two miles without pain." The anger rose inside of her—hotter, faster than she'd ever remembered—and Uncle Cal shot her a warning look, but it was too late. She was tired of being handled.

Her mother's next words weren't a surprise. "You haven't given this new job a chance. You're moving from one thing to the other too quickly—you're not giving anything a chance."

No, that wasn't true. She was giving one person a chance, the biggest chance she might've ever taken. "The clinic was always going to be a short-term solution for me. You both knew that."

"Maybe if you spoke with Daniel," Jeannie suggested. At the mention of her ex-fiancé's name again, Isabelle lost it.

"Maybe if I spoke with Daniel, what? He'd make me see the error of my ways? Remind me that I'm supposed to sit home like some good little scared girl, never going anywhere but the safety of the hospital and then back home to him? I tried that. It didn't work." Her voice had risen and she fought back the sob that formed in her throat, wanting to give in to the pure white hot fury instead.

Before she said something she'd regret, she walked away, past the two-man security team at the front door and out onto the front porch, heard Uncle Cal tell her mother to *give Izzy a minute* as she slammed the door behind her.

She'd need much more time than that. She yanked her cell phone out of her pocket, dialed the number Jake had given her earlier, before they'd left his house that morning to go to the accident. Before she'd cursed at him.

She hated being helpless—he was the first line of defense in stopping that.

He picked up on the first ring. "What's wrong?"

That voice—his voice, floating above her—strong, comforting. Soothing. For a second, she closed her eyes and let his rough tones wash over her as he said her name, and she was in control again. When she opened her eyes her lashes were wet, and when she opened her mouth, nothing came out except a small sigh.

"I'm not a mind reader, Isabelle," he said softly.

"Sorry," she said. "God, Jake, I'm sorry..."

There was a pause on his end, and then his voice again, gruffer than normal and twice as reassuring. "You don't have to apologize to me. For anything."

"I never thought I'd have this kind of bond with anyone," she said as the air bit through the long-sleeved shirt she'd worn under her scrubs, forcing her to pace the porch to try to avoid the wind. "It's intense, so intense. I feel like I know you so well, on a level I can't even begin to explain. Then again, I feel like I don't even have to explain. You just knew. You just... know. And I'm not sure I like it."

She paused, hoping he hadn't heard the hitch in her voice. "That night, when we were lying there and you were kissing me, I pretended that we were on vacation. On a beach, at night, after a long lazy afternoon in the sun. It was like a slice of heaven in the middle of all that hell." She spoke quietly, more to herself than to him. Thinking about that night should've frightened her, but those memories weren't a match for Jake. Most of the time.

"What do you need from me, Isabelle?"

"I need..." *So much.* "I need you to come get me."

"I'll be there in fifteen. Do you need me to stay on the line with you?"

She smiled into the phone. "It's okay—I've got to go pack. I'll see you in a little while."

She clicked the phone off, shoved it into the pocket of her scrubs and walked back inside the house. Her mother and Uncle Cal still had their heads together and so she bypassed them, went upstairs to the room she'd been staying in and began to pack.

"You're leaving?" Her mother walked through the partially opened door.

"I told Uncle Cal earlier—I'm so grateful for everything he's done, for what you've both done, but it's time for me to get on with my life."

"When were you going to tell me this?" her mother demanded of Cal, who stood in the doorway.

"Okay, we all need to calm down." Uncle Cal's voice boomed but Isabelle's temper was too far gone. And it felt good, really good, to unleash it. It was like taking back her power—and a little bit of her life.

"I'm done being calm, Uncle Cal. I've got to heal the best way I know how. And that way is going to be totally up to me. Not you, and not you either, Mom."

"She is so stubborn," her mother said to Uncle Cal. "She's getting worse as she gets older."

"*She* is still in the room," Isabelle said.

"I know that you're a grown woman, and that you can do whatever you like. God knows my interference hasn't helped matters, but I'd really rather if you weren't alone right now," Jeannie pleaded.

"Well, I won't be. I'll have roommates."

Cal shot her another look, which she ignored.

"Roommates?" Jeannie asked.

"Yes. They're men Uncle Cal knows. From the base."

"Soldiers?"

"SEALs, actually," Isabelle admitted. "Part of the team who rescued me."

Her mother was silent for a minute. "Are you . . . *dating* any of these men?"

"I think this is a good time for me to leave you two

alone," Cal said. He stood and left the room quickly, as if hearing about relationships was something he didn't want any part of.

"One of them is very special to me," Isabelle said.

"I just don't think that's such a good idea. I mean, he rescued you, Izzy. He knows..."

"He knows everything, yes," she told her mother. "And he doesn't care. He treats me like I'm whole. Like I'm a flesh-and-blood woman. And why shouldn't he?"

Isabelle wasn't able to stop the flow of tears and her mother pulled her into a fierce hug without reservation. "Of course he should. There's nothing wrong with you. He'd be lucky to have you."

"Then what's the problem?"

"I was just thinking it might be easier with someone who doesn't know what happened. That maybe he's going to be a constant reminder of everything," her mother explained, and Isabelle didn't tell her that Jake was a constant reminder of just how right things could be eventually.

"Nothing about the past months has been easy. But I need to do this. This man just lets me be myself. You don't know how important that is to me." Isabelle let her mother wipe the tears from her cheeks while she waited to hear the rebuttal.

"Honey, I'm sorry. I do know how important that is. I just don't want you to make the same mistakes I made."

It was perhaps the first time her mother had ever admitted anything so personal. Isabelle watched as her mom's eyes grew slightly misty, how she suddenly looked very much like the young woman who'd fallen for a soldier at seventeen.

"Falling in love with my father was a mistake?"

"I was young. He was heroic. Dangerous." Her mother paused, her hand worrying the silver locket she always wore around her neck. "Men like that have secrets. So many secrets. They'll push you away if you try to get too close."

Jake did have secrets—*that* much Isabelle knew. She knew only the basics about what he'd grown up with, could fill in the blanks pretty easily herself, but she had a feeling that what she was imagining was far tamer than what actually happened to the young boy who'd been forced to carry the burden of his stepfather's death all these years.

"You think you can help them. Fix them. Heal them," her mother continued. "But you can't. Military men are just born different. Special Forces soldiers are in a class by themselves. Izzy, I just don't think this is a good thing for you."

Isabelle knew her mother wasn't really talking about her father at all. "I can make my own choices."

"I know you can. But I think this choice is being made for all the wrong reasons, because you think you're safe with this man."

I am safe with him. Those words tried to form on her lips, but they didn't. The words *safe* and *trust* had been effectively wiped from her vocabulary two months earlier and it was a slow, torturous climb getting them back. "I'll be fine, Mom," she said instead. "Really. Just trust me."

"You don't have a lot of experience with men. You spent so much time on school, your residency, your career. You've spent so much time alone. There's a lot left for you to experience beyond your career."

"Being alone was my preference. And I was engaged," she reminded her mother.

"You didn't love him," her mother stated flatly.

"How did you know that?"

Jeannie reached out to put a hand over Isabelle's. "A mother knows these things."

She recalled Jeannie's earlier words. "I don't understand why, if you knew how I felt about Daniel, you'd try to get me to go back with him."

Jeannie pushed some hair off Isabelle's cheeks. Isabelle wound it back impatiently, into a ponytail. She'd pulled it down earlier because she knew that was how her mother liked it, but it was getting in the way.

"You were always so alone. I know you prefer that—at first, I didn't, though. I thought you were lonely, shy. I tried to get you to come out of your shell."

Isabelle remembered that all too well. "You finally gave up." She wondered if Uncle Cal had heard this throughout his lifetime—he was the most solitary person Isabelle knew.

"I did, once I realized that you enjoyed your own company. But I was thrilled when you finally let Daniel in. Or at least I thought you did."

Isabelle's fiancé had treated her well, seemed to deal with her competitive nature—because he had no interest in trying to top her, maybe. He was a pediatrician, not a surgeon, and had no problem with his wife being more successful in her chosen field than he was in his.

He'd been wonderful to her after she'd come home from Africa, more angry at himself that he hadn't insisted on going with her for her MSF tour.

She'd never had the heart to tell him that part of the

reason she'd gone had been to get away from him, to gain some perspective on their relationship, to figure out a way to tell him she wanted to break it off.

Running to Africa. Running to the Navy. She had to stop running, and it appeared that Jake was her brick wall. "I'm going to be all right, Mom."

"I might not be there for you all the time, but I know what you need."

"I know what I need too."

Jeannie smiled, but it didn't reach her eyes. Isabelle knew this fight was far from over.

CHAPTER
10

Jake was already outside, waiting in his car as she dragged her two suitcases past the security team on the porch, brushing off their offers of help.

She'd already said an uneasy good-bye to her mother, who was now on the phone checking in with her assistant. Her uncle's office door was closed, which was good. She didn't want to give him time to think about stopping her again. The conversation with her mother had continued along the same vein of *Please don't go to Africa,* ramping up to insistent yelling until Isabelle had been saved by her mother's ringing cell phone and Jake's honk.

Jake, who was out of the car and onto the porch in seconds. "What are you doing?"

"She refused help," one of the men offered and Jake just shook his head, first at the men and then at her.

He watched her with an unabashed stare, his gray eyes picking up the navy blue of his sweatshirt, making them look deep and mysterious, waiting as if he had a lifetime of patience. Or at least the training to pretend.

He'd wrapped his hair back in a bandanna, much in the same way he'd worn it in Africa. She'd meant to ask him how he could get away with wearing his hair so long, how many times he'd been shot . . . how many women he'd rescued. How he was so brave.

So many things she wanted to know. And he was still waiting for her answer to what she thought she was doing.

"I've got them," she argued, still feeling ornery. She even tried to wrestle one of the suitcases out of his hand while he stood there and stared at her, not releasing his own grip on her bags.

"I don't believe it. You might actually be as stubborn as I am." She relented at his words and he took both suitcases and, despite the fact that he was the one recovering from a bullet wound, carried them effortlessly to the car and threw them into the back of the old Blazer. "Is that it?"

"For now. The rest of my stuff's in storage. I figured I'd have it delivered once I'd found myself a more permanent place." She paused. "Can I drive?"

"No." He opened the passenger-side door for her and she climbed in. He had the radio blasting—some old school heavy metal rock, and when he got in and went to turn it down, she shook her head.

"Keep it," she called, and let herself get lost in the pounding beat of the music. This was the stuff she played

when she performed surgery—the more delicate the procedure, the more frantic the songs, as if the force of the beat
could tamp her nerves down to a manageable place.

She leaned in to turn the music up more as he yanked
the SUV away from the curb, plowed straight through a
snowdrift and shot off down the street.

And somehow, even though his driving methods actually seemed to have gotten worse in the span of a few hours,
she was getting used to them—enjoying the motion, even.
She found herself leaning into the curves, the speed filling
her body, and once they got moving—really moving—on
the highway, she asked, "Can you open the sunroof?"

He didn't blink or question, just rolled it open and
glanced over at her.

In response, she undid her seatbelt and maneuvered
herself so she could stick her upper body completely outside the car.

At first, she hung tightly on to the ski rack on the roof as
she steadied her footing on her seat and the console below.
The wind buffeted her body so hard she couldn't open her
eyes, and so she didn't—kept them closed and let herself
sway with the sensation of the fast moving car underneath
her and the bite of the wind and she was free, without
boundaries.

She let go of her hold and held her hands over her head
and the car moved on a downhill slope of the parkway—
with no one in front of them, Jake was pushing the Blazer
faster, as if he knew she needed a free fall with a net.

Her ears rang, lungs pained with every breath she took
and, as the car barreled along the highway, she opened her
mouth and yelled into the cold night air, as loud as she

could manage against the pressure building in her lungs, over and over until the tension left her body, until her throat hurt.

Until she felt better.

She climbed back inside the car and sat heavily, rubbed her arms to try to get rid of the chills racking her body. She noted that Jake had taken a much different route to his house and realized she'd been up there for longer than she'd thought.

He rolled the sunroof closed and jacked up the heat. "Rough night?"

"You could say that. After I told them that I'd already signed my new Doctors Without Borders commitment contract, the shit pretty much hit the fan. At first, I thought we'd come to an understanding, but the more we talked, the worse things got. My mother told me that I was not listening to reason and Uncle Cal asked how I managed, and I quote, *to take on one of Jake's finer qualities in such a short time.*" She was breathing hard, thanks to the cold air blasting her lungs, and her side ached from her exertion.

He snorted. "I don't think that's a compliment to either of us."

"You think?" She rubbed her temples. "Did you ever get caught up in something without realizing it? And then, all of a sudden, you turn around and you're trapped and you have no idea how you got there?" she asked, didn't wait for his answer. "With the trips—with Doctors Without Borders, I was taking back me. Discovering what I wanted. When I was there, I wasn't a senator's daughter who'd just gotten an offer to practice in a prestigious practice or someone's fiancé. I was just Isabelle. I liked who I was. But that doesn't matter to them. They're going to try to stop me. Any way they can."

She wouldn't let that happen. And she had so much more to tell him—and the words just came out in a rush. "It's just that…I feel better around you. Safer. Comfortable. Is that wrong? Does it mean I'm not healing the right way? What's the right way, Jake? Because if you know the secret, I'd love for you to share it."

"I think you're too hard on yourself. It's all right not to be all right," he said.

"Cresswell women don't fall apart," she said. "That's my mother's motto."

"I think you're going to have to find a new motto." He paused. "You told your mom you were moving out too."

"Of course I did. I'm not a prisoner. But my mother thinks I should move back into her house since I'm not happy at the clinic. I've lovingly nicknamed her place *the compound*."

"That bad, huh?"

"She wanted to assign me two bodyguards after it all happened. I mean, how could I ever trust—" She bit her lip. "No, that's not true. I have to trust."

"You don't have to do anything."

"That's a really good motto. How's that working for you?" She saw the tug of a smile playing at the corner of his mouth.

"Works just fine if you do it right."

"And you're going to teach me how to do it right?"

"Some people might say that I've taught you too much already." He cut her a sideways glance. "What did you have in mind?"

What *did* she have in mind?

"Suppose I want to trust you to touch me? Any way you'd like. Any way that I'd like." The words had tumbled out faster than she could stop them and yet she didn't avert her gaze from Jake's profile, stared at the way his large hands held the wheel easily, with his thumb caressing the braided leather. And she held her breath a little too.

"Rules of the game?" he asked finally.

"What do you mean?"

"Before I go into a mission, I always ask what the rules of the game are. I need to know what I'm allowed—and not allowed—to do."

"And do you always follow those directions?"

His eyes met hers for a quick second—calm and direct in the soft glow from the oncoming car headlights. "For *your* game, yes."

His words took her breath away again. For a few seconds, she couldn't answer him. When she finally did, she tried to keep the tremble out of her voice.

"I don't know the rules. I'm just making them up as I go along," she admitted. "But I want you to keep trying... to touch me."

"You're going to get mad at me. A lot," he told her unapologetically.

"Probably. And I'm sure I'll piss you off again too. But I'll try not to jump onto any more buses without telling you first." She watched as Jake bypassed a slower-moving car from the narrow shoulder left of the fast lane. "Where are we going?"

He pulled into a back parking lot and she saw the neon

diner sign. "I figured you never did get around to eating anything tonight."

"Is this a date?" she asked as he started to climb out of the car. He shut the door behind him without answering, and before she could shift and open her own door, he was doing that for her.

"It's dinner, Isabelle," was all he said.

Jeannie had stormed into Cal's office without knocking. At first he thought her fury—justifiable, of course—was aimed at his allowing Isabelle to move out.

When he actually looked into her eyes, a deep, rich brown that had pulled at him since he was seventeen years old, he knew something much worse had happened.

"He called me...that bastard called me, Cal." Her voice shook, a mix of anger and fear as she shoved her cell phone at him, as if he could trace the number.

It would be a pre-paid cell. "Tell me what he said."

"He said he's coming back—back here. For me, for you and for Isabelle."

"He won't get out of Africa."

"He said he's got his transport out of Africa. He said he's..." She drew in a sharp breath. "Said he's ready to see Izzy again. We need to get her better protection."

"I've got protection detail on her," Cal said.

"A SEAL? One SEAL?" Jeannie let out a harsh laugh and stared at him, and he remembered a time when she'd thought one SEAL would be enough. A time when he might've agreed with her.

"I'm going to ask Jeannie to marry me."

James said it so matter-of-factly that Cal nearly dropped the weapon he'd been cleaning.

"That's fast, isn't it?" Cal asked with a feigned casualness, tried not to think about the way Jeannie had ended up in his bed last night after her fourth date with James. Tried not to think about the way his time with her was running out.

"It's never too fast when you've found the right woman." James had worn a smile Cal remembered clearly to this day.

"Why did you let her go?"

"You were too close to telling her, Jeannie." If Isabelle hadn't stormed out of the house before Rafe called . . . well, he didn't want to think about that.

"I'll give you forty-eight hours, Cal. And then I'm telling her everything."

"Now you're threatening me?"

"It's not a threat. Isabelle deserves the truth. She should've learned about all of it years ago, when I did."

"The truth isn't always the right thing," he reminded her.

"The truth is the only thing I've ever had."

Jake nodded to the familiar hostess and she led him and Isabelle past the noisy main portion of the diner and into one of the side rooms. Quieter, but still large enough so she'd be comfortable.

She slid into the booth and tucked her legs underneath her. He noticed that she'd kicked off her shoes, as his feet hit them when he slid in across from her.

She still wore her blue scrubs, hair up, and if she wore any makeup, he couldn't tell. Even with light smudges under her eyes signaling lack of sleep, she was easily the most beautiful woman he'd ever seen.

He watched the way her hands held the sides of the menu, her fingers playing along the plastic edges as if they couldn't keep still, constantly seeking . . . feeling.

She'd done that along his arm, his thigh the night of the rescue. Her entire body had been shaking, except for her hands, which had been steady and nimble as they'd stroked along his cammies.

Surgeon's hands. Hands wasted working in a clinic doling out Motrin and doing physicals.

Hands he wanted all over his body. Right now.

Jesus Christ, he had to get a grip.

He noted when they'd both gotten out of the car that she didn't even check her six and made a mental note to start reminding her, subtly, to stay more aware of her surroundings.

He was already far too aware of *her*.

"So, when am I going to meet your brothers and which one of them can I blame for your driving technique?" she asked after they'd placed their orders and had taken some time choosing songs from the mini-jukebox that sat on their table.

It was as good a time as any to tell her. "You've met both of them. Devane and Waldron."

"Oh. Yes, I remember them," she said quietly. "From Africa."

"We're brothers by adoption. Chris's dad took me in after my stepfather died. Nick moved in two weeks later. I don't even think the adoption was legal or anything, but at that point, no one argued."

"That's how you were allowed to be on the same team."

"Yes. Although that was more of a fluke. A pretty recent one too. Chris just came back from Coronado a few months ago." He didn't tell her that Nick had transferred out of the mythical Team Six, aka DevGru before it had disbanded. That was still classified information. "They're my brothers, but they're also my best friends."

"My dad was best friends with Uncle Cal. They were on a mission together when he saved Uncle Cal's life. I'm sure the admiral must've told you that story."

They paused while the waitress placed the heavy plates in front of them, winked at Jake and left them alone again. If Isabelle noticed the wink, she didn't say anything, just dug immediately into her food.

"The admiral never talks about his missions, unless it's to give us a specific piece of advice." He took a bite of his turkey club and realized it had been too long since he'd eaten as well.

She swallowed a large bite of her own sandwich before she spoke again. "My father was on a mission with Uncle Cal—when Uncle Cal was still UDT and my dad was with Naval Intel. There was another UDT sailor they were both friends with, a guy named Kevin. I remember him—he came around a lot. For a long time, it didn't make any sense to me, how a man who used to bring me stickers and candy when he used to visit could just turn on his friends."

"Kevin killed your father?"

She nodded. "Uncle Cal found out that Kevin had been smuggling arms and was about to get caught, and wanted to put the blame on my father and Uncle Cal. I guess he tried to kill them both so they wouldn't talk. My dad jumped in front of Uncle Cal to talk Kevin down, and he took the bullet for him."

"And then Cal shot Kevin."

"Yes." She stared out into the dark for a second, the sounds of the jukebox playing softly filled the silence. "I can't imagine what that's like—living with that guilt."

"I'm sure it tears him up, but he's got training on his side."

"How can you train for something like that?"

"It's different for us," he said finally. "We're trained not to think about that—we're trained to react and concentrate on the good of the mission, not the aftermath."

"But you're human."

"Not when we're on the job," he said. "Look, if I worried every second about my team, I'd never be able to focus on the task at hand. You clear your mind and let your training take over. I know it sounds bad, but it's the way it is. We don't take the oath *First do no harm*."

She'd finished her own fries and began to eat his right off his plate. He'd never been one to share—or share well— but he didn't say a word.

"It's actually similar to the way I've been taught to view patients—cool and calm, without emotion," she said. "What oath *do* you take, by the way?"

"Do no harm. Unless someone harms you first."

That made her smile a little bit, and God, he liked making her smile. "You said this would be your fourth trip to Africa with Doctors Without Borders. What was your first time there like?"

She rested her chin in her palm, her fingers tapped the

side of her face. "My first trip lasted six months—I was in the Congo. It's always longer the first time. I guess they figure you're green enough that you'll agree to it. The next few times, you know better—know what you can handle and what you can't."

She drew in a breath before continuing. "The first time you go, it's intense. You have no idea what to expect, even though you've been told over and over. And then you get there and you're immersed and then you come home and you're lost. No one gets it. And it's not their fault and it's not yours, but for a while there's just this huge disconnect."

He nodded, because he got it. Immediately. Wasn't so different from returning from any combat mission. Reentry was always a bitch.

"I wondered, for a while, when things would feel normal. And then I realized that they never would." She shrugged, like it didn't matter, but he knew differently. "It's better the second time. Because you realize that talking about it doesn't change anything. For you, or for them."

"Not an easy life."

"Well, I guess we all chose it," she said.

"You'd be surprised at how that choice is made for a lot of men and women. If you consider the military over jail to be a choice."

"So it was jail or the military?"

"No, not for me. Nick and Chris got themselves into some trouble and got caught. They let it go too far and they had to make that choice."

"And you didn't let it get that far?"

"Right." He stretched his body tentatively, arms over his

head but still conscious of his side. "I never would've made it that far."

"You mean, in jail."

"No, I never would've made it *to* jail."

"I don't understand."

"You don't want to understand," he said. "I was wild, Isabelle. I didn't give a shit about anyone, beyond myself or Nick or Chris, and that wasn't enough to keep me out of trouble in the end. In my world, I didn't owe anyone anything. Not even the people who were good to me, or loyal."

She wasn't saying anything.

"I would've been dead if I hadn't enlisted. I would've been dead and I didn't care. For about the first five years I was in, I didn't care much either. It wasn't a good way to live."

"And now you care?"

"Yes."

"So the military did that for you? Gave you back what you were missing?"

"It didn't hurt." He shrugged. "But that's me, not you. Going back to a third world country as military personnel will be a lot different," he said. "You won't be treating the locals."

"I know. Did Cal tell you to talk me out of this?"

"No. But you have to get how worried he is."

She gave him a small smile and pushed her plate away. She took a deep breath, as if full and sated. Her fingers played along the blade of the dull knife and she kept her eyes focused on it when she spoke again. "Uncle Cal's my biological father."

His head jerked up in surprise, and there were very few things these days that could surprise him. "He never said—"

She shook her head. "He doesn't know I know. Neither does my mother."

"How long have you known?"

"Feels like forever. I was eight when my dad was killed—I still consider him my dad. Always will, I guess." She sat back against the red fake leather seat and stretched her legs out so her feet rested on the seat next to him.

"Do you think Cal knows?"

"He knows," she said quietly. "I was listening, the night he told my mom that my dad was killed. Uncle Cal said, *I tried, Jeannie, but I couldn't save him. I couldn't save him, and I owed him so much for the way I betrayed him, for Isabelle.* It didn't take a genius to figure it all out." She drew a deep sigh. "It's pretty obvious, anyway. Uncle Cal and I are an awful lot alike."

"Does it bother you that they never told you?"

"No. It only bothers me when I see the way my mom looks at him sometimes. She still loves him."

"You've never brought it up to her . . . in all these years?"

"We don't talk about things in my family," she said. There wasn't any trace of bitterness in her voice—more of a vague acceptance of the way things were. "Well, we didn't, although my whole Doctors Without Borders thing has certainly gotten the dialogue moving."

She paused for a few minutes and he knew, just knew, what she wanted to ask him.

He gave her what she wanted. "I didn't know my real father."

"Did you ever think about finding him?"

He stared at her for a long minute, her hazel eyes matching his gaze. "What would it change?"

"Right. What would it change?" She reached across the table—his hand met hers halfway and held it tight for a few seconds, until he was sure he could speak.

"Come on, let's go get you settled in."

CHAPTER

11

It was happening again. Gunfire shattered the quiet, the sound a sharp relief against the eerie silence that always preceded a rebel attack.

Screams plus the steady fire of machine guns came together in a rapid staccato against the pre-dawn calm and Sarah couldn't bring herself to move this time, stood frozen against the back wall of one of the main clinic buildings. There was nothing she could do for these people as the flash of lights and sounds reached a dizzying climax, and still the quiet didn't return.

She stood there, frozen, one person with a weapon against the soldiers would do nothing, but even so, she flashed back to when she was sixteen and the soldiers were breaking in and taking everything—everything she'd always known. In the fury to take back land from white owners, resentment bubbled to an overwhelming blind rage.

She'd wanted to stay, to argue—to beg for her family's farm, but instead pulled her mother and sister hard by the arms, out the back door, to hide in the tobacco crops until the riots died down. She remained in Zimbabwe until she couldn't stand one more set of borrowed clothes and look of pity and she'd stolen a car and driven away.

Now these soldiers were coming closer, and still she was rooted, the boots she wore like lead weights attached to her legs, and every breath felt heavy, almost not worth the effort.

It would be very easy to give up. So much easier, because she'd had nothing to give her family two months before last, and now nothing again.

Sarah had tried to get her family to leave Zimbabwe with her, but they knew no other country. Their grief was still too fresh, too deep. And so they waited, as if their land and their status were going to be restored.

She knew better. Violence mounted around them every day, as did their poverty. Sarah was standing knee-deep in poverty herself, and it was dark and hot and she was not supposed to break down like this. Not here and not now. If she wanted her money, she'd have to get out of here and meet Rafe.

She turned to peer back inside the small house that served as guest quarters for visiting doctors. Empty. A thin trickle of sweat ran between her breasts, between her shoulder blades, and the smell of gunpowder was thick in her nose as she took a hesitant step inside to grab her things.

The hand slapped over her mouth and another strong arm wrapped around her, didn't give her a chance to react before she was lifted off the ground by a brute strength she was helpless against. With her arms pinned solidly to her sides so she couldn't use the gun strapped to her calf, she struggled, until she heard the low American voice whisper in her ear.

"You're coming with me, Sarah."

She nodded to show she understood and the grip around her body tightened even as the hand came off her mouth. He wasn't going to let her go but he'd get her away from the rebels. It was the lesser of two evils, and she was without any choice.

He dragged her away from the camp, through the start of the dense jungles that ran along the back side of the clinic and into a small clearing where she'd parked her car earlier.

He'd been watching her.

Instead of pulling her inside and driving away from the madness that was still too close, he pushed her against the side of the ancient white Land Rover.

His hand wrapped around her throat as his voice came as a low growl directly into her ear. "Where's your friend Rafe? He's supposed to be here with you."

Clutch still maintained a semblance of military bearing— the short hair, nearly white blond, and eyebrows that matched, all standing out in stark contrast to his tanned skin. His eyes were somewhere in between pale blue and green, but closer to a colorless marble that she'd once had in her collection—her pride and joy, the shooter that won her more candy than any other kid in her small school.

So no, Clutch didn't blend here, not by a long shot, but he didn't have to. He'd told her that if he was seen, it was because he wanted people to know exactly who he was—and if he needed the element of surprise, he was good enough that they never saw him coming.

She certainly hadn't. And his hand was far too gentle on her windpipe, as if he knew just the right places to press to make her uncomfortable without actually hurting her. He'd done this before—he could snap her neck easily, if he wanted to.

"I don't know where Rafe is," she managed in a ragged whisper. Shots rang out behind him, but he remained unmoved, didn't flinch as the whoosh from an explosion flashed in the night sky and shook the ground.

"Then I guess you want to stay here—with the rebels. I'm sure they'll find . . . work for you." His eyes dropped to travel her body and she jerked as if she could free herself from him. "Don't fuck with me, Sarah. I know you were working with him."

"He's one of the few who's shown me any kindness," she said, wondered why her heart ached when Clutch looked as though she'd slapped him. Wondered if it was too late for them both.

"If you're looking for kindness, you were born in the wrong country," he said. "If you were looking to get it from Rafe, you definitely went to the wrong man."

"What? Suddenly there's honor among thieves?"

"Do you know what that kind man did to the woman who thinks you're her friend?" Clutch asked, and no, she didn't want to know, squeezed her eyes tight and railed against the hand on her throat. If she didn't know, it wouldn't be real—she could keep lying to herself, keep taking the blood money that Isabelle paid for in the way a woman never should have to pay.

But Clutch wasn't letting up, leaned close and whispered in her ear, told the story over and over, the same one she'd heard whispered rumors of in the bars where other men like Rafe and Clutch gathered, looking for work and company and drink.

Her knees buckled as his grip tightened and she knew for sure that she couldn't take the easy way out.

A rustle came from the bushes behind him and he let go of her and turned his gun on the soldier stepping out into the clearing. Clutch had him down in two shots, but before he could turn back to her, she'd cocked her weapon and had it pointed straight at his broad back.

He froze when he heard the click. "Don't do this, Sarah."

"Drop your weapon," she said quietly, surprised when he did so. She took a few tentative steps toward him, used her free hand to check him for the other weapons she knew he carried. She'd seen him strap up more often than she cared to remember—in order to do this right, she'd have to strip him.

They didn't have the time for that right now.

"Are you going to shoot me or leave me for the rebels?" he asked calmly as she pocketed the gun he'd laid on the grass, along with the one he carried strapped to his ankle. If there were others, she wasn't going in for them now.

If she left him here, he would surely die.

There's no honor among thieves, Sarah.

"I'll get you out of here, leave you off far enough away where you've got a shot at escape."

"I don't want a shot at escape—I want a shot at Rafe."

After what Clutch had whispered to her, he wasn't the only one.

"Your side does hurt."

Jake caught Isabelle rubbing the sore flesh over her rib cage as she stood in the middle of her new bedroom.

"It just aches sometimes," she said. "Probably from the cold."

"Try eight hundred milligrams of Motrin. It's the standard military dose. Solves anything."

"Short of a bullet wound."

"The military claims it covers that too," he said as he put her last bag down in the corner by the large closets.

"Is that what they gave you when you got shot?"

"I didn't need anything."

"Bullshit." The word slipped out before she could stop herself.

"Is that your best bedside manner?" he asked.

"You've seen my best bedside manner."

"I hope you weren't talking about earlier at the scene of the accident."

"Why? Didn't like what you saw?"

"You were yelling. It was obnoxious. It turned me on," he said. Deadpan.

She bit back a smile. "Didn't think I had it in me, did you?"

"I kind of knew you did. You might just make it in the

military after all." He maneuvered his body in front of hers, one hand reaching forward to brush back some of the hair that had fallen forward across her cheek. Just that touch alone was enough to make her belly clench, and he knew it.

Up until this morning, she hadn't seen much of that wildman the world proclaimed him to be. Although the grab-the-guy-by-the-throat maneuver in the bar was impressive, watching him head up the rescue, without being asked, watching everyone follow his direction . . . now, that was something to see.

Nothing about him was overtly pushy or blatant or cocky. He didn't have to be. He moved with the quiet confidence other men envied, tried to emulate and failed. His commanding presence wasn't something to be copied, it was something to be earned. And she'd never been so aware of her own sexuality, the way it pulled her, unrelentingly, toward Jake.

Yes, you're definitely on your way toward healing.

"Remind me to teach you some self-defense moves," he said.

"I know a few—they taught us some before my first trip to Africa. After they took us out to the woods and left us there with a compass and some water and told us to find our way out."

He snorted. "That must've gone well."

"I did better than some of the men." She played with the strings on her scrub pants, stared down at them. "I could probably use a refresher course, though."

"Okay, here's one." He held up his hand, pointed to the butt of his palm. "This can take a man down—here." He held his hand by her nose. "Hard and up. You've got the angle, because you're shorter. Also, here." He put his hand by her sternum. "Slam as hard as you can—take the wind out of them."

He hooked his foot behind her knee and tugged lightly, caught her before she stumbled forward. "Do that and push at the same time—they'll go flat on their ass."

"Anything else?"

"Yeah, scream as loud as you can. I suggest always carrying too."

"Do you?"

"Always."

"Then how about I just hang around with you?" she asked, and watched his mouth tug to the side, the way it always did when she asked something of him. As if he knew how damned hard it was for her to ask for help from anyone.

"I'm here, aren't I?" he said, before he turned to haul another bag out of the middle of the room and place it against a far wall.

Yes, he was here, and somehow, she still couldn't quite believe that he was going to stick it out despite the fact he hadn't given up on her yet.

"I know you think I don't watch my . . . what is it, my *six* enough," she said, and he cocked one eyebrow at her. "And maybe I should. But the thing is, I'm not afraid of random people who are out to hurt me. The person who hurt me is someone I let in. So how am I supposed to be wary of strangers when it's the people you trust who can hurt you the most?"

His gaze never wavered from her face.

"Can he escape? I mean, he's so highly trained . . . Could

a jail hold you?" she asked and then shook her head. "You know what, don't answer that. I don't want to know."

She noticed that he didn't protest—probably hadn't planned on answering anyway.

She avoided his gaze by glancing around the room and noted that there were fresh sheets on the bed. And fresh towels piled there as well. Things she hadn't even thought about needing. "You made my bed?"

He rolled his eyes, like she was making too big a deal of it. "Yeah, well, don't get too used to that. It's like a one-time-only thing. Besides, the stuff is Nick's."

"You stole your brother's sheets and towels?"

He shrugged. "They were just lying around. In his closet."

"I'll buy my own this week and then I'll wash and return them to him."

"Sounds good. You can throw my stuff in with that load too," he said. And he was completely serious.

"You can't do your own laundry?"

"I'm not really allowed to do it," he admitted. "I've broken a few machines. And I tend to turn clothes the wrong color."

"You do realize that I'm a doctor, right? Working full time."

"What's your point?" he asked as he strode toward her. She straightened from where she was putting a few things into the nightstand by the bed as he approached and leaned her back against the wall, just watching him, the way his strong frame moved toward her.

"Being your on-call doctor isn't enough?"

"That's a job you don't want."

"You don't get to tell me what I want," she said, wondered why it was so easy to say things like that to him, why it made him smile when she did. "Do you ask all your women to cook and do your laundry for you?"

"I didn't realize you were my woman," he said, his voice a low, husky timbre that made her want to tell him that *yes,* a big part of her already was his woman, wouldn't be satisfied with anything less.

He saved her from making a complete fool of herself.

"There haven't been a lot of women in my life," he said, then corrected himself when he saw her smirk. "There hasn't been anyone significant."

"I'm sure a lot of women have tried."

He shook his head slowly as he braced his arms against the wall on either side of her. "Whatever you're thinking is wrong. I'm a moody pain in the ass, Isabelle. Trust me on that."

With that, he leaned down and kissed her—a long, hard kiss that went deeper, further than the one last night on so many levels.

This one went on long enough to make her grab at his hair, his shoulders, all while his palms remained flat against the wall, and no, she wasn't wrong. Nothing about this— about him—could be wrong.

He smelled good, like fresh air and salt water, tasted even better and she drew him closer to her, so his body brushed hers. Hers hummed with just that slight contact and he hadn't even touched her yet.

She'd put him in charge of that, but somehow she found

her hands wandering down his chest, winding her fingers through the belt loops of his jeans to pull his pelvis close to hers. She wondered what he'd do if she just stripped him down, right here, wondered if he'd lie still under her inspection.

She was starting things she couldn't finish yet, and this time she wasn't the one to pull away, not like she had last night. Instead, he backed off, slowly, as if it was the last thing he wanted to do, held her gaze for a few seconds before he said, "Good night, Isabelle," and walked out the door.

She pressed her hand over her heart as if she could slow the rate by sheer will. She put her head back against the closed door and rubbed her mouth with her fingers. Her lips felt full and tingly. But the way he'd kissed her, like he wasn't afraid she'd break if he'd really touched her, had nearly broken her.

It was only ten P.M. and she was far too keyed up to sleep. She wandered into the bathroom, which she hadn't looked at the other night when Jake brought her up here to look around, and saw the large Jacuzzi tub and knew instantly that she'd have to give it a try.

As the water ran, she stripped her clothes off and left them in a pile on the floor. There was a full-length mirror that hung on the back of the door and she stared at herself critically, not with a doctor's eye, but with a woman's.

She was filling out again—her curves coming back slowly, her breasts filling out to the size they were in the months before Africa. She'd never been considered voluptuous, but she'd always looked healthy. She made a mental note that she'd need to go shopping for some real food tomorrow and then shook her head as she pictured Jake sitting down and waiting for her to cook him dinner.

Men like that have secrets. So many secrets. They'll push you away if you try to get too close.

Yeah, well, so did women like Isabelle. Jake was letting her in slowly; soon, she'd have to do the same.

She turned the water off and the jets on and climbed into the tub. God, it was nice. Soothing. The perfect way to end the day. Any day.

She let her head loll back against the porcelain and felt her body begin to relax under the kneading pressure of the jets. She spread her legs slightly and realized that besides being relaxed, she was completely turned on. It didn't hurt that Jake was at the forefront of her mind, or that if she closed her eyes she could picture him sitting at the side of the tub actually watching her, and that was some picture.

She angled her body and the hot spray was fast becoming his hands, his tongue and she wasn't sure, at first, that she was going to be able to do this. But she squeezed her eyes tight and pictured his face and let her hand trail between her legs.

"Jake," she murmured, her finger working her hot flesh, her back pressed against the hard tub.

As her fingers circled faster, as the pressure built, she thought about calling out to him, about getting out of the water and walking naked and dripping into his room, the same way she'd walked into his life.

"No," she said loudly. Not like this. She stood and grabbed for a towel.

Jake left Isabelle's door once he heard the water running. His hand had remained on the doorknob; he turned it and he'd felt the door give slightly—she hadn't locked it.

Dammit.

He pulled himself away and headed down to the second floor. He'd already taken a cold shower tonight, after he'd left the bar, wired the house even tighter than it already was, before he'd gone to pick up ˎ ˎelle. He'd made the mistake of taking a nap in his bed and woke up with a hard-on and his face buried in a pillow that smelled like Isabelle's shampoo.

He'd gotten immediately into the shower without bothering to wait until it got hot, knowing all the while that cold water wasn't going to do anything for him.

Forehead pressed to the tile, water pouring down his back, he'd stroked himself slowly. He'd wanted to draw his orgasm out, would have much preferred to not be doing this alone, and it had been too fucking long for him. Nearly four days since he'd been home and two months before that…

Since he'd rescued Isabelle. *Fuck.* He'd paused, hand on his cock, and wondered what the hell was happening to him. If he was losing his edge.

He'd planned on letting her in, just enough to keep her comfortable, safe. But he'd let her in more than he ever had any woman that night in Africa, and there was no taking that back.

But tonight—*fuck*—there was no other word for it, he just *ached*. Everywhere. Like he needed to be touched and touched well. And now, sitting in his room, listening to the water running in the room above his, he still did.

He wondered if Isabelle was thinking about him.

There was no way that one self-serving hand-job was going to be enough. Not for long.

Kissing her again hadn't been the smartest move, either. He rubbed his hands over his eyes and sighed.

There were women he could call, women who'd come over and share his bed at a moment's notice, who wouldn't care that he preferred to sleep alone or not sleep at all. There had always been women, lots of them—from an age when he should've been too innocent to understand. But he'd never been innocent. Neither had Nick, and Chris had grown up along the Bayou with the most permissive parents on the planet. Never mind the fact that Maggie had been a midwife and Chris had been raised around half-naked, screaming women. Screaming for all the wrong reasons, of course, and loud enough to make Chris not all that child-friendly.

Still, Chris had been the first and the only of the three of them to have a serious relationship. He and Jules had dated from the age of fourteen until they'd both turned twenty-three, when she'd gone out on tour and decided she couldn't handle the inherent danger of Chris's job any longer.

Nick had announced a long time ago that he was never marrying. *Never,* he would emphasize, loudly enough that they would all tell him to shut up before he lost his voice. Tracheal operations had done a number on his vocal cords for the first nine years of his life, and they were all protective of it.

But Jake had always hovered somewhere in the middle of thinking that he'd never find one woman who got him and wondering if it was possible. Kenny and Maggie were held up before him as a perfect model, but the despair Kenny had suffered when Maggie died made Jake wonder if maybe it wasn't worth it.

Of course, Kenny always talked about the whole it-is-better-to-have-loved-and-lost thing...but the way Jake had watched Kenny mourn for the last twelve years told a different story.

Just the thought of losing Isabelle made him sweat—and he didn't even have her. Not yet.

CHAPTER
12

Clutch ended up behind the wheel. Sarah split her time between pointing her weapon at him and the single rebel jeep that followed them out to the main road, which partially solved the problem of trying to keep a man as highly trained as Clutch prisoner. He'd have a hard time escaping from her while driving like a maniac to save both their lives, but she suspected he could still do so if he really wanted to.

Machine-gun fire sprayed the car as Clutch swerved from side to side, and she prayed the bullets wouldn't hit the tires or the gas tank. Heart pounding, she fired a few shots of her own blindly for cover out the window and then she stuck her head through the opened sunroof for two straight shots that blew out the jeep's tires. She fired a few more times, watched the vehicle rock, and knew she'd hit the driver.

She sank back down into her seat and held the gun on him again. "Floor it."

He cursed at her order but also gave her a fleeting glance with more than a hint of surprise in it—and a grudging respect, if the morning light wasn't playing tricks on her.

"There's more where they came from," he told her.

"They won't catch us this time. Take the fork left," she instructed.

He did so, swerved to avoid the biggest holes left in the dirt roads from the rainy season and the machine-gun fire that sprayed over them for a few more seconds. She knew these winding paths like the back of her hand—when she drove she could close her eyes and read the red dirt like Braille.

She'd done the same on his body, night after night in the handmade feather bed in his house in Ujiji, with the windows open and their cries mingling with the sounds of the night.

"Go off-road here." She motioned to a break in the dense foliage, one she'd pitched the ancient car through more times than she could count. "We'll lose them."

"And then you think you'll lose me too?" he asked as the vehicle jolted underneath them. He hit his head on the roof and cursed viciously as the car cut a swath through the jungle and finally found some level ground.

She steeled herself against him, the way his voice always seemed to soothe the pit of despair in her stomach . . . the way his hands would stroke her until everything felt just right. "Yes, well, to quote one of your favorite phrases, payback's a bitch, isn't it?"

"In case your memory's gone, you left me, Sarah. You left when I wouldn't train you."

"I left because you kept calling out for Fay in your sleep," she said, tightened her grip around the barrel of the 9mm until her palm ached and burned the way her insides had every time Clutch had called the other woman's name while she'd been lying naked next to him.

She noticed he gripped the wheel tighter, drove harder through the brush as if outrunning his own demons. She could've told him that wasn't possible.

"You never said anything," he said finally. "I didn't know . . . didn't know I did that."

"Now you do. Pull over here."

"Are you going to shoot me if I don't? Do you hate me that much?"

Did she? Sometimes, at night, she'd lay awake, skating on the thin line between hating Clutch and wishing she was back in his arms, before he'd refused her the one thing she'd asked of him.

"What about training me, then?" she asked, and Clutch uttered a short laugh before he realized she was serious.

Once he did, he shook his head sharply. "You wouldn't make a good merc."

"Why not?"

"Because you need the will to live. You lost that somewhere along the way. Find that and we'll talk."

"Fuck you, American boy," she spat. "I know more about the will to live than you'll ever understand."

"You're just pissed that I hit on the truth."

She jerked out of his grasp, rubbed her wrist where he'd held her. "Oh, that's rich. What? You know that poor little Sarah's family lost their land and their money and that I'll do anything to help them? You don't know shit." Her accent grew more clipped, even as she muttered words in native Shona.

"I know enough."

"Do you? Do you know what it's like to have everything taken from you—suddenly? To have the bottom drop out of your world? To lose everything you've ever known, and there's not a single thing you can do about it?"

"Yeah, I do," he said quietly. "Live or die, Sarah. Figure that out first and then the rest will be enough."

And even though she'd believed him, she'd packed her things and left him watching her from his front porch.

"Rafe trained me," she told him.

"I can see that. He also used you. But you can still help," he said, his foot firmly on the gas pedal. He was going to call her bluff.

"Help Isabelle?" she asked.

"Help yourself."

She heard something in his voice she couldn't place. Pity, maybe? Which made her angry and sick to her stomach at the same time.

"The way you helped me? Pull the fuck over, Clutch. Do it now."

He jerked the wheel hard to the left, gears grinding as he brought the car to a stop in the middle of the road.

"There you go, leading with your chin again."

"Is that another one of your cute American-boy phrases?" she asked.

"The American-boy thing gets old fast," he growled, a

low rumble in his chest as she forced a hand she wasn't sure she was prepared to play.

"Get the hell out of my car."

"What did Rafe tell you, Sarah? What could he have told you that would make it all right to turn on a woman who was your friend?" he asked tightly, still not making a move to leave.

I want everyone in that family to hurt, Sarah. I want them to hurt the way I hurt—I know you can understand that. If you could get revenge on the people who hurt your family, you'd do it. I know you would.

"He didn't tell me anything."

"I know you better than that . . . better than you know yourself." He surprised her by grabbing the door handle and kicking his way out of the car and she fought the urge to pull him back. He was giving up on her again.

She ignored the fact that she was the one about to do the running away, same as last year, as she pulled herself over the console into the driver's seat he'd abandoned.

"You still want to prove me wrong about all of this," he said as he dragged his bag out of the backseat and even though she knew it was full of weapons, he still made no move to overpower her. Not with physical force, anyway. "You have no idea what Rafe's capable of."

"Just like you, right?

"I would never do that." He hit the side of the car with his fists and she jumped involuntarily. "Did he hurt you, Sarah? Because if he did . . ."

"What would you do?" she asked with a calm she didn't feel, saw the torment in his pale eyes and wondered what kind of ghosts drove a man like him. Many times she thought about going back to him, begging for something he would never be able to give her.

What could he give her now? Redemption? Hope? Love? He wasn't equipped for any of those things. Come to think of it, neither was she.

W hat *would* he do?

Clutch was going to kill Rafe anyway—there was no way to capture and turn Rafe in to proper authorities. There were no proper authorities here, no law in this country except the one the mercs made themselves. By rights, he shouldn't even be going after Rafe. The other men would tell him it was bad karma to go after one of your own.

His cell phone, set to vibrate, continued to burn a hole in his left pocket, the way it had as he'd driven through the back countryside of Ruyigi. He ignored it, knew exactly who it was and why they were calling—he was two hours late checking in, had been saving Sarah when he should have been reporting for duty and saving his own ass.

They were all being chased by someone, and he'd always known he wasn't the only one being chased by ghosts.

"How do you know what Rafe did to Isabelle? How do you know it's true?" she finally asked him.

"How do you know it's not?" he demanded, and then he softened his tone. "Sarah, don't sell any more of your soul than you already have."

It took a few minutes, but she lowered her weapon. "I'll take you to where he stays. He was supposed to meet me at the clinic tonight. He told me he knew people would start to come after him." She spoke quietly, her voice echoing in the stillness of the car's interior and he remembered making love to her in this car, after he'd watched her sing karaoke at the Impala Hotel last year. "He said that's why he didn't send me money last week—he didn't want to put anyone on my trail."

"Then you should stay back."

"You won't be able to find his place without me," she said, and he wanted to tell her that she underestimated him, that he could track his way through this country, through any country, but he didn't.

The less she truly knew about him, the better. "I've been doing things without you for a long time."

Things the marshals who'd put him in the Witness Protection Program at the age of seven—long before he'd joined the military and Delta Force, before GOST had gotten ahold of him for further training—had told him.

Forget your real name.

No friends to the house.

Don't talk about your past.

Don't expect any long-term relationships.

With those rules in mind and a control that bordered on ruthless, Clutch had nearly thrown Sarah out the first night they'd met, before he'd succumbed to her. She'd been hot against him, her fingers nearly tearing the fabric of his shirt, his pants . . .

Sarah made him lose control, let down his guard in ways he never should have; he'd both loved and hated her for it.

But he remembered every single second they'd spent together, held them tightly, like a treasure he refused to let anyone take from him.

"I almost came back to you." Her eyes held a fresh grief that twisted his gut, and no, he couldn't do this.

"I wouldn't have taken you back."

"I don't believe you."

That made two of them. He studied her in the early morning light, gauging whether or not he could truly trust her.

Last time he'd seen her, her hair had been shorter—spiky and dyed blond with red streaks. Now it was long enough to fall over her forehead in a way that softened her features. He knew there were tattoos along her left arm—practically a sleeve of them—and a sun around her navel.

He'd spent time memorizing that sun with his fingers, his tongue...

Who was he kidding, there was no one left to trust. And still, he got back into the car with her.

Isabelle's hair was still damp when she knocked on the half-opened door and walked into Jake's space. The handcuffs she'd seen on the floor the night before were gone—a pile of papers were pushed off to the side of the coffee table and there were a few big hardback books on the couch next to him.

He'd changed from what he'd had on earlier. Now he wore an old collared shirt, buttoned only halfway up, with a big rip along the biceps, and a pair of sweats. His feet were bare, and God, he had nice-looking feet. Big, same as his hands. Capable, strong.

You're getting turned on by feet. You have problems.

"What's up?" he asked as she approached the couch. "Did you come down to learn more self-defense moves?"

"Do I need them with you?"

"Depends on who you ask." He pointed to his side. "How long does this bandage have to stay on?"

"Fourteen days, usually."

"How long has it been on now?"

"Not even twenty-four hours since I fixed it," she said, and he sighed heavily. And muttered under his breath while she stared at his profile, the strong lines of his nose and chin, the way his hair fell over his forehead.

"I'm never going to make it," he said finally. He reached under his shirt and she heard the ripping of the tape.

"You can't do that," she said, ended up half straddling him without thinking, in a futile attempt to stop him. But he let her grab his wrists and pull them away easily. Too easily. "Did you just trick me?"

"Yes," he said. "The way you wanted me to."

His eyes were heavy-lidded and she had no desire to move off his lap. In fact, she had no desire to let go of his wrists, and so she pushed them away from his body, not caring about the wound on his side or the fact that she might not be ready for this close proximity to him again— caring about nothing but leaning in to kiss him, the way he'd kissed her before.

The old Isabelle wouldn't have made time in her life for a man like Jake—she would've pushed him away. Then again, she knew a man like Jake wouldn't let himself be pushed away easily at all.

Everything she used to do was a lifetime ago; she was a

completely different person than she was before she'd met Jake, and she was never going back.

He kissed her, teased the roof of her mouth with his tongue. She gripped his wrists so hard she'd probably leave bruises, held his hands down by his thighs, even though she wanted—needed—his hands on her.

She didn't stop kissing him, not until she needed to stop for breath.

Still, when she pulled her mouth from his, she kept her forehead against his and her eyes closed. "What would you have done if your team hadn't come that night?"

"I would've run faster."

She couldn't hold back her laugh, but still, she kept her eyes closed, listened to the sound of his voice.

"I told you we'd make it out. I knew we would," he said.

"And you're always right?"

"Yes," he said. "Always."

"Is there anything you do that isn't dangerous?"

"No," he said "But you like it that way, don't you, Isabelle?"

"I love the way you say my name," she said. He jerked his head back away from hers and stared at her. She wondered how the word *love* could scare a man who—to her knowledge—wasn't scared of anyone or anything in this world.

"Say my name again," she said, let her hands stroke the soft cotton of his shirt. His breath caught as she began to undo the buttons, uncovering an expanse of smooth, hard flesh.

"Isabelle, I—"

But she kissed him before he could say anything else,

her palms sliding along his bare chest, skirting his nipples, traveling down his abs. Heat flared to her breasts, pooled between her legs.

He kissed her back, but still, he didn't touch her, as if he knew instinctively that might cause her to become skittish again. And as much as she wanted his arms around her, holding her, she was better this way. Free. In control. Her hands twisted in his hair, her body molding against his, hungry sounds drumming up from the back of her throat to escape as groans into his mouth.

She was shaking, and still she didn't want to stop. He just kissed her, until she could barely breathe, kissed her until her body was one big nerve ending begging for his attention.

The air was warm—*she* was warm—and maybe she should tell him she wanted him, all of him, right now, or climb off of him and go upstairs, locking her door behind her.

She pulled back, not to do any of that, but because she knew she wouldn't be able to go much further than just making out with him on the couch, like a teenager on a first date.

Jake rested his head against the back of the couch, stared up at her, waiting for her next move.

"I feel like such a tease ..." she said finally.

"You're not."

"I mean, that night ... it was different, with you touching me. I mean, you're not different, but I'm still ..." She faltered, not wanting to admit what was already evident.

"You, ah, haven't been able to ... I mean, since ..."

"That *goddamned rescue?*" She tried to keep her tone

light, but it was a heavy subject they'd skirted earlier while driving, and there was no getting around it now. "I haven't been able to. No, that's not entirely true. I haven't wanted to, either."

"I understand."

"I don't think you do," she said, wondered if she could tell him this. If she should. "I was kind of...waiting for you. To be first. I mean, you already were, in a way."

She waited for him to shut down, push her away. But he did none of those things.

"You were engaged," he said.

"I didn't love him," she said finally. It was a relief to say it out loud, without excuses, without the whole *I'm not the same person I was* crap. She wasn't—but she had never been the person Daniel wanted her to be either. "I couldn't... not with him. Not when I wanted you."

His expression remained neutral, but his eyes...his eyes watched her in that all-knowing way he had. "Then touch yourself for me. I want to watch you come. If I can't be the one to do it yet, let me see your face when you do it."

Her cheeks flushed hot at his words. "Jake—"

"Reach behind you, into the drawer of the table," he said. She hesitated, waited for him to say what she'd find in there.

When he didn't, she leaned back and opened the drawer. A glint of silver caught her eye immediately.

She looked between the handcuffs and his face.

"For me, not for you," he said evenly.

"You like being tied down?"

"No. I don't like it at all." His eyes remained steadily on hers. "Take them out and hand them to me."

"But you just said..."

"I know what I said."

She grabbed them and did what he asked. He put them on himself, cuffing his hands behind his lower back before he leaned back the way he'd been sitting before.

"Take off your clothes," he murmured. "I can't touch. I'll just watch."

And somehow, even though this was perhaps far more intimate than making love, it was right. She hesitated only briefly and then she unbuttoned the old flannel shirt she'd thrown on when she'd finished her bath. Her fingers trembled as she worked the buttons out of their holes. She left the shirt closed until the last possible second because she hadn't put on a bra, and when she parted the fabric Jake drew in a quick breath, let his gaze linger on her breasts.

He shifted under her, but made good on his promise and kept his hands down behind his back. He sucked his bottom lip between his teeth for a second before speaking. "Touch them," he said. "Please."

"I've never done anything like this in front of anybody."

"I've always liked being first."

She brought her hands underneath her breasts, and God, they felt so heavy, so ripe under her own touch.

She noted the strain along the fine muscles of his neck, the way his lips parted slightly while he stared at her. The way the hard bulge in his sweats seemed to pulse through the fabric, with a life of its own against her sex.

She shivered as she let her thumbs brush her nipples, and she never wanted anything so badly in her life as she wanted Jake's lips on them.

"Jake, your mouth," she murmured. She braced one

hand against the back of the couch, moved her body closer, poised her breast near his lips. He paused until she said, "It's okay. I'm sure."

She watched as his tongue swiped the top of one nipple. Her mouth dropped, and an involuntary groan escaped. His mouth was hot as he sucked her nipple, until she arched and let her hand slip into her sweats and between her legs.

She stroked herself, the way she'd been doing earlier, and this time she was going to let it happen. Here, just like this, half-clothed on Jake's lap, taking her own pleasure at his command.

"Jake," she moaned, unable to stop saying his name or rocking against her own hand. He nuzzled her breasts with his cheeks before pausing to look up at her.

"You look so beautiful," he murmured, his voice low and rough enough to spear pleasure right through her. "I want to be the one to make you feel like that, when you're ready . . . want to be the one to put my fingers on you . . . my tongue . . . everything . . ."

She closed her eyes as the first wave hit, buried her face against his hair as her entire body stretched taut and then released the pent-up tension with wave after wave of intense pleasure that rocked her from deep inside her womb.

When her sobs started, seconds later, she was as completely unprepared for them as she'd been for her orgasm.

She heard herself telling Jake she was sorry, as he was wrapping her into her discarded shirt and stroking her hair softly, murmuring that it was going to be all right, that *everything was going to be all right.*

For a few, blessed moments, it had been. But she was

crying too hard to tell him that, to convey her relief and her fear as it was all mixed together, into any kind of coherent thoughts.

She was vaguely aware of him carrying her up the stairs and putting her into the freshly made bed, but she did know she clutched at him. "Stay with me. Please."

And he did, outside the covers, stroking her hair until she fell asleep. Her final thought was on the fact that he hadn't needed her help—or a key—to get out of the hand-cuffs.

No one's ever really in control anyway . . .

When she woke the next morning, he was gone from her bed.

CHAPTER
13

With Sarah driving through what were obviously shortcuts she knew well, they got to Ruyigi just before 1600, the wall of silence between them rarely broken. She'd thrown an old Eagles tape into the ancient radio, played it over and over until every skip and crackle of the songs was firmly embedded in Clutch's mind.

She'd taken that tape from him. When she'd left, she'd taken the hope that had started to rebuild in his heart too, and that was something he couldn't let go of.

He couldn't let that matter—he was too busy thinking up plan Alpha, Bravo and beyond. If Sarah was still working for Rafe, he'd... well, he'd come up with something. He'd been mixed up with men far worse than Rafe, men who no longer killed because their lives depended on it, but because they'd begun to enjoy it.

There had been ten taken by GOST from different branches of the military, all of whom were originally under Witness Protection. GOST threatened to expose their identities—and the identities of their loved ones—to the people who'd wanted them dead, leaving the military men and women in the worst possible position.

They'd all accepted the offer, including Clutch. It meant moving to Africa, having their Witness Protection identities officially erased from the system, both military and otherwise.

After two months, the group had been down to eight. One had gone on the run—and gotten caught. Another had killed herself rather than live the way she'd been forced to live.

Clutch's cell phone continued to buzz—every time it did, he rubbed the tattoo on his inner thigh through his cargo pants as though trying to ease the burn.

The Ako Ben tattoo etched on his inner thigh marked him, but only to the people who ran GOST, who knew to check that spot.

Countless times, he'd thought about taking a knife to the tender skin, cutting away the war horn symbol even though he knew it wouldn't do any good—the black ink ran too deep to ever be fully erased.

He pulled his hand away impatiently and tried to forget he'd put Sarah's life in danger in more ways than one—danger far greater than a man like Rafe ever could.

She'd stopped the car.

"We should walk from here," she said. "It's about a

quarter of a mile—he'll hear this hunk of metal coming, if he hasn't already." She was out of the car, around to his side and handing him his weapons as he was still pushing his door open all the way.

Clutch, in turn, stared up at the sky—dusk was coming, but not fast enough for his tastes. Still, waiting until nightfall might be too late, so his choice was made.

He slung his bag over his shoulder and followed her lead through the thick underbrush. Her steps were quick and quiet and sure, her weapon remained drawn—and all of it nearly broke his heart, just when he'd figured it had finally healed.

He should've known better. And when she stopped and pointed, he laid a hand on her shoulder out of habit, out of need. She didn't shrug it off.

"It's on the left," she whispered. "Just past this next clearing."

He dropped his bag behind some bushes and prepared to move ahead toward the freestanding hut in the middle of nowhere. There was no cover around it at all—he'd have to make a run in there.

"You should stay back, let me go in first. He'll bolt if he sees you—he's expecting me," Sarah urged.

He used the hand that was still on her shoulder to give her a light tug. "Stay back here. Stay covered. If anything happens, go back to the car and take off."

"I wouldn't leave you behind."

He didn't bother to remind her that she'd been all too prepared to do so a few hours earlier and instead began to move forward.

She didn't listen, followed at his heels, her own gun

drawn, her body bowed with tension. He humped a fast pace toward the porch, his gut still clenched despite the fact they remained unscathed.

There was a smear of red on the porch railing. Fresh blood. He pointed her outward once they'd made it onto the porch. A lookout.

She nodded, and he went inside.

The air was heavy—thick with the metallic smell of blood and hate and fear, although the only signs that there had been a struggle were the two dead men on the floor. American. They'd had their necks snapped. No sign of Rafe, and the place was sparsely enough furnished for Clutch to know that Rafe was prepared to go on a moment's notice.

Still, this meant the blood could be Rafe's.

He moved toward the opened back door and scanned the wires that ran along the inside of it—trip wires, set up to kill whoever came in through the door.

Sarah was behind him and he put a hand out to hold her back. "It's a trap."

She drew in a sharp breath and when he turned, he saw she'd paled.

Shots rang out over their heads—Clutch pulled Sarah to the ground and together they moved on their elbows across the floor, to clear the open doorway. The windows were long gone and they took shelter in the farthest spot from the shots, weapons drawn.

"Is that him?"

"Could be. These bodies are still warm." He waved the bandanna he'd had stuffed in his pocket and when no shots followed, peered out the window. "If it's him, he's going for the car."

She shot out of the door and back up the path before he could stop her, and he cursed and followed, passing her quickly enough.

His bag was still where he'd left it, which meant Rafe was in too much of a hurry to look around. It meant the man did have some fear. Someone else had put a bounty on Rafe's head, and he was on full alert.

The car was, however, gone, tire marks dug into the soft earth where he'd peeled away in a hurry. Clutch stood in the tamped-down clearing and stared up at the now darkening sky as Sarah ran up behind him.

"Who were those men?" she asked once she'd caught her breath.

"No ID. Looks like former FBI or CIA."

"We've got to go after him. He's headed out of the country—he'd planned to go to the States for a job. We'll grab a car from a neighbor—the closest one is two miles down the hill." She looked at him expectantly, and he prepared to crush her.

"There is no *we*."

"You need me . . ."

"I don't need you. *You* need to stay away from *me*. This is what my kind do—we kill and we hurt innocent people. We take away people's fathers and brothers and husbands," he told her, as though his past was on display, an array of all the people he'd made disappear over the years for no better reason than he was told to do so. It made him no better, in so many ways, than the man he currently tracked.

He turned on her, shook her hard by her shoulders

while she tried to jerk out of his grasp. "This is what you'll become if you stay with Rafe . . . if you had stayed with me. That's why I let you go. You might already be too far gone after what you did to a woman who still thinks you're her friend."

She fell apart in front of him, sank to her knees on the dirt, curled in the fetal position and began to rock back and forth.

He told himself to leave her there, to find a car or a plane, to step over her prone form and go on with his life.

Jake had stayed next to Isabelle for as long as he could, until he thought he'd lose his mind, if he hadn't already. At one point, her head had rested in the crook of his neck, her hair tumbled over her shoulders. Even his own bed wasn't helping—it still smelled like her, like woman and sex and Isabelle's shampoo.

She'd sighed softly in her sleep, murmured his name once and snuggled closer.

Snuggled. And worse, he'd liked it. Still, it was never a good sign when a woman cried after sex—and Christ, it hadn't even been sex.

He needed to get the hell back to work, and fast. Real work. Exploding bridges and jeeps, and flying helos with the Navy fighter pilot who was training Jake to fly the fast birds, the way he'd trained Nick.

He headed for the weight bench and geared up for a light workout. As he started lifting, he noted the bruising on his wrists where the cuffs had been. He'd had both his weight and Isabelle's pressing against them, and at the time, he hadn't cared.

One more rep and he'd be out of his body, flying. Racing up a beach or getting pulled out of the rough ocean to a waiting helo.

He wanted that, needed that. Christ, this wasn't going to work for much longer.

He hadn't told Isabelle everything—but the problem was that she wanted so frigging much. She'd never be satisfied with anything less.

He could keep her distracted for a while. But not forever.

Forever had never been his to give. Not with the job he held now or any job he'd have in the future. Danger was born and bred into him—nature, not nurture—and shit, whoever his real father was, he must've been one hell of an adrenaline junkie.

He hadn't lied to Isabelle last night when she'd asked about his real father—he'd never tried to find him. Jake figured that the odds weren't great that they'd have a warm, fuzzy reunion.

Twenty-four hours. That's all the time he'd ever allowed himself to think ahead. Twenty-four hours could get you through anything. That's all he was going to worry about now.

Nick's ulcer was acting up again, evidenced by the blood he'd just spit into the sink.

Shit.

"Oh, shit, I'm sorry," said Dr. Markham—*Dr. Mark-*

ham?—wearing just shorts and a T-shirt, started to back out of the bathroom and then stopped. "I'm apologizing for being in my own bathroom."

Nick turned, wiping his mouth with the back of his hand. "Your bathroom?" he mumbled, making a mental note to kill Jake.

But she'd already moved forward, stared between the blood and Nick.

"Does it hurt here?" she asked, placing a hand on his chest with a doctor's touch. Nick had to will himself not to jump—his nerve endings were fucked, and even the slightest touch provoked a fight-or-flight response in him if he wasn't prepared.

"What the fuck?" Jake stood in the doorway, still sweating from a recent workout. "Why are you naked?" he asked, like it was a big revelation.

"I'm *always* naked," Nick reminded him. "Besides, someone took all my clean towels."

"Stop, Jake," the doctor said, and *shit,* Jake actually obeyed. "Does it hurt here?"

"Look, Dr. Markham, I know it's an ulcer. A small one. It heals and then it comes back."

"Stress."

He shrugged. Jake sighed loudly. "He's had it from the time he was nine. Because he refuses to take his medicine."

"Are we really going to compare refusals of medical treatment?" Nick asked.

"What are you even doing up here?" Jake asked.

"I come up here sometimes," Nick muttered. "Do you have a problem with that?"

Isabelle could've sworn she saw a flush on Nick's cheeks

and she felt Jake back off his brother instantly. "You can call me Isabelle," she said to the naked man in her bathroom. She figured now might not be the best time to mention the pilfered sheets and towels.

"I'm Nick," he said.

"I remember you."

His voice was rough, as though he'd had some kind of vocal cord damage, and her eyes shifted immediately to his throat. Sure enough, the raised white scar, the hallmark of a tracheotomy, was at the base of his throat, just below his Adam's apple. It would be a hard scar to remove completely, due to the delicate skin around the neck and throat.

Nick was big, powerful-looking and classically handsome—he looked like he should be modeling Armani, not throwing up blood in her sink with a dangerous-looking knife strapped to his biceps despite the fact that he was otherwise completely nude. As if he was expecting trouble at any moment. But his green eyes held an almost reverence in them as he looked at her, and she wondered just what, if anything, Jake had shared with him.

She thought back to the scene at the bar and remembered that Nick had seemed to be good at finding trouble.

"Whose room was this?" she asked.

"Our mom's," a voice rang out from behind them. "It was her office. The place where she used to write songs. Where she used to come to get away from all the testosterone."

"Which never worked," Nick said.

The tall man with two different-colored eyes stared at her, and she knew that he'd also been there that day she'd been spirited out of Africa. Had seen her vulnerable. Hurt.

She straightened her shoulders and his gaze softened slightly.

"It's all right. Mom would've liked you. I'm Chris," he offered.

Chris was good-looking too—but in a much different way than either Jake or Nick. For one thing, the man's eyes made it impossible *not* to stare at him. His jaw was strong, his mouth wide and he towered over the other two, no mean feat in itself. He had to be over six-foot-five.

"Your eyes—that's very rare," she said, because she couldn't stop staring at them.

He nodded, as though used to both the statement and the stares. "Yes."

"Most people born with different-colored eyes have a pigment mixture in at least one eye." She moved closer to him so she could get an even better look. He obliged by ducking down.

No pigmentation in either eye, one a perfectly clear crystal blue and the other a bright green. "It's really amazing," she said.

"I tend to amaze people all the time," he said, a small smile tugging the corner of his wide mouth. His drawl wasn't pronounced, but it was the type that would come out heavier when he was tired, or having sex.

That thought made her turn toward Jake, who stood, arms crossed, a small frown on his face. "That's enough," he said, pulled Chris back. "What are *you* doing up here?"

"Looking for you. Your phone's going crazy." Chris handed Jake his cell, which Jake tucked into his pocket without even looking at it.

"Thanks. Look, Isabelle needed a place to stay," Jake

said, and she noticed that he didn't ask permission or offer any apology for renting the room without asking them first.

"If it's a problem, I'm sure I can find another place," she said quickly. "This is just temporary."

"It's not a big deal," Chris said easily. "Why don't we all leave and let Isabelle get dressed in peace?"

The three men walked out of her bathroom, and she heard their conversation as they went down the stairs.

"And you're not going to walk around naked?" Jake was asking Nick.

"Look, I'll try, but I can't make any promises. Sometimes, it just happens," Nick said. "What the fuck happened to your wrists anyway?"

She gave a small laugh and shut the bathroom door.

T̲he urgent string of text messages was from Clutch.

Jake didn't think Chris had checked them, but the message didn't give much away, not if you weren't suspicious to begin with.

It did, however, make Jake sick to his stomach when he'd cut into his room to shower and let Chris and Nick head downstairs. They'd give him enough shit about this, but he wasn't prepared to deal with it until he'd called Clutch and heard about Rafe's escape.

We'll try to catch him at the airport.

If Rafe was headed to the airport, he was headed to the States, and that was not good.

You're going to have to tell them. And he would tell Chris and Nick—right after he spoke with Cal. He owed his mentor that much.

"Does Cal know she's moved in here—with you?" Chris asked when Jake walked into the kitchen, still half in a daze.

"She's moved in here with *us*. And yeah, Cal knows." Jake drank the last of the orange juice directly from the bottle and forced himself to act as normal as possible. Because when you lived with two human radars like his brothers, you pretty much couldn't get away with having any secrets.

"I like her," Chris stated emphatically, then glanced at Jake. "Not like that."

"Good," Jake muttered.

"Good because you like her?"

"Because she's Cal's goddaughter."

"Yeah, all right. We'll go with that explanation for now," Chris drawled. Jake looked for something to throw at Chris's head while the man continued, "Still doesn't really explain why she's here, though."

"She needed a place to stay."

"You don't usually move in women you like after one date."

"We didn't have a date."

"I can't think of a woman he's liked enough to spend more than a few hours with in recent months. Years, even," Nick said. He'd come into the kitchen and poured and drank a glass of milk with his ulcer medication as Jake and Chris stared. "What?"

"You're drinking milk instead of coffee," Chris said.

"You're actually taking your ulcer medication," Jake said.

"Yeah, your girlfriend's bossy," Nick mumbled.

"She's not— Forget it." Jake knew it was stupid to argue and give them any more fodder, a fact he remembered applied both in real life and in military situations, and one that got blown away when he was around his brothers.

"The admiral gave us the whole *Be nice to Isabelle* speech yesterday," Nick said. "I guess that's the one he gave to you too."

Jake nodded.

"I don't think he meant you had to move her in," Nick continued.

Jake played with the empty orange juice bottle.

"Are we going to talk about this?" Nick asked.

"No," Jake said, and usually, that would end it. A *maybe* was code for, *I'll let you pull it out of me,* but a *no* meant Nick would shut his mouth until—if ever—Jake decided to talk.

But yeah, what the fuck was he doing? This bodyguard-hero-all-encompassing-savior bullshit was grating on every last nerve he had. A lot of people saw him like that, sure. He didn't want Isabelle to.

He'd voiced his concerns to Cal again last night about how his brothers were going to get suspicious quickly, which was why the admiral had casually mentioned to Chris and Nick that they'd be doing him a big favor if they'd keep an eye out for Isabelle.

Jake had been voicing his concerns to *himself* ever since he'd encouraged her to take off her clothes.

Out of control.

Time to bob and weave. "You in today?" he asked Nick, the more likely of the two to let things go.

"Yeah. I've got that ongoing language clinic," he said, motioned to Jake's side. "Did they mention when they'd clear you?"

"Couple of weeks, maybe."

"I wonder if Isabelle's going to be the new doctor for the teams too," Chris mused. "I'll have to ask her when she gets back."

"Where is she?"

"She came downstairs in running clothes and went out the door. So I'd assume . . . running?"

"And you let her go?" Jake demanded before he could stop himself.

Chris raised his eyebrows. "I didn't realize she was under house arrest."

"She's not," Jake said. And *fuck,* this was a total mess, made that much worse when he found himself surrounded by a wall of brothers.

Isabelle hadn't gone running, and he'd fallen for Chris's trick. Much too easily.

Nick didn't waste any time. "What the fuck have you gotten yourself into?"

"You mean, what the fuck has he gotten *us* into," Chris said.

" 'She just doesn't have any other place to stay,' " Nick repeated Jake's words back to him. "Which we knew was complete bullshit, but if you couldn't come up with a better lie than that, we figured you'd let us in on it eventually."

"Cal asked me to watch out for her, same as he asked you guys," Jake said through clenched teeth. "I told you that. Where is this coming from?"

"You've been trying that glare with me since we were eight—it didn't work then and it sure as hell isn't working now."

"She's in trouble," Jake said finally, because he was surprised he'd been able to keep it from his brothers for this long. "Cal asked me to throw some protection her way. That guy—that Rafe guy—he's . . . Cal's looking for him. He's worried that Rafe's coming back for Isabelle."

Chris got up and propped the kitchen door open so they'd immediately see if Isabelle was headed down the stairs.

"Last time I looked, you weren't a bodyguard. You were a fucking full-time active duty Navy SEAL," Nick said with a growl. "What the hell aren't you telling us?"

Chris continued to stare at Jake. "She doesn't know."

"What doesn't she know?" Nick demanded.

"She doesn't know any of it. She thinks Rafe's been caught," Jake admitted.

"How could Isabelle not know she's being protected? Do you know how fucked-up that is?" Nick asked.

Jake pushed past Nick and pulled out a chair. He sat, propped his elbows on the table and lowered his head into his hands. "I know."

The tone of the room immediately softened. He heard the quiet scrape of chairs pull next to him. For a few minutes, Nick and Chris just let him be.

"You've got no distance," Chris said quietly, when Jake lifted his head. "Cal never should've asked you to do this."

"I'm too far in to stop," Jake admitted. "Clutch said the guy's whereabouts couldn't be confirmed, but rumor has it he's headed here."

"You know as well as anyone that the guy could be on U.S. soil within twenty-four hours. We need a plan." Nick ran a frustrated hand through his hair.

"I can't keep her on lockdown."

"You could if you told her."

"I can't do that to Cal," Jake said. "Or to her. Christ, don't you understand, she's barely holding herself together as it is. If she knew, fuck..."

Chris put a hand on his shoulder. "If she's barely holding it together under false pretenses, what's she going to do when she finds out the truth?"

"What good will telling her do?" Jake demanded. "From where I'm standing, she's got nothing to gain from knowing it."

"It's not what she has to gain, it's what you've got to lose," Chris said.

"Did you plan this one at all?" Nick asked, his voice quiet.

"Yeah, I did. But I don't have a lot of options if I can't tell her anything," he answered, his jaw and fists clenched. "Even if I could tell her, I figured I'm safer keeping her here, where I've got backup."

"What are you going to do when she realizes she can't make a move without you there? Are you going to follow her when she goes shopping? To the drugstore?"

"Yes," Jake said simply. "I don't have much of a choice. Cal said it shouldn't take that long. I've got no reason not to trust him. He doesn't want her in danger any more than I do."

"This isn't the time to argue. What's done is done. We'll help," Chris assured him, and Nick nodded in agreement. "But Rafe left her alive for a reason, Jake."

He was going to be sick. Maybe he did have a fever or an infection—or maybe, maybe, he was too far in to see any way out.

Right now, he didn't want a way out. He looked over at Nick. "Clutch said you did some work for him recently."

Chris swore under his breath.

"This isn't about me," Nick said.

"Not yet," Chris shot back.

"It wasn't a big job—I worked pretty closely with Clutch when I was there," Nick explained. "Since I'm still somewhat traceable through the military system, Clutch couldn't chance giving me a bigger job."

"What kind of job did you do for him, exactly?" Jake asked.

"Like I said, this isn't about me now. This is about you taking on something you can't handle on your own."

Jake lunged for his brother, but Chris stepped between them.

"Did you run across this Rafe guy?" Jake demanded.

"No."

"Don't fucking lie to me—not now."

"I never saw him, but I heard plenty about him." Nick kept his voice low, as if he didn't actually want to repeat what he'd heard. "The Africans called him *kivuli*—shadow. They believe in that superstitious bullshit. But if you talked with Clutch, you know all of this already."

"Enough," Chris was still holding Jake by the shoulder. "Jake, you're going to have to back away as much as you can. Let Nick and me deal with her. You work on the periphery."

"I can't do that . . . she'll suspect something."

"Like she doesn't now?" Nick challenged.

"She's jammed up at work—they've got her on fourteen-hour shifts. By the time she suspects anything . . ."

"She doesn't think it's weird that you asked her to move in here after you've known her for, like, a day?"

"He's known her longer than that," Chris drawled quietly.

Nick swore under his breath and stared at the ceiling. "This woman's got you all jammed up, man."

"Yeah, she does," Jake admitted, staring Nick down as if daring his brother to say anything. Chris got things like this, while Nick acted as if getting close to a woman—any woman—was the most inconceivable thing he'd ever heard.

"I'll call in some favors and see what kind of records I can pull," Nick offered finally, but he didn't look, or sound, happy.

"I tried that," Jake said. "They're locked down tight."

"Neither of us has much leave," Chris said, kept a hand on Jake's shoulder to calm him. "We'll do the best we can to keep an eye on her, but we need to figure out our next move."

"What, then—are you going to sleep in her room with her to make sure she's not taken?" Nick asked.

"No, that's not going to work," Jake muttered. "But windows and perimeters are alarmed. And even if she opens them, the screens are wired."

"If this guy wants in, he's coming in."

"This isn't the same as Africa. She didn't have us there."

"If we knew how he took her out of the clinic, it would help," Chris said. "Did she say anything about that?"

"No. What's to know? He dragged her out of there. Had to be in the middle of the night, since it would've been too noticeable during the day."

"Sometimes daylight makes more sense."

"She's in danger when she's on the base too. It's not like

it's hard to get on there, especially if you're in uniform. Especially if Rafe was originally stationed around here. Do we know that?" Nick asked.

Jake shook his head. "I couldn't even get that far."

"Are you up to all of this? You're still recovering," Nick said.

"I'm up to it."

"So you're just pretending to be into her to keep her close?" Nick asked.

He wished he could say yes, but there was no point in lying about anything now. None at all. "No. Not really."

"Fuck," Nick muttered. "Are you sleeping with her?"

"Nick..." Chris sent a warning with his eyes and then turned his attention to Jake. "Then you'll at least keep your distance from her for now. You like her, but this isn't the time for that. Get your head on straight. Think about protecting her, not—"

"Don't say it," Jake said, his tone low and dangerous, even to his own ears. Chris gave a small smile, as if his thoughts had been completely confirmed, and Nick drained the last of his milk before he spoke.

"Go talk to Cal, Jake. We need everyone in this loop."

CHAPTER
14

Isabelle had been quiet that morning when Jake drove her to the clinic, wrapped in her own thoughts, barely saying good-bye to him as she got out of the car. Once again, he'd hung around the clinic without being noticed, watched her take her near daily run down the beach. She'd made it farther this time before she'd been forced to stop.

He'd almost gone over when she'd bent forward, holding her side.

The pace he'd kept to stay far enough behind her wasn't enough to get his heart rate going. Between not being able to work out as hard as he wanted and having no barriers, except mental ones, between himself and Isabelle, Jake was about ready to blow. Hard.

Doing so to the admiral wouldn't be the smartest move, but waiting for the past hour in Cal's office for him to return from a meeting had done little to improve his patience.

Every time he closed his eyes in an attempt to rest, he heard Isabelle crying. Saw Clutch's text message. Eyes opened, he saw all too clearly what was coming down the pike.

The other alternative was the paperwork Saint shoved at him when he'd seen Jake that morning. He paged through the reports, only to realize that even paperwork reminded him of Isabelle now.

He'd had to put down his feelings for the world—or at least the DoD—to see when he wrote the report about the trip out of Djibouti. Not that they would see, but *Christ,* every time he looked at that particular file—before he'd been ordered to destroy it—he was sure they could.

0200
Hostage found. Medical performed.
0230
Held hostage's hand.
0300
Lost my fucking mind and kissed the hostage. Repeatedly.

He threw the folder down on the empty chair next to him and stood to stretch. His side ached less today—the stitches looked good, and despite Isabelle's insistence he hadn't put the heavy bandage on again. The rough scrape of the stitches against his T-shirt was a good reminder of the healing.

He turned the picture Cal kept facing himself on his desk. Jake had actually seen it before, hundreds of times, probably, but it was the first time he looked at it knowing the full story behind the smiling trio of men in their jungle greens.

Callahan. Markham. March. He'd never looked at their names on the small patch on the uniforms. They were standing by the old O-course on the north side of the base, the one closed for repairs. Permanently.

"He's already inside your office, Admiral."

Jake put the picture back where he'd found it as the door opened behind him and finally the admiral strode inside.

"Hansen."

"Sir." Jake nodded, waited until Cal sat and then did so as well.

"I was going to ask you to come in and see me today—you saved me the trouble," Cal started. He clasped his hands together on the desk—never a good sign—and leaned forward on his elbows. "Are you involved with Isabelle?"

"I don't know how to answer that, Admiral. I don't know what we're doing. I'm watching out for her, like you'd asked."

"I don't want you pushing her. She's healing."

"I know that, sir."

"You're going to confuse her. She doesn't know what she wants. Her mother's hoping she goes back with her ex-fiancé when this is all over."

Jake's gut tugged in a way he did not like. It was time to end this part of the conversation. "Rafe was last seen in Burundi."

From the way Cal's neck snapped to attention, Jake

knew the intel wasn't off. "How did you come upon that in-formation?"

"I have sources."

"I told you that you weren't to involve yourself in this aspect of Isabelle's situation."

"I know what you told me. I also know my limits. Having inferior information pushes my limits to their breaking point."

"You are defying my direct order. I had my own men on it."

Jake ran his hands through his hair and prayed for the answer he wanted. "What did your men find?"

Cal paused, a pained expression on his face. When he spoke, his voice was colder than Jake ever remembered hearing. "I haven't heard from either of them in two days."

"My source said he found two men at Rafe's last known address. No ID. Necks broken."

"Did he find Rafe?' Cal demanded, stood, knocking over the coffee mug and spilling the liquid all over his desk.

Jake closed his eyes briefly. "He almost had him."

Cal turned to face the small window on the far side of his office.

"Who were those men, Admiral?"

"Former CIA. I hired them to hunt Rafe—they could get in places other men couldn't," Cal said.

"Who was tailing her when she started working again in Washington?" Jake demanded.

"There wasn't a need at that time."

"Why not? You knew Rafe was still loose then."

Cal closed his eyes for a second. "Because Isabelle's

mother was paying him to stay away. Just like he'd demanded. He refused the last payment—said he'd much rather have Isabelle instead."

"Dammit, Admiral—you're taking her life in your hands and you're tying mine behind my back," Jake said in a voice he had to fight hard to control, because he really wanted to yell as loudly as he could and possibly take the man in front of him down hard.

"You remember who you're talking to," Cal told him.

Jake took a deep breath and forced himself to calm down. He turned away from Cal, faced the wall and envisioned how good it would feel to punch his fist through it. But he didn't. Instead, he did that fucking count-to-ten thing, and knew it wasn't going to do shit. "Paying him in the first place was not a good idea."

"He was threatening to go to the press . . . I couldn't let that happen. Not to the senator and not to Isabelle."

"How did the FBI feel about that?" Jake faltered for a second at the expression on Cal's normally unreadable face. "You never had them in on this, did you?"

"The longer the FBI was in the loop, the more of a chance this story had of leaking to the press. The senator and I decided it would be best to call them off when they'd completed their initial investigation."

"Best for whom? Isabelle's life is at stake—I'd think you'd let everyone who could help get Rafe off the market do so. Do you know this guy's rep? Do you know they call him the shadow, that they say he's impossible to track and capture? That he's broken into the goddamned Pentagon for fucking fun?"

Rafe, who could be everywhere, and nowhere, all at the same time.

He waited for Cal to tell him to get the hell out of his office, out of Isabelle's life, but he didn't. Cal stared at him, and for the first time Jake noted how tired the admiral looked. Worn down, almost. *Shit.*

"I'm on this, Admiral. I'm going to do everything I can to get information on this guy, everything I can to keep Isabelle safe."

There was no breeze, and still Sarah wasn't sure if it was minutes or hours that she'd been collapsed to her knees as if in silent prayer. She remained unmoving, until strong arms wrapped themselves around her and hauled her to her feet. Only then did she let herself open her eyes to look up at Clutch.

She'd lost everything—her cameras, the film, next month's board and food . . . and there was nothing to send home to her family. But somehow, by the grace of God, she hadn't lost this man.

So no, she hadn't lost everything—not even her soul, no matter how many times she'd tried to give that away.

"I've got a car," was all he said. "Are you coming?"

Yes, she would go with him. "Clutch, I . . ."

"I've got your things from the clinic," he said quietly, his arms tightening around her waist. "Your cameras. Clothes. You weren't back in your room when the rebels started their burn and slash today, so I took them out for you."

He wouldn't have left her there for the rebels. Looking back, she wasn't sure if she could say the same thing about herself had the roles been reversed. "You're still watching out for me."

"I couldn't stop. I tried—you have no idea how hard I tried..." His voice hitched and he closed his eyes for a second.

She traced his left eyebrow, the way she used to do, the eyebrow with the small white scar that was nearly invisible against the white-blond hairs, and then she cupped her other hand around the back of his neck, the short hairs tickling her palm as she pulled his face down toward hers. His mouth took hers, hungrily, a kiss without the promise of a future, and still, she wouldn't let go.

When he pulled his mouth away from hers, he continued to hold her close, but his words sent a chill through her. "Sarah, who are you sending money to?"

"My family. So they can buy back their farm."

"No, you're not."

"They were left with nothing."

"No, you were left with nothing," he said. "Your family's gone, Sarah. They didn't survive when their farm was taken over. You were the only one who did—and only because you ran."

"Stop it, Clutch. Just stop it. You don't know what you're talking about." She struggled against him, but this time he was not letting go.

"I checked...I wanted to help. They're dead."

"No!"

"They died the day the land was taken from them. I understand the lies you've been telling yourself, I understand that's the way you've been surviving. But they're gone. Let them go."

Let them go...

"I tried... tried to pull my mother and sister away, but they wouldn't listen to me. They thought they could explain..." She faltered, her voice cracking, and the earth seemed to sway beneath her feet.

"You knew better."

"The crowds were beyond talk."

"It's not your fault that you ran, that you survived." His voice was fierce, and if she could only believe what he said. If she could only believe.

"What have you been doing with the money?" he asked again.

The money—all that money. "I put it into a joint bank account—one my parents could have accessed. I kept hoping that, someday, it would be enough."

He pulled back from her, forced her to look into his eyes—and she saw nothing there but compassion. Understanding. Not a trace of pity or anger. Maybe she even saw love there too.

"It's someday, Sarah. And it's enough. It's always been enough."

Sarah stood in Clutch's arms long enough for the sun to move overhead and throw new shadows on them, letting the strength of his body ease her confusion.

Five years and her secret had finally been revealed. The crushing weight of responsibility lightened, actually made her dizzy as it rose off her shoulders.

"Why did you check on them?" she asked, lifted her head from his chest to look into his eyes.

"I thought, if they were taken care of, you'd give up on your idea of becoming what I am."

"You must think I'm crazy."

"No. Not any more than I am," he said, then pulled her closer, murmured against her cheek, "Sarah, please, you're going to be okay. You have to be."

"Why is it so important to you?"

He brought his mouth down on hers gently, just long enough for the heat to flare in her belly. "You're important to me. From the first time I saw you, I knew you were."

"I was breaking into your house," she reminded him as she reached up to run her fingers through his short hair. "I wanted a shot of the famous American merc."

No pictures . . . ever, he'd told her that night. For a man who didn't bother to blend in, it had seemed a strange statement.

"Funny, that's not how I remember it. One minute, we were fighting . . . the next, we were naked."

"You didn't even take your pants off."

"That's because you were so impatient. *Let's see what the big-time American soldier boy can do.*" He smiled, something she hadn't seen him do in the past twenty-four hours. "Did I meet your expectations?"

She thought about the way he'd cradled her that night, taken her slow and hot against the wall in a way that had shattered her expectations of men—American men . . . any men.

Clutch had ruined her for anyone else. She dared to wonder if she'd done the same for him in the months they'd been separated.

From the way he was looking at her, she had her answer.

"It's going to be all right now, Sarah."

So much truth, admitting her wrongs about so many things. "What I've done..."

"What we've both done. What's been done to us," he said, and she wanted to know what had happened in his past to lead him down this path, something he'd never spoken of during the year they'd been together. She'd searched his house, had attempted to search his soul for clues, but came up empty, except for the woman he cried out for in his sleep.

But he was distracting her the way he'd always done, with soft words and warm hands. Her pulse beat everywhere— her breasts, fingertips, the wet flesh between her legs that had yearned for him every single night she lay alone in her bed and sometimes during the day when someone would say a word a certain way or a man would strut just a little and she would think, *Clutch does that so much better than you...*

He was going to lay her on the soft ground by the car in minutes, and even though her head was swimming, she still had the presence of mind to ask him, "Who's Fay?"

He started, tried to pull away from her. She didn't let him. "Just tell me. Was she your wife?"

"She almost was," he said. "She was killed the night we'd planned to elope."

He wasn't going to tell her anything more now. And when he laid her on the soft ground, murmuring, *I can't wait,* she'd known her memory about how good they were together wasn't faulty.

He'd already reached inside his bag for a condom.

"Hurry, Clutch."

He did, ripped the packet and rolled the rubber on, was inside her within seconds of getting on top of her.

She groaned, grabbed his shoulders at the intrusion—so tight.

He paused, looked at her with a question in his eyes.

"There's been ño one since you," she said shyly, right before his heavy body took hers, primal and fierce and swift, just the way she needed it.

CHAPTER
15

Jake didn't come in until sometime after two in the morning—*oh-whatever-hundred*—and slammed through the kitchen door as if it were two in the afternoon. He wore jeans, a black leather jacket, a black T-shirt underneath, complete with a pair of heavy, black biker boots—he took Isabelle's breath away, nearly made her forget the anger that had grown, irrationally, as the hours passed.

Nearly, but not all the way.

She'd worked a fourteen-hour shift, was already on edge because the phone kept ringing with no one on the other end, and she'd found Chris waiting for her outside the clinic around ten P.M.

"I've got to get a car soon," she'd told the man wearing a Grateful Dead T-shirt with his green camouflage BDUs.

Chris had given her his wide smile. "It's not a problem. Jake's out for a while. He asked me to give you a lift home."

On a Saturday night. At least Jake had been nice enough to arrange a ride for her before going out to get laid.

He'd driven her to work this morning, both of them avoiding any discussion of what happened the night before. At the time, she'd convinced herself that was the way she wanted things, but when he hadn't stopped by the clinic at all, she'd regretted that decision.

Maybe he's just giving you space.

Or maybe he was just busy finding a woman who could give him what he needed. All of what he needed.

According to the younger nurses she'd worked with today, they were expecting to see Jake and his brothers out tonight at the bar called *The Den.*

Still, she wasn't a teenager—far from it—and she shouldn't be behaving this way. She'd fought the urge to ask Chris why he wasn't out tonight as well.

Jake stopped short when he saw her. "You really don't sleep."

"Neither do you." Isabelle tossed the book she'd been attempting to read onto the kitchen table. It had been foolish for her to wait up for him. The only purpose it served was to make her miserable, make her think about the way Jake hadn't been there in the morning when she'd awakened.

Granted, she'd been the one to have a meltdown last night, but he seemed like he'd be able to deal with worse than that.

Still, Jake owed her nothing, not even everything he'd already done.

"What's wrong?" he asked. He'd gone straight for the fridge, downed half a container of juice straight from the bottle before capping it and putting it back.

She fought the urge to lecture him on the spread of bacteria, pushed away from the table instead and prepared to go to her room. "Nothing."

He shook his head as he moved in tandem with her, ended up blocking her path to the swinging door separating the kitchen from the living room area. "I know when a woman's pissed at me."

She pushed past him, muttered, "I'll just bet you do."

She didn't expect the grab, didn't understand how his method of restraining her was so firm and still so gentle. His gaze locked on hers, his body so close.

"I wasn't with another woman."

"What makes you think I care?"

"I know you care. Smell me if you don't believe me," he said. "Women can always smell another woman's perfume, and all that other shit they wear, from nine miles off."

"You probably showered."

"But I didn't."

She leaned into his neck and inhaled, her eyes closed. Her hands fisted his T-shirt, his breath warm against her ear, and no, he hadn't been with another woman tonight. He'd definitely been out at a bar, based on the combination of smoke and mint and if she tipped her head up and brushed her lips to his she might taste whiskey or beer behind the mint.

"Satisfied?" he asked.

"It doesn't matter to me," she lied.

"Sure it does. You don't want there to be someone else."

"I didn't say that."

"You're smelling me like a jealous wife."

"I'm doing what you asked. Now I'm going to bed."

"Going to dream about me?" he asked.

"No."

"Liar."

"Maybe I am, but what does that change?"

That stopped him short for a second. "Nothing. It changes nothing."

"We haven't talked about last night and you've been avoiding me."

"I had things to do."

"Fine. But I didn't think you were into playing games."

"Games? You think this is a game to me?" he asked, his voice a notch below a growl. "You're using me to feel better, to heal. How do I know you're not using me for everything else?"

"You were the one who used the term *game*."

"Don't you get it? In my line of work, my life depends on the rules of the game—it's not a joke to me."

"I'm not...using you." She bit her bottom lip. "I do feel better being with you—I've already told you that. But that's not the reason I want to be around you."

He shook his head. "Yeah, well, I'm not so sure. My self-preservation instincts are kicking in pretty hard."

"Screw you, Jake," she told him, because she didn't know what else to say. Because it felt good to lash out, even if it was misdirected. Because he'd already told her that she never needed to apologize to him for anything.

"That's it, keep trying to push me away. It just proves my point. What happens when you decide you want to be alone again? You told me yourself that you like it that way. Prefer it, even."

"Stop it."

"You're spinning," he said quietly, but she caught the power behind his words. "You don't know what end is up and you're grasping at anything—anyone—to make you feel better. To make you *you* again. But you're not that same person anymore. You never will be. And that's what you're going to have to deal with."

"I'm tired of letting him derail me."

"He's not the one doing that. Not anymore."

"I want you, Jake. If last night didn't show you that...I wanted you. I wanted you in my bed. I want you to let me in."

"I've done that—as much as I can."

"And what, now we've hit the wall and that's as close as we'll get? Are things getting too rough for you?"

"No, things are getting too rough for you," he told her.

"It's not easy—you know that."

"I also know that you don't want easy, or you sure as hell wouldn't have tried to make a go of something with me. But I'm not going to be the one who pushes you. Not like that. I've probably pushed it too far already and I'm not letting myself out on the brink of control again. You can't put me in that position."

"You're the only one who can handle it," she said, feeling the tears rise, sharp and biting. God, he was going to walk away from her if she didn't stop him. "Push me, Jake. Go ahead, I can take it. Give me your best shot."

He stared at her for a few long moments, his eyes steely in the soft light. When he spoke again, his voice was rough. "I saw, Isabelle. The night of the rescue, I saw what he'd done to you."

And she knew exactly what he was talking about, saw the pain in his eyes from that night in Africa that reflected hers. Finding her naked, bound, wounded on the dirt floor. Seeing how Rafe had hurt her, the way he'd forced himself inside of her, over and over, until she'd cried, bled. Jake had seen the way Rafe had taken sex and twisted it into something dark and ugly that made her doubt a man's touch.

Jake saw past what she'd told him to the truth she'd been denying from herself.

For a second she thought about walking away from him, from all of this. But her feet remained rooted to the floor, because she'd asked for this. And it was hurting him as much as it tore at her.

"You saw nothing," she whispered finally, a last defense. "You're a liar."

"I saw everything. I rescued you. I put you into my jacket. I wrapped my T-shirt around you. I saw the blood."

Her breath caught, rasped between her teeth, and he grabbed her arm to keep her from leaving. From denying.

"You've got to start admitting it."

"Why are you doing this to me? Are you trying to break me?"

"No, you won't break. You'll bend, but you won't break. Because until you admit it, it'll never really go away," he said. "You might've taken control, but that man took something from you he shouldn't have. And that's not your fault—whether or not you gave in is irrelevant. Come to terms with it now, Isabelle, before it's too late."

His voice was ragged when he finished, his breathing fast, his hands fisted at his sides. She held her hands up as if in silent surrender and let him go, away from her and back to his room.

When she passed his floor ten minutes later, his door was closed.

She went to her own room, her thoughts swirling, threatening to quickly overwhelm her, and it was only when she crawled under the covers that she allowed herself to think on that time.

The MSF group had been fractured by the time she'd gotten there. Normally, the dynamic was much better—closer—but there had been a major dissension among the ranks, thanks to a broken love affair that had splintered the group, caused the divide right down the middle.

It was a larger group this time around—a clinic, erected two years earlier. She'd been used to working with a small, more intimate grouping, but this clinic boasted an MSF staff of over fifty people. Including Rafe.

A typical day at the clinic began with Irma greeting Isabelle at the main sickroom door. Rafe would be outside already, fixing a car or a machine or transmitting messages over the ancient radio in a hunt for more supplies. He was an expert at that, always getting the clinic exactly what they needed.

Some of the Africans had taken to calling him the miracle worker.

She'd had a feeling that while the actual MSF employees

didn't know who Rafe was, many of the Africans working at the clinic did.

Some of them would whisper *kivuli* when he'd walk out of a room.

"What does that mean?" she'd asked Sarah, who'd told her that they called him a shadow.

But Isabelle could attest to the fact that he was real, flesh and blood, and he haunted her now worse than any spirit ever could.

Those first eight weeks, Rafe had been good to her. She'd been lonely. Once in a very long time, instead of embracing her normal solitude, she'd sought refuge from it. Still confused about her engagement, which was bearing down on her like a lead weight, and caught between the disapproval of her fiancé and her mother at her career choices, she'd been drowning.

Rafe seemed to appreciate the work she'd been doing. He was strong and capable—she'd felt safe with him. That was his job, to protect her.

She'd only been in Djibouti for a week the first time something happened.

The heat had been unbearable, even as the sun went down, and she'd poured water over her head while she was fully clothed. She'd been wearing a thin white T-shirt, and the water had soaked her to the skin, so her bra was visible, transparent, through her shirt. She knew she'd dry fully within ten minutes, and she'd stepped out the back of her tent to try to catch some kind of a breeze.

She'd run smack into Rafe. He stood just a few feet away from her, staring at her—at her face, her breasts. For a minute, she'd considered turning and going back into her tent, but she hadn't. And when he'd walked toward her with that hungry look in his eyes, she'd stripped her shirt off completely and invited him inside her tent.

After that night, he'd moved from sleeping outside her tent to inside of it. On her cot, although he slept less than she did, always seemed to be on guard. He told her about his days in the military, the deeds he'd done in the name of the government.

Sometimes she'd catch him looking at her, surprise and anger on his normally unreadable face.

"I'm a dangerous man doing dangerous jobs in a dangerous place," he'd tell her. "But right now, you pose the biggest threat to me."

He'd taken her hand and held it over his heart.

He was getting too serious and she'd already been struggling with betraying Daniel. More than anything, her affair with Rafe had forced her hand—she planned to tell Daniel things were over between them as soon as she hit Washington.

Rafe hadn't been happy when she'd broken things off. *You don't understand . . . you changed me for the better and I don't want to go back to being who I was. You're my savior.*

She'd been so uncomfortable at the thought of being someone's personal savior on any level that she began to avoid him completely.

Three weeks later, after many attempts to get her into bed again, he'd taken her away from the camps. He'd admitted that he'd fallen in love with her during one of the long hours that stretched into the three days she remained hidden with him until he hurt her. Until the rescue.

Until Jake.

She shook her head as if that would clear the memories, the guilt of her betrayal of Daniel, what she'd actually consented to with Rafe, from her mind.

Being with Jake would be consensual—that was one thing she fully understood. The rest of what had happened with Rafe had become one big jumble in her mind, because admitting she'd lost her power in that situation was too much to bear.

The sob caught in her throat before she could swallow it, echoing in the silent room. She turned and buried her face in the pillow, as if that would block any further thoughts from her mind.

The yells echoed through the house. They were deep, primal. From the soul.

And they weren't stopping.

At first, Isabelle thought she was caught between dreams, where she'd thought she'd woken up but really she was still asleep.

But no, she *was* awake, fully eyes-wide-open, and the yells turned to loud whimpers that wrenched through her.

Within seconds, she was down the stairs; she'd left her door open and so had Jake, and yes, that's where the chaos was coming from.

She entered his room hesitantly. The sounds had softened, but he was still whimpering a little. She knew better than to try to wake someone from a nightmare. No, better to let them shift slowly into consciousness and then deal with the fallout.

Her eyes adjusted to the dark while she stayed close to

the door. She heard the shift of covers and saw Jake sit up. Wrapped in the sheet, he curled in a tight ball, his face pressed to his knees. The only sound in the room was his breathing—fast. Hitched.

In the deepest throes of the nightmare, he'd been yelling *No* and *Stop* repeatedly.

All she wanted to do was walk to the bed and comfort him. Self-preservation told her that was the worst thing she could possibly do, nightmare or not.

Jake knew he was partway out of the nightmare, in that space where he wasn't sure he wanted to wake and deal with it.

Especially because he wasn't alone, and *fuck,* it wasn't Nick or Chris in here with him. No, he'd left his door open purposely, but he'd made sure hers was closed and Chris was on watch downstairs.

Her door was heavy, soundproofed—she never would have heard him. Unless she opened her own door in order to feel safer. She must've run right down to his rooms before Chris could get up to him.

Fuck.

"I'm all right," he said finally.

"I'm sorry—I didn't think you knew I'd come in," she said quickly. "Can I help?"

"No. Go back to bed."

"Maybe you're sick."

"I'm not."

"You could have an infection. Sometimes those bring

on night sweats and pain and nightmares. Even hallucinations."

She hadn't turned on the light, which was good. The darkness between them was one of the only shields he had left. That and the sheet he'd yanked around him, still damp from his sweat, and he was never, ever sleeping again unless Nick was sitting in the same room.

He could count on Nick. Nick never slept. Nick woke him up before the nightmare started, never cared that Jake sometimes punched or kicked him.

But Isabelle—she'd watched the whole thing.

She'd come farther into the room, moved around to the front of the bed, but left a wide berth between herself and the mattress. "Let me check your stitches. You wouldn't let me yesterday."

"I saw the doctor yesterday. I'm fine," he ground out.

"Oh. Well, sometimes these things can happen quickly."

"Not now, Isabelle."

"I'm sorry. I know you're angry with me. But I heard you and I was worried."

He didn't want her to be nice to him, didn't want to have to be nice to her. He wanted to tell her to get the hell out of his room, his life, his memory.

At the same time, he wanted her to run her hand across his forehead to check for fever, to press her lips to his, to cover his body until they were both slick with sweat.

Letting her in would mean letting her in all the way. No holds barred. Revealing everything.

She already knows a big part of it.

"I was a prick to you tonight. That's not your problem, it's mine," he said.

"You were honest. And I asked for that." She sounded strong, sure—in control. "Was it . . . was the nightmare because of me?"

He wanted to say yes, because in a way it was. Triggered by her, but not about her. "Not really. No."

"I never had them. The doctor they had me see said that nightmares were common. And I waited. Wanted them, actually."

"Why?"

"Then I wouldn't have to deal with it during the day." She paused. "When you're captured and rescued, can you talk about it with anyone?"

"With your team. But you don't, because you don't want to add any more guilt or fear to the situation."

"What about a therapist?"

"We're required to see one to be cleared for active duty."

"You don't say much to the therapist, I'll bet."

"I didn't realize we were talking about me." He shot the words at her.

"Mine wanted me to talk about it. Every detail. She said that would give me power over it."

"You kept your power, Isabelle. Don't let anyone tell you otherwise."

"Did I?" She gave a choked laugh. "I was so scared. I didn't know what to do . . . and I knew what he was going to do. I saw it in his eyes." She swallowed hard. "I tried to convince him not to hurt me. He laughed, asked if I thought I could convince him that I wanted him. He'd already ripped off my clothes, and I put my arms around him and kissed him and I let him have me on the dirt floor and pretended he wasn't hurting me. I made myself believe that. All to save my life. And in the end, he tied me up and kicked me until I nearly passed out."

"And you stayed alive," he whispered fiercely in the darkness. "What you did probably saved you from much worse. You have to believe that."

"Do you believe it?" she asked.

He raised his head so his chin jutted stubbornly in the air the same way hers had so many times over the past days. "Not when it first happened. Not for a long time after either."

"What changed?"

"When I first enlisted, my nightmares were so bad I was afraid to sleep at all inside the barracks. I'd drag my blankets out to the beach and sleep there and sneak back in before reveille. My old CO finally figured out what I was doing—I mean, he knew my background. He told me that what I'd done was nothing more than the rules of engagement, and he said it over and over to me every time he found me outside. He didn't stop until he was sure that I believed it."

"Do you believe it now?"

No. Not all the time. But admitting that wasn't going to help her. "Yes. It doesn't always stop the nightmares, though. But you can't go forward unless you acknowledge the past."

"How do you do that—talk about it openly?"

Openly? He was hiding under a fucking sheet. "You've got this picture of me in your mind, like I'm some kind of fucking hero, some kind of saint. And you're one hundred percent wrong about that. You don't know me at all."

"I feel like I do. And I certainly don't see you as a saint. Not even close." Her voice softened. "There's still so much more I want to know, like where you went after I changed planes to come home."

"You went straight home even though you should've been cleared at the closest U.S. base to Africa. Your mom has a lot of pull," he said finally.

"And you didn't come straight home?"

Oh, they'd come straight home, all right, yanked into a debriefing with Washington types before he'd had a chance to wipe the greasepaint off his face or change out of the dusty clothes that smelled like smoke and blood, and they'd forced him to relive every single minute of what had happened.

Relive it, but not tell everything. And then, last month his team had gotten the order to shut their mouths and shred any reference of the rescue in their paperwork for the mission. As if that night with Isabelle had never existed.

As if it was that simple to forget.

"Sometimes, I could swear I remember things from that night . . . things that I can't tell if they happened or not," she said, and his gut clenched. "I mean, I remember hiding. Seeing you above me holding your weapon and you were so still and sometimes I can convince myself that happened in the car after the team found us initially. Other times, I know we were outside and that we weren't alone."

He'd really hoped he'd never have to tell her about the rest of that night, when the team had gotten a mile away before being warned by Max of the soldiers' approach. The new group of rebel soldiers were backup, headed to meet the soldiers the SEAL team had just left behind.

Too many to take on and still complete their mission of getting Isabelle out of the country alive. Rules of the game—no unnecessary risks.

Do not engage. I repeat, do not engage. Max's voice echoed in his ear.

They'd been forced to ditch the ancient Land Rover after cutting out part of the backseat to use as a board to carry Isabelle. They'd strapped her down and he and Nick stayed in between Saint and Chris and Mark for cover. The night had grown stickier, and Isabelle's breathing wasn't easy.

"We had to take a different route out of Djibouti, because you were with us," he said finally.

"Why? What did that matter?"

"You weren't in any shape to take a nice, long swim in the Indian Ocean," he said. Getting to a different LZ was supposed to take an extra two hours. They'd gotten behind, and dawn wouldn't be their friend unless they were already on a helo headed out.

"You passed out. We had to ditch the car—the LZ was miles away. Rebels were coming fast from that direction."

If he closed his eyes, he could still see the scene clearly, could smell the lingering smoke in the air, on his clothes—Isabelle on the ground in between him and Nick, huddled in the rough shadows of the brush, waiting in total silence, weapons readied as the soldiers passed, and all of them praying she wouldn't wake up or moan in her sleep and draw attention to their position.

"You carried me again," she said slowly, as if it was all coming back to her as she sat there in his bedroom, in the dark.

He had—over six miles of rough terrain, nonstop, with his men flanking him, praying that with every step he wasn't doing irreversible damage to her. "The LZ was taking fire," he said. "We had to backtrack."

Caught literally between two opposing rebel forces, the helo had made a death-wish landing, barely touching the ground to allow the five SEALs and Isabelle on before the iron bird took off again.

She'd mercifully remained unconscious through the entire ordeal. "We took off under pretty heavy fire. By the time the sun came up, we were on safe passage."

"I remember waking up when we were in the air. Chris was checking me."

He remembered that too. He'd been hovering until Chris told him to sit the fuck down and give her some air.

"Where did you go after that?" she asked.

He leaned his head back against the pillows, feeling strangely exposed even though his body was still covered. "I came back here. Back to training," he said.

"I was in the hospital for a month."

"I know. I came to see you." There was no reason not to tell her. Not anymore.

"I never . . . saw you there." Her voice was quiet with a slight catch, as if she was trying not to cry.

"But I was," he said. "As often as I could be. Sometimes it was every night."

When she spoke again, it was apparent she hadn't been able to hold back the tears. "Doctors make the worst patients."

"Worse than me?"

"I'd say we're a tie."

"No way. I never tie—I win."

She laughed even as she cried, threw back her head to expose a beautiful column of neck, and he shifted under the sheet. He wanted to invite her inside, under the covers. But he had as much to lose by doing that as she did.

"Go back to bed now, Isabelle."

"Only if you're sure you're all right," she said.

When he didn't answer, she padded softly to the door. He ignored his own disappointment that she'd followed his order so readily, and left well enough alone.

The truck Clutch had borrowed from a farmer a few miles east bounced over the ruts in the road. If the shocks weren't completely shot, they would be soon and Sarah put her hand up on the ceiling of the car so she wouldn't bounce completely up from her seat.

They hadn't had the luxury of lingering together long— she and Clutch had quickly dressed and gotten into the truck and moving toward their ultimate target.

So much to think about, to sort through further, but now wasn't the time.

"Let's concentrate on getting to Rafe—we'll deal with the rest after that," he told her.

"He knew . . . Rafe knew I'd come through the back door of his house," she said quietly, as if saying it out loud would make it more real. "I always came through the back door—up the back path."

"I know."

"He's been to the States," she continued. "He went there about a month after Isabelle's rescue. He said he had to take care of a few things. He went back a few weeks ago too."

"Text that information to the first number on the screen," he instructed her. "Then call the airport."

The betrayal—any betrayal—hung heavily in her heart, even though Rafe had twisted her trust in a far more destructive way than she ever could have imagined. She picked out the letters carefully, stared at them before hitting SEND.

"That's information for the man who's helping Isabelle."

Izzy.

"I stole money from Izzy," Sarah told him. It was within the first hours of meeting the doctor and Sarah found herself sneaking into Izzy's tent that night while Izzy slept, to put it back. She'd closed the door and had only gotten a few steps away when Izzy's voice rose up in the darkness behind her.

"What did you need it for?" Izzy had asked.

"My family."

Isabelle had handed her back the bills. "I understand family."

And from that, the two women, both of whom were used to being alone, both uncomfortable with sitting down and talking, sharing the way women usually did, formed a bond.

Their friendship was different, words often unspoken, as they weren't necessary. At night, they'd sit around the fire and drink bottles of warm Tusker lager—both women dusty, Izzy often still in surgical scrubs.

It had been nice.

"She sounds like a good woman," Clutch said.

"Isabelle seemed so happy," she said finally. "Like if she didn't have to go back to her old life...I mean, she's the daughter of a rich woman, had this whole high-powered life back in the States, but she didn't want any of it at all. I didn't understand that."

"Some people are happy living here," he said.

"Are you one of them?"

"Most of the time, I'm just happy to be living."

She wasn't sure why his words shook her to her core.

She made the call while he maneuvered the stolen truck through the back roads. "Bujumbura Airport's closed. Rafe doesn't have his own plane—he never learned how to fly."

"He knows how to fly."

There was so much she didn't know about either man. "We'd better get there soon—the city still has a curfew," she said, peered up at the night sky.

"We'll be there in ten minutes, so we've already broken curfew."

"Your phone's ringing again. Are you sure you don't have to get it?"

She held it out to him—he glanced at the number on the ID and took the silver phone from her, flipped it open and held it to his ear without saying a word.

"Catch me if you can," was all he said seconds later. He clicked the phone closed with a smile, but the satisfaction of his expression was short-lived, as gunshots shattered the glass of the back window.

The truck swerved as he pushed her head down.

"What the hell's going on, Clutch?"

"Help me lose them."

She'd never, ever heard any trace of panic in his voice, until now. "Take the next hard left and the first quick right—don't miss it."

She held her breath, waited as Clutch did exactly what she'd told him and they heard the other car breeze past them on the other road. "Keep going—floor it—we'll take the longer way to the airport."

His hands gripped the wheel and sweat formed on his brow. She held her gun and looked back even though the jungle closed off behind them, the most effective camouflage for their car there was.

"Who are those men? Who's tracking you?" she asked.

"No one you want to know about. You're going to have to trust me on that one."

*W*ho are those men?

Would Sarah believe him if he told her that he'd been chased by ghosts for years? Probably. She was probably one of the few who would get it.

"I do trust you, Clutch," she said, turned back from watching their six. They'd lost the men, for now. "I know there's more to the story than you've let on. I see how you've lived—like an island. Like me."

Would she understand what growing up in Witness Protection had been like? "I can't do this now, Sarah."

"There might not be time left."

He took a deep breath and he started to tell her everything, as quickly as he could, as though ripping off a Band-Aid.

"When I was seven, my mother turned state's evidence against her husband, my father," he started.

Clutch's dad was a major player in the world of organized crime. After the trial, Clutch and his mom moved around constantly, from the time he was seven until he was fourteen.

"The marshals separated us then. I was getting into trouble in the public school system. They were worried I'd blow my cover. So they sent me to military school." There, he had the normalcy, the discipline he'd craved. He'd been accepted, made friends using the carefully crafted background the federal marshals had given him.

He'd been too young, too full of himself to understand that the rest of his life would always be a carefully crafted lie. And when the marshals put the gun in his hands at age fourteen and taught him to shoot, he'd been sure he'd never feel at risk again. By fifteen, he'd felt naked if he didn't have a weapon strapped to his ankle. He'd graduated from the military academy at eighteen, having specialized in foreign languages and history and had gotten permission to join the military, and for ten blissful years, he'd trained, made rank, hadn't had to worry about anything but his own ass and those of his teammates.

"I would've stayed in forever," he told her. She reached out and squeezed his arm.

"The men who are after you, have they been sent by your father?" she asked.

He shook his head hard. "No, not my father. Not the marshals. Witness Protection sold me out, into a group they'd created—they took highly trained men and women and made them mercs."

He turned quickly to see her face—she was shaking her head and he knew, just knew she'd heard the rumors. You didn't grow up in this country and not hear about a group of government-funded war dogs who'd gone over the edge, so far that even the government couldn't call them back.

"You're part of that group," she whispered. *"Masuka."* *Ghosts.*

He nodded, waited for her to pull away from him or demand to get out of the car, but she didn't do either of those things. Instead, she put a cool hand on the back of his neck and stopped asking him any more questions.

He'd lost his freedom and he'd lost Fay, the woman he'd planned a life with and the only person who knew who Clutch really was. Until now.

Bobby Juniper, we want you back.

It was with a sinking feeling of despair that he realized they might actually get their way.

CHAPTER
16

I sabelle didn't remember the hallway outside of Jake's room being so small. She'd edged toward the window because it was closer than the stairs, and as she stood in the near darkness, the shadows thrown by the trees outside made the hallway a dense jungle, a minefield of endless, hazy memories.

Still, she listened to the shower running, thought about stripping off her T-shirt and joining him, but remained in place as the rain thumped against the wide window behind her.

He'd risked his life more than once for her. He'd been at the hospital. He hadn't left her when things got tough.

And when he walked out of his bedroom, it might've

been ten minutes or two hours later, she was still standing in the hallway, unable to turn back toward his room or go up to her own.

He made the decision for her, covered the small distance between them in seconds with a look of steely determination in his eyes.

Their bodies were inches apart, but he didn't touch her, merely stood and watched and waited, until she reached out and ran her fingers through his shower-dampened hair. At first, he nuzzled his head down against her neck, rubbed his cheek against hers, like a lion attempting to woo his mate. Sweet, strong and dangerous, all at the same time.

"You're supposed to be in bed," he murmured.

"Not yet." She tugged his hair, pulled his face up and let her forehead touch his, the way it had last night . . . the way it had that night in Africa. And then she shifted, put her mouth to his and allowed the heat between them take its course for as long as she could handle it.

She pushed him against the wall while her mouth took his, let her hold his wrists for a few seconds, until he broke free from her grip and put his arms around her.

For a second, a brief second, panic rose inside her throat, tightened her chest until Jake's rough murmur of "It's me, Isabelle. Just me." brushed her ear. And yes, that contact was right. Necessary. She brought her arms up, around his shoulders, stood on tiptoes so she could kiss him harder, deeper.

He kissed her back like he never wanted to stop.

She could take it no further than this—didn't think she could anyway, until his hand slid under her T-shirt. She'd run down the stairs in no more than that and her underwear and now the cool air wafted along the backs of her bare thighs.

His fingers traced slow, lazy patterns along her side, the one that had been injured, as his mouth devoured hers. And slowly, so slowly, he shifted, danced his feet with hers until she was the one with her back pressed against the wall, with barely an inch between them.

"Safe," he murmured, kissed her cheek, her neck. "So safe. Promise."

She was trembling, almost uncontrollably, but she wasn't ready to back down. Jake kept one hand light but steady against her side, the other moving around toward her hip, and he kissed her again, over and over, his tongue teasing hers, soft and sweet and hard and fast, kissed her until her nerves abated and all that was left between them was the scent of arousal and need.

Soon, it was going to be too late to pull back, and he must have sensed her brief moment of hesitation because he stopped kissing her. She caught his wrist before his hands moved off her body completely.

"Go ahead," she murmured, put her hand over his and ran it up along her bare belly.

Her skin burned, his hand a wash of cool relief as his palm traveled upward under her guidance. She nearly forgot to breathe as his fingers brushed the outer curve of her breast, and then she urged him further until his hand covered her breast completely. And when she lightened her grip, encouraged his fingers to play nimbly with her already taut nipple, he tugged lightly until she let out a small moan and opened her eyes.

She hadn't realized they'd been closed, found Jake watching her, lust and concern in equal heart-stopping parts. She caressed his hand as he rolled her nipple and brushed his thumb over the sensitive peak. The sensations burst through her, made her bolder, and suddenly the hallway seemed to break open wider, the big window giving view to the heavy downpour.

Different. So different.

His other hand remained on her hip until she reached for it, and in similar fashion trailed it down her belly. He stopped briefly before he reached the juncture of her thighs but she tugged. And he let his hand move between her legs to rub the silk square of fabric and his breath hitched, like hers.

"Fuck, Isabelle." Under heavy lids, Jake's eyes were a darkened storm cloud color, ready to break along with the weather . . . along with her.

With her hand covering his, he stroked her through the silk, finding a mutual rhythm.

She found the strength to pull her hand away from his, leaving him in control. "Don't stop, Jake," she murmured.

One finger slipped inside the fabric, touched her as a long, low *Oh* escaped her lips. His eyes never left hers.

"More?"

"Yes. More."

Rain pummeled the roof, slammed the windows as if it wanted in, the house shuddering in conjunction with her body. She was as wild and out of control as the storm and she bit his shoulder through his shirt as she came, harder and faster than she'd ever remembered an orgasm taking her.

He didn't stop, even as her knees buckled and her body

sagged, his fingers kept a gentle pressure then built again and she responded in kind by coming again, contracting around his fingers.

She wasn't sure how long she stood there, his body bearing nearly all her weight. When she lifted her head from where she'd buried it against his shoulder, there were a few tears tracking her cheeks again, but he seemed to know they were from relief, not fear. And as his hands cupped her buttocks, hers pushed against his chest to separate their bodies a bit. Her hands played with the string ties on the front of his shorts, unknotting them carefully, assessing her readiness.

She released the strings, her hand playing instead over the impossibly hard bulge. He groaned, let her do so for a few minutes before he spoke.

"You're not ready. It's okay."

Again, she closed her eyes, let her hands drop to her sides.

"I'm bringing you up to bed. You need to rest," he murmured.

"No."

"No? You want to sleep standing in the hallway?"

She shook her head and took hold of a strong forearm and led him back inside his own bedroom. "This way, you can run away from me in the middle of the night and I'll still be close to you."

She'd wanted the same thing the night of the rescue, had cried in protest when Jake had moved away after he'd carried her to the car and gently placed her in the backseat. She remembered stretching out to hold him as the car bumped, feeling his eyes on her in the darkness.

Now he laid her on the bed, and just like the first night

she'd spent here, she first inhaled his scent on the sheets and then tugged at him to move closer. As she stroked his back, her fingers noted raised scar tissue through the thin cotton of his T-shirt in several places. He watched her carefully as she did so, let her hands trail lower and didn't jerk away. He just held a steady gaze until she wished she could bear his full weight on hers without panicking.

Soon, it would happen. Her body knew it—her mind was bucking at the thought.

Isabelle rolled so she was on top of him, his hard length pressing between her thighs, against her still-throbbing sex. Her hands were under his shirt, running up his sides, mindful of the stitches.

"Jake, I want this off." She tugged at his shirt.

"I want *this* off," he echoed as he did the same with hers. Within seconds she skimmed hers over her head and he did the same. She lay back on top of him, skin on skin, her cheek to his chest.

"This is nice," she whispered as his hands stroked her back lightly, then began to knead some of the still unreleased tension out of her shoulders. "Can we sleep just like this?"

"You can sleep here, but you've got to cut me a break," he said, shifted underneath her. "I'll never make it, sleeping like this."

She lifted her head to look at him.

"It's just that . . . I mean, I can wait, but I haven't . . . since Africa."

She finally understood what he was saying. "Oh." She actually smiled as she rolled off him. Curled on her side, she pulled him closer, and that he could handle without needing a freezing cold shower. Yet.

One arm remained under her head. With the other, she ran a finger along his healing scar, along the stiff black stitches she'd used.

"Did you have a tough day at work ... or were you just pissed at me?" he asked finally.

"A little of both," she admitted. "I'm still getting these weird phone calls. Not even hang-ups, really—it's like the person keeps calling to hear my voice. It creeps me out."

"How long has this been happening?"

"Ever since I started." She shrugged. "I try not to dwell on it ... I don't need to be any more freaked out than I already am."

He made a mental note to check incoming numbers for her line, forced himself not to jump up and do it now. He'd promised himself one more night with her like this—just a few more hours before he spilled everything. They both deserved that.

"I also cleared a sailor today for BUD/S. He'd been pulled at the end of Hell Week for a medical leave—stress fractures in his shin."

"He'll roll back in with a different class—and he won't have to repeat Hell Week."

"Well, that's good, at least, right?"

"It just gets harder from there."

"You might not want to admit that you find anything hard to the young men who seem to think you guys are made of steel," she teased.

Jake snorted. "Half those stories are made up to get the guys through all of it. It's not that big a deal."

"Is anything a big deal to you?"

"Yeah, there is something that's a pretty big deal to me." He played with her hair—it had fallen across his bare chest like a fan, tickling him.

BUD/S was something he didn't revisit willingly, although truth be told he didn't remember a whole hell of a lot of it.

When the JAG lawyers who'd questioned him told him that he'd been tied up for over twenty-four hours, he'd argued with them about the timing. He'd also refused to say anything against Master Chief Johnson, known none-too-affectionately by his men as Chief Blood. The man was old school, long since retired from combat having been deemed too tough for this new man's Navy—mostly the chief was doing what was best for the men. The part of him that had wanted to break Jake went way back to Jake's early days of Hell Week, when Blood had argued with Captain Lopez about his place in the class.

Isabelle's gaze held his. "Would you tell me about it . . . if I asked?"

"Are you asking?"

She nodded, but there was hesitance there. Better BUD/S than about his stepfather, he guessed, although it was all going to come out eventually.

In a couple of hours, it would be the anniversary of the day it happened, the night he'd killed Steve in self-defense, and he'd been shoving that into the back of his mind. Some years, it could send him into a mild tailspin . . . others, when he was away on a mission, it was barely a blip on his radar. But here, with Isabelle, it threatened to hit him harder than ever. And that was something he couldn't afford to let happen.

He shifted against her, unable to hide how much she turned him on, and Christ, he'd wanted to take her against the wall earlier, drive into her until she completely lost control. But talking about SERE would be a definite buzzkill.

"SERE stands for Survival, Evasion, Resistance and Escape. It's meant to show you what can happen if you're captured. What it really does is instill into you the importance of never being captured." He checked her expression. "You sure you want to hear about this?"

"Don't stop now," she said, and he resisted the urge to call her stubborn.

"Doesn't matter how physically tough you are. A lot of guys ring out that first day without even realizing they're doing it. They break. It's easy enough to see how it happens. You're hurt, you're tired and you're scared shitless. But if you can stay in the game mentally, you'll make it through."

He'd never been big on authority figures. Chief Blood knew that and rode Jake hard. But no matter what Blood did to him, no matter how much he pushed, Jake didn't break. He was so accustomed to punishment that the torture didn't faze him. But Blood had wanted Jake to show something, some emotion, wasn't going to be happy unless he saw a tear in the fabric. And Jake just couldn't give him the satisfaction. It wasn't in him to break down—he wasn't doing it to drive Blood nuts, but the chief didn't see it like that.

Jake took a deep breath as Isabelle looked at him with rapt attention. "My team was captured after twelve hours. We'd managed to E&E—evade and escape—for a damned long time on that island. Nearly impossible to do. But it's all a big trap, and after a while it's better to just get it over with."

Usually it was the team leader who got the worst of it. But the instructors decided to use him to break apart the team. He was really well liked, well respected by his BUD/S mates, especially after the rumors about how old he really was began to surface.

"The instructors are torturing our team, trying to get us to spill our intel. And nobody's giving in. So the instructors tried the box first."

"The box?" Isabelle asked.

"It's sensory dep stuff. Usually it's built mostly underground, pretty tight space. You crush up into it and they leave you there for extended periods of time," he explained.

"For how long?"

"After a while it doesn't matter."

She nodded, chewed her bottom lip, because she got that.

"After twenty-four hours it was obvious that they weren't getting anywhere. We'd started singing to keep ourselves sane."

The singing had driven the instructors crazy, but had distracted his team from the physical pain. It also covered up the screams coming from the interrogation huts.

"After the box didn't work, they tried a little drowning torture." Then they'd beat him for a while in front of the other men. Jake told the other team members he'd personally take them down himself if they let themselves get suckered. And when the instructors realized that nothing was going to work, Chief Blood decided to show his sadistic side.

"Master Chief decided that humiliation was the best tack to take with me," he said finally. "They stripped me, strapped me facedown to a table and they threatened to rape me for the next twelve hours. And that was in front of two entire platoons, SEALs and instructors."

Isabelle sucked in a hard breath—Jake heard it clearly and realized his fists were clenched into tight balls and that he hadn't taken a full breath in a while.

"What . . . I mean, what did you do?" Isabelle asked softly.

"I did nothing." The boy-toy routine had been done before. It always worked. Always. A two-hundred-pound man could be reduced to tears by that threat alone. "I think if I'd broken, they would have let me go sooner. But I didn't." He hadn't screamed, yelled or cursed, had just disappeared into himself. And he'd stayed like that the entire time.

At first, Jake thought the JAG lawyers who'd come down to talk to him after the incident had their facts wrong. He would've remembered twelve hours of that crap . . . would've remembered every detail in living color. But even now, it was like it happened to someone else. The rescue with Isabelle might've been the first time he'd actually felt something on a mission—either in training or real life.

He still hadn't figured out if that was good or bad.

"When they saw they were getting nowhere, they had no choice but to pass both platoons. And they let the men out before they let me up, just one final dig." His swim buddy, Trey, got to him first, untied him, helped him stand.

When Chief Blood had approached, Jake had snapped to attention.

"Had enough, Hansen?" Chief Blood was shorter than Jake, twice as broad and his fists were meat hooks that had pounded into him mercilessly over seventy-two long hours before Jake had gone into his semi-fugue state.

After a long minute, Jake saluted. "I'll take whatever you've got, Master Chief, sir. Thank you for making me a stronger SEAL, sir."

"It's brutal," Isabelle sputtered. "It's inhumane. How could they?"

Jake ran a hand across her lower back reassuringly, letting her know that he was all right—whatever the hell that meant. "What doesn't kill you makes you stronger. If they didn't do that, we'd never become the men they need us to be."

"No one should ever be held against their will," she said.

"Yeah, well, I signed up for that. You didn't." God, he was such a fucking hypocrite. That was going to end now, the way it should have before things had gotten out of control in the hallway.

"Did you tell me that story to let me know that I might never break through to you?" she asked finally.

He stared into her serious eyes, green flecked with gold and brown, eyes that watched him with nearly the same expression they had that first night in Africa. "I told you so you'd know that you already have."

He watched her eyes mist and wondered if there was some other way around telling her, some other plan he could come up with beyond *Let's run away somewhere together and never look back,* and yeah, that wasn't going to go over well.

No, he couldn't lie to someone he was in lo—*Fuck.* He sat up quickly, pulled his knees into his chest.

"Jake, what's wrong?"

"There's something else I've got to tell you," he heard himself say.

She watched him carefully—she thought he was going to tell her about Steve now, about that night, and if that was all it took to make things right, he would. But there was so much more that needed to happen first, and she was already here—in his bed, in his life and more than partway into his heart.

Dammit.

"I'm listening." She'd propped her chin in her hands, elbows in the mattress, legs crossed behind her and in the air and he almost told her about Steve instead.

Almost.

Minutes after she'd left his room, he'd taken Clutch's call. And then he'd gone to find her—to tell her that Rafe had been on U.S. soil two times during the past two months, that he was headed to the airport . . . that he could be headed anywhere right now but most likely in her direction. But when he'd seen her, half-panicked in the small hallway, he knew it wasn't the time.

It was time now.

"They never caught the guy who hurt you, Isabelle." He couldn't bring himself to say Rafe's name out loud.

She stared at him in disbelief. "That's not true. Uncle Cal, my mother . . . they swore that the FBI caught Rafe."

"They told you what they thought you needed to hear

at the time." He could barely get the words out. "I couldn't keep it from you anymore. I couldn't do this without you knowing the truth. About everything. About what I'm supposed to be doing for you."

That made her mouth drop. She stood hastily, backed away from the bed. "What exactly are you supposed to be doing for me?"

"I'm supposed to be making sure you're safe."

"Safe? *Safe?* I don't know if it's possible for me to ever feel safe again."

"I know." He watched her carefully—her breathing was rapid, her eyes were slightly unfocused and she was either going to have a panic attack or she was going to lash out.

"You know? What the hell do you know? What it's like to have lived a lie for the past two months?" She put her hands to her throat briefly, then crossed her arms over her bare breasts. "I feel like such a fool."

"Isabelle, your mom, the admiral—they wanted you to feel safe."

"And you went along with it? You let them trick me?" She choked back a sob. "This—this whole *I know you don't want to be alone, let me heal you* has all been one big ruse... to what? To protect me without me realizing it?"

"No, it's not like that."

"Then tell me what it's like! Because nothing that happened between us over the past few days has been real. I'm a job." She grabbed the night table for support.

He moved to help her, but she yelled, *"No,"* held up a hand to block him from touching her.

"It was all a lie, wasn't it? Starting with the rescue. Then and now, you were just doing your job."

"No. It was more than that. It *is* more than that."

"I can't believe anything you tell me right now. I've got to get out of here—I need to see my uncle."

"We can call him, but you can't leave."

"There is no *we,* Jake. And I can do whatever I damn well please."

He took a step forward to stop her, but she shrank away from his touch and something inside him nearly curled up and fucking died. He took a step back and she ran downstairs. He was down the stairs in seconds, stopping her by the door, not letting himself care that she'd resisted his touch.

It took nearly everything he had in him to not let her go as she struggled in his grasp.

"Isabelle, listen to me."

"Let me go! I want to get out of here!" she was yelling, hitting him with her fists.

"You can't go. Not now. *Especially not now.*"

"You knew," she said. "You knew and you let me ... Oh, God."

He felt the fight drain out of her suddenly and he let go of her.

She covered her mouth with her hands, then dropped them at her sides. "I was never safe." She spoke softly, to herself, and as the realization hit, she stumbled back a bit.

"You were always safe with me," he told her fiercely, his voice barely above a raw whisper. "You still are."

Clutch swung the car around the back of the tarmac and Sarah was out the door as he hit the brake hard.

He grabbed her arm before she got very far, pulled her

into him with the firm gentleness she'd come to expect. "You can't do this."

But she was bent on taking her revenge—he saw that now. She didn't want to be taken for a fool by Rafe, had to get her pride back, had to make things right. He got that, but still, he wasn't going to let her do more damage to herself.

"Killing Rafe isn't going to help. I don't want that on your head—you have to let me take care of this, Sarah. You have to trust me to do it."

"You'll be careful?"

"I've been up against worse than him."

"Did they follow us?" she asked.

"GOST is always following me. I can't worry about that now. Just stay in the car, keep your weapon ready and—"

"Don't tell me to leave if there's trouble. I won't leave without you."

She climbed back into the car, turned in the seat so she could watch him disappear into the shadows beyond the hangar where he'd parked them and she waited.

The tension was unbearable, the heat equally so even with the window rolled halfway down. She had to keep wiping her hands on her pants so the gun wouldn't slip from her grasp when she needed it.

Clutch's phone rang frantically, the third time in under five minutes and he was still nowhere to be seen. Tentatively, she flipped it open and held it to her ear.

"Bobby Juniper, we wanted you back. You didn't come back. Now we're going to have to kill you."

Her body chilled and she closed and dropped the phone into the seat next to her before she let out a muffled gasp.

It began to ring again, almost immediately at the same time she saw, in the side-view mirror, Clutch heading back toward the car.

She saw the other man seconds later.

He was coming up behind Clutch fast. Sarah had never seen him before, but she was sure he was some kind of former military, could tell by the predatory way he moved.

The *Masuka* had been spoken of in more hushed tones by the Africans than they'd ever spoken of Rafe. And the man she loved had been one of them. And very well could become one of them again.

Clutch sensed the man behind him—he stiffened, reached for his weapon, but he wasn't going to be fast enough. The man clipped him with the butt of his rifle to the back of his head and Clutch crumpled to the ground. And while the man began to bind Clutch's wrists together, Sarah stepped out of the car and fired a clean shot right between the surprised man's eyes.

One down, one to go. And although she didn't want to leave Clutch out in the open and vulnerable, the sound of the plane's engines along the deserted runway warned her she was about to lose her chance to catch Rafe.

"Clutch, please, please wake up." She shook him, tried to untie the ropes with shaking hands until she heard his voice.

"Go, Sarah. Go now," Clutch whispered, because there was no choice. It would be faster for her to get to Rafe now. "It's got to be done. Go!"

His tone didn't leave her a choice. With one last backward glance at him, she ran as fast as she could toward the lights of the plane.

CHAPTER
17

Jake caught Isabelle before she fell.

Her breath came in short, rapid bursts, until he shook her lightly and told her in no uncertain terms that she needed to calm down, sit down and breathe.

She wanted to slap him, and she took that as a good sign. So she sat down instead, pulled on the T-shirt he handed her, then hugged her arms tightly around herself and waited, Jake's words echoing in her head. *You were always safe with me...*

Those words immediately brought her back to a time and place she'd resisted letting her thoughts travel to. But now her mind was already reeling and wasn't giving her the choice of refusal. They were the same words Rafe had spoken to her two months ago, when he'd taken her from the clinic.

"You're not safe here anymore. You need to trust me." Rafe hadn't even let her grab any of her things before taking her arm and pulling her out the back door of her fixed tent and into the night.

He's doing his job, doing what he was hired to do. *She had no reason not to trust him. And she did so, hiding out with the very danger she'd thought she'd been safe from.*

She'd discovered after the rescue that he'd kept her hidden for three days—three days as they camped out in the bush she'd cried and held on to him as though he was her only lifeline. He'd planned carefully in order to get close to her again, after months of preparing to kidnap her for ransom.

She wasn't sure how long they'd walked for, how long Rafe had half dragged, half carried her before finally tossing her across his shoulders like a sack of potatoes and taking off through the hot jungled paths. When he put her down, she saw dawn streak across the sky and realized that once daylight hit, they'd be sitting ducks.

"There's no place around here to hide," she said as he began to move aside some brush and she saw that he'd uncovered the doorway to a small hut in the middle of nowhere. "How did you know about this place?"

"I've been in this area for a while. I always have a backup plan," he said. "Get in."

He'd been rougher to her since she'd stopped sleeping with him—she could understand that and she was still so very grateful he was on her side. She complied gladly, pushed into the small door through the dried brush and stepped into the empty room. Empty. Private. Safe. That was all that mattered now.

Her legs almost slid out from under her, and she grabbed the wall for some support.

"You can sit down."

"We're going to be here for a while?"

"At least until nightfall. Maybe longer. Until I say it's safe."

"Okay." She lowered herself to the ground. "Can you tell me . . . I didn't notice anything. No one threatened me—"

"The rebel soldiers know who you are, and it's not your job to notice things like that."

She looked up at Rafe, found him watching her thoughtfully. "What?" she asked.

"You're tougher than I thought you'd be," he said.

"I guess that's a compliment."

"When I first met you, I thought . . ."

"You thought, here's a woman who doesn't look like she can hold her own," she said. "How did they find out who I was?"

Rafe shrugged. "I guess your luck ran out on that end. You're just lucky it didn't run out on mine."

To her horror, the tears that had threatened from the start filled her eyes and spilled down her cheeks. She put her fist to her mouth and turned toward the wall.

Stop it. Just stop it.

But it was too late. She pressed her forehead against the smooth wall.

"You're okay." His voice was rough, like he wasn't used to giving comfort. But she wasn't in any position to turn it down and when his hands touched her shoulders tentatively, she turned into his arms. Her crying was muffled against his shirt, *and she didn't know how long he let her stay like that before he pulled back. "Toughen up, Isabelle. We're not done yet."*

She pulled in a ragged breath and moved away from him completely. "Admit no weakness, right?"

"I'm not here to baby you. I'm here to do my job."

"Fine." She turned away from him again, lay on the hard dirt floor and cradled her head against her arm. She heard him cock his rifle behind her, was grateful that there was someone to watch over her.

Sleep came in fits and starts. After she'd dozed for an hour, she stretched her tired and sore muscles and then sat up, back against the wall, staring into space while Rafe watched out the small window.

Then she realized she'd quickly go insane doing that. If she didn't distract herself, and soon, she'd have all sorts of unwanted thoughts. She couldn't afford a breakdown now.

"Rafe," she whispered. The only indication he gave that he'd heard her was the shift of his eyes. "It's a good sign they haven't found us by now, right?"

"Not necessarily. They could be waiting to make their next move in the dark."

Fear shot straight down her spine. "Thanks for the reassurance."

"You've got to be patient. You must've thought about the fact that something like this could happen to you. No one asked you to come here," he said. "This is dangerous enough—moreso for a senator's daughter."

"So this is my fault? I'm not supposed to have the career I want because of who my mother is?" She felt the vague stirrings of an unfinished fight in her, and she forced herself back to sleep.

Sometime in the deepest, darkest part of the night, when everything was still and quiet, he'd moved closer to her on the floor where she'd slept. She must've been dreaming, had heard herself cry out in her sleep and struggle against imaginary bonds. When she'd opened her eyes, still halfway between dreaming and reality, Rafe was pressed against her, cradling her from behind, murmuring in her ear.

"It's going to be fine, honey. You're fine. Safe." And even as he spoke, his hand moved across her abdomen, unbuttoned her pants and his long fingers slid inside her underwear.

She spread her legs for him, the way she had so many times before, during her first month in the clinic, whimpered as he stroked her. "Not strong," she whispered. "You said I'm not strong."

"You're stronger than you know," he said before he pulled her pants down to her ankles and took her from behind, entering her in one long stroke that made her cry out from the first pinch of pain, and then from pleasure when he rocked against her.

It was sometime after he rolled away from her that she heard the wheels of the Humvee on the dirt path, peeked out from the small hut they'd been holed up in and saw soldiers.

American soldiers.

They were finally going to be rescued. She turned around, now fully awake, to tug at Rafe, but he wasn't there.

You can't let this opportunity pass you by.

She stood, prepared to run after the car before it got too far away from them. She'd gone maybe ten feet from the house when she heard the click of an automatic rifle behind her.

She turned, slowly, hands in the air, only to find Rafe standing there. Pointing a gun at her.

"*Don't say a word,*" he told her.

"*They're going to rescue us.*"

"*No, they're not. It's not time yet.*"

"*I don't understand,*" she said, heard the car come closer, and felt the cold metal of Rafe's gun pressed against her temple.

"*Not. A. Word. I'll shoot you if I have to.*"

She shut her mouth tightly, not able to suppress the whimper that threatened to become a sob. He clamped a firm palm over her mouth and nose to muffle the sound and the tears poured freely down her cheeks.

The rumble of the Humvee faded into the distance, and Rafe finally released her. She moved away from him, and from his gun, wiped her cheeks with the back of her hand.

"*Why did you do that? You're supposed to help me.*"

"*And you're supposed to have some loyalty, Isabelle.*" He housed the rifle in the holster he wore loose, slung along his chest.

"*I don't understand.*"

"*You're looking to other people to save you—I'm the one who's saving you. And now it's too late.*" He motioned for her to come closer, and she saw that he held a pair of handcuffs and other bonds.

"*No. Please. I'll do anything you ask.*"

"*You brought this on yourself.*" He moved toward her and she stayed frozen to the spot, eyes fixed on the handcuffs.

This wasn't happening.

How could she have been so wrong about him? "*What are you doing? I don't understand . . .*"

"*One day, you will, Isabelle. One day soon, it's all going to become painfully clear that you made the wrong choice.*"

"You're going to hurt me because I don't want to be with you?" she asked. "Rafe, that's crazy."

He grabbed her roughly, but she knew she could still turn this around—he'd told her that he loved her and she could use that love now, even as the thought twisted her insides with guilt and shame.

"Rafe, please, we can fix this . . . whatever it is that's wrong."

"That's what I thought too. But I've let you screw with my plan, my mind, for too long."

His plan . . . She had no idea what he was talking about. "If it's money you need, I can give you money. Is that what you want—to kidnap me for money?"

"I'll get money, Izzy. And much more."

That's when it hit her, like a punch in the stomach. "There was never anyone after me, was there? You took me away from the clinic so you could get me alone like this. There's no one looking for me."

"No, there's no one but me now," he said.

She walked over to him and pushed his chest hard, not caring about the consequences anymore. He didn't budge, just grabbed her wrist and held on while she flailed against him. She was no match for his strength and within a few minutes he had her arms pinned behind her back.

He ripped her shirt a minute later, did the same to her pants. Ripped them completely off and left her naked and helpless in front of him.

"Please, Rafe. Please don't do this," she whispered hoarsely, but she wasn't sure he heard her. He blindfolded her a second later, stuffed a gag in her mouth and carried her, half-naked, back to the safe house.

He removed the gag and the blindfold once they got inside, as if he wanted her to watch what he was about to do.

And she knew what he was going to do with her once he was through, understood that with far too much clarity.

"Take these handcuffs off, Rafe," she told him with the last piece of strength she had. "I won't fight you." And he had, right before he pulled her to the ground.

"Tell me that you want me, Izzy," he whispered.

She swallowed hard, forced herself to smile. "I want you, Rafe. You know that. Please..."

She put her arms around him while he thrust painfully inside of her, in an attempt to make the rape not be what it was, to give herself more power.

She repeated the word no *inside her head the entire time.*

And when he was done, he had the gun out, pointed at her. But at the last minute, he faltered. And that's when his rage boiled over, when he beat her instead of killing her. Told her that he didn't want it to be over yet. That no one had suffered long enough, including her.

"I thought you were the way back," he told her.

Isabelle hadn't realized she'd been telling the story aloud in vivid detail as it played out in front of her. As if she hadn't been the one who'd lived it.

Now Jake had heard the final portion of Rafe's betrayal. How stupid she'd been.

"Do you understand now?" she asked finally. "I didn't tell them that I'd slept with him, not that night, not ever. I consented all those times. I consented the time before he raped me. I consented when he raped me too—*I didn't tell him no, didn't ask him to stop*. And I didn't want to see the look in the eyes of those agents when I told them how pathetically stupid I was. I didn't want them to know...anything."

"You stayed alive. You're not stupid," Jake said. His voice was different. Hoarse—raw even.

She couldn't care. It was all lies. "Did you hear me, Jake? *I slept with Rafe.* Not just while I waited to be rescued, but before that, in the clinic. He was good-looking. Protective. My *hero.* Isn't that every woman's ultimate fantasy?"

"What I saw—the way he hurt you—that wasn't consensual."

She raised her eyes to meet his and finally admitted the truth out loud. "No, that last time wasn't consensual. Not at all. Just like you protecting me." Jake jerked his head as if she'd slapped him.

Isabelle's words hit Jake deeper than he'd thought possible.
She's angry, upset...she doesn't mean...

"You knew, *knew* how hard it was for me to trust anyone, and still you lied to me." She fought for control and lost. "I thought this was a sanctuary—that you were going to help me."

"It was. I am."

"All those phone calls I received—those were from him, weren't they?"

"I don't know. Probably."

"Probably," she repeated, tightened her hands into fists. "Where is he now?"

"He's still in Africa. Last seen in Burundi. Your uncle had people looking for him...now I do as well."

"What do you mean my uncle had people looking for

him?" she asked and then closed her eyes and held up a hand. "No, don't. Don't tell me. I know what he's capable of."

He didn't like the way she was looking at him, like she was comparing him in some way to that goddamned monster. And Jake knew too that on several levels he and Rafe had more in common than he'd ever wanted to think about.

There wasn't much separating either of them from the blade's edge. "Are you sure you never told anyone what you just told me? The FBI, the CIA...?"

She shook her head. "No. I never told them. What did it matter?"

It did matter—it explained why Rafe hadn't taken her sooner than he did. If Rafe was sleeping with her, if he'd developed feelings for her, it made sense he'd put his kidnapping plans on hold. He didn't want to think about what would have happened to her if Rafe hadn't fallen in love with her.

"How long were you sleeping with him?" he asked.

"You don't have any right to ask that. You don't have any rights at all with me."

He held up his hands, a silent surrender to her wishes.

"I need to get out of here. I want to go to my uncle's. I want to hear all of this from him. I can't be here with you anymore—can you understand that?"

"I'll take you."

"I'll get a cab."

"No. You're still my responsibility. I'll take you to Cal's and he can decide what he needs me to do. Go get dressed."

She didn't argue with him.

Clutch lost consciousness again for a few minutes after he'd sent Sarah to go after Rafe. He came to with a start, head pounding, body sweating on the still warm tarmac. His vision blurred and he yanked at his wrists, bound behind him with a thick rope. The knots were tough, though not impossible, but he'd already lost time and Sarah . . .

Sarah was the reason he wasn't dead right now.

He heard more shots ring out overhead and worked furiously on the ropes that bound him, successfully freeing his hands. As he picked apart on the thick knots strung around his ankles, he wondered how many more men they'd send to find him. They had so many ways to torture him . . .

That didn't matter now. As the ropes fell away and his feet pounded the tarmac in steady rhythm to the pounding in his skull, the only thing that mattered was saving Sarah.

Rafe was getting onto the lone jet that was fueled up and ready to take off, despite the lack of lights on the runway—he turned in time to see Sarah coming up the tarmac after him, had his gun pointed at her within seconds.

He was still much faster than she was—a better shot. In the darkness, backlit from the plane's interior, he looked harder, more predatory.

"Are you here for your money?" he called out.

"You betrayed me," she yelled back.

"Remember what I told you, Sarah. Our kind are different—we don't play on the same moral ground."

I want everyone in that family to hurt, Sarah. I want them to hurt the way I hurt—I know you can understand that.

"You lied to me."

If you could get revenge on the people who hurt your family, you'd do it. I know you would.

God, she would, if it meant her family could survive. Anyone who thought differently was a liar and a coward.

And still, the guilt seeped through, the first time in a long time she'd actually felt that emotion. It was real—it was right.

"There's room here for you." He held out his free hand toward her. "Holster your weapon and come with me. There's no one else you can trust. I understand you."

"I know you do," she called back. She pretended to put the safety on her weapon and began to walk purposefully toward the plane.

"Sarah, wait!"

Clutch's voice came screaming from behind her. She turned on him as Rafe began to fire at both her and Clutch, and Clutch returned fire.

She drew her weapon and faced off with Clutch. "I'm going with him," she called, loud enough for Rafe to hear, even as she walked backward toward the plane. "Let me do this, Clutch. I have to do this."

Shots continued to fire over her head, the rational part of her brain telling her that they were too close for mere cover fire. But she couldn't stop.

"Sarah, come back here. Back to me. I'm not letting you go with Rafe."

Clutch knew exactly what she planned to do, and he wasn't going to let it happen. Still, she hadn't expected him to run and tackle her the way he did, both of them landing hard on the ground. Her head hit the pavement but still she drew her weapon, prepared to kill Rafe from where she lay.

Clutch held her down as he continued to return fire on Rafe but the jet had started to move down the runway as the hatch closed.

Her head was heavy. She lay cheek down on the asphalt, the smell of jet fuel filled her nostrils and lungs, the deafening roar of the jet engines drowning her senses.

Clutch held his hands over her ears until there was nothing but silence surrounding them, a silence that bore down on her more heavily than the weight of Clutch's body ever could.

His eyes were red-rimmed as he stared at her. She'd missed, missed her chance to help a woman she'd betrayed. Missed a chance to help herself.

"We didn't get him," she whispered. "Go after him."

"He's gone, Sarah. He'll be out of the country soon. I can't follow him."

"I was going to," she said.

"He would've killed you. Our part here is over." He lifted her off the ground and walked with her across the empty airstrip, back to the truck.

"What about the group that's after you, Clutch?" she whispered as the sirens started up in the distance. "That's not over."

"Don't worry about me. You have your own ghosts to deal with."

"We're strong enough to get rid of the ghosts, aren't we, Clutch?" she asked. He didn't answer her, and she supposed they'd find out soon enough.

CHAPTER

18

Jake must have called Uncle Cal while she'd gotten dressed, because when Isabelle burst through the front door, her uncle was waiting for her.

She slammed the door behind her, in case Jake had any ideas about coming inside. Riding in the car next to him had been difficult enough—it had taken so much control not to look at him.

Cal spoke before she had a chance to. "I would have put Jake on this detail regardless of whether he'd saved you the first time or not."

"Uncle Cal, I'm not—"

"He was following a direct order, Izzy. My order."

"And when he told me, was that part of following your orders too? Doing your dirty work for you?"

Her uncle's jaw tightened before he spoke. "He defied my orders in telling you what he did. He was always adamant about you knowing the full truth. I made the decision to keep it from you. I know you might never forgive me for it, but at the time I felt it was best."

"Not for me, Uncle Cal," she said.

When he spoke again, it was in a tone she'd never heard him use. Normally, he was so in command, so straight-laced. Now he sounded desperate. "I thought I could get that bastard more quickly."

"You had no right to decide that for me."

"You were so scared. In the hospital—every day for the first week you asked if Rafe had been caught. It was only after we told you yes that you calmed down, started to heal. You stopped having to sleep with the lights on," he said, his words a punch in the gut because they were the truth. Knowing Rafe was out there when she'd first come home from Africa had been terrifying. It was equally so now, even though she was far stronger.

"I don't understand. Why is Rafe coming after me now? Why didn't he just kill me when he had the chance?"

She heard her uncle draw in a sharp breath when she said the word *kill.* "Money, Isabelle. He wants money. Don't worry, I just need to make one call and the FBI will come and collect you."

She got the distinct feeling that her uncle was still lying to her. But the need to know something unrelated to Rafe was strong enough to override her concerns about her uncle's agenda. "I need to know why you're still not with my mother."

Cal's eyes snapped sharply to attention, and she realized he'd suspected for some time that she knew. And then his features softened at the mention of her mother, but he didn't answer.

"You had your chance before she married—even after she was and you knew... you knew all about me and you did nothing. And then, all these years..." She stopped, brushed the tears away. "Did you ever love her?"

"Of course I did, Izzy. I still do. That's why I stay away."

"I don't get it."

Cal shook his head, staring beyond her into the kitchen, and she knew he was seeing an entirely different scene than the innocent cabinets and granite and stainless steel. "I'm a bad bet. A good Navy man, but I wouldn't be a good husband. I'm an all-or-nothing kind of guy. I like my solitude too much."

"Too much to think about taking on a kid, right?" she asked.

He reached out but she pulled away, shook her head. "All these years, I told myself that you stayed away, that you didn't admit it out of respect for my father. But it had nothing to do with that—it was all about what you wanted. What was good for you."

"Izzy, you don't understand—"

"Then explain it to me."

"It's too complicated." He walked away from her, leaving her alone in the hallway. She turned to the window and saw Jake on the porch, his back to the large window.

"I've got your mother on the line," Uncle Cal called out

to her from his office. He left, shutting the door behind him once she'd picked up the phone.

"Izzy, honey—"

Isabelle cut her off immediately. "I've heard Uncle Cal's version. I'm assuming yours is pretty much the same. Just tell me why, Mom," she said quietly.

"Cal and I wanted this to go away for you. I didn't want to risk more of an investigation—didn't want to risk the press getting hold of this. We were so lucky we were able to keep it quiet."

Isabelle had no doubt her mother had done everything with the best of intentions—she'd appreciated the lack of media coverage, had appreciated even more when the FBI and the CIA went away and stopped asking her questions.

Of course, she'd thought they'd gone away for different reasons entirely—she'd thought the case was completely closed. Finished.

It wasn't, not by a long shot. And even now, she didn't know if she would have ever admitted the truth to anyone. Knowing she'd been with Rafe wouldn't change anything, wouldn't help them capture him any faster. No, it would just blur the lines.

"We thought we could meet his demands and capture him before you ever found out he was still out there." Jeannie admitted. "But I know Rafe is coming back—it's not an idle threat. He called me. I told Cal I want the FBI involved—I will not take a chance again."

"You spoke with him? Rafe called you?" she asked, slammed a fist on the desk. "I'm not going anywhere with the FBI. Don't you dare let Uncle Cal call them, don't you dare."

"Izzy, please, now that everything's out in the open, you need to listen to reason. There's real danger involved..."

When Rafe left her bound and helpless, his last words had been, *I'll see you again soon, Isabelle. Count on that.*

Count on that. She hadn't, not at all, had foolishly believed that Rafe had been put away for good.

Looking back, she realized that she'd let the idea of Rafe being behind bars comfort her enough to not push past the feelings of anger, of hurt. Of fear.

No, only Jake had forced her to confront those. And still, she was so very angry with him.

"Jake says he can keep me safe." Although she wasn't at all sure she wanted to be back in his company—or if he wanted her in his. Her own words echoed in her ears...

That last time wasn't consensual. Not at all. Just like you protecting me.

The way she'd spoken the words had been purposeful, hateful—meant to strike at Jake's soul. Judging by the way he'd looked at her, she'd been successful, and she hated herself for that.

God, she was so confused. "When you talked about being hurt, the other night at dinner, you weren't talking about Dad, were you?"

There was a long, heavy pause on Jeannie's end of the line. So long, Isabelle broke back in. "I know, Mom. I've known about Dad and Uncle Cal and you for a long time."

"You can't pick who you fall in love with. You can try, but your heart's in charge... I think you understand that."

"You never loved Dad. The man I thought of as my dad."

"I did, just not in the way I should have," her mother admitted.

Isabelle pictured the way her life would've been had she acquiesced to marrying Daniel and staying in private practice, had she not kept fighting, and for the first time she got it with a clarity she hadn't felt since Africa.

"I have to go now, Mom," she said. Jake was standing in the doorway, his broad shoulders filling the space. Cal must have let him in.

"Isabelle, please, I want you to consider protection. Until that man is caught."

"This is something I've got to do my own way," she said. "I'll be in touch. I promise."

She ended the call and held the phone in her palm.

"I'm going in to work," she told Jake. He didn't argue, merely nodded. "I'm still not sure I can forgive you for not telling me."

Again, he nodded.

"So I'm changing the rules of the game," she continued.

"Okay," he said quietly.

"I can't do this—whatever it is that's happening between us. I just can't. I'm not ready. I might never be ready."

"You still have to trust me if you want me to protect you, Isabelle. If you can't do that, I won't be able to do my job."

She wanted to cry at the thought of her being just a job to Jake, but she'd been the one to put herself in that position. She held all the control now, and she wasn't giving it up again only to be hurt. "I know you and your brothers will keep me safe. But I'm not going to remain a prisoner anywhere. Rafe wants to find me—and as terrified as I am about that, it needs to happen sooner rather than later. You can catch him and it will finally be over."

"Yes, that part will finally be over," he agreed.

"You said you wouldn't start that again—that you'd drop pushing me. I'm not ready . . . not now."

"I promised to be honest with you from now on." He remained in the doorway, shoved his hands in his pockets. "Your mom wants you in protective custody."

"She told me. I refused."

Jake nodded. "Did she tell you that Rafe threatened her as well?"

"No, she didn't tell me that." She shook her head. "Why is he doing this? He's trying to hurt everyone I love."

"Your mother will be protected," he assured her. "Still, it's not going to be easy and I'm most worried about you. Rafe's good at what he does—he's traveling alone and he's bent on revenge. You need to start watching your six, learning to shoot . . ."

"I know how to shoot. Rafe taught me how to lock and load during those three days when I was waiting for some mysterious enemy to come get me. His sick way of bonding, I guess. Maybe it gave him a thrill, knowing that I could fight back, but that I'd never win against him."

His nostrils flared slightly. "What kind of weapon?"

"A nine millimeter."

He reached into the back of his jeans and pulled out a gun, held on to the barrel as he presented it to her. "Keep this on you at all times. You don't go anywhere without it."

The set of his shoulders told her everything she needed

to know, but she heard herself asking anyway, "They didn't catch him at the airport, did they?"

"No, they didn't catch him."

"He's on his way here, then."

"Yes."

She forced herself not to cry out. Thankfully, her throat had tightened enough to stop even the smallest sound.

Clutch and Sarah had checked into the nearest hotel to the Bujumbura Airport an hour earlier. Now she stood over him, tending to the worst scrapes on his back and wrists from where the knots had bit into his flesh.

She'd already put what little ice she could scrounge up on the back of his head even though he'd insisted that she'd gotten the worst of it when he'd pushed her down. But she could tell he was in more pain than she was. Not that he would tell her—he would never tell her that.

Before today, she never would have admitted it to him either.

He held out his wrists to her like an offering, watched her as she dabbed the antiseptic and then blew on it to take away the sting, the way her mother used to do when she'd come home with scraped knees.

"Why are you staring at me?" she asked without looking up.

"Because you're beautiful."

"I'm a total mess," she said. She'd rinsed off in the shower first, at Clutch's insistence, while he'd made the call to the States. She knew Clutch didn't want her to have to hear him repeat what happened, the way Rafe had escaped from them both. The way she'd failed Isabelle.

Clutch stroked her nearly dry hair as it tumbled to her shoulders. "You did the best you could."

"No, I didn't. When Rafe got close with Izzy, I assumed the job was off. I got comfortable," she said. "And then one day, Izzy told me she'd broken things off with Rafe, and I knew. I just knew."

She drew a shaky breath. "I almost told her—almost took her from the camp myself and drove her to the airport. She almost had a chance."

"Sarah—"

"No, don't say it. There's nothing you can say that's going to make it right," she said flatly.

"You weren't in your right mind. You were living in a state of constant alert—you were barely functioning yourself. You've paid."

"Will it ever be enough?" she asked. "Isabelle will never forgive me—she shouldn't ever forgive me."

"You need to forgive yourself first."

She shook her head, as if that weren't possible. "I hope she never knows. Is that selfish? I don't want her to ever know what I've done. I want her to remember the good things about our friendship. I don't want her to have any more guilt or pain because of me—I'll be the one to carry that burden."

"I don't think that's selfish," he said quietly.

She couldn't remember the last time she'd slept or eaten and none of that really mattered, not with Clutch safe and in one piece in front of her. As much as she wanted to ask him what would happen now, she wanted him much more.

"Stay just like that," she told him. He remained seated on the edge of the bed, stripped down, wearing just the small hotel towel across his lap. His pupils were slightly dilated—they both knew there was a good chance he had a concussion. Neither of them would do much sleeping that night.

"What are you doing?" he asked as she rummaged through his bag, past the weapons and the computer and God knew what else until she found her camera. She had a full roll of film left—she'd reloaded after she'd taken those last pictures at the checkpoint.

"Just stay."

"I can't stay," he said, and they both knew he wasn't talking about posing for the camera.

She dropped it back down into the bag and walked toward the bed. "You can't leave me again."

She reached out and stroked his cheek, the days-old stubble rough against her palm, and studied him as though looking through her lens. He shifted, visibly uncomfortable with her assessment—his face always looked wonderful on film, his features were contoured enough that light and dark bounced off them, making him look hard and soft, fierce and vulnerable, all at the same time.

"What's your name—your real name?" she asked finally, because she needed to hear him say it.

"Bobby." It sounded like it had been a long time since he uttered it.

"Bobby," she repeated. "I like that."

"Why did you always want to take pictures of me?"

"Because you're handsome," she replied. "Your eyes—

the way you never smile." She reached up to touch his mouth but he blocked her.

"No more pictures," he said hoarsely. "Ever."

"No pictures," she agreed with a whisper, because she could capture all of this with her mind and never let it fade.

His mouth covered hers, tasted like brown sugar and tea, and he tore open the borrowed shirt of his she wore. She heard the light scatter of the buttons hitting the floor as he yanked the shirt off her shoulders, without stopping kissing her, hungrily, like he'd been thinking about it the way she had for the past hours.

She grabbed the towel off his lap impatiently and she attempted to climb him, to get him inside of her immediately.

But he wasn't having it. Instead, he stood, grabbed her around the waist and pushed her up against the wall. He took her with his fingers, circling the hot, wet flesh, his tongue dancing on her nipple as she writhed with her back pressed against the wall.

And then he lowered himself slowly until he was on his knees. He kept one of her feet on his shoulder, held it there as he tongued her sex until she grabbed his hair and shuddered to a hard, fast climax against his mouth. But he didn't stop, his tongue working her clit over and over until she was crying out his name... *Bobby. Oh, God, Bobby...*

She was still shuddering as he carried her to the bed. His body covered hers, his heavy weight pinning her against the soft mattress.

He put his head down, nuzzled against her shoulder, and for a minute she let the overwhelming feeling of trust wash over her.

Jake took Isabelle straight from Cal's house to the base clinic—that's what she wanted and even though all of this was against his better judgment, it wouldn't be for much longer. Rafe would be found soon.

He hadn't bothered to tell Isabelle that this kind of game, the one that Rafe was playing and the one that he and Isabelle were dancing around never really had any rules to begin with.

What the senator had told him earlier had kicked him in the gut nearly as hard as the look in Isabelle's eyes when she'd learned he'd betrayed her.

"You're no match for this man," the senator said, and Jake wondered how the women in this family knew exactly the right way to cut him to the quick.

"I'm a match for Rafe in every way, Senator. Make no mistake about that. But I won't go against your wishes."

"I'll make the arrangements—the FBI will take her into custody tonight."

Jeannie Cresswell's tone wasn't debatable and he hadn't bothered to argue with the woman—Isabelle was her daughter—although certainly, when the time came, it would be Isabelle's choice. And she'd made her decision.

Based on Clutch's calculations, Rafe could be on U.S. soil already—it would be a stretch but Jake wasn't taking chances. He refused to leave the clinic, hung out in one of the empty office cubicles in the back, where he had a view of the rear parking lot.

Both Nick and Chris had offered to take tonight's shift for him, because his brothers knew what day tomorrow

was. A day he never wanted to relive, and one he did, bru-
tally, in his dreams.

It was a night for ghosts, living and dead.

Dammit, his body felt sore from underuse. He wanted
to run along the beach, let his bare feet pound the rough
sand until there was nothing else but the rhythm of his
body taking over every recess of his mind.

Everything was far too raw.

CHAPTER
19

Although she hadn't seen Jake around much, Isabelle sensed his presence more strongly than ever. True to his word, he'd driven her to the clinic early that morning—she'd spent the day clearing new recruits and bandaging up some female Marines who were nearly through boot camp. They walked and talked with tight swaggers, similar to the male posturing she'd seen among young soldiers.

She wished she felt half their confidence, had been faking the *I'm doing fine* thing all day long. But every time the clinic got too quiet, all her own doubts about her safety came rushing back to her.

She'd been barely holding it together when she thought Rafe was in prison—now that she knew he was running free, and coming back for her, her tenuous grip slid perilously out of control.

At six, toward the end of the twelve-hour shift, she grabbed a stack of files and noted the small package that had been laid on the corner of her desk. Plain brown envelope, addressed to her with a return address of Norfolk, but no name.

Without thinking, she opened it, figuring it to be medical books or supplies, but when the red kanga—the same cloth she'd used as a blanket in Africa—stared up at her, the dizzying fear overwhelmed her. When she opened her mouth to call for Jake, nothing came out. She tried again and found herself hyperventilating.

Her office phone began to ring, and even though she didn't have the breath to speak, she picked it up, waited for the silence to greet her.

This time, she was greeted by something far more sinister.

"I've got your SEAL, Izzy."

Isabelle wasn't sure how she managed to stay standing after she heard Rafe's words, but she was, firmly on her own two feet and dialing Jake's cell phone.

She held her cell to her free ear, and within seconds she heard the ringing phone calling through to Jake. But she didn't hear the ringing phone on Rafe's line. "You're lying."

Rafe laughed, a soft sound she used to enjoy. Now it made her blood run cold. She closed her cell phone before Jake could pick up and reached for the gun that she'd put in the bottom desk drawer, unlatched the safety and backed herself against the wall.

"He's no match for me. He knows it too. Did you like

the present?" he asked. "Remember how I used to wrap it around you when the nights got chilly?"

She did remember that—remembered all of it, no matter how hard she tried to delete it from her memory. "You bastard—you left me for dead."

"You're a fighter. I knew you'd make it. Just like you knew I'd come back for you," he said, and then the line went dead. She threw the receiver down on the desk, hard enough that it cracked into pieces and tumbled to the floor in a mess of plastic and wires. And then she held the gun by her side and walked out of her office as the claustrophobia got worse.

Jake appeared in the doorway before she reached it.

"Where are you going?" he demanded. She stared between Jake and the gun. "Isabelle, what's wrong?"

She still couldn't talk, merely pointed at the kanga lying on the desk. He looked toward it and then at her, helped her to take a few steps out of the office and into the fresh, cold air.

"Is it . . ."

"It's got a return address in Virginia," she managed. He released her for a second and let her stay in the opened doorway while he walked over and grabbed the brown package.

"It's postmarked New York."

"That doesn't mean he's in New York now."

"No, it doesn't. Let me take you—"

"How does he know about you?" she interrupted.

"What are you talking about?"

"He called me. Called here. But this time he talked to me." She hated that her voice shook.

Jake immediately pulled her away from the open doorway and inside the office with him. He stared at the phone on the floor and then back at her.

"He said, *I've got your SEAL.* How does he know everything?"

Jake shrugged. "I have no fucking idea. But we're not going to stand around here and figure it out. He's never called you at the house, right?"

She shook her head hard. "No, not there or on my cell phone either."

"Then he associates you with this place. We're out of here."

The Blazer bounced over the ruts in the backwoods, a trail not made for a car, but Jake didn't seem to care about that.

The farther away they got from the base and the clinic, the worse she felt.

"Please, pull over—I'm going to be sick," she told him.

He did so immediately, and she pushed out into the brisk night air and just breathed.

She heard Jake get out of the car. He hadn't cut the engine, stood instead in the beam of the headlights and watched her.

The nausea subsided after a few minutes, but the woods closed in around her, dark and dank . . . and when was all of this going to be over?

"He knows where I work, maybe where I live, even. He's coming back for me and no one seems to be able to stop him."

You're no match for this man, Lieutenant Hansen.

"I won't let him get to you. He's not going to be able to get through me, Isabelle. He knows that. He'll try a different tactic this time."

"My mother. Or Uncle Cal," she whispered.

"Yes. That's what we're thinking. We'll go back to the house."

"And then what? I sit inside like a prisoner, waiting for Rafe to make his next move? Dammit, Jake, I can't do this."

"I know how hard it is for you, but you're going to get through this. I know you're strong enough."

She swallowed hard. "What do you know? It's so easy for you—you're not scared of anything or anyone. You're made of steel, remember?"

"If you're trying to push me away, you're doing a damned fine job, so keep it up."

"And what about you? After you fix me, what guarantees are there that you're going to hang around?"

"Funny thing, Isabelle. You haven't asked me to hang around. You've asked me to be there for you, to touch you ... but you talk about being solitary and about going back to Africa. Then you told me to back off completely. The one thing you never talk about is how you really feel about me. You dance around it, talk about our bond ... you wonder if it's just the rescue, and hell, I don't know how to move past that."

She didn't answer him. Couldn't. It didn't matter—he was angry enough for both of them now.

"What does it take to earn a spot in your inner circle, Isabelle? What does it take to earn your trust? Because I've got to know if you're in this with me."

"What does it take to earn yours?" she shot back.

He didn't hesitate, untucked his shirt, yanked it roughly over his head and threw it to the ground. He turned around slowly, put his head back and squared his shoulders and she squeezed her hands so hard into fists to keep from gasping that she was sure she cut her own palms.

"Go ahead, Doc. I know you felt them. Maybe even saw them in the shadows, so go ahead—now's your chance."

He stood silently, almost proudly as she stared at the map of crisscrossed scars that traveled along his shoulders and down to his lower back.

She took a tentative step and then a few more quick ones so she could see up close. Her fingers traced the raised scars—there were many, so many crisscrossing his back. She knew what instruments would make each mark, identified chains and belt buckles. How the hell had he survived this?

"Yeah, I have no idea what it's like to be afraid, right, Isabelle?" He jerked away from her touch, turned to face her.

"You think showing me these scars is enough? Everyone's seen these scars—every woman you've ever been with. But how many of them know the story behind them?"

"None of them."

"None of them, including me. That's a great defense."

"Don't you dare talk to me about defenses."

"Hits too close to home?"

His chin rose. "You think it's all about sex...about breaking through that one particular barrier, but it's not. It's about breaking through all your barriers. It's about you breaking through all of mine. So just get back into the car, Isabelle. I need to get you over to the house."

"You don't get to tell me what to do."

Jake's hand tightened on the door handle as Isabelle's voice floated up from behind him, echoing in the dense woods. Her normally soft, smoky tone, the one that drove straight through him when she whispered his name when she came, or when he touched her, was couched in pure steel.

He wondered how far he could push her tonight—how smart a move that would be, with danger right on their six.

He turned to her fast, made her start. "Get in the car. Now."

And still, she held her ground. "You may be running this show, Jake, but I'm in charge of my life. You don't get to give me your speeches and then walk away with no more than a peek at your past."

And there it was—the real anger was rising up from the fear.

"Now we're getting somewhere. Now we're getting to it, past the *I'm going back to Africa* bullshit and down to the real issues."

"Drop it, Jake."

"I'm not dropping anything. Why don't you tell me what's really bothering you?"

"I know you think..." She faltered for a second. "I know I did the wrong thing by going with him. But even if I didn't, he had all that training."

"His training wasn't the problem."

"So what, he didn't have to use his training? All he had to do was say the word and I went along for the ride?"

"Yes."

"I was vulnerable."

"Yes."

"I won't make that mistake again."

"What he did was unconscionable. You let him do it to you over and over every time you let him stop you from really living."

"It's so easy for you ... your monster's dead." She went to push past him, to get into the car.

"I thought you were going to stay and fight."

She whirled back around to face him. "Fight? How am I supposed to fight against someone who's not in front of me?"

"You're doing a good job of fighting—you're going to work, doing what you need to. Making plans." He paused. "What would you have been doing for the past couple of months if Cal hadn't lied to you?"

"Now you agree with what he did?"

"Answer the question."

"I would have ..." She stopped, shoulders slumped, defeated momentarily. "I think I hate you."

She pushed him hard, with the butt of her palms against his chest, just the way he'd taught her. And then she took him down at the knees.

He fell with the grace of someone who was ready for it, ass in the mud, and she was on top of his chest within seconds, her arm across his throat, barely seeing straight through her anger.

She pummeled his chest with her fists, as hard as she could. He didn't stop her and she hit him harder.

"You're not going back to Africa to prove to yourself that you're healed, you're going back as if that can turn back

ime, like that can make you the person you were before
Rafe hurt you. But that's not going to happen—I don't
want it to happen. Don't you get it? If you go back to the
way you were, you might never have been able to let me
n."

"I haven't let you in anyway."

"Yeah, you have. You've let me into your dreams.
Halfway into your bed, halfway into your heart. This—*this*
s life beyond survival, getting past the fear and getting an-
ry."

"And then what?"

"If necessary, you do it all over again. You did that when
ou wanted me to kiss you. That wasn't an act of despera-
ion, it was an act of life. That's when I knew you were go-
ng to fight to get your life back. That's when I knew..."

He stopped, mid-sentence, as if his words were too
powerful for him to say them out loud.

"That's when you knew what?"

"Now's not the time."

"What's it the time for, then? You want me to be strong,
ake? Okay, how's this? Come and get me, you bastard! I'm
ight here, out in the open! Come on out!"

He lunged forward to grab her, to shut her mouth, be-
ause everyone knew you didn't invite trouble, but she was
grabbing at him too, and somehow, in between the anger
nd hate and mud, they were kissing, passionately locked in
fierce tangle of arms and legs and mouths.

It was dirty and hot—so hot, even though their breath
urned white between them. He tried to stop her, to pull

her away, but her hand went between his legs, slid down th
front of his jeans and circled him.

That effectively killed any thoughts of throwing her off
of him. "Isabelle, please, not like this."

"Yes, just like this. I want you to lose control—the wa
you've made me lose control."

"You've already done that to me—don't you under
stand?"

But still her fist stroked him, his hips bucked and he le
a hoarse cry escape his throat. She'd used her other hand t
unbutton and unzip his jeans and the cold air did nothin
to deter his cock from throbbing, pulsing, needing with
life of its own and not listening to his protests.

He gave up, closed his eyes and let her kiss him, ove
and over until he didn't care about anything that was hap
pening in the world beyond this little patch of dirt in th
middle of the woods. She was teasing his nipple with he
mouth, sucking hard and setting the perfect rhythm witl
her hand and he covered his eyes with his hands and le
himself come with a ferocity that had him seeing stars.

He lay there for a few seconds, panting, her hand still o
him. Then he sat up and pushed her away, gently.

"I'm not him, Isabelle," he managed finally. "I'm not th
man who hurt you."

She sat back on her heels. "I know that—don't yo
think I know that?"

"I don't know what you know. I'm just a man who
falling in love for the first time in his life, a man wh
doesn't know the rules of the game and who thinks he's go
ing down this road alone. And then I remember, alone i
how you like to do things." He stared at her as if he realize

e'd revealed way too much, but he didn't take any of it
ack.

"My God, Jake, I'm..."

"I told you that night I picked you up from Cal's—you
ever have to apologize to me. Don't let anyone stop you
rom taking your power back, Isabelle. Not even me."

CHAPTER
20

"What the hell happened to you two?" Nick demanded when Isabelle and Jake came through the kitchen door.

Isabelle ignored him and pushed past them to go up to her room. Jake started to follow but she turned on him. "You don't have to..."

"I do. Every time. Let me go first."

"Nick's been home."

It didn't matter. He needed to check for himself—Nick would understand.

He took the stairs two at a time until he reached the third floor—he checked the windows and doors, the bathroom, the closets. All clear. He went to the fourth floor—

the converted attic that Chris called home, and checked there too—and finally he swept the back staircase.

"You're all set. Keep the windows closed. Keep your weapon with you. Even in the shower. And keep your door open."

She gave him a mock salute before she turned tail. He headed back down the stairs and found Nick waiting at the bottom of the flight leading to Isabelle's rooms; his brother's face was set in serious lines. "I found something."

"Tell me."

"I've got Rafe's file," Nick said quietly. His fist was tight around the side of the thick brown folder, so much so that the material was bent from the tension in his hand.

"How?"

"You don't want to know."

Jake stared at him. "I'm not letting you get into trouble—"

"I broke into Cal's office."

"Christ." Jake propped his elbows on the stair behind him and stared at the ceiling. Why Cal was still hiding things from him was the biggest mystery of all, and the part that bothered him the most. He needed every ounce of ammo to fight this bastard. "Do I want to hear this?"

"No. Especially not today," Nick said.

"But you'll tell me anyway," Jake said firmly.

"But I'll tell you anyway," Nick repeated. "Rafe was raised in foster care after his father died. At least six of them, from the time he was eight until he was seventeen. His mom left when Rafe was still an infant—they couldn't find her."

Jake curled his fists, didn't want to hear this. None of this. But he had to. "Go on."

"It's not pretty."

"Beatings."

"Yes."

Jake screwed his eyes shut. "There's more."

"Yeah, there's more." Nick paused. "He was severely molested in one of those places."

"None of that is an excuse for what he did," Jake said fiercely.

"I'm just giving you his psychology. Like you asked."

You have to know your enemy.

"That could've been..."

"No. That's not you. It never will be."

"If it had gone beyond beatings..."

"You would've gotten through it. You're not him, Jake. You never could be. You're not damaged."

"Yeah? Why is he damaged and I'm not?" Jake demanded.

"I know what you're thinking."

"I know you do."

"You're wrong." Nick stared him down as he rubbed the small, white scar at the base of his throat the way he always did when he was angry or upset.

"Why? Because you say so?" Jake grabbed the folder out of Nick's hands and twisted it between his own as if to destroy it. "If Steve had taken things further..."

"It wouldn't have mattered. That's still not you."

"And it wasn't Rafe either. Not until when he finally snapped."

"In case you forgot, you already snapped," Nick reminded him, not unkindly. "And that wasn't your fault. That wasn't just blind rage, Jake. Steve tried to kill you."

Jake didn't answer him.

"I could kill Cal for getting you involved in all of this," Nick muttered. "You lived through it and came out stronger. You put it behind you. What happened with Isabelle has brought it all back."

"If she brought it out, that means I never really put it to rest in the first place. Means I've been pretty damned good at lying to myself."

"You haven't been lying to yourself. I think you're falling in love." Nick's voice grew hoarse. "Jake, you're the final defense for Isabelle against Rafe. That's always the most important, because it's the hardest one to breach."

Jake nodded, because he knew that, stared down at his hands, which were still clenched around the file. He eased his grip, slowly. "It doesn't make sense—to get through the Delta screenings, the psych evals . . . they would have picked this up." He steeled himself and opened the file, flipped through the too familiar social work papers and police reports.

"Screenings aren't perfect. They missed this one—picked it up two years into his work with Delta. That's when they discharged him, dishonorably. Defying a direct order."

But Jake had stopped listening, was staring down at the page in front of him so hard the lines of type began to blur. "Rafe's dad was military. He was killed."

"Yeah, when he tried to kill another sailor. Shot in self-defense. What does this have to do with anything?"

"Kevin March killed James Markham. Kevin March is Rafe's father."

Nick's eyes darkened. "Rafe's father killed Isabelle's dad?"

"It's worse than that. Cal was the one who killed Rafe's dad." Jake closed his eyes as the picture on Cal's desk flashed in front of him; the only sound breaking through the roar of blood between his ears was a small, stifled gasp.

He turned swiftly to see Isabelle standing at the top of the staircase, wrapped in a blanket. She'd heard every damned word.

"Isabelle . . ."

"Is that true? What you just said, is that true?" she demanded as Jake took a few steps up toward her.

"It's in the file. I recognized the name from the picture on Cal's desk."

Nick put a hand on Jake's shoulder before he stood and went quietly down the stairs, leaving Jake alone with Isabelle.

"Did Rafe talk to you about your father?" Jake asked her.

"Yes. He asked questions," she said slowly. "About my father. Uncle Cal too. I just thought he was making conversation." Her voice grew thin, trailed off. She stared straight ahead, her eyes focused on nothing.

Jake sat as still as he possibly could. Hard, when all he wanted to do was reach out and hug her. Tell her it was going to be all right.

Except that he didn't know what all right was anymore.

"So Rafe came after me specifically—it was more than just kidnapping the daughter of a senator for money." She grabbed for his arm, as if that would ground her, as if that could stop everything that had been set in motion far too long ago. "Doesn't he know that his father was the one who did something wrong? My father, Uncle Cal . . . they were the victims."

Jake didn't say anything.

"They were the victims, just like I was."

"You were a victim, yes," he said.

"You think there's more to the story?"

"I don't know—something doesn't seem right about all of this."

"Rafe is crazy—look at his background!" she yelled and then she took a step back as if trying to take back her words.

Of course, she'd heard everything, heard him talking with Nick about Rafe's background, and *Christ,* he was losing his touch if he could let an untrained woman sneak up on him like that.

Nick was obviously losing it too, was too close to this, the way Jake was.

"Jake, please, I didn't mean—"

"Not now, Isabelle."

"You're not like him." She grabbed at his shoulders, and he resisted her touch for the first time ever.

"Not now. Just go downstairs . . . go to Nick. Please do that for me." He barely ground out the words, hers echoing in his head, over and over.

Rafe is crazy—look at his background.

He clenched his fists, trying desperately to hold it all in, hold it together until she left the room.

Finally, she nodded, obviously upset, and went past him down the stairs.

You're nothing like him . . .

Jake knew he was nothing like Rafe, and yet he was always waiting to see if the good inside of him would continue to prevail. His controlled temper was one indication of just how tightly he'd learned to hold himself in check—and right now, he knew he wasn't going to be able to do that.

He waited until she was out of his view before he went into his room and let it out by trashing the bookshelves, the coffee table, flipping the couch—because screw counting to ten. No, this release was so much better than that.

But this full-blown explosion by his own hands could overtake him until he was beyond caring. Beyond everything.

He'd betrayed her by not telling her the truth, and somehow he ended up feeling like the one who'd been betrayed.

Rafe is crazy—look at his background.

But Isabelle had done nothing wrong, and he'd done everything wrong from the start.

Isn't a man more than the worst thing he's ever done, his old CO's voice whispered in his ear.

He stopped cold, tried to fucking breathe. None of this was helping. Nothing would help except getting rid of the man who was still coming after Isabelle—would keep coming after her until he got what he wanted.

Jake still couldn't figure out what that was, and Cal wasn't helping. But this blind rage was taking his eye off the prize. His first concern was Isabelle's safety, had to be. He'd deal with everything else later.

When he flexed his fists open, and shut and then open again, his blood was still running too far above a boil for anyone's comfort, including his own.

Cal sat with his back to the windowless wall, the Sig Sauer in his hand as if waiting for the inevitable. And when the phone finally rang, he picked it up without hesitation.

"I need to know why."

"Yes, I understand," he said. In his hand he held the journal he'd found in the mail. It had come in a plain brown envelope—return address, Norfolk, Virginia.

Kevin March's old address.

For the past hour, before the phone rang, he'd forced his hands to stop trembling, to hold steady while he read the journal, and he knew there was no turning back, dread filling him with every turn of the musty, yellowed pages.

All those years, James had known about Cal's betrayal and he'd done nothing but love Isabelle as if she were truly his biological child.

All these years, Cal had never thought about how he'd ripped a father away from a son, John James March, when he'd killed Kevin.

His name had been changed when he'd been adopted briefly by his second family. The family he'd been taken from after the molestation happened. And still, he'd kept that name, hadn't gone back to the name Kevin had given him.

Had Rafe known this entire time? Could he have waited

patiently, planned his revenge in order to strike at just the right moment—in the process hurting everyone Cal had ever loved? It didn't seem possible, and yet still, Cal had always known what happened in Africa would come back to haunt him.

"The truth's going to come out—all of it."

"I'm going to lose everything. I'm prepared for that," Cal said. It had never been his anyway. Not really. Not when it was all built on lies and deceit. A house of cards.

"Yes, you're going to lose everything."

"I'll do anything you want, Rafe—you just keep your goddamned hands off of Isabelle."

"You're not the one giving the orders anymore, Admiral. And I'm not making any promises." Rafe cut the line and Cal did the same, turned his cell phone off and threw it to the side.

He laid the gun down on the desk, grabbed his car keys and prepared to pay for his crimes, prepared to turn himself in and deal with the Uniform Code of Military Justice. Dealing with his own conscience would be far worse.

He didn't have time to react when the cold, hard steel butt of a gun came out from the shadows and caught him on the side of the head.

CHAPTER
21

The noise coming from the second floor—Jake's rooms—echoed throughout the house.

"What is he doing up there?" Isabelle asked Nick, who ignored her in favor of staring out the door. It was only a few minutes later, when the noises stopped and Chris came into the living room, that she got some answers.

Chris's right cheek was red, looked like it would swell soon, but he brushed it off. "It's nothing. He's all right."

"He's not all right. None of us are all right."

"He's as all right as he's going to be," Nick said tightly. "Drop it. Let's concentrate on what we have to do."

"I need to go to him," she said.

"Now's not a good time," Nick started, but Chris cut him off.

"Now might be the best time. Go ahead, Isabelle. We've got this covered for a while. We're not going to let anything happen to you. But you've got to start making some decisions about your safety, before we get called in and can't help you anymore."

She nodded, left the kitchen and Nick and Chris behind, hesitated briefly before heading up the stairs, and again with her hand on the doorknob leading to Jake's room.

It was time for her to put an end to this confusion once and for all. Nick and Chris would keep her safe while she resolved this. That part of it—her safety—was out of her hands now.

Resolving things with Jake wasn't.

The door wasn't locked. She pushed it open without knocking and found herself looking across the room at him.

He'd just come out of the shower, wore only a towel around his waist. He'd tried to keep the area with the stitches dry. It looked raw and ugly, but it was on its way to healing.

Everything was on its way to healing.

He didn't say a word, stared her down—and that should have warned her away, but it didn't. She closed the distance between them so she could run a finger along his wet bicep. She watched the water run along the rivulet left by her touch.

"It's not a good time." Something in his tone should've scared her, should've turned her away. But she stayed.

"You're not all right."

He laughed softly. "No, I'm not. Not today. By tomorrow, everything will be back to normal."

"I keep trying to tell myself that too, but it's not working," she said. "I don't think it's working all that well for you this time, either."

"What the hell do you want from me?"

This was a different Jake—not the calm, cool man who'd helped walk her through a lot of her fears. No, this was the man who, at this moment, was trying his best to break any bond there was between them.

She paused, not sure if she was going to be able to get the sentences out. But she pushed back her tears and her anger and she asked him what she'd wanted to from the night she'd met him. "I want to know everything. The whole story. Why you did what you did. Why you understood. Why you cared." She paused. "I want to know why you have those nightmares."

"Today's the anniversary of the day it happened. The day I killed my stepfather," he said. "Tomorrow, it'll be over and I won't have to think about it for another year. So yeah, my monster might not be breathing, Isabelle, but he's definitely not dead."

His body was sleek and hard without a hint of give. Even the scars seemed to be in the right place on him, giving him the appearance of a warrior, scars from a different kind of combat, but combat nonetheless. Fights he'd survived. Fights that had made him stronger.

Yes, she could follow his lead.

Barely breathing, she traced the scars on his back with

two fingers the way she hadn't done when they'd been out
side in the woods earlier. And he stood stock-still and le
her do so. When she got to the large one that ran straigh
across his lower back, she finally spoke.

"This is why...when you said you didn't like doctors
The questions. They all must ask so many questions..."

He didn't answer, his biceps flexed, the only thing giving
away just how hard it was to stand still under her inspec
tion.

"When?" she asked, shook her head as she stared, ran
tentative finger across one of the thick, roped stripes—
maybe from a belt—and then along a thicker one across hi
lower back—from a chain, if she had to guess...God, she
should at least be as strong as he was.

"Started when I was little. Lasted until I was fourteen.

"When you—"

"Yeah."

She swallowed, hard. "I...I don't know what to say."

"You don't have to say anything."

"Why? Why would he do this to you?"

"He was a drunk, Isabelle. They don't typically need
lot of reasons."

"I don't understand how someone could do this to
child."

"Don't bother trying—it'll never make sense," he said
"It's over. Done with."

"Except in your dreams," she said and he drew in
hissed breath and jerked his head toward her. She repeated
his own words back to him from the night of the rescue
"Sometimes admitting it the first time's the hardest."

When she said she'd remembered everything about tha

ight of the rescue, she'd meant it. Every single word he'd
poken. She'd held on to them like some kind of Holy
Grail, because they'd kept her breathing, moving, able to
ope with life beyond those seventy-two hours Rafe kept
er hostage.

"And sometimes it's the worst thing you can ever do."
His tone didn't hide the pain well at all, as if he'd given up
trying to hide that from her. It was a good sign.

"Your stepfather's dead. There's nobody who can hurt
ou. Why can't you just tell me..." She trailed off, because
f the look in his eyes. She'd hit on something. "You've
ever actually told anyone this story, have you?"

He shook his head and turned away from her, faced the
window while he spoke. "I never had to tell."

"But Chris and Nick..."

"They lived it with me. Saw the cuts and bruises—I
ever had to tell them. They saw the aftermath of that
ight, but they never asked me about it."

"The police must have asked."

"They did." His voice was taut. "I told them that I
idn't remember anything."

She put her lips to his bare shoulder, to keep from sob-
ing, because that wasn't going to help him at all. He didn't
ack away from it, or flinch, but he didn't respond either.
He drew in a ragged breath and he continued, staring
traight ahead.

"I remember most of it, but the end...I was uncon-
cious. The police were able to piece together what hap-
ened, based on what they found that night."

She lifted her head. "What did they find?"

He turned and hesitated briefly before dropping the

towel. Her eyes took a slow travel down his body—a mag
nificent body of hard muscle, and even so, her eyes imme
diately caught on his hip, on the raised, still angry red sca
surrounded by a ring of white that looked...

"Oh, my God," she whispered. "That can't be..." Sh
dropped to her knees so she could take a better look at i
ran a shaking finger over it the way she had all his othe
scars. But this—

"This is a brand," she said.

"Yes."

She continued to trace the raised welt of skin, maybe a
big as a man's fist, and not fresh. But the memory of how i
happened was still fresh in his mind, at least for today.

Tomorrow this will all be over.

She closed her eyes for a second, pressed her lips to th
spot, and this time Jake's body jerked under her touch,
nearly imperceptible motion, but she'd moved him.

His naked body was still wet and he hadn't so much a
shifted. What must it be like to have that kind of control
That kind of... patience?

No, she'd been wrong about that one—Jake Hansen wa
far from a patient man... except when it concerned her
That touched her to the very core.

"How do you explain the scars to other people?" She re
mained on her knees, her fingers outlining the rough shap
of the brand.

"You mean, to other women?" Jake asked harshly
"They assume combat and I don't tell them any differently
Some think I was in a gang. Others don't give a shit as lon;
as I make them happy."

"And you're good at that, aren't you? Making women happy?"

"I used to be."

"As long as there was an expiration date." He nodded and she bit her bottom lip. She didn't want to think about like with other women. She had apologizing to do. "God, m sorry. I didn't mean to . . . before, when I told you about afe. I shouldn't have . . . I never should have compared you him . . . I was upset."

"You had a right to be."

"I don't know what I have a right to anymore," she dmitted, her hand still on his hip. "Have you ever seen a doc-r about any of these? There are some newer techniques—"

"You want to fix me, *Doc*? You think taking the scars way is going to make everything better? Going to erase my ast?"

"I know it won't do that," she said. "You were the one ho showed me that lying to myself was the worst thing I uld possibly do."

"I spent my childhood giving someone permission to eat the shit out of me. Spent my teenage years pretending hat my life was great until my mother died. I was the mas-r of lying to myself. And I know better than anyone how uch pretending can come back to bite you in the ass. But didn't say I knew how to make it go away."

She got up off her knees and faced him. "You know it ill never go away fully, but you can still make it better. You art by telling people. Telling me everything you do re-ember, the way I told you everything."

"Don't push this," he warned, and he meant it, but she

pushed anyway, pushed him beyond his breaking poir The same way he'd done to her.

"Or what, Jake? What are you going to do?"

His voice was a low growl. "Push back."

"You wouldn't dare."

"Try me."

She paused a minute before slamming his shoulde with her palms as hard as she could. He didn't move at a but he did bare his teeth at her. So she did it again. An again. Until tears were running down her cheeks and h teeth grit together so hard that her head ached, until h caught her wrists.

"Stop it, Isabelle."

"No. I won't stop. I don't want to stop. I can help you. can fix your back. It won't be perfect—"

"And neither will I," he said fiercely. "Don't you get i This doesn't matter to me. It always matters to everyor else. If you take the scars away, nothing will change."

"Everything will change," she said quietly. "You'll hav let me help you. You'll have gotten rid of something th you shouldn't have to carry around for the rest of your life

He grabbed her by the shoulders. "You don't get to te me what I'm allowed to carry around. Do you understand You don't have the right—"

"I have *every* right!" She pushed at his chest but h wasn't letting go. She struggled against his grip, but when was apparent that was futile, she took his face in her hand instead. "I love you. And it's not because you saved my lif I'm not going to walk away from this. Even though yo told me that you knew I wasn't ready," she said.

He stopped, let go of her shoulders and put his hand

on her wrists to pull hers off his face. "When I told you that, I meant that you weren't ready for me."

"Maybe you're the one who's not ready for me." She heard her own breath catch in her throat and realized that he'd taken another step closer to him rather than away. "Maybe you still see me as a victim. Maybe you'll never be able to get past that."

"I don't see you as a victim. Not at all," he said, his voice holding that low, couched danger. "When I see you, all I can think about is touching you, running my hands along your breasts. Putting my mouth between your legs and taking you with my tongue until the only name you think about is mine."

She swallowed hard, the heat between her legs pushing her right into Jake's arms, making her want to tell him that his *was* the only name.

"Is that how you want me to see you, Isabelle? Or is it naked? In my arms? Riding me?"

A low whimper escaped the back of her throat, and the only thing she could do was nod yes.

Heat flooded her body, her cheeks flushed with desire and embarrassment at being found out so easily. He knew her the way no one did, saw right through her, and now, after tonight, he would literally know her inside and out.

She wanted nothing less.

"I'm going to take you now, Isabelle. Right here. On the floor. The couch. The table. So if you don't want that to happen, you'd better leave."

For a few seconds, Jake let go of her completely and watched her face. She stood, her breasts pressed to his chest, not sure whose heart was beating faster, hers or his.

There was so much danger waiting for her outside tha door; tonight, she only wanted what was about to happer between these four walls.

And then she let her hand move between them to circl his hard, thick length. A low, fierce rumble rose in his ches and for a second she saw the sudden loss of control in hi eyes.

She stroked him, wanting to see the glaze of pure desire For her. Because of her.

His palms closed in again on her lower back, locking he in place. The mood changed, his arousal pressed against he belly and she knew that Jake Hansen wasn't going to b gentle with her. And when he put his mouth on hers, h kissed her like he owned her.

"Jake," she moaned against his mouth.

He pulled back, stared down at her. "You're mine Tonight you're all mine."

"Yes. Yours," she whispered. She'd been his since tha first time he'd taken her into his arms, in Africa, when he' covered her up so gently.

Tonight, he was taking her clothes off, uncovering he Seeing her in a new light.

He yanked her shirt over her head and threw it asid and then roughly undid the clasp of her bra. His eyes neve left hers as he did the same to her jeans and underwea pushed them down her legs until they puddled around he feet when she shrugged her bra off and they stayed like tha for a second, skin on skin.

And then his hands reached around, each one grabbin an ass cheek and forcing her off her feet, pushing his arousa against her sex. She moaned at the contact, ran her hand across his shoulders and down his biceps and he took her down to the ground until his full weight was on hers, thick carpet at her back.

"Open your eyes, Isabelle. Open them and look at me," he said. She hadn't realized she'd closed them, saw his serious gray eyes probing hers.

"I remember everything...every single thing about those months in Africa," she said. "The way the earth smelled different in the heat than it did after a good, hard rain. The way I could never get my cornmeal to stick together the way the African women could. The way they all wanted my American things—my flip-flops and my sunglasses. I remember when he touched me, that first night, that it was different. I mistook different for good. I know better now. I know so much better."

"I'm the man in your bed tonight. Do you understand?" Jake asked fiercely. In response, she twined a hand in his hair and roughly pulled his head down toward hers, kissed him, felt his groan vibrate through her entire body.

Jake couldn't tell if Isabelle was shaking with anticipation or with nerves, or if that shaking was coming from him, but he'd be damned if he was going to stop now.

She was so soft against him—wet, willing, her legs spread, and God, he hoped this was the right thing to do. It didn't matter anyway. He couldn't stop now if he tried.

His hands moved between her legs as he bent his head to suckle a nipple. Her body jolted and bucked against his, and he circled her clit with the pad of his thumb before he slid a finger inside of her, and then another.

"I can't wait, Jake—please..."

He couldn't either, pressed himself inside of her without stopping and his cock jumped as her wet heat contracted around him almost immediately. Control was gone, replaced by an insatiable urge for her taste, the feel of her skin on his, warm and sweet. He sank in between her legs and took what he'd wanted, laid claim to Isabelle with a fierce, overwhelming desire that seared through to his core.

In her haze, she didn't realize she'd climbed him, her thighs clamped around his waist, her arms tight to his shoulders, her body heaving upward into his involuntarily. She'd already begun to shudder. His hand traveled down her belly, to brush the soft curls between her legs while she gave those low whimpers of pleasure.

"Let it go, baby," he urged. "This is what you want... what you need."

"Jake—oh, God, Jake!" She cried out his name over and over, and Christ, he loved it, urged her to say it louder still.

He didn't care that she ran her hands down his back, along the harsh ridges of scars, hard plains of muscles tensing, twisting under her caresses. Her touch was a cool wash of relief even though he knew the worst wasn't over—not by a long shot. But right now, in this space, there was nothing but Isabelle and her pleasure.

He wanted to explore every inch of her, discover every single sweet spot she had and find some she didn't know about herself... the ones that would make her cry out in surprise, and the ones that made her fingers tighten at his hips, the way they were now, digging into his flesh with a sharp, biting pain he welcomed.

And even though he was the one on top, in charge, he

knew he'd never been more out of control in his entire life than he was lying between her legs, cradled in her arms, buried deep inside of her.

Everything in his body was screaming for sweet relief, but it was too soon. He hadn't waited this long for things to end this quickly.

He closed his eyes, rested his forehead against her shoulder, tried to ignore the way she impatiently pushed her feet against his ass to drive him in deeper—and oh, yeah, this was good. Unbelievable, with her soft, wet heat pulsing around him, driving him out of his fucking mind.

She was still coming, his name on her lips in stuttered gasps, when he pulled out of her, put his mouth between her legs. His cock throbbed in response to the warm, sweet flesh he licked and sucked until she came again—and again, while he held her thighs apart.

Her back arched up off the floor, her hands clawed at his shoulders, the rug, anything to gain some purchase against the assault of pleasure raining down on her body. Every sensation heightened, a renewal.

His touch was dominating—potent. Her body surged toward his and it was incredible, he was incredible. Firm and fast and hot and slow all at the same time, so many different sensations buzzed through her that it was almost too much to process.

She watched as he kissed his way back up her body. She wanted him again—but more than that, she wanted him to lose control the way she had.

"Please..." She pulled him back on top of her. She hadn't been sure she'd ever be able to handle the feel of someone's full weight on her again. But now she just felt protected . . . safe . . . sexy.

She let it all go. Finally. Let herself open her eyes and watch Jake as he drove into her with equal parts ferocity and tenderness, wondered briefly how much pain this was causing him thanks to his side and promptly forgot her own name when he lifted her hips off the floor to thrust inside of her at a new angle.

She didn't forget his name, was yelling it so loudly—and he seemed to like that, encouraged it. Asked for it.

No, it had never been like this. Ever. Connected—pushing and pulling back—and she was lost, filled with him. Overwhelmed with the intensity and the pleasure and her whole body was warmth and tightness. His swollen length stretched her, pushed her past any limits. Skin damp from exertion, his shower, but still she clung and he was inside her, filling her, her legs over his arms so she was helpless against his thrusts.

She was never letting go.

CHAPTER
22

Clutch woke up calling out Fay's name, while Sarah remained wrapped around him. For a few seconds, he thought he was back in Ujiji, back in California, back in bumblefuck anywhere. Back in the life he had before he was seven years old.

And yet, there wasn't judgment in Sarah's eyes—only pain. She'd been watching him while he slept, waking him every half hour to make sure he was still conscious. This time, he'd woken himself.

"You're haunted, Bobby." Her voice was low, throaty. She shifted and found her cigarettes on the bedside table and lit one. For a little while, the silence hung thick between them as the smoke curled toward the ceiling. "You're being hunted in your dreams."

"Yes."

"Why did they kill Fay?" she asked. "Did she find out who you really were?"

He sat up, his stomach lurched and he drew in deep breaths so he wouldn't get sick right in front of her. Sweat slicked his body and he felt the covers being drawn up around his bare back and shoulders, Sarah's strong arms holding him. "I told her everything... the way I told you. We were going to run together. God, I was so young, so fucking stupid to think I could escape them—or my past."

"We can do this together, Bobby," she told him. "I'm not letting you go now. Not after all of this."

"Don't you get it, Sarah? They took Fay and they killed her. They did horrible things to her—told me what they'd done in blow-by-blow detail before I agreed to go back to work for them." Things he saw in his dreams, thanks to the pictures they'd forced him to look at. As if what he'd imagined wasn't horrible enough.

She called out for you the whole time, one of the men told him.

"After they took her... Why did you agree, Bobby? What was left?"

"It was the only way to insure my mother stayed alive." He waited for more questions, but none came. Instead, she spoke the words he thought he'd wanted to hear from her—words that broke his heart.

"Where is your mother now?"

He looked directly into her eyes. There was nothing else to hold back. "I don't know. I'm not allowed to know."

"She might not even be alive."

"And she might be living happily-ever-after somewhere," he said. "Which is more than I can hope for myself."

"It doesn't have to be that way."

"There's no other way out, Sarah. These men don't play by any rules. Just like this country. Just like the man I'm going to be forced to become again."

She caressed his shoulder. "Then we'll run—together."

"That's what Fay said, that's what we were doing. Don't you see, Sarah? They won't stop until they get me back. I can't do this to you."

"You can't leave me behind either. They know who I am now."

God, she was right. He'd stripped her of any protection she might've had when he left her with his phone, when she killed one of the members of GOST. A man named Dave, recognizable by the skull-and-crossbones tat on his inner right wrist.

"We can get lost in this country," she said.

"We're already lost. Don't you get that?"

She was still smoking, staring up at the ceiling. "Yes, I get that, Bobby. I always have."

Jake wanted to sleep, to lose himself in Isabelle's slow, easy breaths, to pretend that there was nothing wrong outside his door. And he could really sleep next to her now—it wouldn't matter if he had another nightmare. She'd seen it and it hadn't fazed her, hadn't scared her away.

Nothing he did could scare her away. The problem was, her nightmare was still out there.

He was going to have to let go.

The last thing he wanted to do was slide out of the bed, but he forced himself to extricate his limbs from the warm tangle of arms and legs, leaving her clutching the pillow and murmuring his name sleepily.

"Don't leave, Jake. Please."

He had to go, had to figure out how the hell he was going to keep her safe and capture Rafe at the same time.

He didn't want the answer, probably didn't have any right to it, but he needed to know before he let himself in any further: "Were you in love with him?"

"No." She said it immediately, shook her head at the same time. "But I think he did have feelings for me. Which is why I ended things. It wouldn't have been fair. I was already engaged." She stopped. "My God, what you must think of me."

"I think you're human. You were lonely and scared and you turned to him for comfort," he said, and it took so much for him to remain rational.

"I'm not . . . that's not what I'm doing with you."

He didn't answer, dropped his head and stared at the floor. He heard the rustle of the sheets as she moved closer, touched him tentatively on the shoulder.

"Jake, you have to believe me. This is different. So different. I don't know how to explain it, but it just is. The way I knew I didn't love Rafe or my fiancé, not the way I was supposed to . . . that's how I know—"

He stood, knocking her hand off his shoulder by his movement. "Not now, Isabelle. It's not the time."

"It's the best time to tell you that I'm in love with you, Jake. Not with the SEAL who saved me, but with the man who, little by little, made me whole again."

She had him by the shoulders. Shook him almost urgently.

"You didn't need me for that. It would've happened in its own time," he said.

"Maybe. But I didn't want it to happen with anyone else."

"You keep saying that—"

"I'll be like your old CO and say it until you believe it. You deserve to be happy. We deserve to be happy."

He shook his head as he pulled on jeans. She spoke again before he could get out the door.

"I never want to be the one who upsets you this much. Don't you get it, everything I thought I knew, it just shifted out from under me . . . I lost everything and you came in and gave it all back to me."

When he answered, his own voice sounded calm—cold. "I'll kill him. Do you understand, Isabelle? I'll fucking kill that bastard for laying a hand on you."

"I know," she said quietly. God, she hated seeing the pain in his eyes, the way his fists clenched and his breathing was heavy, the same way it had been during his nightmare she'd witnessed. "I don't want that burden on you."

"It's too late for it to be anywhere else."

"He's really here," she said, more to herself than to him.

His phone rang insistently. He answered, listened intently, and snapped the cell closed.

"What's wrong?"

He didn't mince words. "Cal's missing. Not answering his beeper or his phone. Nick went to his house—no sign of him or his car. No signs of a break-in."

"What are you saying, that he just disappeared? He wouldn't do that unless Rafe forced him."

"If he's with Rafe, all signs point to him going willingly."

"Why would he do that?"

"I think it's time to ask your mom some tough questions," he said finally.

She reached for her phone and he got up to leave. "I want you to stay for this." She dialed, put the phone on speaker and laid it on the bed. He sat down so the phone was between them.

Jeannie picked up on the second ring.

"Mom, it's me."

"I know—Izzy, are you all right?"

"I'm all right. I'm still with Jake. But Uncle Cal's missing," she said, heard the sharp intake of breath come across the line. "Mom, you've got to tell me what happened the night Dad died."

Jeannie wasn't going to tell her—not without a major push. There was a thick pause and then Isabelle realized why. "I've already asked Uncle Cal why you and he aren't together. Dad's been gone a long time—there's something keeping you two apart. Something beyond guilt at having had an affair."

"Sometimes, for the people you love, you do things that you think you should be incapable of doing—things that seem impossible. You do what's best."

"And what was best at the time, Mom? What are the secrets that are going to get all of us killed?" Isabelle asked, and wondered how much she'd regret getting the answer.

Cal was strung up by his wrists, feet barely able to keep their grip on the earth. His shoes had been stripped off and he was forced to balance on his toes or find himself hanging painfully by his arms.

He'd thought his days of physical torture were behind him, but his mind had never been free. And that day in the barracks loomed in front of him as the beginning of the end.

"I'm in big trouble, Cal." James, shorter and stockier than Cal, paced the small area for a few seconds before stopping to face his friend. James's hair was so blond it was almost white, and today his bright blue eyes looked washed out, his skin pale from worry. "I don't know what the hell to do."

"It's the gambling, isn't it?" Cal asked, unable to keep the anger from his tone. He'd bailed James out of gambling debts twice over the past six months, nearly wiped out his own savings account paying the bookie and helping James with his rent.

The friendship that had seen them from childhood straight through Cal enlisting in the Navy and James following soon after was straining to the breaking point. Between Cal's guilt over the affair and James's growing gambling addiction, Cal wondered if the friendship would—could—survive. And whether he wanted it to, after all of this.

"I needed the money." James punched the side of his fist

lightly against the closed door. It was lunchtime—the rest of their platoon was at the mess and Cal had no appetite now anyway. "I've got rent. Jeannie's school..."

"Does she know?"

"No."

"She's not stupid. She's got to know that you're bringing in more money than you should be at times and running short on others."

"I told her they're stipends. Overtimes. She believes me. But with the baby..."

Cal stared straight ahead—he knew that Jeannie knew. "How much do you need?"

"It's a lot this time, Cal. They let me in on a high-stakes game—I told them I was good for it. And now they're going to send men after me if I don't pay in full by the end of this month."

"How much?" *Cal repeated, blanched when James told him the amount—more than the two men's yearly salaries combined.*

"James, there's no way in hell."

"You have to help me, Cal. If you don't, I'm a dead man."

How could Cal refuse him? His betrayal of James weighed heavily on his chest. Beyond that, he'd be helping to take away Jeannie's husband, the baby's father... "I'll help. I don't know how, but I will."

James had come up with his own way two days later. Cal and Kevin were sent on an overseas mission with the UDT, which pre-dated Cal's SEAL days—James was offshore, on ship, their intel guide. And James had gotten a contact that allowed him to buy surplus weapons from

Russia on the military's dime; all Cal had to do was make the actual trade.

He'd done so, kept Kevin distracted with a little false intel from James's side. A week later, James sold them to an African warlord in what had been Zaire at the time.

His friend had kept Cal out of the process as much as he could, but Cal was still complicit, had known exactly what James had done. He'd justified it by telling himself that there were so many worse things done in the name of war . . . so many worse things done in the name of love.

When they were caught six months later, all the evidence pointed squarely at Kevin. Which was exactly the way James had set it up, unbeknownst to Cal.

"It wasn't me," Cal said slowly. "I didn't sell the guns. It was James. And when Kevin discovered what had happened and threatened me, James jumped in front of me—confessed."

"I don't understand. If James confessed, what happened?" Rafe's voice shook and Cal wondered for just a second if he could turn the boy around, like he'd done so many times before for the young men who'd passed before him, the ones who'd lost everything and found themselves through the military. And then the rational part of his brain told him that Rafe had already taken a path where there was no road back.

"It happened so fast."

"You blamed my father. You killed him, let him die disgraced."

"I owed James. I didn't think about the consequences to your family." Cal swallowed hard.

"And if you had, what would that have changed?" Rafe's

voice hardened. "You've known about your daughter all these years and you did nothing."

"I'll take all the blame, the way I should've years ago. The way I wanted to take care of it when it first happened. Nothing good ever comes from lying. From betrayal."

"You'll take all the blame? You'll take what I'll tell you to take." Rafe's voice was low and menacing against the cold Virginia night.

Cal had already started to shiver slightly, his arms stretched to their breaking point overhead, his toes barely touching the ground. "Kevin was a good man—he wouldn't want you to do this."

"He didn't want to die by his friend's hand either." Rafe shoved the gun up under his ribs. "And I'm not one of those boys you mentor, Admiral. I don't fall for that bullshit so easily."

No, Rafe wouldn't fall for any of it—none of them should have. Cal had never had a right to dish out advice to any of his men, hadn't deserved to have the last twenty-three years of freedom he'd managed. "I should have found a way to make this up to you."

"But you didn't. And when one of my father's team-mates shipped his things to my first foster home, I was so ashamed of what the military told me he'd done that I couldn't look through any of it. I dragged it from place to place, kept it until the week before I was due to go through my final phase of Delta training. And then I opened it, prepared to put the past behind me. And you know what I discovered, Admiral? That the past really could have set me free."

Now that he knew the reason behind Rafe's rage, Jake just had to figure out where the hell the guy had taken Cal.

Using the passwords Max had given him that morning, he got into Cal's records. The mission where James and Kevin had been killed happened in Africa—outside the Horn of Africa.

Was Rafe going to try to drag Isabelle back there? Or was Isabelle just an unexpected complication in Rafe's plan for vengeance?

The FBI was searching for Cal, but he knew Isabelle would be worried sick.

He looked up from the screen. "She told you about going into protection."

"I didn't think you heard me come in."

He shifted, turned the chair around. "I hear everything. Even things that are unsaid."

Isabelle walked over to him even as he stood and closed the laptop so she couldn't see what he'd been searching for.

"I'm not angry that you didn't tell me." She squeezed his hand tightly. "I'm going to go."

"You don't have to do that."

"I'm not helping any of you by staying here—I'm in the way."

You're no match for that man. "Then we should get you packed. They'll be here soon."

"I'm not giving up on you by going with the FBI."

"I know that."

"No, you don't." She took his chin in her hand; any

other person who'd ever done that had not found themselves in a good position. For her, all he did was tighten his fists and stare at her. "If I stay with you, you might be forced to do something you shouldn't."

"Do you really think I'm going to sit back and not do anything to catch this guy?"

"I don't want you to do anything. I don't want that on my conscience. Or yours."

He didn't bother to tell her that no way was that happening. If she needed to believe it, so be it. And so he took her hand and led her back up the stairs and to the third floor, where he'd helped her move in just a few short days earlier.

And now she was leaving him, on her own steam.

Still, he had to let her know that he understood, and while she carried clothes from the dresser to her suitcase, he stood in the doorway and spoke. "You know, I get it now."

"What's that?"

"That move, on the bus... that wasn't you spinning out of control. That was just—you."

She flushed as if he'd caught her, discovered something about her that no one else ever had. And in that second, he knew he always wanted it to be like that.

"You got pissed at me because I didn't get it. I should have gotten it," he continued.

"You did... eventually." She paused before dropping the clothing in her hands and pressing herself against him easily, as if she'd never been scared of doing so. Like they'd been doing this dance forever, and his body responded instantly. "I was scared. Getting onto the bus, that was the start of me taking something back. You kissing me that night forced me to get back in the game, but not in a bad way. Not at all."

"This isn't the bus, Isabelle. There isn't time—"

"There's still time. Even though I'm worried about Cal, I know, more than ever, that there's always time," she said. "If my mother hadn't lied to me, Rafe still wouldn't have been caught. And maybe, who knows—maybe I would've stayed close to my old job, maybe I would've even found myself in a marriage I didn't want. I wouldn't have had the courage to leave everything behind the way I did and start over."

"But starting over was a lie."

"No, not really," she said. "Not on my part. I wanted a change and I got a change. All my options are still open. The only thing that's different is that I realize I'm in danger. And that I'm still angry as hell for what I let Rafe take from me. I'm not going to let him do it again. There's no point. Not when I've found what makes me happy. I'm never letting go of that. So you can try—keep pushing me away, but my heart's not going anywhere."

She leaned in, dragged her mouth lightly along his jawline. He'd tried to brace himself against her touch, was completely unsuccessful as she ran her hands up under his shirt and tugged at it until he helped her take it off.

He sighed her name while she ran her tongue over a smooth strip of skin, along the back of his ear, while her hand traced his pec, rounded his nipple and pressed it between her finger and thumb.

"I want you," she repeated in a husky voice against his ear. "Don't deny me this."

His upper body rocked slightly as she tweaked the other

nipple. He regained control briefly, but she didn't wan
that.

"I want you, Jake. More than I've ever wanted anyone,
she whispered. "I want you to lie back on this bed and le
me make love to you. To show you that I've made m
decision—that it's the right one. That it's not based on fea
or ignorance."

Her surgeon's fingers traced the contours of his fac
with a light precision, as if she was searching for something

One finger over his lips. Another down the bridge of hi
nose. One along each cheek.

He'd never been more turned on by a touch in his life
He willed himself to calm down, the way he'd been taught
but it didn't help much. The urge to buck up into her wa
too strong.

"Jesus." He gave a short laugh, ran his hands through
his hair before he stared at her again. "You don't treat m
like I'm made of steel. You know I'm not and still you trea
me like..."

"Like what?"

"Like you could really love me."

"I do love you."

He swallowed hard. "That scares me more than any
thing. But fuck, Isabelle, I do love you."

She smiled, the first real smile he'd seen all day, since th
insanity began. " *'But fuck, Isabelle, I do love you'*?" she re
peated. "You know, only coming from you could that actu
ally sound romantic."

And he laughed and she laughed and that felt good
Real.

He took the gun out of his pants and laid it on the table

"The safety's not on," he said, and then he let her push him so he was flat on his back on the bed.

And she kissed him, everywhere, trailed down his neck, his nipples, and let her tongue run lower still as she roughly undid his zipper and yanked hard on his jeans, pulling them to his hips and lower.

He tensed, then his hips rose off the mattress toward her as she took him inside her mouth, sucking and swirling with a maddening rhythm. His hands twined in her hair and he couldn't stop the long, low moan that escaped his throat. Her hands gripped his hips, like she was trying to hold him in place.

"Isabelle, please—not like this." He was so close, but he wanted inside of her. He shifted and she kissed her way back up his abs, his chest, until she was straddling him.

She'd wiggled out of her pants at some point when he'd been incoherent and now she positioned herself over him, sank slowly onto his cock, balanced against his chest with her palms down on his pecs, her hair tumbling down over her shoulders, her eyes heavy-lidded with lust, and she didn't regret a thing about what was happening between them. He could tell by the way her thighs clenched around his body, the way her sex contracted around his cock, prepared to milk him until he cried out her name.

She moved to the rhythm she'd set, long and slow at first and then she moved harder and faster until he gripped her hips because his balls tightened and he didn't care about control anymore.

He shifted, drove up into her, a long, slow thrust that pushed her over the edge to an orgasm that rocked her body first, and then finally, finally, he lost himself in her.

CHAPTER
23

Sarah woke with her cheek pressed to the pillow and stretched contentedly with her eyes closed. It was the first time since she'd left Clutch's house six months ago that she'd slept so soundly, surprisingly so, considering everything they'd discussed the night before. But after his nightmare, he'd urged her to sleep, told her that after today they'd both be sleeping with one eye open.

She'd assured him she was ready for that, as long as they could stay together.

"You could handle life without me, Sarah. You already have," he said, his eyes looking even more translucent in the lamplight from the night table.

"I could, yes. But I don't want to."

He'd seemed strangely content by that, had pulled her into his arms and taken her slowly on the bed, over and over until her limbs were weak from pleasure, whispered what she needed to hear. That he loved her, that he'd do anything to keep her safe. That she would be safe.

"We'll be safe together," she said.

She'd fallen asleep wrapped around him, but he wasn't in bed with her now. Instead, the bathroom door was slightly ajar and the sound of water from the shower echoed through the small room.

She pulled back the dark shower curtain and found herself staring into an empty tub of running water.

"No, no, no . . ." she heard herself say out loud as she turned, near frantic, and prepared to throw on clothes and run out the door. And then she turned again and put her hand under the water spray—freezing cold. When she went to turn the water off, she realized only the hot tap was turned on.

He had a lead on her—maybe not much, but she'd have no idea where to even begin to look for him now. When she sank down to sit on the edge of the tub, she spotted the paper on the edge of the sink.

Her hands shook as she read the note he'd left underneath the keys, his house keys.

Bobby Juniper is going back.

"Oh, God, Bobby, no," she whispered.

Clutch had left Sarah the keys to his house—a place that was already paid for. He'd left her instructions, where he'd hidden money. The business he ran would close, but she'd have someplace to stay and she would have enough cash to get by for quite a while. He'd send her more, because he wasn't going to need much.

GOST wouldn't go after her—she'd be safe, because he was going back to them. He hadn't planned on it, hadn't wanted to leave her while she slept so peacefully, but at some point last night, when they'd been making plans, he'd known what he needed to do.

"*You'll come with me, then,*" he murmured. "*Into the wild, never looking back?*"

"*Yes.*"

"*You can't sell any more of your pictures. You won't even be able to take them for pleasure. How can I take that away from you?*"

"*You're not taking anything from me. I'm giving it up willingly.*" She stroked his back, cradled his head. *And that's when he made up his mind, wrote a note that gave her some idea of the kinds of crimes he'd committed. Anything to make her fall out of love with him.*

"Bobby Juniper, reporting for duty," he said quietly to the man who'd met his car at the border of the DRC.

"There are some men who are very angry with you, Bobby."

"I'm here. That should be all that matters," he said.

"You killed one of your own. Sources say you had help."

"Those sources are wrong." Clutch kept his facial expression neutral and stared at the man.

"Why should I believe you?"

"I agreed to this life, that's why. And you agreed to leave anyone associated with me on the outside alive."

A life for a life, and Sarah's was always the more impor

tant. She could continue with her photography, go to school. Get married, have a family, get the hell out of this country, if she wanted.

She'd forget about him. And that would be the best thing she could do.

He wouldn't forget anything about her for the rest of his life, though, no matter how long that was.

The man, John Caspar, stared him down for a second before shaking his hand. "Then the deal is done. Welcome back, Bobby."

Clutch nodded, could swear he felt the last piece of his soul breaking off as he left the borrowed truck behind and got into John's car.

Jake was sitting at the bottom of the staircase that led from his rooms to Isabelle's when he heard the doorbell ring. Still, he didn't move from the spot, heard Isabelle rustling around in the room behind him, packing her things as he leaned against the wall and let the memories of this house comfort him.

He knew every creak, every way to get in and out without being detected. This house had been a haven to him when he'd needed one most. He still remembered that trip, all of them loaded into Kenny's old Suburban. They'd left in broad daylight, Maggie not caring that she was taking one boy away from a foster care system and another from his family.

Neither foster care nor Nick's family had come after any of them.

But this house couldn't keep Rafe away.

Even though Jake didn't hear Nick coming up the stairs, his brother was now standing in front of him. "The FBI's here," Nick said.

"She's expecting them. Bring her down."

"You can still fight this, you know," Nick said. "You can grab her, take off—"

"Bring her down."

"And where are you going to be?"

"I can't do this," he said. "I can't . . ."

"I haven't heard you say *can't* in a hell of a long time."

"I'm in love with her, Nick. I've got to do the right thing here."

His brother stared at him, opened his mouth, and then thought better of it. For a second, Jake thought Nick would refuse, but he didn't.

"I'd better get her now, then," Nick said instead. "Chris and I just got called in. Training."

"Training," Jake repeated.

"Yeah. That's where I'll be. What about you?"

Jake stood, prepared to head down the back staircase, one they rarely used anymore. "You know what I was thinking about today? Remember when you stole the principal's Caddy?"

"Borrowed. I borrowed it," Nick said quietly.

"I promised her mother I'd keep her safe," Jake said finally.

"The only promises you should be making are to yourself—and to Izzy." Nick shook his head, but he didn't try to stop Jake. "I'll bring her down."

"She'll be all right," Jake said, repeated that to himself over and over as he went down the steps, away from her.

I'll be all right.

The FBI agent waiting in the foyer was tall, with dark hair, and his eyes were kind.

Isabelle hated him on sight. And even when he picked up her bags and brought them out to the car, she didn't follow, stood next to Nick inside the front foyer.

"You've got to trust him, Izzy," he said, and she knew he wasn't talking about the FBI agent.

"Like you do."

"I trust Jake with my life, have for a long time."

"He said you were the one who saved him—the night his stepfather died."

Nick shook his head. "Jake saved himself. All I did was bring him down to the ambulance because the EMTs weren't moving fast enough."

Agent Harris cleared his throat from where he stood in the doorway. "We're ready, ma'am. The senator's been apprised that we're taking you into custody."

"You'll be all right," Nick repeated. She had no choice but to believe him as she let Agent Harris escort her out of the first place she'd felt safe since Africa and into the black Town Car.

He introduced her to Agent Callum, the man behind the wheel, who wasn't nearly as friendly. His head was shaved bald and he barely turned to glance at her before he pulled the car away from the curb.

His driving style was safe. Calming.

She was miserable as she huddled alone in the backseat,

her bags next to her. And even though she didn't want to, she turned and watched out the back window until she could no longer see the house.

The men in the front were listening to the radio and drinking coffee—coffee, like this was any other day and she was of no real importance to them.

"I think I want to go back," she said. No one heard her—or if they did, neither one answered. "I said, I think this is all a mistake..."

"No mistake, ma'am," the man who'd taken her from the house to the car said, his voice slightly more slurred than it had been earlier. "Your mother..."

He trailed off and slumped to the side, his head hitting the window.

"Oh, my God, he passed out—you need to stop the car." Isabelle pulled herself up in between the front seats as the other man didn't slow the car down.

"Your mother wanted it this way, Isabelle."

Her hands tightened on the seats and her mouth opened, a silent O. Her breathing became harsh, her world unsteady as the car picked up speed.

"I told you I'd be back for you. And I always keep my promises."

*H*ostages taken. *Mission Status: Ready.*

Let the war games begin.

The team room, where the lockers were located, was loud to the point of raucousness. Someone had cranked up the radio and Chris and Zane were singing and dancing as they readied for the training op.

Nick had moved away to get into his own space—dressed quickly and efficiently with first-line gear and all the trash he carried and moved on to the war paint. He wrapped his hair in a cammy bandanna to keep it out of the way, applied war paint with his fingers, covered every square inch of skin above the neck—becoming invisible under the greens and browns and blacks. He painted down lower than normal since he tended to rip the collar of his T-shirts purposely—couldn't stand shit around his neck, and so he covered the skin leading to his chest as well.

Survival mode.

There would be a time for stripping down and cleaning off layer by layer. Now was about covering up. About protection.

Less than five minutes later he was hauling ass up the icy trail with a forty-pound ruck. It was close to pitch black, the snow had started to slow and his NVs did shit, but he was still headed in the right direction. Instinct coupled with years of experience told him so.

Prisoner, six o'clock, he motioned. Chris nodded, as if he already knew. He always already knew.

The night of Isabelle's rescue, Nick had gotten to the meeting place with only a slight delay—he'd had to reroute thanks to enemy fire, because he hadn't had time for it. And Chris had already left to find a car.

His brother claimed it was just a symbiotic thing, that he knew the men so well. Nick wasn't going to be the one to break it to him that the guy was probably even more psychic than Kenny was.

Tonight's prisoner was a downed pilot in enemy territory. Being played by a Navy pilot—and former SEAL—Glen Sinclair. Chris's ex-girlfriend's brother.

You couldn't spit in the Navy without hitting someone you were related to, dated or went to high school with. Privacy? Fuck privacy. Nick was still shocked—and grateful—that his own background had stayed as under wraps as it had.

The name change helped. Having best friends who could keep their mouths shut like steel traps when they needed to was even better.

Shots overhead and he and Chris hit the floor, rolled to find cover.

"Goatfuck," Saint muttered from his right, and Nick knew this was the part of the exercise the SEALs hadn't been privy to. The part where they got captured and sent to an impromptu SERE-like training for a few hours or a day, and there was no way Nick was dealing with that well.

None of the SEALs did, which was why having them to participate in a SERE-like evolution always involved a trick or two from the top brass.

"We're not getting fucking captured today," Mark Kendall, the team's senior chief whispered. "We're grabbing the hostage and getting out."

"Let me," Nick said quietly. He'd pulled this trick with Jake more times than he could count... this time, he'd do it with Chris and it would be as effective. The old bait and switch.

He began a slow commando crawl toward the house where the prisoner was being held. Halfway there, his phone began to vibrate against his thigh. When he checked it, he saw that he'd taken Jake's phone by accident.

When he checked the message, he realized it was no accident.

Isabelle's legs barely worked but she forced herself to move along the wooded trails so Rafe wouldn't have to touch her. He'd tied her hands again, and she'd bitten her lip so as not to beg him.

But when she tripped over a tree root and lost her footing, he caught her. She resisted, but he held her, turned her body into his. She heard the shots in the distance, the yells of men and women all around her—*war games,* the female Marines had told her earlier at the clinic. *Mass confusion. No one knows what's going on . . . you'll see a lot of action tonight.*

Rafe had known about all of it. And even though she had to swallow hard to force down the retch, she looked him in the eyes.

In turn, he yanked the gag out of her mouth. "This is just like old times, isn't it?" he asked. "You and me, together, alone in the jungle."

She didn't answer him, didn't know what he wanted to hear—or what would throw him even further over the edge.

"I had a plan, Izzy. It was all going to be simple. Kill you and watch your mother and Cal suffer. And then I saw you and everything changed. And when you decided you were done with me, I came up with a new plan. None of them will see the red light."

She kept her mouth shut, and he kept talking.

"Your SEAL's not going to come out of it alive. Neither is Cal. But you could." He paused, ran a hand over her hair, and she tried not to flinch.

"You could come with me, Izzy. Run away into the jungle with me—let me keep you safe there." Rafe's voice was a deep, hypnotic timbre that chilled her. "Or I could take you there without your consent. In time, you'd learn to depend on me, to need me. To want me. And until that happens, I'll just take you any way I have to."

"No!" She screamed it, so loudly she startled herself, a primal sound that came from somewhere so deep she felt it reverberate in every fiber of her being.

He attempted to stuff the gag back into her mouth and she bit his finger hard. He hit her across the face and she went down. She tried to crawl away from him but he grabbed her again and yanked her along, his hand on her throat this time.

This would not be a repeat of what happened two months ago. She refused to give him the satisfaction, refused to cry.

He'd let the FBI agent die right in front of her. And she had no doubt he planned to do the same with Cal.

"What have you done with my uncle? I want to see him," she demanded.

Rafe restrained her easily by the shoulder. "Don't worry, you'll see him soon enough. He's not dead—yet. I wanted you here first, to hear his confession."

"I know everything, Rafe. It's not going to change anything."

He shoved her down to the soft earth and she fell hard

on her hip. She backed away from him, still on the ground, in the direction of the woods.

You're strong, Isabelle. You can do this.

"You can't blame your life on other people," she told him.

He took a few steps toward her, grabbed her ankles and began to chain her to the nearest tree. He grabbed her already bound wrists and wrapped the metal shackles around them

"Your father and your uncle—or should I say, your two fathers—ruined my life. Do you know what kind of monsters raised me, Izzy?"

"I know you had all the chances in the world to make something of yourself. I know that every man's worth more than the very worst thing he's ever done—it's not too late for you, Rafe."

"It's been too late for me for a long time, I just never realized it," he said and she felt the sinking dread in the pit of her stomach at his words, as if perhaps it *had* always been too late for Rafe. This was what he'd been living for, surviving for, the last few years. That had twisted his soul in ways Isabelle couldn't begin to comprehend.

"After I finish with you two, I'm going to get your mother. I'll enjoy showing her exactly what happened to you and Cal. She thinks she's safe—just the way you did. I hope you finally realize that there's no such thing as being safe."

But she knew better. She'd had safety in the palm of her hand, warm and comfortable, and with a desperation she couldn't control, she began to yell for help, continued yelling even after he slapped her across the face and stuffed a rag into her mouth.

"It's almost true confessions time for the old man. Time for the whole base to hear his betrayal."

"Back away from her, Rafe."

The sound of Jake's voice reverberated through her. There was nothing she could do or say, helpless against the bindings and the gag.

And when Rafe whirled around, weapon drawn on Jake, she closed her eyes and began to pray for all of them.

The woods were dense, dark as hell, and normally Nick liked it that way, could get lost in here and come out the victor.

Tonight, no matter what happened, there would be no victory. These woods, this training ground represented everything that could go wrong.

His team was lying in wait, the war games halted. Saint had discovered trip wires encircling much of the training ground—live ones—and Nick skirted off, leaving Chris to explain what was going on with Rafe.

It was the only explanation as to why the base was rigged.

Along the way, Nick had passed some IEDs that, on further investigation, looked to be controlled by remote detonators. He'd reported back to Saint, who sent their senior chief to jam the signals, and then he'd kept going. He'd also taken note of several safe places where there appeared to be no explosives—areas with enough cover to withstand most explosions.

It hadn't taken him long to get to the old O-course. The first person he spotted was Rafe, the man waiting to take his revenge any way he could get it. Waiting to take Isabelle from Jake, and there was no way that was happening.

His own breathing slowed, the way he'd been taught—sniper slow.

Isabelle was struggling against her bonds. But that was unnoticed by Jake and Rafe, who were concentrating only on each other.

"How the hell did you find me?" Rafe demanded.

Jake gave the briefest hint of a smile, as if to make Rafe lose his cool even more. "I was in your trunk."

Jake had been in the principal's trunk the day Nick had borrowed his car as well.

CHAPTER
24

This was wrong—killing from anger was wrong—and Jake hadn't felt this kind of rage since the night Steve tried to kill him and his own survival reflexes took over. All the anger he'd been pushing down for years had come to a boil, the pressure of pretending everything was all right exploding, and now there were consequences he'd have to live with for the rest of his life, even if no one in the free world would convict him on any charges.

Self-defense. Rules of engagement. Yes, most likely, from what little of the incident he could remember. The searing of the brand had rendered him unconscious with rage and pain. When Jake woke up in the hospital, Nick told him hat Steve was dead, a broken neck from falling backward over the kitchen table.

More than likely, the man had been pushed.

So yes, they could say self-defense or rules of engagement, coat it any way they'd like—in Jake's mind, he'd always remember it as the day he killed his stepfather. He'd known he was going to do it before they walked into the door of the apartment that night, knew that Steve was going to push him over the edge. Jake had been close a time or two before, now that he was nearly as tall as Steve and stronger, because the alcohol had been weakening Steve's body . . .

But now Rafe's voice forced him to tamp down anything resembling emotion and turn around with a barely there control.

"This is where it all began . . ."

His fingers tensed around the familiar grip of the gun, his breathing as nonexistent as his body would allow and still let him function. It didn't matter that the woods were nearly pitch black—Jake didn't need his NVs. Rafe's shadow was clearly defined, and even though all Jake wanted to do was run to Isabelle, who was less than twenty feet from him, he refused to take his eyes off the target.

"This is where it all ends," Jake told him.

"So you're Cal's golden boy."

"Stand down and I won't have to hurt you."

Rafe laughed, a harsh sound. "But you want to hurt me. You've wanted to hurt me since you first met Isabelle."

Jake didn't answer, held the gun steady as sweat formed between his shoulder blades.

"Senator Cresswell and her husband took my father. I

figured I'd take something near and dear to her heart," Raf
continued.

"It's not your job to do that."

"It's mine if no one else has the balls to do it," Rafe said

Jake hadn't lowered his gun, hadn't let his arm twitch o
his hand shake, the muzzle aimed straight at the man
head.

All he had to do to end this was pull the trigger. Bu
there were so many questions Isabelle would want answer
to . . .

"Isabelle's innocent," he said.

"Yeah? So was my dad. He never did anything but serv
this fucking country. In exchange, he was betrayed. Killed.
Rafe paused. "Isabelle's a nice piece of ass. Doesn't mind he
sex rough. But I bet you already know that."

"I know that you love her," Jake said. If Rafe was sur
prised by this, he didn't show it. "You're not going to ge
her."

"No, but I can make sure she doesn't get you."

"Stand down."

"I'll fight you for her," Rafe said.

"She's mine, Rafe. I'm already the winner in this game
But if you want the satisfaction of knowing that I can kil
you with my bare hands, I'm all for it."

"Fuck you."

"Stand down and I won't have to hurt you."

"I'm not going to stand down. You and I are going t
play a big game of chicken, until one of us decides to shoo
We're both fast. No matter what happens, we'll both b
dead within seconds. So make your peace."

Jake knew he was faster—could and would take Raf

out. And when Rafe shifted, an almost imperceptible motion, Jake's brain screamed, *Go!*

Two shots and Rafe slumped to the ground.

Two shots, neither one of them fired by Jake's gun.

Nick emerged from the bushes, his face covered in full cammy paint.

"I would have done it," Jake said, but his voice sounded rough, ragged to his own ears.

"I know. But you shouldn't ever have to make a choice like that."

Only after Nick pressed Jake's arms gently did Jake disengage, realized he was still holding the weapon pointed at the spot where Rafe had been standing seconds earlier.

"Is he..." Jake asked, even though he'd seen enough dead men to know that Rafe was gone the second the bullet had entered him.

Still, Nick bent over Rafe's body, fingers on the pulse point of the man's neck. "Yes. He's gone. It's over."

Over? No, it wasn't. It was all just beginning.

But before he could move over to free Isabelle, who he heard crying through the gag, Nick grabbed his arm.

"That's the detonator." Nick pointed to the Talkabout Rafe wore taped under his shirt around his waist. The mechanism was covered in blood, half-crumpled from the shot Nick had fired—Rafe had worn it close to his heart.

Jake's breath caught, and even as his gut screamed for him to free Isabelle, his training took over. "Isabelle, honey, listen to me—everything's going to be fine, just hang in there and stay still. We'll get you out of there soon, but you've got to stay as still as possible."

Isabelle stared at him. She'd already moved earlier to try

to get his attention, so he didn't think Rafe had trained an infrared detonating device at her or on her.

Still, he wasn't taking a chance.

That meant neither he nor Nick could cross the line to get to her until they were sure they wouldn't trip anything.

"He's got this place fully wired," Nick said quietly. "We found some over by the training ground. It's chaos back there. Between the war games, the IEDs and the infrared sensors he planted, no one knows what's ready to trip and what's not. This must've taken him months to do."

"Yeah, two months." Jake wouldn't let himself think about the IEDs that were elsewhere, easily camouflaged in sandbags or trash cans around base, homemade devices that could be pure dynamite or synthetic C4 or a deadly combo of both. Instead, he knelt next to Rafe's body for a close look, and then stared up at his brother. "This one could be a secondary. If that's true, he's got something rigged that could take the whole base down."

"Saint, we've got a big problem." Jake spoke into Nick's mic and prayed he'd hear his CO's voice respond. That explosion he'd heard seconds before Rafe died had come from the direction the teams were training.

"Jake, what the hell's going on? We've got men down here." Saint's drawl was clipped.

"The base is wired to blow—IEDs all over the place, trip wires . . . the works. We got the guy who did it—he was using a Talkabout—rotating the frequency to key the mic—but I have no way of knowing what the device he was holding controlled. It's not the only detonator."

Saint confirmed his worst fears. "Some of these IEDs are still live. We're having trouble jamming their frequencies."

He heard Saint call out to the team, "We've got to find the primary—until then, assume that every wire, every mine, every IED is wired to blow. Jam what you can, back away from the rest."

And then Jake heard another explosion, both in his ear and in the distance, heard Saint cursing and yelling, and *shit,* it sounded like Rafe had set up IR bombs in strategic locations, on top of everything else.

He didn't even want to think about what Rafe had planned for the finale.

"Where the hell is the other detonator?" Jake muttered to Nick.

"Where the hell is Cal?" Nick asked.

They stared at each other for a second, and then looked toward the old concrete structure used for Close Quarters Battle practice, which was about ten feet from where Isabelle was tied up.

Jake scanned the exterior without moving, spotted the motion alert device on the rooftop, pointing east.

"I'll go," he told Nick. "We've got to get it before someone comes down that path. Don't go near her. Not yet."

Nick nodded, and Jake moved slowly, threaded around the side of the structure and ended up on the roof, above the IR. With a flash of a knife's blade, he had it disabled and he motioned *all clear.*

He stopped dead when he heard the voice. It was calm and capable, even though it shouldn't have been. And it was coming from inside the structure.

Nick was staring at him, knew something was up.

Don't scare her, he motioned to Nick, because he knew exactly where the originating wires were located.

Cal was wired to blow.

He was the main source.

Isabelle didn't dare move, didn't dare breathe—and didn' know what to think when Nick finally walked over to her

"It's okay, Isabelle, you're going to be fine," Nick said his rough voice calming her as much as she could possibly be at this moment. He took the gag out of her mouth, and from the corner of her eye she saw Jake climbing carefully across the roof of the one-story building.

"Tell me what's happening." Her voice was hoarse from screaming. "Is my uncle in there?"

Nick didn't stop what he was doing, just nodded *yes* and continued to work on the handcuffs that bound her arm together in front of her. For the first time, she noticed the fine wires woven in between the hard metal that bit into her wrists, as Nick's fingers flew on the wires, clipping then carefully, precisely and with a confidence she was grateful for.

She turned her attention back to Jake, watched him stop, saw his lips moving. Saw him nod and knew by the set of his shoulders that he was in full battle mode.

If Uncle Cal was inside that building, he could be a wired up as she was. Maybe even more so.

"Rafe told me that you'd never see the red light," she whispered, more to herself than to Nick.

"Rafe was dead wrong," Nick told her. "Don't you dare give up on us now."

And then she was free. All she wanted to do was collapse, but she knew that it wasn't over. Not at all.

"I won't give up," she whispered. Nick took her hand and held it and together they watched Jake on the rooftop.

"I'm wearing a homicide vest with a detonator. There's an IR positioned right at me. There's only one way in, and there might not be a way out." Cal's voice was steady as he laid it on the line. Jake remained poised on the roof, above the only door leading into the structure.

"You're going to have to walk me in, Admiral. I can disable it and then the rest will be easy."

"There's a problem, Jake."

"Tell me."

"He wired the primary to my cell phone."

"I'll put out a no call order—"

"It's scheduled to ring a reminder for me to take my medication. Every night. Exactly at 2100."

Jake checked his own watch. 2055:42 and counting.

"Is Izzy out there?" Cal asked. "Rafe said he was bringing her here."

"She's here, Admiral," he said, turned to glance back at her, standing next to Nick, looking uncertainly up at him.

"Then you take her, Jake. Take her and get out of here. Tell her that I've only wanted to keep her safe. Do this for me."

Jake kept his eyes trained on Isabelle as Cal spoke. Nick would trade places with him in a second. He knew that.

He owed both men more than that—owed himself and Isabelle as well. "Get her the hell away from here, Nick," he said firmly. "Go now."

Isabelle was screaming, "No, no no!" even as Nick lifted her from the ground and took off in a dead run for the woods, the way he'd come originally, back to an expanse that was too dense for Rafe to wire.

He could've argued with his brother, could've insisted on taking his place on that fucking rooftop. But Jake had trusted him with maybe the most precious thing in his life—and Nick wasn't going to blow that.

The next explosion shook the ground—pushed them both forward. He lost his breath momentarily as his body shielded hers, held her down even as he repeated silent prayers in his head.

And Izzy was still screaming.

She just didn't realize that she was doing it for both of them.

Isabelle fought like hell to get out from underneath Nick, began to kick and scratch, heard him curse softly when she caught him between his legs.

"Izzy, I'm on your side."

She heard the tone of his voice, realized that he was just as worried about Jake as she was. "We have to get him."

Nick wouldn't let go of her wrist. "If he's gone, that's not something you want to see, Izzy. Not that way."

Halfway between twisting herself out of Nick's grasp,

she turned to him. "You saved him once. And now you saved me."

"Jake saved himself. All I did was get him to the hospital quicker. All I did for you was what he asked." Nick eased up with the pressure on his wrist. "He's all right."

"How do you know that?" she demanded.

"Because he's standing right behind you."

She whirled around to find Jake less than a foot from her—how he'd come through the woods so silently, with Cal by his side, was something of a miracle in itself.

"How did you do that?" she asked Jake.

"Only with Cal's help," Jake told her.

When the floodlights came up simultaneously with the sounding of a centralized alarm, she saw that both men were covered in dirt and mud and blood and she managed to hug them while simultaneously checking to see which one of them was bleeding.

"Cal needs medical attention," Isabelle told Nick. And somehow, Chris was there, telling her not to worry, and there were two other men there in full gear and then it was just her and Jake, standing together in the midst of the old O-course. Just like the picture Uncle Cal had in his office. Where it all began so long ago for her family.

Where it was all going to come full circle now.

"You were in the trunk the whole time...you never really let me go."

"I didn't know Rafe was in the car—I would never have let you go through that. Never. I would've taken him out before you got to the car."

"What were you going to do?"

"I wouldn't have let them take you away from me, Isabelle. I never go down without a fight."

"You would've known where I was the whole time."

"Yes. I would've followed you to your first safe house—and your second—kept watch for however long it took. But once I got out of the trunk and saw where the hell we were, I knew something was really wrong."

"This is why he waited two months...he'd come here, probably right after I came back to the States. He needed to plan this out. Set it all up. He was here...when I was here, he was here, on the base..."

"It looks that way. But he's not now."

"I know. It's over—it's really over."

"You're shaking." He pulled her close, into a warm embrace. His heart beat so fast against hers and she buried her face against his shoulder and hung on as tightly as she could, not leaving any room between them for doubt.

"Jake, I still...I still need to go back to Africa."

"I know that," he said. "I know that you have a lot of things you need to do, and that they might not include me."

"What are you talking about?"

"You don't owe me anything, Isabelle. Not because of the rescue, not because of what just happened."

"I know that—"

"No decisions about us now," he said fiercely.

"You don't get to tell me what to do anymore."

"Dr. Markham, I've got two men down on the other side of base—they need your attention stat." Saint's drawl was heavy as he crashed through the woods. Jake's CO looked at him. "We're still finding wires, but so far, they're all defused. The area's been swept for mines. I'll keep her with me—she'll be safe."

Isabelle took Jake's hand and he turned his attention to her. "Go now. Go do what you do best," he told her. "I'll get Cal out of here, make sure he's all right. And I'll contact your mom."

She squeezed his hand tightly before she took off with his CO, thankful she'd found a man so willing to give her back all of her strength, plus so much more.

CHAPTER
25

It was hard to come down from what had happened on base—the enormity of the consequences, for Cal, for all of them, had Jake tamping down his emotions in order to deal with the debriefings and the senator. To the outside world, this was merely a training exercise.

You rescued me again, Isabelle had whispered to him when they'd met up much later that evening in the clinic. He'd wanted to say something, but wasn't sure how to respond.

The night he'd rescued her in Africa, he knew they'd survive because he hadn't had that gut-clenching feeling he'd gotten once before, on a mission where he'd literally thought it was all over.

He'd come so close to the edge that night in the Sudan—his first mission as a platoon-based SEAL, eighteen years old and thrown into the fire. Which was where he'd wanted to be, had trained to be, fought to be.

His swim-buddy and teammate lost his life that night and there was nothing Jake could've done to stop it. And as he and his teammates went into the sea, dragging Trey's body with them because they would not leave him behind, Jake learned the real meaning of *no way out*.

They'd all come so close that night—too close. All because of a man who Jake couldn't stop thinking about. And he found himself standing outside on the deck, well before dawn.

He took out his phone and dialed.

"I was wondering when you'd call."

Jake smiled into the phone. "Like you didn't know, Dad." He paused, shuffled his feet on the deck and pretended Kenny was right in front of him, the way he'd been the night Jake told him he needed written consent to join the Navy. "How do I know I'm doing the right thing?"

"You know, Jake. You've always known," his father told him. "You're a good man. Nobody can ever take that away from you."

Jake stared straight ahead, tears in his eyes, but a small smile of pride played on his lips.

"The doctor, she's all right?" Kenny asked, and Jake didn't bother to ask how he knew. It could've been through regular means, through Chris or Nick, or he might've known from the start, but it didn't matter.

"She's all right."

"And she knows everything."

"She does." He paused. "She says that she loves me."

"You understand, probably better than anyone I know, about what can happen to a man to make him go bad," Dad said. "You can forgive that. And yourself."

Jake clutched the railing, wishing it was that easy.

"It is that easy," Dad said quietly.

Isabelle remembered working on the three men nearly simultaneously, all of whom had made it to surgery and survived and then she'd slept for almost two days straight. She'd been vaguely aware of Jake and Nick and Chris fending off any stray law enforcement and media and anyone else who wanted to bother her, including the FBI.

All she'd known was that she was free, finally, gloriously free, and her body had revolted by insisting on rest. Jake insisted on her eating as well, woke her every once in a while and pushed food on her.

She called him bossy at one point.

The thing was, he wasn't sleeping next to her. She mentioned that to him too, but he hadn't responded. And she'd been too exhausted to fight him.

This time when she woke, it was still dark in the room but her eyes actually stayed open. She glanced at the clock and stretched.

After a long, hot shower, she dressed in Jake's sweats and wrapped herself in a big warm blanket and wandered downstairs just before dawn.

She found the three of them—Jake, Chris and Nick—outside on the back deck, in the cold. Watching the sun rise over the water, the way Jake had the morning after the bus accident.

Three men of honor, who'd all saved her—and themselves, in their own way. She watched the proud set of their shoulders and felt her own heart swell with pride.

Chris turned first and saw her, motioned for her to come out onto the deck with them. It was such a moment, a bonding ritual, that she didn't want to disturb them. Didn't want to intrude, but Jake actually broke away and opened the door and brought her out.

He didn't say anything. None of them did, just watched the orange globe slowly rise, the way it did every morning. Consistent and comforting.

And when it was all the way up, Nick and Chris went inside, left her and Jake out on the back deck alone.

"You should go in—it's cold," Jake said finally.

"Not yet, it feels too good to be out here."

He nodded, turned to look at the morning sky again. "Cal's going to face a formal inquest," he said. "It might affect your mom. And you, peripherally."

"I figured as much," she said. "What about you and Nick?"

"There's an investigation pending, but the JAG who handles legal matters for the teams doesn't think it's a problem. We should be cleared by the time we're due to move out."

"Will that happen soon?"

"Maybe."

This is what it's like. This is what it'll be like. "You do this every morning, don't you?" she asked finally.

He nodded, and for the first time since she'd come

outside she noticed that his gray eyes were lighter. Happy. "For as long as I can remember. If I made it to the morning, then I'd survived another day. That's all that mattered then. It's all that matters now."

"And Nick and Chris?"

"Well, it kind of became a tradition for all of us. And for my dad."

"I'd like it to be one for me too," she said. "But after everything we've been through . . . I mean, I'd understand, Jake. I'm not going to hold you to something you don't want to be in. I don't want you to do anything out of a misguided sense of loyalty."

"That's not it, Isabelle. That's not it at all." He paused, drew in a deep breath. "Don't you see, I've done so many more dangerous things . . . been places that were hell on earth. And I could get past them. Until you. I can't get past you."

"I don't want to be the one who haunts you."

"It's too late," he said. "I don't want you to stop." His hand caressed the back of her neck for a second before pulling her gently toward him. He kissed her softly, sweetly.

"The thing about sunrises is, you don't have to be in the same place in order to share them. You can be anywhere in the world and still be connected," he said quietly, and she knew she and Jake would have more than their share of sunrises together.

If you loved
HARD TO HOLD,
don't miss the second book in Stephanie's
blazingly hot trilogy

TOO HOT *_{TO} HOLD*

Coming from Dell Books in December 2009

And don't miss the third and final novel in
the series,

HOLD *_{ON} TIGHT*

Coming January 2010

Read on for a sneak peek inside
TOO HOT TO HOLD . . .

CHAPTER

1

"That which does not kill us makes us stronger."
—**Friedrich Nietzsche**

The car wasn't moving fast enough. Eighty miles per hour would be fine for most men, but Nick Devane wasn't most men, and never would be if he had anything to say about it.

The midnight black Porsche Turbo shook when it reached 110 and skidded onto the curved expanse of highway on two wheels. His breath came in short gasps, heart slammed in his chest, fingers curved around the steering wheel. The rush spread through him like a fever until he was no longer thinking, the possibility of danger vibrating his soul, the catch in his throat urging him to push past the brink of fear.

Some people might say he hadn't changed a damned bit from the wild kid he'd been. Built for speed and trouble, and his pulsing drive for adrenaline seemed to feed on itself, increasing exponentially through his early years and culminating with an outlet as a member of the elite Navy SEAL Teams.

It was a job he planned on keeping until they threw him out on his ass. A job he'd gotten because of his need for speed and trouble.

Hotwiring a judge's car and taking it for a joyride ten years ago might not have been the smartest idea, but Nick had to say it was the best thing he'd ever done.

Seventeen, cocky as hell and without a care in the world, he'd pushed the borrowed Porsche Carrera to the limit on that darkened stretch of highway along the Virginia–Maryland border, pushed it so hard the gears groaned and the chassis shook and he'd been sure the car would either explode or take flight off the pavement. At that point, he wouldn't have given a shit either way. If he'd had to make an honest assessment of himself as a disowned teenager of wealth and privilege, death would've been an easy option.

But it would've made things easier still for the man he refused to call *Father* anymore, and that special brand of screw-you Nick had been born with, and continued to reserve for authority, had been too deeply ingrained in him to quit anything. Especially living.

That night, he'd slowed the car, turned off the engine and rolled the sleek silver baby up the long driveway. He'd been prepared to leave it ridden hard and put away wet where the judge had parked it, no worse for wear—save the near-empty gas tank.

He'd never expected Her Honor, Kelly Cromwell, to be standing there as though she had all the time and patience in the world. Which, he would discover later, she did.

"End of the line," he'd muttered to himself, had gotten out of the car and swaggered over to her, because he did not run.

Not anymore.

When given the choice between jail or the military, he'd chosen wisely.

Tonight, the black Porsche was his, but there was also somebody waiting for him when he slammed into the back lot of the diner and eased into the last available space.

No, nothing had changed inside of him. But on the outside, the façade, the carefully concealed past was a tightly woven secret that he refused to let unravel.

Which was exactly why he needed to meet Kaylee Smith and do what he'd promised six years ago to the man who saved his life.

Don't get yourself into trouble, his CO had warned earlier that evening. Nick had almost said, *Too late,* but figured the wiseass remark was better kept to himself.

A brutal, three-month mission overseas and the team's combined injuries—consisting of a bullet wound, two broken ribs and a broken nose, none of which were his—added to one week stateside, and a twenty-four-hour window of R&R practically screamed for a night out.

He had expected to get into trouble that evening—hadn't expected the trouble to actually find him.

When his CO put him in charge of the team's behavior, his enthusiasm lessened considerably, but didn't change his opinion that drinking, dancing and the loudest music known to man were still the night's best options. He'd planned on heading to the Underground, a place senior officers rarely frequented and where he could be semi-assured none of his team would get into a brawl. Although with most of the team in tow, including his two adopted brothers, the odds weren't on his side.

Trouble always comes in threes, Kenny Waldron, the only man Nick called *Dad* now, would always say when Nick, Jake and Chris were together in the same place.

Nick's plans had been altered when Max, a captain in Naval Intelligence, called with an urgent message.

Hey, Devane, someone's been running your name. What the fuck is that all about?

Max was the man who brought the teams home—all the SEALs owed him a hell of a lot, and somehow the chits seemed to come up in Max's favor even when the teams were on dry, safe land. Relatively speaking.

With Nick's blessing, Max had gotten in touch with the guy from the Department of Defense who'd initiated the search on Nick, put the fear of God into him and gave Nick the name and number of the woman who'd been hunting him.

Kaylee Smith.

Nick hadn't heard of her.

She's heard of you. Find out why and shut it down had been Max's final words.

He knew why now. Shutting it down was the final step.

Kaylee Smith had come to the diner early, to have dinner and to frame out some of the stories she had on deadline—

piece on a cache of weapons found at a women's shelter, and another piece where she'd gone for a ride-along with undercover policewomen. The investigations had been exciting—the writing not as much, although if she was in the right mood, she could get that partial sensation of still being in the moment.

Tonight, she couldn't get herself to that place. She hadn't eaten, was on her third cup of coffee as she tapped her pen restlessly and stared out the window that faced the back parking lot where she hoped Nick Devane would pull in. She wanted to see him before he saw her, to assess who was coming at her. To attempt to know her target on sight, since the only way she could identify him was by his voice.

"Who is this?" The voice on the other end of the line was a rough growl, had made her start initially.

"Who is this?" she asked back, even though she suspected exactly who it was, with a more than sinking pit in her stomach. Her search for Nick Devane had triggered something in the system, especially since she'd had a friend in the DoD search for his birth certificate. Her friend had come up empty.

According to the information Kaylee had, Devane was Special Ops. Navy SEAL. That was six years earlier—he could be discharged by now. Working for the CIA or FBI was a definite possibility for a man with his background.

Either way, he was a man who didn't want to be found.

He didn't answer her question—not fully. "You've been looking for me. I need to know why."

"Your name . . . it's on Aaron's list," she said quietly. There was silence on the other end, so long that she'd checked the display screen on her phone to make sure they were still connected.

The call had registered as an unknown number on her cell phone's caller ID. Untraceable.

"You want to meet me," he said finally.

"I want to meet you," she agreed. "To talk about Aaron."

"City Diner, on Maple Street. Tonight, 2300."

Military time. He was still in. "I'll be there. Don't you want to know my name . . . or how to recognize me?" she asked before he could hang up.

"That won't be a problem."

What Nick didn't realize was that anything to do with Aaron was a problem—a large one that threatened her career, her past . . . her life.

Nick had known more than her phone number—he'd known what state she lived in. And he was coming to her.

"Honey, can I get you some more coffee?" The waitress didn't bother to wait for an answer before she topped off Kaylee's cup. And when she walked away, Kaylee noted that a black Porsche had pulled into the lot during that brief interruption, and the most handsome brick wall she'd ever seen in her life was standing directly in front of her.

She'd called Aaron's entire list, man by man. Each had come willingly to meet with her. Each of them told her that Aaron had been alive when they'd left him, that her ex-husband had saved their lives.

That Aaron had refused to answer questions as to whether or not he was affiliated with the U.S. military.

Nick was the last man on Aaron's list, and he was definitely not least. If she'd been writing an article about him she could already picture the opening paragraph:

Every bit the warrior. Tall, broad shoulders, an aristocratic face—handsome . . . and it is as though Nick Devane should be

*nodeling menswear instead of running around the world with
weaponry.*

But she knew differently. Underneath the calm, cool
and collected man who stood before her was a hint of the
fire inside he couldn't control. The heat in his belly that
drove him to hit harder, fly higher, to risk his life for the
sheer need of it.

It was something she both understood and hated. And
right now, with Nick standing in front of her, she was convinced that she hated him as well.

For being on Aaron's list. For being a part of the same
military that had taken so much from her.

For turning her world upside down in the space of mere
seconds.

So yes, Nick was the last man on the list. The last one to
see Aaron alive.

And maybe the one who knew how he died.

"You must be Nick." Her voice was thankfully calmer
than she'd expected. He merely nodded in response.

The men she'd met over the past days had been succinct
as well, but this man was a whole different animal.
Taciturn. Not the buttoned-up type who called her *Ma'am*
and expressed sincere apologies for her loss.

Yet, somehow, she had little doubt that whatever came
out of his mouth would be sincere.

"Thank you for agreeing to meet with me. Please, have
a seat." She motioned across the table to the empty half of
the booth, a booth she'd picked specifically to watch both
the entrance and the lot. A place where her back could stay
against the wall—the first rule of combat in the world according to Aaron.

"Not here" was all he said before he turned and strolled out.

She had no choice but to follow. Hurriedly, she threw money on the table to cover her bill, then caught up with him halfway up the street.

He didn't turn to acknowledge her presence, had assumed that she'd follow him to wherever he was going.

And he'd been right.

Yes, he was definitely proving to be the most arrogant of the bunch.

"Aaron was your husband," he said once he finally stopped at the entrance of an alleyway between two buildings at the corner where the lamppost had blown out. Then he gazed at her and corrected himself. "Ex-husband."

She was going to have to give answers to get answers from this one. "Yes. He was my ex for a long time before he died."

"You were young."

"Too young," she agreed. "Just eighteen when we married." Aaron had been a way out. She hadn't known that she'd been running into more of what she'd left behind, after being deserted by her mother and left with a grandmother who neither wanted nor had any love for Kaylee.

Her life was so much different today. She'd molded herself into a cold, ruthless undercover reporter who was both respected and feared.

No guts, no glory.

No emotions, except when it came to Aaron. Her first love. Her first everything. And most of those emotions ran between nostalgia and hatred.

"I met him in Africa," Nick said finally. His rough voice

shot up her spine like a direct caress, the way it had on the phone this afternoon. But it was so much better in person.

"I know. In the DRC—the Congo," she said. If he was surprised that she had that information, he didn't show it. She hadn't expected him to anyway, but just as she wondered if there was anything that could break through the façade, he swallowed hard, then rubbed the base of his throat with two fingers as he stared at the night sky as though reliving that time in Africa.

"Aaron saved my life."

"The list of men he left for me to find—he said that he'd saved all their lives. Except for you."

Nick looked at her with eyebrows raised, waiting. So patient, but somehow impatience radiated off him in waves.

"He said you would've done fine without his help," she finished. "Is that true?"

"You want me to use twenty-twenty hindsight on something that happened six years ago?" he asked, his voice tight. "Hell, I don't know how to answer that."

He stuck his hands in his pockets, the leather jacket flaring out to the side, and she half expected to see a gun holster.

"I tried to get him to come back with me, on the helo," he said. "He refused. He said that there wasn't a way back for him. And then he gave me this—told me to give it to his girl when she came looking for me."

She felt the tears jump to her eyes, hot and too fresh as Nick took a hand out of his pocket to place a worn circle patch, a gray background with a black symbol crudely sewn in, into her palm. "You've kept it all this time?"

"I always keep my word."

That was so much more than she could say about Aaron.
"When you saw him last...I mean...how was he?"

Nick nodded as he spoke. "He was all right. I was the
one who'd been shot."

"He was a good Ranger." She couldn't bring herself to
say *man,* even though the military seemed to think the two
terms were synonymous. She knew better.

"I believe you."

"How did he look?"

"I don't know what he looked like before. I have nothing to compare it to."

She pulled a picture out of her bag, the one of a non-
smiling Aaron, fresh out of Ranger School and in full uniform. The day it had been taken, the moment, actually,
she'd known it had been the beginning of the end for them.

Nick took the picture from her and stared at it. "That's
him. His hair was longer. He had a beard and he looked like
he'd been through hell."

He stayed close to her, both of them leaning against the
side of the brick building as the words tumbled out of his
mouth.

"I met him when we were both only fifteen. I barely saw
him after we got married—he went to Ranger School and
then he went off to save the world. *Leading the way,*" she
said, unable to keep the sarcasm out of her voice as she used
the Ranger creed.

There was none in his. "Not easy for a military wife."

"The military would've made me a widow by the time I
was twenty-six anyway." She'd gotten notice of Aaron's
death from the Army four years ago—gotten his personal

effects, which included a key to a safe deposit box that contained the list of names, and Aaron's final words.

I'm sorry.

In her estimation, that wasn't nearly enough.

"How long have you had my name?" he asked finally.

"I didn't open the safe deposit box until two weeks ago—I didn't know he had a list in there." Her words came out nearly a whisper, but she felt as if she'd shouted them.

"And then you had your friend at the DoD tracking me to the ends of the earth."

She tilted her head to stare up at him. "Why are you such a hard man to find?"

He ignored her question and fired back his own. "Why did you wait four years to open that box? What changed two weeks ago?"

Would he believe her? She barely believed it herself, but she'd come too far to quit now. "I got a phone call from a dead man."

CHAPTER
2

Nick was doing a piss-poor job of shutting this one down, could just imagine the shit his brothers would give him if they knew where he was and what he was doing. Thankfully, he'd managed to slip out the back of the ba when they were both too distracted to notice.

They'd notice soon enough.

"Hold on a minute—you think Aaron called you? Dead Aaron?" he asked Kaylee.

"Yes. Maybe. And you can stop speaking to me like I'm crazy."

He let his eyes flicker over her—he had the advantage was used to working in the dark even without the benefi of night vision goggles. She thought she was hidden, didn' realize how much her body language, her expressions, gave away.

Even now, she sucked her bottom lip lightly between her teeth—something she'd done often and well in the ten minutes he'd known her. It drove him crazy every time.

She was telling the goddamned truth, for sure, and he dragged a hand through his hair and wondered why he wasn't running for the escape hatch.

"What did he say?" he heard himself asking, against his better judgment.

"He said, *Happy birthday, Kaylee*. The line was all crackled—I asked him where he was and he didn't answer. And then he said, *I'm sorry, KK*." She paused. "He was the only one who ever called me KK. Always in private."

"It's a mistake. Someone playing a trick, a horrible trick, on you."

"I never saw a body, Nick. I didn't go to the funeral—I don't even know if he had one."

"What exactly did the Army say when they notified you?"

"They told me he was KIA," she explained. "The problem was, the list of names he left me was dated . . . the dates begin a year later than the Army claimed he died."

She might not have known that Aaron had gone over the hill, but how could the Army not have known? "Aaron was AWOL when he saved me."

She shook her head in complete disbelief. "No, not Aaron. The military was his life. He loved being a Ranger. Loved it more than anything else."

"Including you?"

"Yes, including me. To be fair, I didn't do much to try to keep him from that."

The way Kaylee looked should have been enough. She was all long-legged, hot as anything, with dark auburn hair, long and wavy and kind of wild, like the woman herself. He'd noted the black leather pants and vintage AC/DC T-shirt the second he'd laid eyes on her, and yes, Kaylee Smith might just be the most dangerous thing he'd run across on a non-mission basis. Part angel, part hellcat, and shit, it was not cool when he realized that one night wouldn't be enough time with her. Not even close.

She was trouble.

"I know what happened that night, on your mission," she told him. "Aaron wrote down more than your name. He's got a whole report. He called it a Situation Report."

Damn, that couldn't be good. What had Aaron been thinking, writing up a SITREP?

This had gone from being a favor for a dead man to something much different. "If you've got the whole story, why am I here?"

"For your side of things. I want to fill in the gaps, to know what Aaron really did for you. Please."

Whether or not Aaron had deserted, a plea from a widow couldn't be ignored. Nick could tell her the story without telling her the whole story.

There are such things as false truths and honest lies, his dad would say.

He shifted away from her and began to walk slowly toward a small playground beyond the apartment buildings—mostly grass, with a swing set in the middle of the area. And he laid down, flat on his back, arms folded behind his head, and stared up at the night sky and wondered why the hell all this chose to come down on him now, after all this time.

He closed his eyes and tried to recall his memories from that night, pulling it into sharp focus.

Six years ago, he'd been Petty Officer Third-Class Devane, twenty-one years old and on his first mission with his original SEAL team. And members of the militant militia group he'd been sent to recon in the Congo were trying to kill him.

Near death had happened to him before, mainly when he was younger and was not expected to live past his first, second, third birthdays, and he'd honestly never thought he'd make it to legal age.

But still, lying there, just beyond the row of tin-roofed, pastel-colored houses in a small town on the outskirts of Kisangani, he'd been going down hard, and he remembered how badly it had pissed him off.

"That mission was supposed to take under six hours from start to finish," he said finally, more to himself than to her. In at dark, out before the dawn.

"American helo arrived in the DRC at 2200, just outside Kisangani," she said, and she was speaking from memory rather than from paper.

She'd lain down on the grass next to him, despite the fact that the air was chilled and the ground even colder. Like him, she stared up at the sky when she spoke.

He'd always made it his practice to not look backward, to keep moving forward and to try not to make the same mistakes twice. Apparently, that wasn't in Kaylee's plan.

You owe this to Aaron, he told himself, because he understood what it was like to not want to be found, even as the other half of his brain told him that he didn't owe anybody shit beyond what he'd promised. And he'd kept that promise by handing over the patch to Aaron's girl.

He didn't like thinking about Kaylee as *Aaron's girl*.

"Six men inserted into the LZ," she continued. "Blue on Red fire began immediately, forcing the group to split. Blue on Red means you took on enemy fire, right?"

He nodded in agreement. Six SEALs from his team were prepared to insert just below their intended target for recon of a potential new terrorist cell that utilized monies and resources from the militant militia. A completely classified, locked-down mission with the highest priority.

The helo had traveled up the Lualaba River toward Isangi—a small town outside Kisangani and their ultimate destination—would drop them over ten miles away along a deserted part of the river and far away from any checkpoints and towns, save for the smaller villages.

As soon as the last man, Wolf, had fast-roped down to the ground and their ride left, the team had begun taking on enemy fire.

The shadows seemed to surround them from everywhere and anywhere, their howls echoing through the jungles, to start a chain of events that would spiral quickly out of control. An ambush of goatfuck proportions.

The militia wanted nothing more than to make examples of more American soldiers, the more elite, the better.

Nick remembered Wolf radioing for a Quick Action Force, remembered Brice and Jerry and Tim going east to try to get behind the enemy.

Nick had split west behind Joe and Wolf, covering their six as the rapid fire of AK-47s rang over their head.

Divide and conquer, Wolf had said.

"Man number six caught artillery fire to the chest after killing two militia and launching a grenade to push back the enemy." Kaylee's words echoed in his ear and he could hear the sharp impact of the shots echoing in the night—the bullets that tore through his shoulder had taken him down briefly.

Joe had already gone down—a shot to the thigh that had him cursing and still firing as Wolf had been dragging him to safety, while Nick had been trying anything to buy them some time.

"Man number six is separated from his team."

When the bullets hit, Nick had been knocked backward and unconscious—woke seeing stars, but he'd still been able to feel, and move, fingers and toes and he'd known that there had to be a reason he wasn't moving. Because the sound of renewed automatic machine-gun fire in his general direction had been as real a wake-up call as he was going to get.

Fight or flight had been ingrained in him from the time he could walk—that response wouldn't desert him now without a damned good reason.

He raised his head slowly off the dusty ground, a bare-bones movement that sent a shot of pain through his skull and nearly knocked him out again. By the time he put his head back down, he had his answer.

The damned good reason was a loose wire attached to a claymore that he'd fallen on when he'd passed out. If it had been a tight wire, he wouldn't have had a shot in hell. As it was, the mine was less than twenty-five meters from him and it was live, lethal—and tangled in his gear.

So fight or flight had now become be still or die.

Fucking motherfucking clusterfuck.

His radio was long gone—smashed when he'd slammed to the ground. His only way out right now was himself.

He kept his breathing shallow, by design more than choice, given the wounds he'd sustained. They were closer to his shoulder than his chest—at least that's what he kept telling himself, but he couldn't be sure of anything. The fact that he was conscious and breathing was the best sign.

He closed his eyes and listened to the quiet surrounding him, searching out any scrap of intel.

This is the best adrenaline rush you'll get this side of legal, *his old CO had boasted during training.*

Yeah, this was a real fucking adrenaline rush. Complete with the dizziness and dry mouth, life flashing before his eyes. His body was too far gone to feel much pain—his nerve sensors were pretty much destroyed, so much so that in order to feel any physical pain, he'd have to be hit pretty damned hard.

He'd been hit pretty damned hard.

Carefully with his right hand he reached into one of the utility pockets for his Ka-Bar knife—once he had it firmly in his palm, he cut the loose wire on the right side. It probably took less than five seconds but it felt like he'd been swimming through oil to get the job done.

He transferred the knife to his left hand and prepared to cut that wire, when he realized that someone had come behind him—someone as covert as he'd been trained to be, and that was the only reason his senses went on alert.